# Lights, Camera, Christmas Town

## Heartwarming Christmas Town Series

Mistletoe Memories

A Daring Little Christmas

The Lights of Christmas

Her Second-Story Santa

Christmas Take Two

Cocoa Kisses and Marshmallow Hugs

Red, White & Blue Christmas

Catering Christmas

ChelseaBeth Publishing

Mistletoe Memories, Copyright © 2023 by Anna J. Stewart

A Daring Little Christmas, Copyright © 2023 Beth Carpenter

The Lights of Christmas, Copyright © 2023 by Melinda Curtis

Her Second-Story Santa, Copyright © 2023 by Cheryl Harper

Christmas Take Two, Copyright © 2023 by Liz Flaherty

Cocoa Kisses and Marshmallow Hugs, Copyright © 2023 by Tanya Agler

Red, White & Blue Christmas, Copyright © 2023 by LeAnne Bristow

Catering Christmas, Copyright © 2023 by Cari Lynn Webb

Edited by Melinda Curtis & Cari Lynn Webb

Sweet Romances By:

Anna J. Stewart

Beth Carpenter

Cari Lynn Webb

Cheryl Harper

LeAnne Bristow

Liz Flaherty

Melinda Curtis

Tanya Agler

# Dedication

A long, long time ago, I had an idea to write connected holiday novellas and asked two other authors to join me in pitching the idea to Harlequin for their Heartwarming line. With the help of Anna Adams and Anna J. Stewart, we created Christmas Town, the gazebo, and the idea that sweet holiday romance collections are that much sweeter when the stories are connected. The next year, we recruited nine more authors who wrote for Harlequin Heartwarming and a tradition was born. Every year, our connections and collections grow. We challenge ourselves and we support each other.

This year, I'd like to dedicate this set to every author who has written in the collection, whether it was one time or several. You truly hold the meaning of Christmas in your hearts and bring the magic every time. Happy holidays, ladies!

~ Melinda Curtis

# Foreword

*Believe in the Magic.*

This is certainly a popular saying around Christmas Town and one of my personal favorites. It was with a little bit of luck and stars aligning that I was asked to be a part of the Christmas Town collection years ago. And it was with a not-so-subtle nudge from my writing crew that I accepted (and I'll be forever grateful for their support and encouragement that continues to this day). When I wrote my first novella, *A Gift of Home* for the collection, *A Heartwarming Christmas*, I never imagined what Christmas Town would become. Or how much the world (and the authors who've contributed to its creation) would come to mean to me. I'm so fortunate to collaborate with such talented authors and more than a little excited each time I get to revisit Christmas Town and imagine what comes next for a place I truly adore.

When we gathered for our brainstorming session this year, it only seemed natural after all this time that Christmas Town should finally star in its own movie. With the direction set, the story ideas came together for *Lights, Camera . . . Christmas Town*. I've often said that I write about characters I would like as neighbors and friends, people I would want to spend time with, and never is that more true than in Christmas Town. And this year's collection is certainly no different. From the wonderful cast and crew of the movie filming in town to the delightful locals, Christmas Town is truly abuzz this season. And of course, the Knotty Elves are on hand to remind us to believe in the magic. After all, it's the heart of the holiday season.

Here's your ticket to our movie. We've saved you a front row seat. Grab a cup of hot chocolate, a candy cane (or two) and make yourself comfortable. The action is about to begin.

Merry Christmas, Christmas Town Readers and Fans. May this be your best Christmas yet!

~ Cari Lynn Webb

# Contents

# Mistletoe Memories

## Book 1: Lights, Camera, Christmas Town

### Anna J. Stewart

ChelseaBeth Publishing

# Prologue

*November 24th<sup>th</sup>*

*Over the River Retirement Home, Christmas Town, Maine*

"That's a wrap." Odette King grinned the day after Thanksgiving, silently congratulating herself for working a film-making reference into the conversation with her two closest friends. She straightened her red-sequined, mistletoe-adorned sweater. "And I do believe we've outdone ourselves."

Prudence Parker fluffed the long ends of a silver-and-blue satin bow on the countertop flocked Christmas tree they'd picked up from Murphy's Tree Lot. "Posey isn't going to want to leave her new apartment." The one she'd moved into at the Over the River Retirement Home. "She might even retire and enjoy life more." Instead of being so hands-on at the restaurant she owned—Posey's Diner in Christmas Town, Maine.

"Transitioning to a retirement community is tough." June Baxter turned on the small string of snowflakes they'd hung in the windows. They sparkled like June's gaze behind her owlish glasses. "The support of friends and family is vital."

"Her place feels like home." Pru's gaze drifted over the living room. Satisfaction drifted through her words. "I wouldn't mind living here for the holidays."

"That's good to know." Odette chuckled. "Seeing as you live down the hall. Only two doors away."

June set a small snowflake light spinning like a disco ball. "We certainly needed to make it special for her."

"You know what's going to be special?" Odette mused, gathering empty decoration boxes. "Having a real movie filmed right here in Christmas Town."

Pru fussed with the ice blue and cream-colored stocking they'd knitted for their friend, trying to get it to hang flat from the mantle. "It all came together so quickly, makes me think there was more than a dash of holiday magic involved."

"That and some very determined folks like Mayor Banning." Odette attempted to nestle all the empty ornament boxes within each other. It didn't work. With a sigh, she started over.

"Don't forget Lark Matthews." June tapped her glasses into place, set her hands on her thin hips and gave the room one final inspection. "That sweet girl has turned her producing dreams into a reality."

Pru nodded at the mantle as if satisfied with the stocking's outcome. "Do you think she's forgotten her personal dreams? Especially the ones that included West Coogan."

"Always was a spark between those two." June tucked the scissors and tape into the craft tackle box marked as: *Property of Mrs. Claus.* "Nearly a decade later, and West is still single. Do you suppose..."

"I do." Odette straightened, satisfied with the manageable nest of boxes. "Sometimes sparks just need a little encouragement, *just a nudge*, to flame bright again."

"Knitting, Christmas decorating, and nudges toward love." June settled the craft bag strap on her shoulder and headed toward the door. "The things we Knotty Elves have a knack for."

"I do enjoy a bit of good-natured nudging in the love department." Pru sighed wistfully. "I suppose we should make a list of singles in need of a love nudge."

"I've already compiled a list of the production crew and cast that will be here this week to begin the filming of *The Christmas Carousel*." June's thin eyebrows perched higher on her forehead. "Our idea to give couples matching knit goods is brilliant, just one more reason for them to chat."

"A sweet ice breaker," Pru agreed. "I do hope we'll be cast as extras in the film."

"Good thing we have appointments at Carols and Curls this week." Odette bumped the bun on top of her head back to center.

"Plus, they always have the latest gossip about the town's singles." Pru opened the front door and ushered her friends into the hallway.

Odette knocked her elbow into June's bony side.

"Ouch." June rubbed her ribs. "What was that for?"

"I'm just getting warmed up for all those nudges we're going to be doing soon." Odette chuckled.

"It's going to be a busy December for certain." Pru stretched her arms out in front of her as if warming up too. "What with the second annual Bake-Off happening. Our usual influx of tourists. And now a movie."

June rubbed her hands together. "It's a December of opportunities, ladies."

"We'd best get to it then. Let's get our knitting supplies and that list of eligible people." Odette smiled at June and Pru then added, "'Tis the season in Christmas Town, ladies. There's no better time for believing in holiday magic and nudging the lonely toward love."

# Chapter One

*D*ecember 1ˢᵗ

"Morning, West!"

"Morning, Gina." West Coogan acknowledged the owner of The Tea Pot while she filled his travel mug with an extra-large, triple shot mocha. He avoided looking outside at the gazebo in the town square. Instead, he pretended interest in his surroundings.

There was a line nearly out the door at The Tea Pot, despite it snowing outside and it being before seven on a Friday morning. Idle chit-chat, the sounds of espresso and latte machines, along with calls for a Merry Christmas blended with the chorus of *Holly Jolly Christmas*. Behind West, a long wall was decorated with old logging tools and pictures of Christmas Town from a century ago—loggers, bakers, Santa Claus standing in the town square gazebo.

*No escaping that gazebo.*

West sighed.

"Here you go, West." Instead of handing him his coffee mug, Gina came around the coffee shop's counter, retaining possession of West's much-needed caffeine. Her short, white-blond hair had a bit of a frizz to it and her brown apron had streaks of flour on the front. "I was wondering how you're doing. You're a long-time resident and a first-time proprietor. Christmas Town business owners are a tight-knit bunch. We talk about all kinds of things—business, tourists, the holiday and...personal stuff." Finally, she handed him his mug. "Are you okay?"

"I'm definitely settling in at the Workshop. But okay? I'll tell you after I balance November's books." How he hated admitting it. After three years of planning, West had purchased the Christmas Town Workshop, the town's original hardware store. He had big shoes to fill. The previous owners—Gus, Barty, and Marv, otherwise affectionately known as the Three Wise Men—had made their mark in the community. West had plans, big plans, to grow the landmark in his hometown. "Did Nick tell you I've applied for a permit to expand?" Nick being the mayor and Gina's husband.

*I Saw Mommy Kissing Santa Claus* filled the air as another wave of Christmas Town workers entered the shop, stomping snow from their boots and removing snow-dusted caps before moving into the order line.

"Nick didn't tell me." Gina smiled, brushing the flour on her brown apron. "But he doesn't tell me everything. Expansion? That's great news. Anything else going on?"

"Nope. Everything's fine." It was a good feeling for a fellow-business owner to be interested in West's plans, satisfying, like finally making an elite, prestigious team. "How are things with you?"

"Oh, the usual. Husband, kids, Christmas, baking. I'm blessed with a never-ending line for pastries and coffee." She waved an arm at the line and the jolly customers wishing Merry Christmas to each other. And then she looked at West with compassion in her eyes. "You know Nick and I are here for you, right? If you need to talk."

"Thanks?" Did she know something he didn't? About the Workshop? About something that was going to muck up his plans. He'd been in a bubble lately—working, working, working. "Is there—"

"Gina!" A worker pushed through the kitchen door. "The oven timer's buzzing!"

"Gotta go, West. You know where to find me." Gina bolted for the kitchen faster than Rudolph led Santa's team of reindeer in the wee hours of Christmas morning.

"*Oh-kay,*" West drew out the word. That was weird. And now that West thought about it, people were looking at him oddly.

He moved toward the door just as a van from Over the River Retirement Home was unloading. A middle-aged man helped three elderly ladies out. They were decked in thick jackets, red and green knit caps, mittens, and scarves, and carrying bags nearly overflowing with yarn and knitting needles. The Knotty Elves had arrived.

West held the door open for them. "Hey, Pru, Odette, June. And goodbye." He flipped up the collar of his fleece lined jacket and ducked out into the steadily falling snow.

"Oh, West." June fluttered after him, her large, round glasses giving the impression of an owl bundled up for the holiday season. "Merry Christmas. We made you this." She handed him a knitted drink cozy that was large enough to fit around his already insulated travel mug. It would give it double the insulation. It was green with candy canes all around it. "We'll be here all morning if you want to talk."

"Thank you." West slipped the cozy over his mug and wondered why so many people suddenly thought he was a talker. He turned away from the gazebo and the town square and headed in the other direction—toward the Workshop.

"Merry Christmas, West!" The high school principal gave him a quick wave as he passed on his way to school. "Doing okay?"

"Yeah." The weird factor increased. Folks weren't usually overly concerned about his well-being. West turned and walked backwards a few steps, watching the principal disappear around the corner, in case he expanded upon his concern.

And while he was walking backward, he bumped into Lisa Richardson.

"I'm sorry. My fault. All these people coming to town have my head spinning." Lisa juggled multiple three-inch binders, blond hair blowing beneath her blue cap. Still, she managed to finagle a hand on West's arm. "John and I have been thinking about you. You need anything, you let us know, okay?" She scurried across the street toward city hall, deftly avoiding the icy patches.

West paused in front of Dockery's to drink some of his coffee and take a good look at himself in their store window. There was nothing smudged on his face. He bared his teeth in a smile. Nope. They were clean. His jeans weren't on backward. His work boots were neatly tied. Granted, he did have a dusting of snow on his blue knit cap and the shoulders of his black jacket, but it was snowing.

*Could something have happened at the Workshop?*

A pit formed in his stomach, and he hurried on his way.

*If something happened, I would have gotten a call.*

From the fire department, the sheriff's department, someone on his staff, or the Three Wise Men, who spent their so-called retirement hanging out on the front porch of the Workshop, the same as they always had. Unless...

That pit in his stomach dropped to his toes.

*Unless something had happened to Barty, Gus, or Marv.*

He ran, shouting out, "*Fine!*" whenever someone asked him how he was doing.

The Christmas Town Workshop came into view. Unscathed. The Three Wise Men sat outside on the front porch in their wooden rocking chairs, bundled up against the cold so they could greet townspeople and collect gossip. Also unscathed. Relief flooded through West.

"Morning Gus, Marv, Barty. How are you doing today?" West kicked the toe of his boots against the bottom step before taking them two at a time. "How are things in the store?"

"We beat Raymond here." Marv huddled over a steaming mug of hot chocolate that fogged his thick glasses.

"Opened everything up, right and proper," Gus said from beneath what looked like several layers of blankets.

"Fulfilled Troy's order." Barty rocked his wooden chair furiously, as if he held a fussy baby. "Where've you been?"

"Getting my morning coffee." West held up his cup with its candy cane cozy, peering at each wise man in turn. They all looked hale and hearty to him. "Anything going on that I should know about?" Had there been a fire in the storeroom? Was there a shortage of replacement Christmas bulbs? Had the cat he'd adopted from Holly Haven Animal Rescue decided he didn't like being the

Workshop's mascot? West glanced in the store and then back at the men. "I feel like something happened since I left yesterday."

"Yeah, about that..." Gus, his bald head covered by a thick wool cap, rocked forward, and narrowed his eyes as if examining West through a microscope. "How you holding up?"

"Okay." Abandoning his plan to balance November's accounts first thing, West leaned against a porch post and looked at each of the elderly men in turn. They might just as well have been playing poker. Their expressions offered no clue to...anything. West dug his cell phone out of his pocket. There were no messages. "What's going on? Did we get robbed? Did you donate my stock of tree light timers without asking again? Do I need to call someone...about...something?"

"Weren't robbed," Gus said tersely. "Folks wouldn't do that to us."

"Donations are always good for business." Barty didn't slow his rocker. And there was something tense about his expression, something making more wrinkles than usual.

"But you could call your mother." Marv slurped his hot chocolate, glasses still steamed so thick that he probably couldn't see a thing. "Heard her mention the other day that she has to take a number to get a sliver of your time."

"And so..." West took a big slug of his coffee, wishing it had something stronger in it. "Why are you looking at me as if I found coal in my Christmas stocking?"

"I don't think he knows." Barty stopped rocking and stared at West.

"How can that be?" Marv set his hot chocolate on a wood crate, removed his fogged glasses, wiped them clean and then put them back on, only to stare at West in slack-jawed amazement. "Well, I'll be."

"You're gonna need to sit down." Gus patted the empty rocking chair next to him.

West stayed put.

"Merry Christmas." Sam Collins, the local handyman, hurried up the steps. His hands were shoved deep into his wool-lined, denim jacket. "Pretty cold this morning, huh?" He stomped his work boots on the porch and nodded at West's coffee mug. "Should have stopped at Gina's myself. Heard you were just there. Wanted to talk to you about some special orders if you have time. Unless you aren't up for it."

"Why wouldn't I be up for it?" West's patience was wearing thin.

The Three Wise Men coughed dramatically into their gloved hands, but Sam didn't seem to notice their warning. "Marnie told me over dinner last night. That's gotta be rough."

"Marnie told you what?"

"About Lark Matthews coming back. Today, I heard." Sam looked completely shell-shocked. And when Sam was shell-shocked, he tended to babble. "You know, she's here to work on that TV movie about John and Lisa Richardson. Happened all of a sudden. String of luck for the town's economy. Bad luck for you, though."

The trio of old men's coughing sounded like a sudden influenza outbreak.

West's ears rang louder than a cavalcade of bells on one of Haverford Stable's sleighs. "Lark's coming home?"

The coughing chorus went silent.

"Oh, boy." Sam tugged off his knit cap and slapped it against his thigh to remove the snow. "You didn't know."

"I did not know." There was an ache in his chest, an ache that still had a jagged edge, even after nearly a decade. "So, this is what's got everyone tiptoeing around me like I'm a broken Christmas ornament."

"Well, can you blame us?" Marv picked up his hot chocolate mug and took a sip. Almost instantly, his glasses fogged again. "That girl turned you down and bolted out of town so fast she barely left tire marks in the snow."

*True.*

"And after all your planning, too." Barty returned to his fast-paced rocking. "Can't recall anyone ever hiring the Victorian choir to sing backdrop to a man's marriage proposal."

"And you invited all your friends." Gus tsked. "Did you have no idea that she'd say no?"

"No." And that was the source of that jagged pain in his heart. He and Lark had dated for a few years in high school. They'd told each other those three magical words—*I love you*. They'd talked about their dreams—hers to make film, his to run a business in Christmas Town. Sure, in the back of his mind, West had suspected those dreams didn't jive. But he'd loved her. He'd had faith that they'd find a way to make a life together. And what had he gotten in return for his faith? An indelible image of her running away and a broken heart.

"And there it is." Barty stopped rocking once more, staring at West. "That expression of yours... That's what we've all been worried about. You and Lark Matthews."

What the entire town had apparently been worried about.

"I'm fine." West sipped his coffee, as if he needed a jolt of super-charged caffeine to sell the concept of well-being. "Let's go over that order, Sam."

"You're fine?" Marv removed and polished his glasses again, as if needing to see for himself.

"Absolutely." What a lie. It took all West's effort not to look up at the sky for the lightning bolt headed his way.

"If you say so," Gus said in a sing-songy voice.

"I do say so. I've moved on. I'm sure she has, too." But his gaze drifted to the street, looking for Lark's determined walk and her bright blond hair, because the reality of Lark's return was sinking in.

*Lark is coming home.*

Maybe he'd finally get answers as to why she'd said no and ran.

Maybe the jagged hurt would finally smooth over the way scars were supposed to.

———❄———

"How is it nothing has changed?" After nine-hours and sixteen minutes—they'd hit at least two accidents on the drive up from New York—driving into Christmas Town almost felt like passing through a time portal, straight into the past.

A past Lark had spent nearly ten years avoiding.

Lark's chest crowded with vestiges of grief. She forced herself to look at her hometown with the eyes of a film producer, not with the eyes of the girl she'd once been, the girl who assumed her parents would live forever.

There was Dockery's. Although Lark had tried to contact everyone in advance with a warning about the ugly Christmas sweater dinner scene, there was bound to be someone who'd request something different. Dockery's always had a broad selection of corny Christmas wear. There was The Tea Pot, looking busier than ever. The cast and crew tended to thrive on caffeine. And the snow... They'd need lots of that for the exterior scenes, especially any filmed on the town square and in the gazebo where...

Lark gulped and pressed the brake too hard. The production company's motorhome lurched at the stop sign. The dancing reindeer tangled in Christmas lights she'd attached to the motorhome's dashboard shimmied. "Sorry. I was distracted by the time capsule." She'd just unearthed a sharp memory of the look on West's face when she'd uttered the word, "*No,*" after he'd asked her to marry him.

"Looks the same to me, Aunty Lark." Nine-year-old Molly sat in the front passenger seat. Her long, dark hair was mussed from sleeping through the night, but her eyes were bright and her smile wide. "Grandma Posey always says Christmas Town is a winter wonderland. Now it gets its own movie."

*Only because the other location I chose fell through a week ago.*

Lark made the turn to navigate the border of the town square, giving the motorhome some gas and feeling it lumber along as if it was as awe-struck as she was.

Nearly a decade should have meant some transformation, shouldn't it?

No. Lark sighed. Time always stood still in Christmas Town. A time that, up until a few days ago, she'd have done anything to avoid returning to. Now her hometown was the only thing that could save her professional bacon.

"Don't blow this, Lark." That was the last thing her studio chief had told her when he rightly anticipated her protests against using her hometown for the shoot. "We've been wanting to film a TV movie in Christmas Town for some time. You had this script written based on a true story in Christmas Town. Whatever bad memories you have, turn this broken egg into eggnog."

*Bad memories?*

Lark's fingers trembled on the wheel. The dashboard reindeer swayed as if encouraging her to let go and lean into the Christmas joy, not the pain.

*But my life shattered here.*

She gripped the hard plastic wheel tighter.

Her parents had died here during her senior year of high school. Her uncle Harold had blamed Lark at the funeral. Her best friend Faye discovered she was pregnant around that time and her high school boyfriend wanted nothing to do with the baby. And then, West had proposed after graduation, as if getting married at eighteen and giving up on her dreams would make Lark feel whole again.

It had all been too much. Lark was afraid it still was.

*There's the ice skating rink where Dad took us skating.* There'd been joy swirling around on that ice for hours on end. Pride too when she'd finally been able to skate backwards. The dashboard reindeer wiggled.

*There's the school gymnasium where Kaleb used to play basketball.* Where she'd cheered for her brother from the bleachers, surrounded by friends and family. The dashboard reindeer bobbed.

*There's the cemetery up on the hill where Mom and Dad are buried.*

She tapped the brakes on memory lane and concentrated on the road in front of her. The one that led to the Pine Tree Inn and RV Resort and the continuation of her career as a producer.

Lark pulled into the parking lot of the RV park and instructed young Molly to stay put while she registered. The desk clerk wore a Christmas sweater with a wreath on it and matching earrings. People in her hometown went all in on the holidays. There'd been a time she'd led the Christmas cheer charge. Now it was a dashboard reindeer and holiday scented soaps for her. There was nothing wrong with a more subdued approach to the season, even if the locals would disagree. The clerk gave Lark a registration slip for her windshield, pointed out her space, and wished her a Merry Christmas.

If Lark could finish this film by December twenty-fourth, she'd feel very merry indeed. After that, Christmas Town wouldn't have the cast and crew disrupting their warm and fuzzy traditions.

*Like kissing or receiving a marriage proposal beneath the gazebo.*

*Stop it.*

Time to get to work. Time to think about something other than her memories and mistakes. There was a movie to make and eggnog to taste. Lark drove to her space and pulled in.

She and Molly glanced around. There were other trailers and motorhomes they'd arranged to use here as accommodations, some with holiday decorations. Since everything was last minute, one of the biggest challenges during this holiday season had been lodging. Lark was staying in the production company's motorhome, not her vacant family home.

"I see Mom." Molly's long dark hair draped across her shoulders as she stared out her window. "She's parking behind you." Molly had ridden in the motorhome so that she could sleep on the bed in back.

Faye was Lark's best friend since forever. She ran a film set catering service and also doubled as Lark's production assistant when she didn't have other work.

Lark unbuckled her seat belt and moved into the motorhome proper, intending to review list of the tasks needed to get the film off the ground. Instead, she stopped and stared out the back window, imagining if the trees hadn't grown so tall that she'd be able to see West's house. Or perhaps that barely visible gable was his. "You should go get your things, Molly."

"Aww." Molly turned her familiar *I don't wanna* pout on an immune Lark. "Why can't we stay in the motorhome with you, Aunty Lark?"

"Because I'm going to be working most of the time and it isn't conducive to little girls sleeping or doing their homeschool studies."

"I could sleep in your bedroom while you work." Molly's grin warmed Lark's heart. Man she really loved this kid. "I don't take up much room and I'll be quiet. I don't snore like mom does."

"You'll be staying in a real house. My old house. There are so many ornaments and lights stored there. I give you full permission to bling the place out." She was certain her parents would be happy about that.

"I guess that's okay." Molly dragged her feet to the back of the motorhome.

"Congratulations. We arrived in one piece." Faye pulled open the door and all but fell up the stairs as the wind and snow flurries pushed her in. Her light brown hair swirled beneath her knit cap. "You ready to go, Molly? I could use food and a nap before Aunty Lark puts me to work."

"I'm packing," came the subdued voice from the back.

"Ah, the sound of an excited child never fails to make her mother smile." Faye dropped onto the leather sofa across from the dining booth and then flopped onto her back. "How are you holding up?"

"Okay." But Lark hadn't moved. She was still staring out the back window, unsure if the roofline she saw was West's or not. And wondering why it mattered so much. She pulled her head out of the past and focused on the task ahead. "I just need you for a few hours after your nap. I could use help making sure everything is running smoothly. I lost my intern when we changed locations." She'd been offered a romcom shoot in Miami.

*Why couldn't I get those jobs when I was first starting out?*

She'd interned on horror films at sea during rough waters, in the Mojave desert during June, and in the Louisiana Bayou in July. Then, somehow, she'd landed a job at a production house that made romances for television and streaming services. Happily-ever-afters had become her stock in trade.

*How ironic.*

Few at work—but everyone in Christmas Town—knew that Lark had run away from her own happily-ever-after.

"We won't work long, I swear," Lark told Faye, once more distracted by thoughts of West. "We're both tired."

"I always have time for you, my friend." Faye stretched out with a sigh. "But I told Grandma Posey we'd stop by to eat as soon as we got to town, even if it's too late for breakfast and too early for lunch."

"Are we having peppermint pie?" Molly swung into view, holding onto the doorframe, and leaning diagonally.

"A true Christmas Town tradition," Lark murmured, wondering what had happened to West. He was probably married with two kids, a golden retriever, and a minivan. He'd probably kissed some other girl in the gazebo and whispered, "*Together, we can get through anything.*" But she didn't know. Lark didn't allow herself to reconnect with the past—not on social media, and not with Faye, who visited Christmas Town at the holidays. West wasn't a conversation her heart could handle. Now, thinking about him, her heart pounded. And she couldn't slow it down. "I need to work."

"I need *pie*." Molly's eyes sparkled. "You don't know this, Aunty Lark, because you never come home, but Grandma Posey sometimes lets me have pie for breakfast or lunch. Can we, Mom?"

"It's Christmas Town and we'll be with your great-grandmother," Faye told her daughter. "What do you think?"

"Awesome!" Molly disappeared back in the bedroom. "Don't help me find Elmer the Elf this time."

"Wouldn't dream of it." Faye closed her eyes. "We'll leave you alone just as soon as I can feel my butt again. That was a long drive."

Still haunted by the past, Lark stretched some of the kinks out of her spine and sifted through a box of paperwork on the dinette seat. "Word is Abilene and Cyrus got in late last night." She sorted through the same thick stack of papers she'd been reorganizing over the past few days—cast and crew accommodations, shooting schedules, budgets, invoices and contracts. "Why can't I remember where they're staying?"

"Abilene is at Over the River." Faye sat up and pressed her hands against the base of her back. "You know, the retirement home? Didn't you read my email?"

"No." Lark blinked. "Does...ah... Did Abilene know that's where we found her a room?" The older actress had once been so famous that she'd become known by a single name. It had taken some kind of miracle to land her for the role of Lisa's grandmother in the film. Lark hoped she wouldn't feel slighted and quit.

"She didn't know. But since she's young to be playing an adult's grandma, maybe she'll just consider it part of her preparation method."

"That's my story." Lark smiled. Her smile felt rusty, but welcome. "And I'm sticking to it."

"I'm ready, Mom." Molly wrestled one large suitcase and two backpacks from the bedroom.

"Take a breath and come to Posey's with us," Faye urged Lark, hefting Molly's suitcase.

"Into town?" Lark kept her gaze pinned to her papers. "No. Thanks." What would she say if she saw West? It was too soon.

*What do I say if he has a wedding ring on?*

Lark sucked in a breath.

*What do I say if he doesn't?*

Air left her lungs in a rush.

Molly skipped down the steps, opened the door, and lost hold of it when the wind whipped past.

The loud bang and resulting snow flurries snapped Lark out of her funk. This TV movie was supposed to be light and breezy, with all the feels. To deliver on that, Lark needed to be light and breezy, as enamored with Christmas and Christmas Town as she had been as a child.

"You can't hide in here the whole time, Lark." Faye moved more carefully down the stairs with the suitcase while Molly bunny hopped across the snow with the backpacks.

"I don't plan to hide." Lark couldn't. She had to be in ten places at once as the producer. Hiding wasn't an option. Avoiding wasn't an option either.

There were introductions to be made. Thanks to be handed out. Cast and crew to check on.

But it still took Lark a long time to venture out into the snow.

# Chapter Two

Lark stepped into Posey's Diner and firmly back in the past.

The restaurant was decked out to the holiday nines with fresh, thick pine garlands, spiked with glistening silver and gold tinsel, no doubt courtesy of Murphy's Tree Lot. Ornaments Posey had collected from customers since the day the diner opened dangled from the boughs while seasonal music drifted from the overhead speakers. The air was filled with sugar, spice, and everything nice. With the gentle snowfall hitting the Christmas Town sidewalk on the other side of the frosted windows, it was absolutely looking a lot like Christmas.

Lark indulged in a second deep breath, thinking perhaps she might be feeling Christmas, too. The tiniest stir deep inside her. It was a start.

Faye met Lark at the hostess stand, frowning. "We didn't expect you. We already finished eating."

"I got busy with paperwork." *And stalling.* "Besides, I'm not hungry."

"It's okay to say you need a distraction. Or company." Faye wrapped a knitted, reindeer-patterned scarf around her neck and kept silent.

"Ms. Odette and I found Elmer, Aunty Lark." Molly tugged on her gloves, bounced in her snow boots then motioned to the elderly trio of walking Christmas cheer headed toward them. "Ms. Odette and I hid Elmer in a super-good, super-secret spot too."

It was tradition in Posey's to find the small elf, who resembled Santa and wore green overalls with a red hat. He was hidden amidst the plethora of Christmas decorations. Whoever found him earned a free piece of peppermint pie and the honor to hide Elmer elsewhere.

Faye re-introduced Lark to the elderly trio Molly had charmed and explained, "Odette, June, and Pru call themselves the Knotty Elves."

"We knit." Odette tapped her nose like Mrs. Claus with a really good secret. "Pru, don't you have something to welcome Lark home?"

"That's not necessary." Lark opened the door and the small group spilled out onto the sidewalk.

"Oh, it is," June insisted, studying Lark the way she used to study students when she was the high school principal.

Pru dug in a cloth bag stuffed full of yarn and knitting needles. "Aha!" She handed Lark a green knit cozy decorated with candy canes. "You'll be grabbing coffee on the run. This will keep your drink warm and your spirits bright."

"That's... It's... So kind," Lark managed to say. Film producers weren't always recipients of gifts unless something was expected in return. That faint feeling of Christmas cheer from earlier built inside her, soft and welcoming. Maybe she could do this—be home and be okay. She gathered the reins on her hope before it got away from her and said, "I'll be sure to use it." She tucked it in her jacket pocket.

"Molly and I got personalized hats." Faye adjusted the slouchy red elf hat on her head and flicked the white pom over her shoulder. "Now, Molly and I need to pick up the keys to your old house, Lark. I guess your brother Kaleb has been renting it out. And it's popular. We have to be out of there on Christmas Day." Faye looked up and down the crowded street. "And Bailey Real Estate would be..."

"Chase's office is that way." Pru tipped her head toward Comfort and Joy, a quaint shop. "We'll walk with you." Prudence dipped her chin at Lark. "You too, Lark."

"We've lots to discuss with you about your film," June added in a tone that left no room for argument.

Lark embraced the transition back to work. It was where she was most comfortable.

"The Knotty Elves have ideas for the opening sequence of the movie." Faye glanced at Lark, laughter in her gaze. "I told them they really *must* share every single thought with you, *too*. You always welcome new ideas."

*Not always.* Lark was more of a lone wolf when it came to her job and her life, depending on no one but Faye. But even then, she tried to protect Faye and Molly from worries about the future, taking on that burden herself.

"We believe it'll be best if we show you our ideas." Odette linked her arm through Lark's, bundling Lark neatly at her side. "We want to give you a visual walk-through of the opening sequence for the movie."

*Oh, boy.* Lark's cheeks hurt and not from the cold. *Just keep smiling. Just keep smiling.*

"We've several options in mind." Pru stepped to Lark's other side and bumped her shoulder into Lark as if to nudge Lark where she wanted her. "The entire town is quite thrilled about the movie, as you can imagine."

Lark suspected that was true—the entire town, minus one. West most likely wasn't thrilled about the movie or Lark being back. She managed a dutiful, "I'm glad to hear it."

"You'll be even more glad to know we've spoken to the business owners," June explained. "They've agreed to allow their businesses to be filmed. You can't imagine the excitement."

Lark suppressed a weary sigh. "But I can imagine the paperwork."

"Paperwork can be quite tedious, can't it?" Odette tsked. "It'd be so much easier if everyone just agreed to get along."

If Lark and West simply agreed not to go digging around in their past, would that be enough for them to get along while she was in town? There was that hope again. Still, that required a conversation. With West. Who probably never wanted to speak to her again.

"Rules are meant to be followed," June chided, still the school principal, even in retirement. "Same as protocols meant to keep people safe."

But where was the protocol that kept hearts protected? Lark touched her forehead, trying to keep her guard up because the past was surely waiting to jump out at her. Already, she could feel the gazebo and the cemetery demanding her attention.

They reached Comfort and Joy. Its window display was intricate and beautiful, featuring a very large Victorian village, including a miniature steam engine, a ski lift, and a horse-drawn sleigh circling the church in town.

Lark's smile came more easily. "The Victorian Christmas Village has doubled in size. I remember coming to see it with my parents every year."

"It's nice to have holiday traditions," Pru said quietly.

"And to make new ones." Odette nudged Lark with her shoulder, as if they were good friends. "Traditions bind us and help us heal."

Once upon a time, Lark had a family and holiday traditions galore. Her favorite was always helping Mom display her antique Santas. Even Lark and West had their own tradition. They'd cuddled up on a couch and watched *Love, Actually* together, followed by *Die Hard*. Both were favorite Christmas movies.

Something in Lark's chest eased. For once, the memories didn't burn. They soothed. And Lark wanted to linger and lean into the good, if only for the moment.

"Look!" Molly had moved to the window of Fingers and Feet Sock Shop while her mother went into Bailey's Real Estate. "Look at all the funny socks. And there... There's Santa in a hula skirt." She laughed as Lark joined her.

Lark recalled West's laughter when she'd gifted him a pair of socks for Christmas one year. Teddy bears. He'd worn them to the winter dance and claimed they were his favorite gift that year. She could still remember how safe she felt with his arms around her that night.

Lark's soft exhale steamed the window.

"Wouldn't it be lovely to open the film with vignettes of each of these charming shops?" June asked, her voice suddenly soft and unassuming.

"People bustling past with bags filled with wrapped packages." Pru patted her overstuffed red velvet shoulder bag, which gave off Santa sack vibes.

Lark took in the earnest faces of the well-meaning trio. Her smile wavered as she revised her assumption that this project would be a trial. Her fingers curled around the yarn drink cozy in her pocket, easing into its comforting softness.

"Chase wasn't inside, but his assistant found the keys to Lark's house." Faye shook a small key ring as she joined them.

Lark gave Faye a look that pleaded for her not to leave her alone with the elderly knitters. She'd only just admitted this project might be fun, but that hardly meant she wanted to play tourist with the Knotty Elves and rediscover something like her Christmas spirit.

"Oh, you'll be fine, Aunty Lark," Faye teased, shaking the keys so they jingled like sleigh bells. "Come on, Molls. Lark's house used to be Christmas Town central for us. Your Aunty Lark doesn't know what she's missing." The pair scurried off happily.

"You aren't staying in your family's home?" Pru pulled a small metal tin from her bulbous bag and offered Lark a meltaway candy as if peppermint soothed the way for those hard truths.

"No." Lark hadn't been back since she'd run away from West and had no intention of going inside now. She hadn't even known it was a short-term rental until they made housing inquiries in town for the film. She'd left the details of handling her parents' estate to her older brother Kaleb. She popped Pru's mint into her mouth. "The production company provided me with a motorhome."

"But..." June's eyebrows twitched behind her eyeglass frames. "What about a tree? Hanging stockings? Baking cookies?"

"I won't have time for that." She'd barely have time for sleep. "This is my big break, you see. The first film I've been put in charge of."

"And it features a couple who rediscovered love years after things fell apart, right here in Christmas Town." Pru snapped the mint tin closed with a decided click. "The very place you've avoided for years. How...prophetic."

"It's not like that. You're all familiar with Lisa and John's story." It wasn't Lark and West's story.

*But it could be.*

The peppermint dissolved completely, but she was feeling anything but a cooling and refreshing sensation. Lark frowned.

"Will you look at the time?" Odette glanced at a silver watch on her wrist. The crystal-accented snowflake face revealed it was eleven-thirty. "The lunch hour is upon us. And I've just recalled that Lark hasn't eaten. She looks like she needs sustenance, doesn't she, ladies?"

"Yes." June marched ahead. "Let's head over to Three Elves Sandwich Shoppe. We can point out some of our finer window displays along the way."

---

West found it impossible, despite his best efforts, to focus on anything related to work.

He chatted with his morning customers, helped at the counter, answered questions and booked appointments for clients looking to do some remodeling, which as an architect, he could help them with while also increasing sales of materials at the Workshop. And yet, he wasn't excited. West listened to Elvis sing *Blue Christmas*. But always, in the back of his head, he could hear the thump-thump-thump march of the inevitable.

*Lark was back.*

He heard people talking about the motorhome that had rolled into town this morning, an RV that had headed straight for the Pine Tree Inn & RV Resort, which offered both rooms and RV spaces for rent. He heard others talk in excited voices about the movie that was to be filmed. Someone from the film crew came in to check out their merchandise and bought several sawhorses. Funny how the movie hadn't been on his radar before, but now it was all West heard about.

"I'm taking lunch," he announced at eleven-thirty, unable to stay inside any longer. He told the same thing to the Three Wise Men on his way out.

"Going to meet Lark?" Marv stopped his chair from rocking, looking curious.

"Are you coming back after?" Gus asked, looking concerned.

"Do you need backup?" Barty demanded, looking fiercely protective.

West felt the weight of being under a microscope. He faced them in order to answer the Three Wise Men each in turn. "No, I'm not meeting Lark. Yes, I'll be back in thirty minutes after I grab a sandwich. And no, I don't need backup.

I probably won't see Lark. If I do, I'll keep things civil." Even if another piece of his heart broke off in the process.

West headed out into the falling snow. He wanted to keep his head down and hunch his shoulders. Instead, he kept his head up and on the swivel, looking for a woman with a purposeful walk and hair so blond it rivaled the gold star he put on his tree every year. He didn't have his hopes up. He was a pragmatic businessman now. But even pragmatic businessmen needed closure.

But no one caught his eye as he walked through town. No one made his heart skip a beat.

He entered the Three Elves Sandwich Shoppe and moved into line.

"Look who's here, Lark. West Coogan, as I live and breathe."

West turned to face the Knotty Elves and Lark.

"He's early," he thought he heard June mutter. She received an elbow from Pru.

It dawned on West that he'd fallen into predictable habits. Coffee in the morning from The Tea Pot. Lunch at the Three Elves Sandwich Shoppe. Dinner at home. If he had dinner.

"Hey, West." Lark's gaze collided with his, wide and expressive.

"Hey, Lark." Did it hurt that he read vulnerability in her gaze but wasn't certain of its cause? He decided the ache in his chest meant it did.

West took a good long look at Lark. She'd changed her hair. It was shorter now, more stylish with its angular cut just at her chin. She still huddled into her jacket, hands tight in her pockets, shoulders hunched as if she needed to brace herself against life, a habit she'd developed after her parents died.

"I'm about to order," West said in a carefully neutral voice. "Why don't we eat together and catch up?"

*Best get it over with.*

Lark gave a jerky nod.

The line inched forward. The Knotty Elves kept their circled wagons around Lark, perhaps fearing that she'd run.

West feared that, too. Lark ran away from problems and conflict. She'd run away from him after he proposed and then she'd cut him out of her life, along with her brother Kaleb.

They ordered separately and waited for the sandwiches to be made while the Knotty Elves made small talk. In no time, their orders were up. They'd ordered the same thing—a soda, a bag of chips, turkey with sour cream and cranberry sauce.

"We'll let you two get reacquainted," Pru said to them before leading the Knotty Elves out the door. "Merry Christmas!"

"The Knotty Elves told me you bought the Christmas Town Workshop." Lark unwrapped her sandwich and dug in. She'd never been shy about food. Or talking about how she felt, which was why running had always perplexed him. "They very carefully worked you into the conversation about which stores and locations downtown offered the most holiday charm for my film."

"I own a business." He had no appetite. But West dutifully unwrapped his sandwich and took a bite, chewed, swallowed, tasted nothing. "I didn't think the Workshop came with Three Wise Men."

"How could you think any differently? They've hung out there since we were kids." Lark tucked a stray tomato more firmly between her bread as *Run Rudolph Run* played from the speakers. "I'm going to address the elephant in the room. Looking back, we had decidedly different dreams. I wanted to create film and you wanted to run a business in our hometown."

"Who'd have thought we'd both be achieving those dreams before we turned thirty?" Alone. "Here's to dreams." He raised his soda cup.

"To dreams." She tapped her cup against his, smiling a little. "It's good to see you."

He smiled more broadly, not wanting to let on that the scars on his heart were cracking open again. It was as if he'd merely duct taped it together all those years ago. "It's good to see you, too. To see for myself that you've been thriving."

"Thriving?" Lark took a bite of her sandwich, gaze slipping toward the windows and the foot traffic. "Does that imply you have a personal life?" She gave a wry laugh at his nod. "Do people who thrive stop to smell their Christmas trees? I wouldn't even have a Christmas tree if it wasn't for Molly and Faye."

He chuckled. "If you're thriving like I am, we're both too busy making sure everyone who depends upon us has a holly, jolly Christmas ahead of our own. How did we get to this point in our lives?" He shook his head. "Remember how we used to have all the time in the world to help each other's families decorate for the holiday?"

At the word *families*, Lark stiffened, set down her sandwich. Blinked. Cleared her throat. "I... That was a long time ago." And it didn't seem as if she'd reconciled herself with the past.

Did that mean she hadn't reconciled her feelings for West?

"No one blames you for anything, Lark, least of all me," West said softly. But those were the same words he'd told her nearly a decade earlier. She hadn't believed him then and it was obvious that she didn't believe him now. "This is a fresh start for you here."

"You can't start fresh pushing a luggage cart full of baggage," she said in a guarded whisper. "There's you... My parents... Kaleb..."

"You can continue to ignore everything," he said gently, wishing that she'd accept his help—or anyone's—to stop running and face the hard things. "Or you can take hold of someone's hand and look the past in the eyes."

"I hurt you," Lark admitted. "When I left. The way I did."

The music switched to Bruce Springsteen's version of *Santa Claus is Coming to Town*.

Lark crumpled her sandwich wrapper and began to slide out of the booth.

West caught her hand, staring at it instead of into her eyes because he didn't want her to realize that he still loved her. She needed to hear something different. "When you love someone, you try to find a way to forgive them. When you left, it hurt. But I picked myself up. The same way you did," he assured her. The same way he'd pick himself up after she left.

"I envy you," she said quietly. "You've found peace with the past."

He hadn't. But he would after today.

He'd let Lark go. And he'd create a new dream for his life in Christmas Town. One with a woman who could stay, lean on him when need be, and love him come good times or bad. Lark was too independent, her hard shell protecting that soft heart he'd once known so well.

He let her go.

Or he would have if she hadn't recaptured his hand, tugged him up and said, "Walk with me."

# Chapter Three

"D o you ever hear from your brother?" West asked Lark as she towed him down the street at a brisk pace, dodging people on the sidewalk like she was a race car driver in a video game.

She was trying not to take in their surroundings. But the memories of Christmas Town were flooding back to her. The town square came into view. She'd sung in the school choir during the Christmas pageant, beaming out at her parents and grandparents in the audience. She'd told Santa her Christmas wishes there and he'd told her to lick her candy cane three times to make them come true.

*My parents...*

"Slow down," Mom used to tell her. "Life comes at you fast, but that doesn't mean you have to go at that pace."

She and Kaleb had volunteered to deliver Christmas presents to kids spending the holiday in the hospital. Christmas Town General's roof was visible in the distance. She'd built a snowman on the snowy green with Kaleb. He'd taken her sledding and...

*My brother...*

"Breathe deep twice," Kaleb told her when she'd been upset over Uncle Harold telling her one Thanksgiving that her ears were too pointy. She'd been five or six and devastated, although it seemed silly now.

"Lark?" West's low voice brought her back to the present.

"Kaleb used to call and text but I..." Lark was ashamed to admit that she didn't stay in contact with her older brother and hadn't since he'd left after her parents' funeral. He'd left her, barely eighteen, in a house full of memories. He'd left to grieve his way and left her struggling to manage hers. "Do you ever talk to him?"

"Every once in a while. Kaleb has a good life in Texas working on an oil rig. He's a real go-getter, like you."

Was West dragging his feet? She risked a glance at him. At his tall, straight posture and chin held high. He had nothing to run from in Christmas Town. His steady brown gaze hadn't changed. There was warmth there. A tenderness she didn't deserve. She couldn't talk to her brother. She couldn't set foot in her childhood home. She didn't know what had happened to her mother's beloved antique Santas.

But this... *I can do this.* Be honest with him. Lean on him the way he wanted her to. At least for the next few minutes.

"Family is a prickly vine," Lark told West, not slowing down.

"You can always trim those thorns." West's voice was deeper now, richer. "It's never too late. The last time I saw Kaleb, he asked me if I'd heard from you."

Lark swallowed thickly, crossing the street, and heading toward the community center. "And my uncle?"

*This is your fault, Lark. All your fault.*

"Your Uncle Scrooge?" That was her family nickname for the sour, glass-half-empty paternal uncle. "He left town not long after you did. Good riddance, I say."

His words made her smile. "Still loyal to me after all this time?"

"I'm always Team Lark," West said in a husky voice. "Your uncle should never have blamed you for your parents' *accident.*"

Lark kept marching forward, stomping her feet as if she could smash her uncle's accusations out of existence.

"Stop." West dragged her to a halt. There was a cup half-filled with candy canes in front of Glad Tidings Floral Shop with a collection tin beside it. "This conversation requires candy canes." He plucked two from the bin and tucked a five dollar bill in a slot.

"You're over-paying." That was producer Lark talking, the watcher of budgets.

West handed her a candy cane, shrugging. "It's for holiday meals for shut-ins, a good cause. Besides, we used to sit in the stands when Kaleb was on the championship basketball team and devour candy canes. Remember? No one can be stressed or blue while eating a candy cane."

Lark was stressed and blue. She unwrapped the straight end of her candy cane and bit off the long end. No eating slowly for her. "Not to mention it keeps breath minty fresh."

"There's nothing like candy cane kisses after your team wins." West took the lead, dangling his hand behind him for her to take if she chose.

*I choose.*

They walked past the community center, which had a sign promoting a gingerbread contest on the front door. That was new.

Lark crunched her candy cane. West sucked on his. Block after block. She barely registered memories now. She was looking at the town with the eye of a producer. Which locations offered charm and had easy access to electricity. How much snow was too much snow. It was good that circumstances had led her film production here. Christmas was authentic in Christmas Town.

But there was one more thing to face before she started this film.

The graves of her parents.

West seemed to know it, too. That's why when she hung back, he kept moving forward. And now the entrance to the cemetery came into view. The iron gates. A winding road up the hill. Instead of looking grim and somber, the snow gave it a cozy impression. *You're reaching.* Lark shoved the snarky back where it belonged. Her parents were resting here overlooking the town they loved, the town where they'd found love.

The town their children no longer lived in.

The sky seemed to darken, and the snowflakes increase, falling with a dramatic hiss.

"Oh." Lark's steps slowed. She wasn't ready. "I need to head back."

West didn't listen. His steps didn't falter. His fingers around hers didn't release.

And only then did his words from the sandwich shop come back to her. *You're thriving.*

She wasn't. She was missing out on so many things as she pushed herself forward in this career, dragging Faye along with her.

A line of dialogue from this film came to mind: *When I was working, I didn't stop to appreciate the sights the way I would have if you were there with me.*

And now, West was here with her, helping her to move forward and appreciate what she had and what she lost.

"Faye has been telling me for years that I need to come back and make peace with the past. I knew that in my heart. I knew that I had to come here."

"You carry your parents in your heart." West gave her the kindest, most loving look. "I'm sure you think of them often."

*Every day.* Lark took a steadying breath. *Just like I think of West every day.*

The wind blew. The snow fell. Time ticked past. It had been ticking past.

Something inside of Lark burst out, something that had been suppressed for too long. *Love.* For her parents. For West. For Christmas Town. For her brother Kaleb. Love for the familiar and the past.

Suddenly, there was more love in her heart than there were regrets and grief and guilt.

"This is some candy cane," she whispered, passing under the cemetery gates.

---

Lark found the graves far more easily than she imagined she would since she'd only visited twice before. Once on the day her parents had been buried and the second on the day she'd left Christmas Town. They'd been her last goodbye. Fitting as she had been theirs that winter's day.

"I miss you both so much." There were no tears. How could there be when she'd already shed a lifetime of them? But there was still tension pressing down on her. She'd called them to pick her up that night. She'd put them in the path of that drunk driver.

She squeezed West's hand and moved closer, drawing on his warmth and strength, wanting to feel something besides grief and loss, wanting the happy memories to return. She needed those recollections to fully heal, no more running.

She and West didn't speak. The snow fell. Somewhere far off, bells jingled. Lark tried to recall memories of her parents at Christmas, tried to see their faces, hear their voices, feel their love. At first, there was nothing but images of the funeral, their pictures displayed on their caskets. And then, memories came flooding back.

And those memories. Good memories. Laughter. Mugs of hot chocolate. Her parents often spiked theirs. Cookies in the oven. The smell of a fresh Christmas tree and turkey roasting in the oven.

"I'm home, guys," Lark whispered. She used to shout those words every time she burst into the house. "Merry Christmas."

"Merry Christmas, Mr. and Mrs. Matthews." The tender smile on West's face was as familiar as his hand around hers. "Good to see you again. You'd be proud of Lark. She's still a hard worker, rushing to get ahead. She's one of the youngest producers in the industry."

Lark did a double-take. "How do you know that?"

"I have access to the internet." West's smile grew into a grin. He gestured further up the hill. "My family has a plot over there. I stop by to pay my respects to your parents from time to time. I remember how they were always such good listeners. They still are."

Lark's phone pinged. Work was bringing her back to reality. She wasn't ready. Not to let go of this feeling of peace. Or to let go of West's hand.

"I think I need another candy cane. I have some in my RV. Can you spare me a few more minutes?"

"Sure. After I say hello to the folks up the hill."

# Chapter Four

They didn't talk much on the walk to the RV park. West thought Lark needed space to fully embrace the feelings she'd discovered in the cemetery. He was waiting to talk more when they reached the motorhome she was staying in.

But when they reached Lark's RV, her expression changed, from pensive to determined.

*Work mode.*

"Home sweet work home." Lark handed West a candy cane. But then she became engrossed in her cell phone and shuffling around papers she removed from a box.

West could feel her nerves pinging off the walls of the RV like a runaway elf. Was this her normal?

While taking note of the small amount of Christmas decorations in the vehicle, West received a text from Gus: *We're here for you.*

Ah, yes. By now, the entire town would know they'd taken a walk together, holding hands. He could handle the questions. But could Lark?

Sucking on his candy cane, West caught sight of a piece of paper with some scribbles on it, peeking out between two blue file folders. He tugged it free. Whoever had drawn it had little artistic talent although he could make out something that looked like Tinkerbell and the words: Pixie Pop. "What's this?"

Lark glanced at it, pausing, emotions flitting across her face—guardedness, sadness, longing. Lark ran a hand over her short, blond hair, letting it fall to swing loosely around her chin. "That is...probably a pipe dream."

That was more emotion than he'd seen from her since they'd come inside. "Tell me about it."

She hesitated, the guardedness shadowing her blue eyes.

"Dreams are fragile things," West told her in a low voice. "I was brave enough to tell people I wanted to run a business in Christmas Town, but I wasn't brave enough to tell them which business I wanted. What if they laughed?" He watched the weight of his words touch her, waiting to see how she'd react. But she looked away, out the motorhome's back window. "I love you, Lark. I always will. But dreams often take a village to bring to life, which means your odds of achieving them are better if you tell someone. We used to be able to tell each other everything." Before her parents died, that is.

Lark closed her eyes. "I wish you hadn't said that."

"What?" He played dumb anyway, waving his candy cane around. "That we used to be able to share things openly? Or that dreams take village?"

She opened her eyes in a magnificent eye roll. "You've helped me work through stuff today. But now... Are you making this difficult on purpose?"

"Nope." Oh, yes, he was.

"Liar," she murmured with a regretful smile, taking her scribbles from him. "You want me to talk. And...Pixie Pop. It's my own production company. My dream. I've talked about it for years but only with Faye. When I reach a certain level of success, I'd strike out on my own with Faye. She loves to cook and cater, but she loves project logistics, too. Every producer needs someone like Faye." Lark shrugged nonchalantly, not fooling West. This was important to her. "Anyway... I'm not sure how close it is to reality these days. Work's been complicated. And financing..."

"It'll happen." West was sure of it. But he was also certain that if it did, that would be the end of the hope that they'd ever be a couple again. "I believe in you."

He didn't mean to make her cry. But Lark's eyes filled and just as quickly spilled over. "I never meant to hurt you, West. I hope you know that. Turning down your proposal..."

"I'm proud of you, Lark." West stood and wiped away her tears before taking hold of her hand. "I'm so proud of everything you've done. You went after your dreams."

"But I left you behind. I loved you. So much. But after Mom and Dad—"

"I never should have pressured you." It was the apology he never thought he'd get to make. "Proposing like that in front of the entire town, it was selfish and the fact you said *no* only shows what a strong person you are."

She stared at him for a long time. "You aren't mad?"

"Not anymore." Talk about laying himself bare. "Not for a long time. And time... It gave me perspective. What did either of us know about forever promises? If you'd said yes, we might not have even made it together. You'd have resented me after you didn't go chasing your dreams and I'd have foregone college to keep you as happy as I could." He shook his head. "You did us both a favor, Lark. You made a hard choice."

"I wanted to say yes." She squeezed his hand. "There have been a lot of days when I wish I had."

"Yeah." He nodded. "Me, too. But you didn't."

"And now I'm back."

"And now you're back." West crunched his candy cane, something he never did.

But it was fitting. Because like Lark's time here, the candy cane joy wouldn't last.

---

After closing the Workshop for the night, West walked through Christmas Town, no longer the object of concern.

That was because the town was filled with strangers. West suspected they were part of the cast and crew of Lark's movie. But he saw a lot of locals out and about, too.

Movie madness had taken over concern for West. Talk of the production had seeped into every nook and corner, every store and business. Word was they'd be using locals as extras, and some of their businesses were about to be featured front and center.

Before heading home, West stopped for a hot chocolate from the hot drinks cart at the corner of the town square, intending to walk slowly past the ever-increasing decorations lighting the snowy green and gazebo, and soak up Christmas. He'd no sooner taken his first sip than he turned and spotted Lark standing in front of the old Christmas Town Savings & Loan. She was illuminated by the golden glow of a street light. He quickly bought a second cup of hot chocolate and hurried over before she moved on.

"Hey, Lark." He handed over the cup. "Thought maybe you could use this."

She smiled down into the mountain of whipped cream before looking up at him and accepting. "Well, that's lovely, thank you." She reached into her jacket pocket and pulled out a candy cane cozy that she slid on her cup. "If the Knotty Elves see me, I'll earn points. They gave this to me this morning."

"They gave me one, too." His travel mug was sticking out of his coat pocket. He tugged it free, revealing a matching cozy. "They must have made a lot of these."

"But we match." Lark carefully sipped her cocoa, returning her gaze to the bank. "What happened to this?"

"New building." West pointed to the other end of Main Street. "Got its own parking lot, so it made sense to move. Shame about this building though." As an architect, he'd always loved the art deco design of the building. "It's been vacant going on about two years now." It was too bad. It was perfectly located across from the gazebo and the town square. Smack dab in the middle of all the action. The right business hadn't made a play for it yet. "I know you're busy, but... Do you have a minute?" At her nod, he took her hand and crossed the street to a bench with a clear view of the gazebo.

They sat, still holding hands. Still holding hot chocolate.

They sipped, still silent. Still staring across the street at the bank building.

West looked at her. At wispy blond hair that belied her strength. At bright blue eyes that didn't hide the wheels turning in her pretty head.

"Hey." Impulsively, he moved closer and kissed her. Softly, carefully, briefly for fear of scaring her off. But he kissed her and then almost immediately drew back to give her space. "When we were in your motorhome, you changed the subject about Pixie Pop. I felt like you had more to say about that dream."

Lark's gaze drifted toward the bank with its For Rent sign in the window and then back to him. "It's...I don't know," she said in a small voice, the kind that spoke of vulnerability and powerful dreams. "It's more than just a production company. I want to do something for small towns like ours. I want to produce movies that use them, that spotlight them and support them. I want to help preserve them by bringing attention to them. People like to visit or even move to film locations, which helps preserve and sustain small towns."

"I bet Faye loves that idea."

"She doesn't know." Lark tried to look away, but he caught her chin with a gentle touch of his finger and shook his head. "I haven't told her more than about me wanting to start a production company. The film business is hard enough without adding a higher purpose to it. If I tell Faye, she'd worry." Her voice grew smaller still. "Like I do. But someday... I'm going to make it happen and we'll do it together. Just like we've done everything."

Years ago, West had been in Lark's circle, along with Faye. Now he was on the outside looking in. How long ago that seemed. "Why wait?"

"Oh, um, money? Location? Employees? Scripts?" Lark laughed, then sipped her hot chocolate. "We live in New York, so saving isn't exactly easy. It'll take a while, but it'll happen."

"I'm sure it will." He had no doubt. "You're Lark Matthews. It's what you do."

She blinked at him blankly.

"You'll build your village, and your dream will come true," he said softly.

"No." Her expression turned serious, and she repeated, "No. I'm not a village-builder. I tear things down. My family. My relationship with you. I have to do this on my own. Thanks for the hot chocolate and...thanks for listening." And then she walked off alone.

"Someone must have hit you with the biggest stupid stick in Christmas Town, Lark Matthews." Faye paced the narrow aisle in the RV on Saturday morning, steam coming out of her ears. She'd left Molly at Posey's to work on movie logistics with Lark. "Let me get this straight. You had a second chance with West, right at the gazebo where it all fell apart last time, and you walked away? Because he said you should ask people for help making your dreams come true?"

"Uh, yep." Lark pretended to be checking wardrobe budget numbers. But inside, she was reliving the gentle, familiar feel of West's lips on hers and longing for longer kisses.

"*Yep? Yep?*" Faye spun to face Lark. "What is the matter with you? He's right and he still loves you!"

It wasn't the reaction Lark had expected upon sharing the details of her cocoa confab with West. As she'd shared the details, Lark had barely stopped herself from reaching up and touching her lips. They'd kissed. Her and West. After all this time. And it had been... perfect.

No, nothing about this was perfect. There was reality to deal with. So, she argued, "We live in different states, Faye. It's not practical. And you know as well as I do that the chance of a female producer under the age of thirty getting funding to start a production company is nil. If it's going to happen, it's on me. Only me."

"Lightning strikes. Miracles occur. People win the lottery." Faye dropped onto the sofa. "Forget your dreams for a second. Why are you closing the door to love when it's only just been opened again?"

"Is that why you were so excited about filming here when my other location fell through?" Lark hadn't had time to really stop and think about it before. "Were you intent upon trying to get me and West back together?" To kiss one more time?

"Of course not," Faye snapped. Then she shrugged, expression turning guilty. "Okay, maybe a little. But you have to admit, the film's romance happened here. Authenticity will be good promotion for this movie."

Lark took a deep breath. "You wanted me to go through the emotional wringer when I have to produce a film that could make or break me?"

"If you put it that way...it does sound bad. But you still love him." Faye looked at her with misty-eyed frustration. "You've loved West since we were in third grade, and he thumped Billy Wilding in the playground because he hit you too hard with a dodgeball. You've loved West since he tried to teach you hockey even though you kept tripping on the stick. You've loved West since he wore those emasculating teddy bear socks to the winter formal. He would move heaven and earth for you."

Lark bet if she unwrapped a candy cane and took a bite, she'd remember more times that West had watched over her.

"You think I don't see it?" Faye went on. "That you were hurt when we left on so many levels that you used an all-out pursuit of your dream to protect you from getting hurt again? You think I don't know that you wanted to protect me and Molly?" she added softly. "You pretend to be so put-together and career-driven, needing no one, but you care for people. Why go it alone? Why not let others care and support you for a change?"

Lark's back was stiff. Her midsection, her shoulders, her neck. She felt attacked. Did that mean Faye was right?

"I love Molly," Faye continued in that soft tone of voice. "And yes, I'm lonely. But when I'm old and gray, I'll still have her. What will you have, Lark? A film production company that you run alone."

"Faye, I've never gone it alone," Lark said quietly. "I've always had you."

"To a point." Faye shook her head. "But what if someday you don't have me? My grandmother is slowing down. She moved to Over the River because she couldn't keep up with her home's maintenance. What happens when she needs me here and you have to leave?"

Lark didn't know.

"He loves you." Faye sighed and stood up. "You love him. Molly's father didn't love me. Do you know what I'd give for that?" And with that, Faye left.

Lark stared at the door she'd gone through for a long time. Thinking.

West sat in his office Saturday afternoon, his accounting program open on the computer screen in front of him.

As a boy, he'd had a dream about owning a business in Christmas Town. But as he grew, he didn't want to run a gift shop or a diner. He'd always enjoyed building things with his dad and grandfather. After his relationship with Lark fell apart, he'd signed up for an architecture college course with his roommate. He learned that building things that lasted started with a good foundation and solid walls. But before that, they started with a plan.

His plan to expand Christmas Town Workshop was to add on in the back, building a showroom with displays of building solutions. He wanted to help people make their houses and businesses, old or new, more functional and aesthetically pleasing. But he was already doing that now. Without the showroom. Without a plethora of samples, extra staff, or fancy computers to bring his plans to life.

Which brought him back to the money he'd set aside for expansion. For permits that he'd already applied for and materials he hadn't yet purchased.

West had dreams about life, just as Lark did. He'd bought a business. She'd become a film producer. He wanted to expand. She wanted to be her own boss. She wanted to help small towns thrive and survive.

Heaven knew, small towns were disappearing. She could be their lifeline.

West stared at the figures on the computer screen.

He could help her and by association, help others in small towns.

But if he was going to help her, it had to be without strings.

And after kissing her yesterday, he wasn't sure he wanted to cut that tie.

# Chapter Five

"Morning, West." Posey appeared at his booth shortly after his arrival at the diner. "You don't usually come by for breakfast, even on Sundays."

"I usually sleep in on Sundays." But he'd slept fitfully. A decision had yet to be made. His dream or Lark's. West glanced up at Posey, who always seemed to be working when he dined here. "Did I hear a rumor you might retire?"

"Bite your tongue." Posey snapped her order pad closed. "I changed my address. If one more person asks me about retirement, there'll be no more pie for that person. Not. Ever. Again."

"Warning noted." West handed her his menu, registering the sound of youthful laughter but unable to place its source. "Can I get a waffle and a side of bacon? And coffee." Oh, he needed so much coffee. He noticed a dark-haired little girl peeking out from behind Posey. "Hello there." There was no mistaking those big dark eyes or that pert little nose. "I bet you're Molly. Faye's daughter." The Three Wise Men had mentioned her yesterday at the Workshop.

"Uh-huh." She nodded but clung to her great-grandmother.

Posey tucked her order pad in her apron pocket. "Molly, this is West Coogan."

"West!" Molly's eyes lit up and she stepped closer. "You're Aunty Lark's old boyfriend."

West smiled. "Yes, I am. Her *former* boyfriend." He wasn't that old.

"Mom says Aunty Lark's dumb because you kissed her and she's not giving you a second chance and Aunty Lark is going to be an old maid."

West's ego boosted significantly. "I've always thought your mom was smart."

"Do you need help marrying Aunty Lark?" Molly was completely oblivious to the fact that everyone—and by everyone that included the Knotty Elves in the back booth and the Three Wise Men sitting at the counter—was listening. "You know, Aunty Lark does everything I tell her to."

Posey made a sound that eroded the validity of that remark. "I think we'll get your coffee now." She ushered Molly away.

"But Grams—"

"Good strategy if you ask me," Gus said from the counter. "You get Molly in your corner, you increase your odds of Lark saying yes this time."

"Can't ignore those sparks you two were setting off at the gazebo yesterday," Odette chimed in from the other direction. "Hotter than an overblown Christmas tree bulb from what I hear."

*It was a peck.*

Marv coughed. "If you ask me—"

"I didn't," West cut him off before the rest of them could go overboard.

"Leave him be," June said gently, adjusting her glasses to give every would-be love advice specialist in the diner a firm look. "Let the man eat breakfast first. Thinking and advice-taking require fuel. So, eat fast, young man," she added when his coffee arrived courtesy of Molly. "And then we'll get to work."

"No thanks." West turned toward Posey, who was clipping his order ticket to the order wheel. "Posey, make that order to go."

---

"Darn it." Lark huffed out a steamy breath. She'd had an idea. A crazy, impulsive, out-of-this-world idea shortly after three this morning, right after she'd had a dream about saying yes to West inside the gazebo. A lot of her impulsive, far-reaching, out-of-this-world ideas arrived at about that time and very few of them had ever paid off. Yet.

But this one... Oh, this one had her out of bed too early on a Sunday. Only to see the bank building no longer had a For Rent sign in the window.

"Well, Pixie Poop. Maybe it fell off the window."

"We have got to stop meeting like this." It was West, carrying a coffee and what looked like a to-go box. "I could hear those mental wheels of yours turning all the way over at Posey's."

"Could you?" She smiled. How could she not? He was her kind of charming. Not to mention, she'd spent a long night pondering Faye's words about her tendency to do things solo, including her not-so-thriving personal life. She'd decided her independence traced back to the accident. If she didn't ask for help and took on the responsibility for others, no one would get hurt. But now, West stood in front of her, having referenced the heavy thinking going on in her head. "What was I thinking just now, West?"

"About Pixie Pop. About how to make that dream of yours come true when it's only you."

Lark smiled. "That's right. I sent off a request to meet with an equity firm about financing Pixie Pop. It's a long shot, but after talking with you and Faye, I realized I have to try."

"Yes. Try." West stared at her oddly, not as if waiting for her to say something more, but as if he was wrestling with words of his own. He blinked, then set his coffee and to-go box on the curb. "You just need to be ready to accept help. In this case, my help." He reached into his pocket and withdrew an envelope, staring at it for a moment before holding it toward her. "My dad and grandfather left me quite a bit. Being the only child and grandchild has its perks, I guess. And...I didn't spend it all buying the Christmas Town Workshop." West extended it closer toward her. "Open it."

Lark's heart pounded and her hands shook. Whatever was inside that envelope felt like... felt like the responsibility that came with a village. Not only would she be worried about not letting Faye and Molly down, but she'd also be worrying about West, too. "I don't—"

"Open it, Lark. It's my way of saying I'm letting you go. You're free to dream as big as you want."

She didn't want to let him go. "You can't just do this without thinking it through."

"I have." West cleared his throat and said again, in a stronger voice, "I have. I spoke with my attorney yesterday and asked him about the risks involved with investing in a new film production company. We agreed, given your experience and your determination and ability to get things done, that it was worth taking a chance on. *You're* worth taking a chance on. I want to invest in Pixie Pop Productions, Lark. Good luck. Be happy. Thrive."

This felt impossible. Improbable. And so completely West.

The sidewalk beneath Lark's feet felt unsteady. West was going to help her achieve her dream. West was making an offer with no strings, except future profit, if any. She should be grabbing hold of that envelope with both hands. She should be hugging him and thanking him and telling him she'd have her legal people call his legal people. That's the way this business worked.

Lightning struck. A miracle had happened. She'd won the lottery.

Except she hadn't. She couldn't. Not without him.

Tears spilled onto her cheeks. "I was going to come to the Workshop later," she whispered, "to ask if we could talk about the future. To see if we could..."

"To see if we could what?" West still held that envelope out.

She'd hurt him before. Deeply. And she'd hurt him yesterday, too, when she'd walked away. Faye was right. Lark was afraid, wrapping herself in her work and working hard enough that she never had time to heal. That wasn't thriving.

Lark took a step forward, lowering West's hand, the one holding that envelope. "I wanted to see if we could start over. To discover if maybe there was a chance—"

"There is." He nodded and rested his forehead against hers. "Whatever chance you want to take, I promise you, I'm here for it."

"I'm not who I was," she whispered. "I need you to understand that. I've changed."

"Good." He nodded. "So have I."

"I'm more stubborn."

"So am I."

"I want to try," she whispered. "I want *us* to work."

"Okay." He moved back, inclined his chin toward the gazebo standing behind them, still holding that envelope. "Then let's do it right this time." He slipped his hand down to hers and they walked down the short path, and then up the stairs. He held her beneath the sprig of mistletoe hanging from the dome ceiling and kissed her.

She clung to him, sobbing a bit, laughing more.

"Lark Matthews, will you—"

"Don't propose." She couldn't stop herself. It was too much too soon. Panic rose in her throat. "Not yet."

He laughed, shaking his head. "I wasn't going to propose marriage. But make a promise. For the future. Lark Matthews, will you promise to take a chance on us? Will you promise to have faith in me and believe that I want nothing for you but for all your dreams to come true?"

She nodded and sniffled. "Yes. And for the record," she murmured when he brushed his lips against hers. "I want yours to come true, too. I love you, West Coogan. Now and forever."

"Now and forever." He handed her the envelope. "I'll have my lawyer contact your lawyer."

"You have changed." But Lark loved it. She took the envelope, knowing she had plenty of time to look at it later. "Did I see you had breakfast ready to take home?"

"You did." He was having a hard time containing that happy smile. "Do you want to go home with me, Lark?"

"I do."

The End

# A Daring Little Christmas

## Book 2: Lights, Camera, Christmas Town

### Beth Carpenter

ChelseaBeth Publishing

# Chapter One

*D* *ecember 4th*

The sun was just inching over the horizon, but in a barn about a mile down the road from the carousel building in Christmas Town, conversation buzzed like a wind-up Santa toy.

The set dresser made a few last-minute adjustments on the carousel workroom set, while a man with dancing penguins on his sweater tested the lighting. Today was the first day of filming for *The Wedding Carousel*, and Miranda Paxton, assistant to supporting actress Abilene, could feel the swell of eager anticipation filling the cavernous space that had, up until last week, served as a storage unit for Christmas Town's holiday decorations.

Miranda had almost forgotten what it was like, being on a film set. The excitement, the nerves, the pressure. Her mission was to anticipate the bumps and make Abilene's return to acting as smooth as possible. At the drinks table, she ignored the selection of teabags Faye Burlew, the movie's caterer, had set out. Instead, she opened a tin she'd brought along and spooned a special blend of dried mint leaves into a diffuser ball. Abilene—Abby to friends—wouldn't complain about teabags, but Miranda knew Abby preferred this mint blend. She dropped the tea ball into Abby's travel mug, added hot water from Faye's urn, and let the tea steep.

A sudden breeze sent all eyes toward the sliding doors, where Faye's young daughter, Molly, was helping her mom push in a cart loaded with breakfast pastries. The furry ball on Molly's Santa hat bounced as she skipped inside and called out, "Merry Christmas, everybody!"

"Merry Christmas, Molly," the crew and cast replied, almost in unison. The assembled workers seemed like a great team, ready to make a great movie.

Miranda hoped so, anyway, since she'd been the one to urge Abby to accept this role.

Once the tea brewed, Miranda stirred in honey and snapped a lid onto the travel mug. She made her way through the crowd to the trailers outside. Abby's dressing room was tiny, at the end of a row of six and she had to share it. Miranda knocked on one of the two doors. "Abby, it's me."

"Come in." Abby glanced up from her script and met Miranda's eyes in the mirror. It was weird, seeing Abby in a white wig, made up to look thirty years older, and yet still her beautiful self. Miranda handed over the mug. "Your peppermint tea."

"Thank you. Have you seen that scarf I was wearing this morning? Those knitting ladies gave it to me."

"I have it here." Miranda retrieved it from her tote, where she also carried an extra copy of the script, Abby's favorite lip balm, a tourist map of Christmas Town, a set of earmuffs with reindeer antlers on the headband, and a dozen other items that might prove useful. She had wondered about that scarf, knitted from sparkly silver, fuchsia, and teal green yarn. Abby would never in a million years have chosen such flashy colors. "Are you cold?"

"No, but I thought the ladies might get a kick out of it if I wear it for filming." Abby took a sip and set her cup on the desk. Beside her, the bottom of the accordion screen separating her dressing room from the next one was a few inches off the floor, probably for better heat circulation, but not ideal for private conversations. "Did you check with wardrobe?"

"Yes. They okayed it."

Abby draped the scarf over her costume coat. "What is it they call themselves? The Knitting Sprites?"

"The Knotty Elves," Miranda corrected, smiling to herself at the quirky name. She'd only been in town for a few days, but from what she had seen,

Christmas Town was full of colorful characters. "It's nice of you to think of them."

Abby winked. "I'm always nice."

A snort of laughter, gallantly covered by a fake cough, emitted from the room next door.

Grinning, Abby reached over and folded back the divider, exposing Cyrus Nash, Abby's on-screen soulmate in this film and off-screen ex-husband. He lounged on his couch. He was attractive, charming, and at the ready whenever an opportunity to talk to Abby presented itself.

"Here." Abby thrust her tea toward Cyrus. "It sounds like you need this more than I do. Hope you're not catching a cold."

He waved the mug away. "No thanks. I'm fine. Never better."

The tension in the air was palpable. To Miranda, at least. The phrase that came to mind was: *Get a room.* But the pair always claimed to be *just friends.*

"Would you like to run through your lines once more before we shoot?" Abby asked him, her voice dripping with innocence that didn't fool Cyrus or Miranda. "At your age, the memory starts to go, they say."

The corners of his brown eyes crinkled in amusement. "And yet, I still remember your birthday, which makes me a month younger than you, I believe."

"Ah, but women's brains age more slowly," Abby replied good-naturedly. "It's a scientific fact."

He chuckled.

Someone knocked on Abby's door. "Abilene, we need you on the set, please."

"Coming." Abby stood, releasing the accordion screen, which sprang back in place.

Miranda straightened Abby's scarf.

There was a similar knock on Cyrus' door. "Cyrus, we need you on the set, please."

Abby and Cyrus each stepped out their own door.

Miranda followed Abby, stood in the doorway and watched them.

Cyrus offered an arm to Abby. "Ready?"

"As always."

The pair exchanged a glance and somehow, using nothing but posture and expression, they transformed from a pair of middle-aged actors made-up to look older to an eighty-something-year-old couple still very much in love. It was almost like a magic trick.

Miranda grabbed Abby's tea and coat before following. When she was six, her parents had taken her to their hometown theatre to watch *Christmas Moon*, starring Cyrus Nash and Abilene. It had been Miranda's first time in a theatre, and the story mesmerized her. Later, after her parents' bakery failed, they moved away from that small town to a city, and then to another. And another. And yet, whenever she caught a rerun of that movie, Miranda was transported back to when life was simple, and movies were magic.

Consequently, Miranda had jumped at the opportunity to be Abilene's assistant several years ago, not long before the decision was made to cut Abby's part from a television series for no better reason than that she was getting older. Abby had handled it with grace, but Miranda could tell she was hurt. Shortly thereafter, Abby's aunt in Vermont died and Abby had moved into her house, claiming to be taking a creative break. Miranda went, too, continuing to work for Abby, first helping to organize her aunt's estate, and then assisting her in running a tearoom. The tearoom flourished, but occasionally Miranda caught a glimpse of something unfulfilled in Abby's life, a restlessness and melancholy.

Several months ago, Abby's agent had sent the script for *The Wedding Carousel*, not to Abby, knowing she wouldn't read it, but to Miranda. It was a lovely story, of second chances, of Christmas, community, and family. Abby was perfect for the role of Nana Elaine. And, Miranda figured, once the movie was successful, it would show those shortsighted execs in Hollywood just how wrong they'd been to turn their backs on the talented Abilene.

It took some convincing, but eventually Abby agreed to take a risk and accept the part. Ironic since Miranda herself abhorred risk. She always had, ever since her father's poorly timed expansion had bankrupted the family bakery and forced them to move away from Yarrow, Kansas, the town she adored. But Miranda had a plan, and it was about to pay off.

For years, she'd been hoarding every spare penny. Those savings, combined with a nice little nest egg she'd inherited from her grandparents, had grown to almost enough to buy a modest home in Yarrow. For cash, so that she would never have to worry about losing her home. Of course, she would first need a secure job, and judging by the want ads in the electronic version of the *Yarrow Weekly Bugle*, suitable jobs in that small town were few and far between. But finally, the perfect position had opened up.

The moment she'd seen the listing of administrative assistant for the county tax assessor, Miranda had applied. What could be more secure than taxes? Last week's Zoom interview had gone well. Now she just had to wait for the job offer. This was another reason she'd urged Abby to take this role. After this, Abby could return to acting or retire on her own terms, and even though she was a generation younger, Miranda wanted Abby settled and happy before she left. Once the film was in the can, Miranda could seek her own happy place without feeling like she was letting Abby down.

Inside the filming barn, Abby and Cyrus approached the set. In one corner, a paper-mâché carousel horse, this one a Clydesdale, had been painted and textured to look old and cracked, with peeling paint. A half-finished mural leaned against the walls in the background. In the center of the set was a mockup of the mechanical gearing of a carousel, and that's where the two stars of the show, Macy Winter and Fox Baylor, found their marks. They were playing John and Lisa, a young couple working together with a ragtag group of volunteers to restore the carousel before the sixtieth anniversary of Lisa's grandparents, played by Abilene and Cyrus.

The camera assistant snapped the clapboard, and director Alexis Dorsey called, "Action." In this scene, John and Lisa were discussing whether restoration was even possible. Toward the end of the scene, Abby and Cyrus strolled into the workshop, personifying loving grandparents. They delivered their lines flawlessly.

"And cut," Alexis called.

And just like that, Nana Elaine disappeared, and Abby was back. "I'll take that tea now, please, Miranda."

Miranda hurried over and handed her the mug. Alexis went to talk with the two stars while a beautiful woman with short, dark hair fluttered around, brushing hair and powdering faces. "Nice job. Let's do it again, just like that." Alexis returned to her spot behind the camera. "Places."

Miranda and the other support people moved away from the set and the actors assumed their assigned positions. The clapboard sounded, and the scene began, but only two lines in, Alexis called, "Cut! What's that green and red thing on the horse?"

All eyes turned toward the Clydesdale. Sure enough, a small doll wearing green overalls and a red Santa hat was perched like a jockey on his back. One of the prop people hurried over and removed it. "It's an elf."

Miranda heard a small gasp from Faye, the caterer, who had been refilling the coffee urn. She hurried toward the prop guy. "I'll take that." Faye whisked the offending elf away.

"Let's try it again," Alexis called. "Places."

Filming went smoothly for the rest of the morning. When they broke for lunch, Miranda helped Abby remove the costume coat. "I'll take this to wardrobe. Do you want to change before you eat?"

"By all means." Abby reached for her own coat, but Cyrus took it first and held it so that she could slide her arms into the sleeves.

"I believe I saw Mulligatawny soup on the lunch menu," he mentioned.

"Mulligatawny soup." Abby smiled. "Like the soup we used to get at that little hole-in-the-wall in Manhattan, when we were in that awful play together?"

He chuckled. "The play was awful, wasn't it? But the soup was good. I'll meet you in the catering tent."

Abby had a little smile on her face as she and Miranda walked to her trailer, but she sighed when she stepped inside, glancing around. "I do miss my darling Duchess."

"Me, too," Miranda admitted as she hung their coats. When Duchess, Abby's Pomterrier, passed on, Abby had been devastated, swearing she would never go through this heartbreak again.

So it was a complete surprise when, with her head still inside the sweater she was pulling on, Abby declared, "I believe I'm ready for a new canine companion." She pulled the turtleneck over her head and looked in the mirror to arrange the collar. "I saw a flyer for a bake sale benefitting a local animal shelter."

Miranda had seen it, too, for a place called Holly Haven. "Would you like me to arrange an appointment with them around Christmas, when you're due to finish filming?"

"Why not today?"

"Today?" Miranda did a mental check of the schedule. "You're needed back on the set at one-thirty, and you won't be done for the day until after six. I don't imagine a shelter would be open that late."

"I'd really like to do it today if we possibly can." There was a wistfulness in her tone.

Miranda started to point out all the practical reasons this couldn't happen, but she hesitated. Abby had been beside herself after she lost Duchess. If she felt she was ready for another dog—well that was a good sign. It meant she was moving forward, and that Miranda had been right in encouraging Abby to take this role. "I'll see what I can do."

# Chapter Two

"Come on, Jolly. Sit." Dustin Burnside held a treat just in front of the big red dog's nose and moved it slowly backward. Jolly's furry haunches hit the snow, and Dustin handed over the treat. "Good boy."

"He's coming along." Lia Logan, his friend and the director of Holly Haven Animal Rescue where Dustin was volunteering, stepped outside, holding the leashes of a trio of small dogs. One, a Chihuahua, let out a string of barks. Jolly immediately leapt to his feet, but Dustin waved another treat in front of his nose. "Sit, Jolly."

The dog looked from Dustin's face, to the Chihuahua, and back at the treat. With an exaggerated sigh, he sat.

"Good boy." Dustin rewarded him with the treat and an ear rub. "Yeah, he's still a big puppy, but he's starting to settle down. Let's practice walking."

Lia started walking the three little dogs in a clockwise circle. Dustin and Jolly fell in line several yards behind. Dustin had been working with the big dog for a while now, and Jolly was finally getting the hang of this. They passed the small pen where Dustin had left his own ten-year-old golden retriever, Nugget, who acknowledged them with a sweep of her tail. Dustin stopped and allowed the two dogs to sniff noses.

"So, what's the progress on the zipline?" Lia asked Dustin.

"It's officially done." Dustin and Jolly resumed walking. "The inspector signed off yesterday, and I'm planning a grand opening soon. I just hope somebody shows up. I mentioned it to the snowshoers this morning, and a couple of people seemed interested. Can I put a flyer on your bulletin board once I set the date?"

"Sure." Lia stopped and had the little dogs practice their sits. "Do you really think Christmas Town tourists are the adventure type?"

"I sure hope some of them are," Dustin said. "Between the fat-tire bikes, sporting equipment, and zipline, I've invested a lot of money in this business."

"Lia?" Juliana, the volunteer receptionist, was standing at the door. "Someone's here to talk to you."

A woman with loose reddish-gold curls held back by a set of furry white earmuffs with reindeer antlers stepped outside, peering at them with wide blue eyes. Or were they green? Dustin needed to get closer to tell.

Lia handed the little dogs' leashes to Dustin and walked over to the woman. "Hi. How can I help you?"

"I'm Miranda Paxton, here with the movie we're shooting in Christmas Town. Do you know Abilene, the actress? I'm her personal assistant."

Dustin edged a little closer. He'd heard they were filming a movie, but he didn't know much about it. Might there be some promotional opportunity for his new adventure business there? He was just starting out, and he needed all the publicity he could get.

Lia seemed excited. "Abilene, who starred in *Christmas Moon*? She makes all those public service announcements to encourage pet adoption."

"That's her. She noticed you're having a fundraiser this week, and she asked me to bring you this." Miranda handed over the folded check.

Dustin drifted a little to the right. From this angle, Miranda's eyes looked more green than blue.

Lia glanced at the amount, and her eyes widened. "That's very generous. We can do a lot with this. Tell her thank you."

"I will," Miranda told Lia, "but that's not the only reason I'm here. Abilene would like to adopt a dog."

"Great." Lia smiled at her. "She'll need to fill out an application and—"

Miranda interrupted. "I can do all that."

"*Ok-ay,*" Lia said slowly, "but to adopt, she will need to come by in person."

"She wants to," Miranda assured her. "The trouble is, she won't be done filming until six-thirty, and I wondered if you could possibly let her come then. I know it's an imposition, but she's very eager to adopt."

"I wish I could, but I'm working at the bake sale on the square later," Lia said carefully, no doubt not wanting to offend. "Maybe next week?"

Miranda's face fell, but before she could say anything, Dustin stepped up. "I could do it." He'd planned to spend the evening handing out flyers for his business on the square, but this might be an opportunity to find out more about the movie and see if he could find any cross-promotional opportunities. Besides, he hated to see the sparkle dim in those beautiful bluish/greenish eyes.

"I thought you had a moonlight snowshoe outing." Lia frowned.

"That was yesterday," he answered, trying not to sound overly-eager. "I'm free this evening."

"All right, then. Thanks." Lia turned to Miranda. "Let's get started on that paperwork. If she qualifies, Dustin can get the final signatures this evening."

"Great." Miranda flashed a smile in Dustin's direction. Turquoise, he decided. Her eyes were the exact color of the bracelet his grandfather had bought for his grandmother on a vacation in Santa Fe. "I owe you one."

Dustin grinned. "I'll keep that in mind."

———

That evening, Miranda drove carefully along the dark country roads to Two Sticks Farm where Holly Haven was located. Meanwhile, Abby wiggled on the seat beside her like a six-year-old waiting to unwrap a Christmas present. "I can hardly wait!"

Miranda forced a smile. This afternoon, she'd received bad news from Yarrow. The assistant tax assessor position had been filled. However, they'd added in a personal note that a similar position might be coming up in the next year or two when someone retired, and that they would keep her resume on file. So the dream was still alive, just delayed.

But Abby didn't know about any of that, and Miranda intended to keep it that way. Abby had enough on her plate. "You're pre-approved for adoption," she told Abby, "and they have several adorable little dogs." Personally, she had her money on one named Sugarplum.

Ten minutes later, Miranda parked in front of the shelter. The wreath on the door featured wooden cutouts of dogs and cats chasing one another. Before she could knock, the man she'd met earlier opened the door. He wore a knitted cap over his thick, brown hair, a green quarter-zip pullover with rows of ice-skating reindeer racing across his broad chest, and a wide grin. A handsome grin. "Merry Christmas."

Miranda couldn't help grinning back, her earlier disappointment forgotten. "Merry Christmas to you, Dustin. This is Abilene."

"Call me Abby." The actress offered her hand and the smile that a movie critic had once called *pure starlight*.

Miranda had seen men stop in their tracks under the full force of that smile, but Dustin just shook her hand politely and turned his eyes back to Miranda. And just like that, Miranda could feel her cheeks heating as though she were the one in the spotlight. Their gazes held.

Abby cleared her throat. "Are the dogs through here?"

Dustin gave a little shake as though he was pulling himself out of a trance. "Yes, right this way."

Miranda hid a smile, rather enjoying the idea of being the one to make the handsome shelter volunteer lose track of what he was doing.

Dustin stopped in front of a cage holding the dog Miranda had mentally chosen. "This is Sugarplum. She's a Cavapom, we think. A Cavalier King Charles spaniel crossed with Pomeranian."

"My sweet Duchess was a Pom mix." Abby knelt down in front of the gate. "Hello, Sugar."

Sugarplum pricked her fringed ears and wagged her plume of a tail. Dustin opened the gate, and Sugarplum climbed into Abby's lap and licked her cheek.

Abby laughed. "What a sweetheart."

"Isn't she?" Miranda smiled to herself. A perfect match.

But after a few minutes, Abby returned Sugarplum to her pen and moved on to the next dog—a terrier mix—and then to a Chihuahua, and to three more dogs. Each received petting and sweet words. Once they reached the end of the row, Dustin announced, "That's all our small dogs."

"What's over there?" Abby asked, looking toward the next row of kennels.

"Our three larger dogs."

"I'd like to meet them, too."

Dustin led the way. The first pen held a black Labrador who jumped for joy at their visit, crashing into the gate with both front paws. Abby reached through the mesh and allowed him to lick her hand, which sent him into spasms of delight. Next was a German shepherd cross, who eyed them suspiciously from the back corner of his pen.

"Donner just came in today," Dustin explained, "and he's a little over-whelmed. He'll need some socialization before he's ready for adoption."

"I understand. You'll be in a good home before you know it," Abby quietly assured the dog.

Finally she moved to the last pen, where a dog with a wavy red coat, bigger and furrier than the Lab, stood watching them with his head cocked and a doggie grin on his face. Abby cooed at him, and his tail wagged, beating faster when Dustin stepped nearer.

"I've been working with Jolly," Dustin explained, "and he thinks we're going for a W-A-L-K."

Abby clapped her hands. "We can't disappoint him, then. Let's do that."

"Dustin is giving up his time for us," Miranda pointed out. "We should stick to the dogs you're seriously thinking of adopting."

"I agree." Abby turned to Dustin. "Do you have a leash handy?"

*Uh-oh.* Duchess had fit nicely into Abby's professional life, but this dog would take up most of a dressing trailer by himself, not to mention need long walks and extra care. "What about Sugarplum, or one of the other little dogs?"

"They're sweet, and I'm sure someone will come along who wants to adopt them, but not too many people are up for a dog this size. What is he, about eighty pounds?" she asked Dustin, as he snapped a leash to the dog's collar.

"Probably a little more," he admitted, "and I'm not sure he's done growing. He's only about a year old." He walked the dog to a rear door that led to the enclosed area and handed the leash and a handful of treats to Abby. "I've been working on leash manners, but he forgets sometimes. He's still a puppy in a lot of ways. You might want to consider an easier dog to handle."

Ignoring his advice, Abby began a brisk walk, and the dog stayed right beside her, watching the hand that held the treats. Miranda turned to Dustin, ready to enlist his help in steering Abby back toward Sugarplum. But before she did, she noticed the patch on his hat and read aloud, "Christmas Town Adventure Tours?"

"That's me." Dustin grinned. He had a smile that lit up his face, a beacon that drew Miranda.

"You work for an adventure tour company?" Abby wouldn't have thought Christmas Town was big enough for something like that.

"I *am* the adventure tour company, right now at least." His face lit up with enthusiasm. "This winter, I'm offering snowshoeing, cross-country skiing, ice climbing, bike tours—"

"Bike tours? In the winter?" *Brrrr.*

"Sure. I have a fleet of fat-tire bikes that can ride on the snow. It's a wonderful way to get out onto the trails, breathe the crisp winter air, and get in a good workout while you're at it. And starting soon, guests will be able to zipline over snow-covered trees."

"Wow." It was obvious he loved what he did. She'd never held a job that lit her up like that. But job security was more important than thrills. "How long have you been doing this?"

"I started about a month ago. So far, so good." He paused. "Although I'll need to hire some people soon, to staff the zipline." He looked into her eyes. "Have you ever done one?"

"Me? A zipline?" Miranda laughed. Her idea of adventure was trying out a new flavor of tea at Abby's tearoom. "No."

"You should try it," he urged. "I'm not ready to open yet, but if you wanted, I could take you—"

"I don't think so."

"A lot of people are hesitant, but I've never known anyone who tried it who wished they hadn't." He held her gaze. He had such expressive, compelling eyes. "Come on. I dare you."

She scoffed. "I don't do dares." Although Dustin's enthusiasm was hard to resist.

"Well, the offer's open." From his jeans pocket, he pulled out a crumpled flyer featuring the same design as the patch on his hat, with stylized mountains and a Christmas tree behind the company name.

"Nice logo."

"Thanks. Zoey Hansen, a local designer, did it for me. My number's in there if you change your mind, or you know, if you need someone to show you around Christmas Town."

Miranda took the flyer. So now she had his number. A risk-taker's number. Her heart thumped, as though she was on that zipline, ready to—

"Miranda, could you come over here for a minute?" Abby called.

Miranda turned with a start. She'd been so caught up in her conversation with Dustin, she'd forgotten about Abby and the dog. She hurried to where they had stopped just under the main floodlight.

"Sit." When Abby held up a treat, the dog immediately sat and gazed up at her with obvious devotion. "Good boy." She gave him the treat. "Just look at those eyes."

Miranda had to admit, the dog had beautiful eyes, warm and brown. They almost looked as though he was laughing. In fact, they reminded her a lot of Cyrus' mischievous eyes which, now that she thought about it, explained why Abby had chosen this dog over Sugarplum.

Miranda could relate. The way Dustin had looked into her eyes as though he saw something fascinating inside her, something no one else had ever seen... Well, it lit a spark. A spark that almost made her want to throw caution to the wind and use that number he'd given her. But no. She had a plan to settle down in Yarrow, and a Christmas Town adventurer didn't fit into that plan.

"Here." Abby handed her the leash. "You hold him while I go sign whatever it is I need to sign, and then we'll take him with us."

Miranda's mind immediately jumped from Dustin's handsome face and adventure-loving nature to logistics. "You can't possibly take a dog this big to your suite at Over the River."

"Oh, I hadn't thought of that." Abby pressed a finger to her cheek. "Could he stay in your hotel room for the time being? Assuming the Pine Tree Inn allows pets?"

"They do," Miranda admitted, although she wasn't sure how she and Jolly were both going to fit in her miniscule room. According to the story she'd gotten when she made the reservation, a new furnace installation had necessitated robbing several feet from a standard room, leaving a tiny single that they only rented out in emergencies.

Dustin joined them. "We could keep Jolly here until you're done filming your movie and are ready to go home."

"Oh, no. I need a dog with me while I film. Dogs are so calming and affirming, don't you think?" Abby didn't wait for an answer, just beelined for the shelter, adding, "Miranda can take him for walks while I work, and he can nap in my trailer in between. Where do I sign the papers?"

"In here." Dustin held the door open. After Abby and the dog passed through, Miranda started to follow, but he laid a hand on her arm to stop her. "Are you okay with this?" he whispered. "Because if you're not, I can be the bad guy and say I can't release him until she has a fenced yard or something. He really does need a lot of exercise."

Despite her coat, Miranda swore she could feel Dustin's warm touch on her arm. She smiled. "It's okay." Sure, she'd be a little cramped, but now she understood that no dog would do for Abby except for Jolly. It was nice of Dustin to be concerned, though.

"But—"

"Really, it's fine. My job while we're filming is to look out for Abby and keep her happy, and it's clear she wants Jolly. After Christmas, once the movie is shot and she takes him home, she's got a great setup with a fenced yard. Believe me, that dog will never want for attention. In the meantime, I promise I'll take good care of him and take him out for exercise every day. Christmas Town does have a dog park, right?"

"Yes, near your hotel, on the other side of Mistletoe Park. It's called Prancer Park."

"Named after the reindeer?"

"Of course." Dustin grinned.

"We're good then." She touched the hand that still rested on her arm. "But thanks."

# Chapter Three

The next morning, Dustin decided to give Nugget a play session at Prancer Park in between his cross-country ski outing and this afternoon's fat-tire bike trek. He threw a tennis ball, and Nugget trotted after it. In her younger days she would have galloped, but she still enjoyed a game of fetch. No sign of Jolly or Miranda yet. Not that he was looking for them or anything.

Okay, he totally was.

Last night, he'd gotten so caught up talking with Miranda, he'd forgotten to explore the opportunities with the movie. It'd be great if they needed an activity location. But Abby and Miranda probably weren't the right people to talk to, anyway. The film presumably had a set location person he could contact.

Suddenly, a familiar red flash zipped past him and ran toward Nugget, leash flapping behind him.

"Jolly?" Dustin turned toward the gate, to see Miranda running after the dog, her loafers slipping and sliding on the packed snow. Dustin reached out to steady her.

She looked up. "Oh. Hi."

"Hi. You okay?" Reluctantly, he let go of her arm.

"I'm fine. I was in a hurry to get Jolly out of the trailer before he had an accident, and I forgot to change into my boots." She glanced toward the dog, who was dropping into a play bow. Nugget indulged him by feigning a couple of lunges in his direction. "Hamlet! Come."

"You're calling him Hamlet?"

Miranda shrugged. "Abby's idea. But I don't think he's caught on yet."

Dustin whistled. The dog looked his way. Dustin pulled a treat from his pocket and held it up. "Come."

Jolly shot across the snow and came to a sliding stop at Dustin's feet.

Miranda watched in amazement. "How did you do that?"

"Magic." Dustin handed her a handful of treats and whispered, "Dried liver."

"Eww."

"Try it. I mean, don't eat it. Show it to him and ask him to sit."

"Hamlet, Jolly, whatever—sit." She held up the treat, and Jolly smacked his haunches onto the snow. "Good boy." She grabbed the leash and smiled at Dustin. "Thanks."

"You're welcome. Why not let him play with Nugget for a while and burn up some energy?"

"Good idea." She unclipped the leash, and Jolly dashed in circles around Nugget, who seemed to be laughing at him. "Did you say your dog is Nugget?"

"Yes. She's ten, old for a golden, but she still loves to play." That familiar pinch of sadness welled up in his chest "She was my grandfather's dog."

"Was?" Her eyebrows drew together in concern.

Dustin swallowed the familiar lump in his throat. "I lost him two years ago. Grandpa left me his dog, his workshop, and his cottage with ten acres just outside Christmas Town."

"I'm sorry, but it's sweet that he left you his home. You must feel closer to him, living there. You have some great houses in Christmas Town." She pulled a paper from her pocket, a sales flyer for a saltbox-style home close to the square. "Like this one."

Dustin recognized it. "My third-grade teacher used to live there. It's a nice house. Are you thinking of buying it?"

"Oh, no. I just like to look at real estate flyers." Her voice grew quieter. "Hopefully before too long, I'll be shopping for my own home in Kansas."

"Kansas?" Dustin had never been to Kansas.

"Yes. I want to get back to the town where I was born. It's called Yarrow." Oh, her tone was wistful.

"What's it like?" Dustin threw Nugget's ball again, then turned to look at her.

"A lot like Christmas Town, actually." She smiled. "Minus the uber-Christmas stuff. I haven't been there in years, but there's a town square with big old elm trees, a community pool, and a movie theatre. Actually, I read the theatre closed, but someone is thinking of buying it. People greet each other on the street, and when something goes wrong, they step in to help. Just like here in Christmas Town, when the company that was supposed to restore the carousel went out of business and the townspeople stepped in and restored it themselves in time for Christmas."

"Yeah, that was awesome. That's what this movie is about, right? The carousel?"

"Yes, and about John and Lisa and the people who came together to help."

"I volunteered a few hours on that project, but I'd already committed to other activities so I couldn't put in a lot of time. My grandfather did some of the restoration work," Dustin said. "He knew all about it, because back when the amusement park originally brought the carousel here, he helped install it."

"Wow. See, that's what's special about living in a small town. Connections."

"So you've kept your connections with Yarrow? Do you have family there?"

"Two cousins." Her smile clouded. "We're not particularly close, but I hope to change that. My grandparents owned the Yarrow Bakery. They died when I was a baby, and my parents took it over. But when I was ten, the bakery went out of business and we moved to Wichita, and then St. Louis, and then San Diego. After that, I've always lived in cities, at least until I went with Abby to Vermont. It's in a lovely little town, but it doesn't feel like home."

Dustin knew that feeling. He'd never understood why his parents had chosen to move south. Sure, there was no snow to shovel in Florida, but their condo there didn't feel like home, either. As far as he was concerned, there was no place like Christmas Town.

But before he could comment, Miranda looked up and gasped. "Oh, look!" She pointed up. The cloud on her face had gone, replaced by wide-eyed wonder. A large bird soared gracefully across the open sky. "I think it's a hawk."

"A red-tailed hawk," Dustin confirmed. "You see a lot of them around the Blue Spruce Resort."

"Wouldn't it be amazing to be able to soar like that?" she whispered, and he could hear the longing in her voice.

They continued to watch until the hawk had disappeared into the distance.

"How long have you been Abilene's assistant?" Dustin asked, wanting to know more about her. All about her, truth be told.

"Almost six years. I went to work for her when she was still acting, and then she hired me to come to Vermont and go through her aunt's estate. She had a huge house full of stuff, ranging from priceless to worthless. After that, when Abby decided to buy a tearoom, she asked me to stay and help. When I convinced Abby to take this role, I promised I'd come along and make sure everything runs smoothly."

"She seems..." he hesitated briefly. "Nice."

"Oh, she is." Miranda wrinkled her cute little nose. "But occasionally she gets these sudden enthusiasms."

"Like adopting Jolly."

"Exactly. When she gets excited about something, she's like a little kid, who wants it to happen right now." She smiled. "It's a good job, and it pays well. I've almost saved up enough to buy a house in Yarrow, someday."

"Someday." Dustin chuckled. "I kept saying I was going to start my own adventure tour company someday. Until a friend pointed out that you can wait your whole life for 'someday.'"

"What did you do before?"

"I worked for Parks and Recreation. It was fine. I got to be outside a lot. But sharing my love of the outdoor life with other people—that's what really makes me happy."

She gaped at him. "So you just quit your job and started a business?"

"Pretty much." He nodded.

She gave a little shudder. "See, I can't imagine doing that."

He studied her face for a moment. "You don't like taking risks, do you?"

She didn't hesitate. "No."

She seemed uncomfortable, so Dustin decided to change the subject. "How did Jolly...er...Hamlet, do in your room last night?"

"He was fine. Fortunately, Pawsitively Merry was open late, so I was able to pick up a bed for him. Unfortunately, he preferred mine. Eventually we compromised."

"How so?"

Miranda smiled. "I let him have it and moved my blanket and myself to his bed, which was surprisingly comfortable."

Dustin laughed. "Well, as long as you showed him who's boss."

An alarm on Miranda's phone chimed. "Oh, got to go. Abby will be done with makeup shortly and she has two scenes to film today." She clicked something on her calendar. Dustin needed to get organized like that. Right now he was using sticky notes on a paper calendar to keep track of his schedule and clients.

"Jolly!" Miranda waved a treat. Jolly bounded to her. She snapped on the leash. "Nice to see you again, Dustin. Thanks for the help."

"Anytime." He hesitated, and then went for it. "You know, I think you'd love the zipline if you tried it." She just laughed and shook her head, but as she and the dog passed through the gate, he called, "Life's more interesting if you don't always keep both feet on the ground."

# Chapter Four

"Did you get a picture of me at the top?" Sasha, one half of the couple Dustin had just taken ice-climbing, asked her husband, Milo.

"You bet I did." Milo leaned forward between the two front seats to show her. "Just look at this shot."

"Oh, wow, you got the whole frozen waterfall, too. Send that one to my sister. She'll never believe I climbed all that ice."

"So, you had fun?" Dustin asked, as he pulled up in front of their bed-and-breakfast. The couple had done some rock-climbing in the gym, but never any ice-climbing before.

"We rocked!" Sasha pumped a fist. "I'll be leaving five-star reviews all over the place."

"Thanks. That really helps," Dustin told her. They all climbed out of the van, including Nugget.

Sasha bent and stroked the old dog's head. "So, will we see you at the big ice-skating thing?"

There were always people skating over at Reindeer Meadow, but Dustin hadn't heard about any particular event. "What ice-skating thing?"

"You know they're making a movie, right? Well, I heard the mayor invited the stars from the movie to come skating, or at least to sign autographs at the pond this evening," Sasha explained.

Dustin had little interest in autographs, but he couldn't help but wonder if a certain assistant might be there. By the time he'd put away the ice-climbing gear and fed Nugget, he'd convinced himself to check out tonight's event. Besides, it was a good opportunity to hand out flyers.

The parking lot at Reindeer Meadow was almost full, but Dustin found a spot at the back. A few people skated, but most of the crowd had gathered near the concession stand. He slung his skates over his shoulder and headed over. He waved to June Baxter, his former high school principal and one of the Knotty Elves, an elderly trio with the apparent mission of outfitting everyone in Christmas Town with some sort of knitted object.

Macy Winter and Fox Baylor, the stars of the movie, sat at a table autographing photos for eager fans. Empty chairs next to them probably meant Abilene had already finished signing autographs and been driven home by Miranda. Disappointed, Dustin was debating whether to skate or just go home and catch up on some paperwork when he noticed Sasha and Milo waiting in line.

Sasha spotted him at the same time and waved him over. "This is the man I was telling you about," she told the next couple in line. "Dustin, these are the Novaks. I was showing them pictures of our ice climb today."

"We're not up for ice-climbing," the woman told Dustin, "but Sasha said you do snowshoe treks. Do you take kids? We've got three." She pointed to the pond, where two boys who looked to be late elementary school age and a girl two or three years older raced across the ice, narrowly missing a middle-aged couple who were skating hand-in-hand around the edges of the main group.

"Sure, I can take kids snowshoeing or on fat-tire bike treks. I've got openings for tomorrow morning, leaving from the town square, if you're interested." They immediately signed up and paid in advance.

"Did you say you offer winter bike tours?" a man further down the line asked. "I do."

Twenty minutes later, Dustin had five more people registered for the afternoon fat-tire bike trip. Business was taking off. He stuffed the sticky notes with their information into his pocket. He hoped he'd correctly remembered the number of people already signed up for the trek, or he'd be a bike short. If necessary, he could borrow one from his neighbor, Luke, who was a bike enthusiast any time of year. He made a note to check as soon as he got home.

"Dustin!" June Baxter called, waving a shiny green bag at him. "We have something for you!"

"What's this?" Dustin walked over, accepted the bag, and looked inside. "Socks! Thank you!" He pulled them out. The socks were red, with green toes and a white band near the top. On one sock, the band had a row of red hearts, on the other, green Christmas trees. Odd that they didn't match, but still, "These are awesome!"

"They're wool," June preened. "We figure you need to keep your feet warm, being outside so much."

"Absolutely! I'll try them now." Energized, he found an unoccupied bench and changed into his new socks before putting on his skates. More people, having gotten their autographs, were skating now. He joined them, gliding over the ice, waving to a few friends. Then he spotted Miranda, near the skate rental booth, standing alone and holding onto Jolly's leash.

Miranda wore a thick knit hat with a green pom-pom. A matching scarf wound around her neck and halfway up her face, but there was no mistaking that glowing red-blond hair. Dustin skated to the edge of the pond and skidded to a hockey stop. "Hello, there."

"Hi." Her mouth was hidden under the scarf, but he could hear the smile in her voice. "I didn't know you'd be here tonight."

"Last-minute decision." He took a few awkward steps across the snow to stand closer to her. "Why aren't you skating?"

"I don't skate, not ice-skating anyway," she said. "I've done a little rollerblading."

"Then why are you here?"

"Abby is skating, but she didn't want to leave Jolly alone." She waved her hand at the ice, and Dustin realized that Abilene was one half of the couple he'd seen almost collide with the racing kids.

"Who is that with her?"

"Cyrus Nash. He plays opposite her in the movie."

Dustin watched for a few minutes. "She's good. They both are."

"Abby grew up skating in Vermont, and she taught Cyrus to skate for *Christmas Moon*, a movie they were in together a long time ago. They're doing the same moves they did in that movie."

"Nice." Dustin offered Miranda a hand. "Skate with me. If you've roller-bladed, you can ice skate."

For a moment she looked tempted, but then she shook her head. "I need to stay with Jolly. And Abby might need me."

That sounded like an excuse to Dustin. "If she needs you, you'll be right there with her on the ice. I'll ask her if she minds if you skate." Dustin stepped back onto the ice.

"No, don't—" Miranda started to object, but Dustin pretended not to hear.

He skated across the pond and joined Abby and Cyrus. "Hi."

"Hello." Abby smiled. "Cyrus, this is Dustin, who set me up with a new canine love."

"Always good to meet a fellow dog lover," Cyrus said with a smile that charmed. "I have an elderly Boston terrier back home. He's staying with a neighbor for now."

"That's great." Dustin turned on his smile. "Say, Abilene...I came to see if you needed anything. If not, I was hoping to get Miranda out on the ice."

"Excellent idea." Abby gave him an approving smile. "Just what she needs to get her mind off things. I'm afraid Jolly was a bit of a trial for her today."

Dustin grinned back. "You decided not to call him Hamlet? It's totally up to you, but he'll always be Jolly in my head."

"He didn't seem to care for the name." And Abilene didn't seem at all upset about it. "I think that may be why he shredded tomorrow's script and chewed one of my leather gloves when we left him alone for a few minutes. And of course it fell on poor Miranda to replace everything. Jolly didn't know any better, but you could see in his eyes he was terribly sorry. Such a sweet boy."

Dustin bit back a chuckle. He was very familiar with Jolly's sad-eyed, repentant look. "I'm sure he'll settle down, but you know, if you decide a smaller dog would suit you better—" Not to mention making Miranda's life easier.

Abby shook her head. "No, Jolly and I have bonded. You and Miranda have fun. Jolly can wait in the car while you skate."

"I have a better idea." Dustin skated over to the concession stand and flagged down one of the Knotty Elves. Once she had agreed to dog-sit, Dustin wasted no time returning to Miranda. "You have Abby's blessing. Let's get you some skates."

Miranda, tentative soul that she was, reached for another excuse. "What about Jolly?"

"Help is on the way." He nodded toward the Knotty Elves making their way along the bank toward them. "What size shoe do you wear?" he asked, eager to get her out on the ice for the first time. To share that feeling of gliding free. To see that smile again.

"Uh, seven."

Dustin made his way to the rental booth and came back with a pair of white skates. "Here. Sit on this bench and I'll lace them for you."

"You don't have to do that," Miranda protested, but she sat and pulled off her snow boots, exposing her red socks. Hand-knitted socks, if he wasn't mistaken. He pushed her pants legs higher to slip on the skates and wasn't terribly surprised to find a white band with hearts in the pattern on one foot, and Christmas trees on the other.

"These were a gift—" Miranda began.

"From the Knotty Elves, right?" When she looked surprised, Dustin pulled up his own pants leg, exposing the band of hearts on the top of the sock. "Me, too."

"Are yours mismatched as well?" Miranda asked.

"No." Dustin showed her the Christmas trees. "They match yours."

She laughed, and Dustin decided he needed to hear more of that laughter. He tugged the laces snug. "That's not too tight, is it?"

"No, that's fine."

The Knotty Elves arrived, and Ms. Baxter took Jolly's leash. "You two go have fun."

"Thanks." Miranda got to her feet and wobbled. "Although, I'm still not sure about this."

Dustin took her arm. "It will be easier to balance once you're moving." He helped her to the edge of the pond, and together they stepped onto the ice. Her skates skidded, but he braced and kept her upright until she regained her balance. "Here, give me your hands." He held her gloved hands in his and began to skate backwards across the ice, pulling her along. "How's that feel?"

"Not bad." Some of the tension left her shoulders as she started to move.

"Want to try pushing a little? Just like you would on rollerblades." He let go of one hand so that he could move to her side.

"Okay." Miranda pushed with one foot, and then the other, and soon she was gliding smoothly over the ice.

"See. You're a natural."

She smiled at him. "You're good at this. Are you a skating instructor, too?"

"No, but maybe I should add it to the lineup." They made another lap around the pond, waving to The Knotty Elves as they passed.

"This is fun." Miranda laughed. "I'm glad you talked me into it."

"See? Sometimes taking a chance feels good." Dustin twirled around as they skated so that he could look at her face, but he didn't let go of her hand. It fit just right in his. "How was filming today?"

"Good, although they're in a tizzy because the pristine meadow where they're supposed to film later this week isn't so pristine anymore. Someone drove a tractor across it. They really wanted that virgin snow for a background shot."

Suddenly, he had a great idea. "You know, I think I can find you a new film location."

"Really?"

"Yeah, I know of a perfect place. I can call the owner tonight and ask." He raised his chin. "If you'll do something for me."

She eyed him suspiciously. "What's that?"

He was going all in, daring her to give him a chance. "Try the zipline."

She recoiled, nearly tumbling backward before he caught her arm. "Oh, no—"

"Come on," he urged. "I'm talking about a perfect location, untouched snow with forest and mountains in the background."

She stopped skating and braced her feet wide apart. "Can you really get it?'

"Let me make the call." Dustin phoned his neighbor, Gwen, and explained the situation. As he expected, Gwen was agreeable to letting the film crew use the snow-covered herb field between her house and the river. "Done. About that zipline..."

She hedged. "Are you sure it's safe?"

"The inspector said so just last week."

Miranda hesitated for a long moment. Dustin was about to tell her to forget it when she said, "When would you want to do it?"

"The zipline?" His heart beat faster. "How about now?"

She shook her head. "I can't go *now*. I have to drive Abby back to her place and walk Jolly."

"Afterward then." He wasn't going to let a little thing like dog-walking get in their way. "Bring Jolly with you. He and Nugget can play in my yard while we do the zipline."

"In the dark?"

"I installed floodlights."

She sucked in a long breath. "What if I get to the top and can't do it?"

"Then you'll have tried." Just like he was trying to find out what it was that made her so irresistible. "That's all I'm asking."

"Why?" She tilted her head. "Why is it important to you that I try your zipline?"

*How could he explain?* He wanted her to try the things he loved, to discover the joy, the freedom. To take a chance. He was convinced once she'd tried it, she would love it, just like she was loving skating.

In the end, he just shrugged and said, "Because of the way you were looking at the hawk. I want you to know what it's like to fly."

# Chapter Five

"Jolly, am I out of my mind to even consider this?" The big dog had been sulking in the backseat since they dropped Abby off, but now he raised his head and gave a little whimper. Miranda wasn't sure if that was a yes or a no. "I mean, it's a zipline. In the winter. In the dark!"

As a child, Miranda had preferred the carousel to the Tilt-A-Whirl, much less the roller coaster. And yet, here she was, following a winding country road past an herb farm to Dustin's house, behind which, he claimed, was a brand-new, not-too-scary, zipline. Yeah. Right.

Still, she trusted him, and trust didn't come easily for Miranda. She was usually slow to warm up to people, and yet somehow it felt like she and Dustin fit together, like those mismatched socks the Knotty Elves had given them. He'd been right about skating. Even though she'd never ice skated, once she was out on the ice, she'd felt comfortable. Mostly because Dustin was right there, holding her hand, ready to catch her if she fell.

Five minutes later, Miranda pulled up in front of a Bavarian-style cottage that looked like it belonged in an animated movie, with pale stucco walls, heavy timbers, and steep gables. A porch light illuminated an arched wooden door-way displaying a pine and holly wreath. Forest green shutters framed the two front-facing windows, with matching window boxes filled with evergreens and twinkling Christmas lights. Overhead, carved brackets supported the balcony that ran across the entire front of the house, and icicle lights dripped from the roofline.

Best of all were the bird feeders. Miranda counted five visible within the light from the porch, designs ranging from a red roof over a feeding tray to an elaborate church complete with stained glass windows. The one nearest the porch was a miniature of the Christmas Town gazebo. While Miranda was still getting out of the car, the front door opened and Dustin stepped out, followed by Nugget. "You made it."

"I did. I love the bird feeders."

"Thanks. My grandpa made most of them. You should come back sometime when the sun is shining. This place is bird central in the daytime."

Miranda wasn't sure if that was an invitation or an offhand remark, but she hoped for the former. She would love to spend more time with Dustin at his fairy-tale cottage. Jolly whined and scratched at the window. She opened his door. Before she could snap on his leash, Jolly pushed past her and ran to Nugget.

Dustin opened a gate and the dogs trotted inside. Immediately, Jolly was off, dashing through the snow in big circles while Nugget looked on, her mouth open in a doggy grin. "They'll be fine." Dustin latched the gate. "Are you ready to zipline?"

"I guess." She followed him to the edge of the woods. He lifted the cover of a box on a pole there and pressed a switch. Instantly, the path in front of them lit up, making a bright tunnel through the trees. They followed it until they came to a circular staircase spiraling around a sturdy pole. Dustin flicked another switch and floodlights lit the whole area.

Miranda looked up. That staircase seemed to climb forever before it reached a wooden platform. Two thick cables ran above the platform. She gulped. "Are you absolutely certain this is safe?"

"Absolutely. It wouldn't be good for my insurance premiums if I killed my first customer."

"Your first?" she squeaked.

"Other than myself, some friends, and the inspector from the fire marshal's office." Dustin grinned. "He rode it three times for fun after inspecting it, if that makes you feel better."

"Maybe a little." Of course, fire marshals also ran into burning buildings. Miranda pulled the wool cap more securely over her ears and climbed the first step. And then another, and another until she'd reached the wide platform with two heavy cables running overhead.

Dustin had just stepped up beside her when a cooing sound came from somewhere nearby. Dustin tilted his head. "Did you hear that?"

"What is it?"

"An owl. Listen."

Miranda waited, and soon the sound repeated. "Whoo-whoo-whoo."

"Great horned owl," Dustin whispered, pointing at a tall evergreen just behind them. "I think he's in that tree."

"That's cool."

"Uh, huh. Are you ready to—"

"Not yet." Miranda grabbed the railing near the stairs.

"I was just asking if you were ready to put on your harness and helmet."

"Oh. Okay." Putting on the gear didn't commit her. She removed her knit cap. He helped her step into a series of straps and adjusted them until they fit snugly. Then he put another harness on himself. "You're going, too?" she asked.

"Yeah. There are two parallel lines. That way I can help you on the landing platform."

"Landing? How does that work? Like—what if I miss the landing platform?"

He laughed. "You can't because the line ends there. There is an automatic braking section just before you get to the bottom that will slow and then stop you. Super easy."

He selected a helmet, set it on her head, and buckled the strap under her chin before putting his own on. "Now come over here." He led her to a spot a few feet from the edge and snapped her harness to a big ring hanging from the line. Handlebars like those from a bicycle dangled above. "You just hold onto the handles, step up to the edge of the platform, and when you're ready, jump." He put an arm around her shoulders and tucked her up against him, whispering, "I know you can do this." For an instant, his confidence seemed to spill over onto her. Then he let her go and it drained away.

She grasped the bars but made sure her feet stayed firmly on the platform. "What happens if I lose my grip?"

"Nothing. The handles are just to keep you facing forward. All your weight is on the harness, which is attached to the pulley by this big 'ole carabiner." He demonstrated by snapping his own harness to a ring identical to hers.

"Oh." She was running out of excuses. "I'm not—"

"It's okay. Take all the time you need." He smiled encouragingly, and some of that confidence seeped back in.

Still, Miranda hesitated. Dustin was probably sorry he'd brought her here. She glanced over, but in his eyes, she saw nothing but patience and encouragement. She took a deep breath. "Here goes." She jumped.

For a nanosecond, it was sheer terror, falling into the unknown, but then she was sweeping forward, soaring over the trees. Dustin cheered from behind her. The treetops below rushed by at incredible speeds, and yet, what she felt wasn't panic. The unaccustomed rush felt more like—freedom.

Suddenly, she caught movement from the corner of her eye. It was the owl, cutting through the air on silent wings, keeping pace with her. She was flying with birds, just like Dustin had promised. Too soon, she was slowing down, and the owl swooped by to disappear into the forest. She came to a stop. Seconds later, Dustin arrived beside her. He pulled himself up, unclipped his harness, and helped her onto the landing platform. She stumbled a little, and he pulled her closer. His scent mingled with the piney smell of the forest, fresh and clean.

He unclipped her from the zipline, led her to the middle of the platform and unfastened all the snaps and buckles so that they could step out of their harnesses. Once they were both free, he took her gloved hands in his and searched her face, his expression anxious. "You're awfully quiet. Did you hate it?"

"No." She gave a happy sigh. "In fact, that may have been the most incredible experience of my life."

Relief mingled with joy in his expression. "Oh, yeah?"

"It was just like you said. Flying." Their gazes met and held. "And then with the owl and all—"

"The owl?"

"Didn't you see it? The owl was flying along beside me."

"No way! That's amazing." He squeezed her hands. Slowly, he leaned in. She raised her face to his. Their lips touched, sending a little shiver of excitement zinging through her body. He dropped her hands and reached around to pull her closer for another kiss, this one long, and sweet, and every bit as thrilling as the zipline.

An eternity later, he broke the kiss and gently touched her cheek.

She sighed. "Dustin."

"Yes?"

"Thank you for bringing me here."

"It was nothing."

"It wasn't nothing. You urged me out of my comfort zone. Never in a million years would I have tried something like this if not for you." It felt so good in his arms. If only Christmas Town was a little closer to Yarrow, say seven states closer. But it wasn't, and she was going to have to keep a tight hold on her heart. Because it would be far too easy to fall for this wonderful man.

He leaned in for another kiss. "I'm glad you did."

# ChapterSix

T he next morning after the snowshoe outing, Dustin couldn't find any place to park his van near the square. "Looks like something big is going on. I may have to drop you a block or two away."

"No problem." Mr. Novak grinned. "How about near that bakery with the incredible cheese and rosemary muffins?"

"And peppermint hot chocolate!" one of the boys yelled.

"The Tea Pot? Done." Dustin had a weakness for Gina's lemon scones.

"I heard that movie is filming on the square today," Mrs. Novak remarked.

"Oh." Would Miranda be there? Dustin found a parking spot a few doors down from The Tea Pot. Once all the passengers were out of the van, he followed them inside and perused the pastry case. He'd pick up something for Miranda too, he decided, a little sweetener to add to the invitation he planned to offer.

"Hi, Dustin." Gina flashed him a grin. "Let me guess. Two lemon scones?" She didn't wait for his answer before transferring them into a sack.

"Yes, please, and—hmm, what would Miranda like?" he muttered to himself, distracted by a rousing version of the *Twelve Days of Christmas*. "*Five golden rings.*" He grinned at Gina. "Best part of the whole song."

"Agreed." Gina nodded, silver-blond hair brushing her shoulders. "If this is for the woman you were skating with, she's a big fan of pecan shortbread."

He looked up in surprise. "How could you possibly know about her? You weren't even at Reindeer Meadow last night."

Gina nodded toward a table where the Knotty Elves had settled in with their knitting. "I hear things." She slid two of the snowflake-embossed shortbread cookies into a tiny pink box and handed them over, along with his scones. "Enjoy."

"Thanks." He paid and then made his way to the square.

Some people huddled in a small group. Maybe they were actors since someone was fixing their hair and touching up their faces. Others set up tripods with reflectors or diffusers or whatever they were. Dustin didn't see Miranda at first, but he finally spotted her, carrying a tray of hot drinks.

He started toward her, but a man stopped him. "Sorry. Only authorized people on the set."

"Dustin! Hi," Miranda called. "It's okay, Griffin. He's with me." Miranda passed out the drinks to a group that included Abby, and then walked over to meet Dustin.

He smiled at her, loving the sparkle in her turquoise eyes. "Good morning." He handed her the bakery box. "For you."

She peeked inside the box. "Oh, wow, I love this stuff. Thanks!"

"You're welcome." He touched her arm, drawing her attention back. "Are you free for dinner tonight? Say, six-thirty?"

Miranda shook her head. "Sorry, we shoot until seven, and I can't take off early."

"We can make it after seven."

"But I'll still need to take Abby home and feed and walk the dog." She bit her lip. "I might not be done until eight or later."

"Then come at eight or whenever you can. I'll wait," he assured her. "And bring Jolly. We can walk the dogs together after dinner."

"Places!" someone called.

Miranda glanced over her shoulder. "I have to go."

"Okay, but will you come tonight?" He couldn't keep the eagerness from his voice.

Miranda nodded, smiling a little. "I'll be there."

Between the bike tour and preparations for dinner, the hours flew by. But by eight-thirty, Dustin was beginning to wonder if he'd been stood up. Maybe he shouldn't have kissed her last night. What if—

Before he could speculate further, his phone rang.

"So sorry, Dustin." Miranda sounded breathless. "Filming ran late, and then there was a problem with the buttons on Abby's costume for tomorrow. It reflected flashes at the camera, and... Well, you don't need all the details. Am I too late? Want to reschedule?"

"No!" He continued in a more normal voice. "No need to reschedule. Can you come now?"

"I still have to drop Abby, but I can be there in twenty minutes."

"Perfect."

———❀———

Miranda found Dustin's cottage every bit as charming on the inside as it was on the outside. A staircase with snowflakes carved into the banister lined one side of the entryway. Underneath the stairs, shelves held old books and snow globes. In one corner of the living room, a roll-top desk was piled high with papers, instrumental Christmas music played from a smart speaker nearby, and wonderful smells were wafting from the kitchen.

"Dinner from my friend's restaurant at the Blue Spruce," he told her as he took her coat. "Pork osso bucco, polenta, and roasted root vegetables. Plus fresh salad from my neighbor, Gwen's, greenhouse." He grinned. "One of the advantages of dating a local, like me."

Miranda blinked. Dating? She couldn't date Dustin. That wasn't part of the plan. She couldn't let anything get in the way of her eventual return to Yarrow. But wait—he'd been smiling when he mentioned dating and he knew she was only in town for the movie. He was kidding, she realized.

She relaxed.

Fortunately, Dustin had been busy hanging her coat on a bentwood rack and hadn't noticed her inner turmoil. He turned and leaned in for a quick kiss. "Dinner is ready. I'll put the dogs in the backyard. Have a seat." He nodded toward a round table covered with a white tablecloth, and set with red napkins.

A silver bowl of holly sat in the center. After she took a seat, she noticed the china, a beautiful pattern with cardinals, nuthatches, and chickadees.

"I love these plates!" she called.

"My grammy loved birds," Dustin told her when he returned, carrying a full serving tray. "Thus, all the birdfeeders. Grandpa gave her these dishes for Christmas about ten years ago.

The food tasted every bit as good as it smelled. "I never expected food like this in a small town," Miranda told Dustin. "It must have been fun, growing up in Christmas Town."

"It really was. I enjoy traveling, and my parents have moved south, but for me, Christmas Town is home."

"It's a beautiful place, and the people are so friendly. Not to mention, you live in a cottage right out of a fairy tale."

"I know. I'm so lucky to have inherited this place. That's one of the reasons I'm working so hard: to make sure I can make the payments on the mortgage I took out when I started the business."

She sat back. "You risked your home?" He'd been handed the perfect storybook cottage, and he risked it on a business venture? Didn't he realize he could lose it all? Just like her parents had lost their business and their home in Yarrow when they took out a loan to expand the bakery just before a recession hit.

"The interest rate was way lower than for a business loan," he explained.

"But this beautiful house—"

"It's still mine. I just have to make mortgage payments, like everyone else in the world."

"I guess." She stopped herself from saying more. It really wasn't any of her business. But she just couldn't conceive of his risking his grandparents' cottage. If she had been lucky enough to inherit a place like this, she would never risk losing it.

"Are you ready for dessert?" Dustin asked. "I have two slices of Posey's famous peppermint pie. It's practically the official food of Christmas Town."

"Sounds great," she said, but she couldn't seem to generate the enthusiasm she'd felt earlier. "Didn't I hear she was retiring?"

"Don't let her hear you say that. She takes it like an affront on her ability to keep going forever."

"Good thing I didn't ask her," Miranda replied, trying to make polite conversation.

"I loved going to Posey's when I was a kid," Dustin said as he set a piece in front of her. "If you were the first to spot Elmer the Elf, you got a free piece of pie. In third grade, I won twice in one week." He grinned. "That was a good week."

"I'll bet." She tried a bite, and immediately understood why this was a favorite. Smooth, sweet, and creamy, but punctuated with a cool nip of peppermint. Delicious.

Dustin toyed with his fork. "Um, it sounds like your job was a little stressful today."

She shrugged. "A few hiccups. I just felt bad that I kept you waiting." All afternoon, she'd been looking forward to coming to Dustin's house, thinking about those kisses on the zipline platform. But she hadn't realized the price of that zipline could be his home.

"I didn't mind," Dustin assured her. "Do you like your job?"

She nodded. "Abby has been very good to me."

He set down the fork. "What if you had the chance to do something else, and to live in a place like Christmas Town?"

She looked up at him. "What are you talking about?"

He sighed. "I'm trying to ask if you would be interested in working for me. I need a business manager, someone to take calls, handle paperwork, keep track of activities and guests, maybe set up some social media, things like that. You're amazing at organization and—"

"Can you afford an employee?" She experienced a rising feeling of panic. "What about your mortgage payments?"

Dustin wrinkled his brow. "I need someone with strong organizational skills to expand the business. I thought you'd love a new challenge."

For a few seconds, the panic receded. Miranda was tempted. She *was* good at organization, and if Dustin was going to grow his business and meet his bills, he needed someone like her. She couldn't imagine anyone she'd rather spend every day with. But what if his business folded, leaving her without a job? She wouldn't even have Abby to fall back on. The risk was too big. The panic tide began to rise again.

"I'm flattered." She flailed around for an excuse that didn't hurt his feelings. "Dating coworkers is a bad idea. There are so many pitfalls."

"We'd be fine," he insisted, waving away her concerns.

"You don't know that." She set down her fork. "That's what you do. You just jump off the edge and assume the zipline will catch you. But what if it doesn't?" What if the bank foreclosed? What if he lost everything? Or what if she went to work for him and lost her heart and never made it back to Yarrow, where she'd been so happy?

His face fell. "So that's a no?"

"It's a no. Nothing personal, but—"

He held up a hand. "Say no more. It was just a thought." He was trying to shrug it off, but she could see the hurt in his eyes.

She put her hand over his. "Dustin—"

"It's fine. You haven't finished your pie." He withdrew his hand and took a sip of water.

Miranda couldn't take another bite. She hated that she'd hurt him, but did he really expect her to say yes? He knew about her plan to return to Yarrow. Tears welled up, but she willed them away. Abandoning her pie, she walked to the door to let Jolly in and put him on his leash. "I have to go."

Dustin didn't try to stop her.

# Chapter Seven

The next morning, Miranda opened the passenger door and waited for Abby to settle in. "They changed the buttons on your costume for today's scene, and they sent over some minor changes in the script." Miranda handed over a travel mug with tea and the pages before shutting the door and moving around to climb into the driver's seat.

"What's wrong?" Abby asked as they started forward, patting Jolly's head when he leaned forward to give her a nuzzle.

Even though Miranda kept her eyes focused on the road, she could feel Abby's penetrating gaze. "I'm fine."

"You're far from fine. You came fifteen minutes earlier than scheduled this morning, these pages are out of order, and you forgot to put honey in my tea." Abby put her cup in the holder.

Miranda blew out a long breath. She never made mistakes like that. "I'm sorry. I'll make you a new cup when we get to the set."

"I'm not concerned about the tea. I'm concerned about *you*. Did something happen on your date last night?"

Miranda twitched her shoulders. "Dustin offered me a job." She expected Abby to scoff, but instead she seemed intrigued.

"Doing what?"

"Business manager for his fledgling adventure business. I imagine it would involve everything from answering phones to wrangling guests to bookkeeping."

Abby laughed. "Sounds like your job now."

"It does, a little. But at least you can afford to pay me."

"And he can't?" Abby seemed surprised. "I heard people at the skating pond singing his praises."

"I think Dustin is good at what he does. I'm just not sure Christmas Town can sustain a business like that year-round. Do tourists come here in April?"

"I don't know, but the shops and restaurants seem to be thriving. It might even be more fun to get a taste of Christmas in the middle of summer."

"Dustin certainly believes in it." Miranda wished she could believe, too. That she could have faith in Dustin's business. That she could accept his job offer. But even if she were willing to risk her job, she couldn't risk her heart. Not when she was planning to move to Yarrow at the first opportunity. She sighed. "He actually mortgaged his house to get the money for bicycles and trailers and to put in a zipline."

"A zipline!" Abby sounded delighted. "No one told me there was a zipline in Christmas Town."

"It's not open yet. Besides, I think your contract forbids it."

Abby sighed. "Too bad. I've always wanted to try a zipline. Maybe we should have our wrap party there. Have you ever done one?"

"Once," Miranda admitted.

"How was it?"

Miranda couldn't help but smile, remembering the thrill of flying. And of the kiss that sent her flying even higher. "It was incredible."

"See, some things are worth the risk. If I hadn't taken a risk, I would never have become an actress. Or opened a tearoom, for that matter. The safest roads don't always lead in the direction you want." Abby touched her arm. "I admire this young man of yours. It takes a lot of courage to give up something good in order to chase after something great."

"I suppose so." Miranda didn't bother to tell Abby that he wasn't "her young man" anymore, not after she'd crushed his heart with her refusal. It was for the best. So why didn't her heart agree?

"Have you made any progress toward your dream?" Abby asked, apropos of nothing.

"What dream?" Miranda had never shared her plan with Abby.

"The one where you move to a small town like where you grew up, buy a pretty cottage, hang a dried flower wreath on the door, and build a little free library shaped like a hobbit house for your front yard."

Miranda blinked. "How could you possibly know—"

"If you don't want people looking at your Pinterest boards, you should make them private." Abby smirked.

"Fair enough. But if I wanted to live in just any small town, I'd stay in Vermont. My goal, ever since I was ten," she admitted, "has been to return to Yarrow."

"I see." Abby nodded. "Tell me about Yarrow. What makes it special?"

"It's a pretty place with brick buildings and a town square where we would have holiday celebrations," Miranda answered, just as they arrived at the corner of Christmas Town Square.

People wandered along the sidewalks as thousands of Christmas lights twinkled on the huge tree, while the candy-cane light posts illuminated pots of poinsettias, very lifelike plastic poinsettias. More lights outlined the graceful lines of the Christmas Town gazebo. It was beautiful.

"And?" Abby prompted.

"The people in Yarrow are friendly." Miranda stopped at a crosswalk to let a family across the road.

They waved their thanks and called, "Merry Christmas!"

Abby rolled down her window. "Merry Christmas to you," she replied, then turned back to Miranda. "What else?"

Miranda resumed driving. "The people are kind. They're willing to pitch in to help their neighbors."

On the sidewalk, an older woman pushing a small cart filled with grocery bags got a wheel hung up on a snowbank. Two teenagers stopped, gathered up the cart and grocery bags, and followed the lady up the street.

"It sounds like a special place all right." Abby chuckled. "Kind of reminds me of another small town."

"How are you doing this?" Miranda demanded, gesturing outside the car.

"It's not me," Abby assured her, eyes twinkling. "It's the magic of Christmas Town."

Okay, she had a point. Christmas Town was every bit as special as Yarrow. Miranda just wanted to get home, but where was home? Was it the place that made it home, or the people? Or one special person?

Dustin's handsome face came to mind.

Abby pointed to an empty parking spot. "Let's stop at The Tea Pot. I'm in a skinny vanilla latte sort of mood this morning, and since you were early, we have time."

Miranda parked behind an old station wagon with the back gate open. A blond woman was loading up an armful of potted rosemary plants, pruned and decorated like little Christmas trees. Miranda held the shop door open for her. The Tea Pot was usually bustling, but they seemed to have caught a quiet moment between the early morning workers and the mid-morning snackers.

"Thanks!" The woman set the little trees in the window and turned back to see Abby follow her inside. "Oh, wow. You're Abilene! I loved you in *Christmas Moon*. I'm Gwen. May I please have your autograph?"

"Of course." Abby turned to Miranda. "I believe we have some photos in the car, don't we?"

"Yes." Miranda hurried out to grab a few headshots the publicity department had provided, along with a pen. When she returned, Abby and Gwen waited by the front counter while Gina made Abby's latte.

"So you get a lot of tourist traffic year-round, not just at Christmas?" Abby asked Gwen as she accepted the drink.

"Yes, especially in the summer," Gwen said. "The local stores sell as many of my herbal soaps in July as they do in December."

"I'll have a peppermint mocha, please," Miranda told Gina. "I'm curious. Do you think the new Christmas Town Adventure Tours will be a success?"

"For sure," Gina replied, as she made the drink. "Dustin has been coordinating camping trips and hikes since high school, and I'm always meeting tourists who want to spend time outside."

"Dustin lives just down the road from me," Gwen volunteered. "He let me ride his zipline last week. It was a blast!"

Abby autographed the photo and gave it to Gwen. "Guess what?" Abby said to Miranda. "Gwen, here, is an herb farmer, and she's getting married in two weeks. Her husband-to-be will be moving in with her after the wedding."

"Luke will still be using the workshop on his property, but he's talked about renting his house, and Abby said you might be interested," Gwen told her. "It's right next door to my farm. Let me just find a picture." Gwen pulled out her phone.

Miranda raised her eyebrows and looked at Abby. "Are you trying to get rid of me?" she asked in a low voice.

Abby wrapped an arm around her shoulders. "Miranda, my dear, you make my life easier in a hundred ways, but at some point, it will be time for you to move on and start your own life. Maybe the time is now. I'm sure if I explain the circumstances, the people at Over the River would make an exception and let me bring Jolly there."

"If I did go—not that I am, but if I did—I'd stay on for you and Jolly until filming is completed." Miranda owed Abby that much.

"That's a relief." Abby winked.

Miranda shook her head. This was crazy. She couldn't just abandon the plan she'd held for so long and relocate to Christmas Town, could she?

Before she said anything, Gwen handed over her phone for Miranda's inspection. An adorable beagle posed beneath a dried herb wreath which hung on the red front door of a classic gray saltbox. Black shutters framed the windows, which each held a glowing candle nestled in greenery. There was even a split-rail fence with a corner post that would be the perfect place for a free little library.

Miranda sucked in a breath. "It's gorgeous."

"Shall I have Luke call you?"

Why not? Even if she didn't decide to stay, it was an excuse to look inside a historic New England saltbox. "Yes, please." Miranda wrote down her name and number on a napkin and handed it to Gwen.

"Great." Gwen smiled. "I can't wait to have you for a neighbor."

———⚹———

"Here's your change. Ten, fifteen—just a sec," Dustin ducked into the van and fished four quarters from the ashtray. "Sixteen. Sorry, I'm out of ones." Dustin needed to get to the bank for change as well as to deposit the cash he'd collected the past couple of days.

"That's okay. Keep the change." The man was a last-minute addition to the snowshoe outing this morning. "Can I get a receipt?"

"Sure." Dustin found a book of receipts in the glove box and hand-wrote one. He really needed help, and Miranda would have been great, but he'd totally messed up his approach last night. Worse, by offering her a job, he might have blown their chance for a relationship. He only hoped he could salvage the situation.

As soon as his customers were gone, he texted a few friends and neighbors who were likely to be out and about in Christmas Town, asking if they'd seen Miranda. Almost immediately, his phone started to chime.

From Gina: *Left The Tea Pot twenty minutes ago.*

From Gwen: *Saw her parking by Comfort and Joy ten minutes ago.*

From Lia: *She's walking Jolly at the town square.*

And finally, from June: *We will surveil until you arrive.*

Dustin grinned. The Knotty Elves were on the case. "Come on, Nugget. Let's roll." The retriever climbed into the van, and Dustin wasted no time getting to the square.

Prudence Parker, June Baxter, and Odette King fussed with the decorations at the gazebo, with red and green knitted scarves wrapped to obscure their faces. Ms. Baxter jerked her head toward the far side of the square. He spotted Jolly and Miranda there, Miranda's bright curls billowing from under her hat. Dustin let Nugget out of the van, tucked the folder he'd brought under his arm, and headed her way.

Jolly saw them and almost pulled Miranda off her feet, dragging her across the square. Dustin reached out to steady her when Jolly skidded to a stop. She looked at him with a tentative smile. "Hi."

"Hi."

"Listen, I wanted to apolo—" Dustin began, but Miranda spoke at the same time, "Dustin, I'm glad you're here because—"

They both stopped talking. Miranda waved her hand. "You go first."

"Okay." Dustin took a deep breath. "Miranda, I'm sorry. You'd had a long, exhausting day, and then I sprang that surprise job offer on you last night without any warning."

"It's okay, I—"

"No, let me finish. I realized after you left that even though it feels like longer, we really just met. You don't really know me, not yet. So, I wanted to show you this." He handed her the folder in his hand.

"What is it?" She opened it to the first page.

"It's a business plan. I may have given the impression that I just jumped into this business, but I actually spent two years planning before I pulled the plug on my old job." He turned a couple of pages. "As you can see, I have a full budget allocated for marketing and staff, including part-time workers for the zipline and a full-time business manager."

"I see." She looked over the page, and then met his eyes. "Why are you showing me this?"

"Because I want you to have the facts. Fact 1: I like you. A lot. And I want to get to know you better. Fact 2: I also believe you would be a huge asset to my business. But that's not the most important thing. You're right, mixing work and romance is risky. But even if you have no interest in working for me, I want you to understand who I am. Yes, I take risks, but they're calculated risks. I take care of the people and places I care about. And Fact 3: I'm starting to care about you. I know you have a plan to return to Yarrow, and if that's what you want, then that's what I want for you. But if you should decide to stay in Christmas Town, well, I'd do everything in my power to make sure you never regret it."

She blinked but didn't answer. Maybe that was answer enough. Dustin sighed. "Okay, that's what I came to say. The ball's in your court. You have my number."

He turned to go, but she grabbed his arm with a gentle but firm grip. "Wait. You really think I would be a good business manager for Christmas Town Adventure Tours?"

"I think you'd be awesome. But it is a new business and that's always a risk."

"But not as big a risk as I'd feared." She returned the folder to him.

"Still, if you feel like dating someone you work with is too risky, I understand. And I withdraw my job offer."

"Well, that's awkward." Miranda grinned. "Because I've already given notice to my current employer that I'll be leaving to take a new job. With you."

"You quit your job?" Dustin nearly dropped his paperwork.

"That's right. I'm taking a risk, and it's kind of a thrill." She tossed her head and laughed. "Almost as thrilling as zip-lining."

He chuckled. "We may have awakened your inner adrenaline junkie. Keep in mind zipline access is one of the major perks of working for me."

"How about zipline kisses? Are those included?"

"Only for you. In fact, if you like, we could do a little signing bonus right now."

She stepped closer. "Yes, please."

He pulled her close, but before he kissed her, he took a moment to admire the curve of her cheek, the way the morning sun reflected off the coppery highlights in her curls, the intoxicating mix of blues and greens in those bright eyes. "You're beautiful," he murmured.

"Quit stalling." She laughed and reached up to tug him closer so that they could kiss, a kiss he felt all the way to his toes.

He couldn't have said how long it lasted, but when they were done, Nugget and Jolly were sitting side-by-side, their heads tilted as they watched. The Knotty Elves were also watching from near the gazebo, scarves covering half their faces. Odette gave Dustin a thumbs-up.

Miranda turned to see what he was looking at. "Aren't those the Knotty Elves?"

"Yes, but don't stare. They think they're incognito with that scarf disguise of theirs."

"Incognito? Why?"

"I didn't want to disturb you at work, so I sent out a few texts to see if anyone had spotted you around town. The Knotty Elves decided to follow you until I could catch up."

Miranda's beautiful eyes sparkled as she laughed. "I can't imagine anything like that happening in the city."

"Welcome to Christmas Town." Dustin kissed her again. "You're going to love it here."

The End

# The Lights of Christmas

## Book 3: Lights, Camera, Christmas Town

### Melinda Curtis

ChelseaBeth Publishing

# Chapter One

*D*ecember 7ᵗʰ

"Christmas is all about lights. And I'm all about *lighting*." Movie lighting contractor Dave Walsh told Esther of Esther's House, a B&B in Christmas Town. He pressed the hidden button in the neckline of his ugly holiday sweater. Rudolph's nose blinked a cheery red.

Esther chuckled, fluffing her shoulder-length, pure white curls. She had the friendly air of Mrs. Claus and the efficiency of a drill sergeant. After a week spent at the bed & breakfast, Dave thought Esther ran Esther's House and its restaurant with an iron fist and a heart of holiday gold. "You fit right into Christmas Town, Dave."

"Is that because of his love of Christmas or his penchant for dad jokes?" Betsy Anne Gleason appeared beside Dave, looking as stunning as always, despite the fact that it was only six a.m.

Her smooth, short black hair curled gently at her delicate chin. Her big brown eyes were expertly accented and highlighted. There wasn't as much as a blemish showing on her face, although her make-up wasn't thick or cakey. And her lips... Well, they were kissably red.

Dave modulated his excitement at seeing Betsy Anne because for years he and the hair and make-up artist had been—*much to his dismay*—just work friends. "You don't like my dad jokes?"

"You're not a dad." Betsy Anne smiled at Dave, and then at Esther, holding up one finger to indicate how many were in her party.

"With Dave's Christmas enthusiasm, he's among friends here, no matter the corn in his jokes." Esther smiled broadly. "In Christmas Town, we celebrate the spirit of Christmas year-round. You movie people are straining my breakfast capacity. I'm putting you together. But the good news is that we've just started serving breakfast for the day and you get a window overlooking the town square." She led them into the elegant dining room. "If no one's told you yet, our gazebo out there is famous as a place where a kiss at Christmas foretells of a wedding in the new year."

Practically everyone in town had told Dave this fun fact.

*If only I could convince Betsy Anne to step in that gazebo with me.*

"I've been enjoying looking at the lights on the town square before bed and again at breakfast." Unaware of Dave's thoughts, Betsy Anne sat at the table, staring out at the pre-dawn darkness. "I'm from New York, Esther, where we have a different kind of light show."

"Ours are one-of-a-kind," Esther said, looking pleased.

"And we appreciate you opening for breakfast an hour early." Betsy Anne was doling out compliments the way Santa handed out candy canes. "My room is adorable. How did you know I love a pink-flocked Christmas tree?"

"When they told me you were the head of the hair and make-up department, I took a guess." Esther handed them menus before returning to her station.

While Betsy Anne alternated glances at her menu and at the lights of the town square, Dave alternated glances at his menu and her.

*Ask her out.*

Dave's mouth was too dry to form words. He hadn't been expecting to see her until they were on set later.

*Ask her out.*

He couldn't. Once a shy nerd, always a shy nerd. It didn't matter that he was sitting across from the most beautiful woman on the film crew of *The Wedding Carousel*. Dave revised that thought—*on any film crew*. Instead of working up his nerve, he perused his surroundings with an appreciative holiday eye.

Esther's was a contradiction of class and schmaltz. Classic Christmas music played softly in the background—Bing Crosby's version of *White Christmas*.

The windows in Esther's dining room were elegantly trimmed with garland and twinkle lights on the inside. There was a small, white-flocked Christmas tree in the corner with big, colorful lights. The tablecloths were white and the china expensive. But that's where the class ended, and the schmaltz of Christmas began. The salt and pepper shakers were Christmas characters—Rudolph, the Abominable Snowman, Santa and Mrs. Claus, angels, and snowmen. Instead of being black, the cloth napkins were printed with whimsical, holiday gnomes.

Dave liked Esther's. He liked the cast and crew on this film. He liked Christmas Town. He suppressed a sigh, thinking about the other thing he liked in town—Betsy Anne.

"Dave, you must be in heaven on this film." Betsy Anne set her menu down, shook out her napkin, and laid it in her lap. "More so than usual since there is Christmas on set and Christmas off set."

"I'm thrilled. It's better than that time we shot the Christmas movie in Miami." He smiled across the table at his dream girl, the woman who never saw him as more than a work buddy. Dave pushed his new, plain black glasses higher on the bridge of his nose. "I thought you liked Christmas, too."

"I do. And I love all this snow. But I'm stressed. This is the first film I'm doing without a business partner." Betsy Anne had run what was now Gleason Hair and Make-Up with her on-again/off-again boyfriend and partner Marcel, providing services to productions ranging from theatrical film to television. "Every decision is mine."

"You know, you can bounce things off me if you need to." Dave had his own crew to manage. "Vent or whatever. I know how hard it is to run a business *in this* business. You can't always predict where the next job is coming from or where you'll be working or how many employees you'll need."

"Yes. That's why I want to do a good job for Lark." The movie's producer. Betsy Anne touched her right cheek with the back of her hand. It was a gesture she used sometimes when she was nervous, not that Dave understood why. "If I go above and beyond for her, I could be the first hair and make-up artist she calls for every project."

Dave nodded. "I'm hoping that, too. Since she's new to being the top producer on a project, she'll be looking to assemble a team." Her team. Not someone else's.

A lock of his hair fell into his eyes, behind the frames of his new glasses. He brushed the hair away. "Do you need a ride over to the location today? I've got to get there early to set up the lights. I'll be leaving after breakfast." He smiled up at the waitress. "The oatmeal breakfast, please. With fruit and strong coffee."

"And you?" the waitress glanced at Betsy Anne, who seemed distracted as she ordered the same.

*I hope she's not still heartbroken over Marcel.*

---

*Fa-la-la-la-la. Hunka-la. La-la.*

Betsy Anne was having a Christmas-themed hottie alert.

*When did Dave Walsh become so attractive?*

He tossed that black hair off his forehead like a romance movie star. And those Clark Kent glasses were really working for him today. Who didn't find Clark Kent sexier than Superman?

Not her. She'd never been a woman who liked a man in tights. Not Robin Hood. Not Batman.

Betsy Anne glanced skyward. Or in this case, toward the ceiling, which happened to have a sprig of mistletoe pinned above their table. In fact, mistletoe was pinned above every table in the formal dining room of the charming Victorian.

"Betsy Anne? Are you all right?" Dave leaned forward and was Dave again, the friendly lighting guy who binged Christmas movies like other people binged episodes of *The Bachelor*. The sweet, nice, not-attractive-to-me Dave once more.

Betsy Anne breathed a sigh of relief. "I just need my first coffee of the day."

A very large mug appeared before her, along with a small milk pitcher shaped like a Victorian home and a Santa sleigh filled with packets of sweetener.

"It's like my every wish is their command." Betsy Anne doctored her coffee, still fighting the lingering effects of Dave's unexpected wow-ness. Given her track record with relationships at work, best keep things on a professional level. "How are you lighting the set today?"

"Funny you should ask." Dave held his steaming mug beneath his nose and breathed in deeply. "We're doing the ugly sweater dinner scene at Lisa's grandparents' house." Lisa being the lead character in the romance, not the actress who played her. "The script calls for a combination of family warmth, Lisa's melancholy over John shipping out on Christmas, humor over John's ugly sweater, and John's tentative admission that he never truly appreciated Christmas until he left Christmas Town." He pressed his tan sweater's neckline, causing Rudolph's nose to blink. *Classic Dave.* "That requires a lot of different set-ups—soft lighting, letting the light from a Christmas tree surround our two stars in an intimate glow, a clear shot of eight reindeer on John's sweater requires bouncing light, and..." Dave paused, sipping his coffee. "I should have just said I have my work cut out for me today. I'll be shedding this sweater sometime in the first hour because I'll be sweating from moving all that heavy equipment."

"*You should have said...*" Betsy Anne smiled. "What's that all about?" He could string together a monologue on the ins-and-outs of lighting the shortest of scenes, which was oddly comforting because his eyes didn't glaze over when she did the same about hair and make-up.

"Abilene asked me how I was going to light her during a scene at the carousel and I..." He sipped his coffee again, looking self-conscious about mentioning a conversation he'd had with the actress playing the heroine's grandmother. "You know how I get when I talk about two of my favorite things. Christmas and production lighting."

"You go on. And on." It was endearing. *Dave* was endearing. And what with this sexy vibe those new glasses of his had triggered, Betsy Anne could imagine herself building on that feeling of endearment. But, unlike Marcel, Dave was the kind of guy who'd want an honest relationship, one where he and his girlfriend told each other everything, including the vulnerabilities they covered up so that people would like them. "I wouldn't worry about it, Dave."

"But I do. Abilene told me—*in a very nice way*—that I talk too much." Dave set his coffee down, tapping the mug with one finger.

"And so, based on the word of an actress, you're going to talk less?"

"Well, it wasn't just her. There was that local trio of old ladies who knit." Dave laughed uncomfortably. "They gave me a hand knit, ugly Christmas sweater. Which I love."

"The Knotty Elves." Betsy Anne nodded. "They gave me a sweater, too." It qualified as an ugly sweater, as well.

"Their comments reminded me that I started this year with several resolutions. And I realized over the summer that I hadn't achieved any of them. But I got busy with work in February and..."

"You lost track of yourself." She'd done that as well. Or rather, Betsy Anne hid her real self from the world. All the time. She brushed the back of her fingers over her right cheek and the birthmark hidden by layers of make-up. She didn't want to talk about herself. "What were your resolutions, Dave?"

There was color high in his cheeks, highlighting his good bone structure. "Well...er... One of them was that I didn't want people's eyes to glaze over when I talk."

He was sensitive to others and perhaps in need of a confidence boost. Betsy Anne nodded. "Hence you taking this recent advice."

Dave smiled. "I wanted to start exercising, which I've done. Working out is hard to fit in when on location but I'm no longer twenty-five."

"You're thirty-five." The same age as Betsy Anne. With everything going on, she'd been having trouble keeping the weight off, too. It didn't help that pastry, pie and cookies were everywhere on this set. "Anything else?"

He nodded. "And I wanted to start dating. Although... that one I've made no progress toward. It's hard to date when you work ten-hour days and you're on location four-to-six weeks, or more, at a time."

The lock of hair fell over his eyes again.

And Betsy Anne had the strangest urge to brush it back in place.

# Chapter Two

"We need to block this scene," Alexis said in a loud voice, one that carried through the large, old Victorian. The director clapped her hands. "Let's go, people."

The actors playing John and Lisa came forward, followed by various crew members, including Betsy Anne, who wore a utility belt filled with whatever she needed to touch up hair and make-up.

After giving Betsy Anne a you-got-this smile, Dave moved to stand near Alexis, ready to change the lighting to better please the director because she was always changing something, usually for the better.

John and Lisa walked through the entry hall and into the living room.

"That's good. Keep close but not close enough to touch," Alexis said in her commanding, director's voice. "Remember that you're still longing for each other but believe that love is lost. Stop. Dave." Alexis gestured to him. "Their faces are a little stark here."

Dave assessed the room, taking in the brightness coming in the east-facing windows. He'd set up the lighting when the sun hadn't yet risen. Now it was too bright in this corner. "Quinten, we're going to need filters over those windows. There's too much sunlight streaming in, amplified by all that snow." There had to be three feet on the ground outside. "You'll find the filters in the van. Right side."

"Got it, boss." Quinten, his *best boy*, hurried outside to retrieve the equipment and make the adjustment.

"Great. Let's continue." Alexis waved her arms from the principal actors to the Christmas tree in the corner. "Lisa and Dave talk about the past and head toward the Christmas tree, ostensibly to admire it but it allows you a few moments more alone together. Stop." Alexis waved toward Betsy Anne. "Is it me or do Lisa's lips seem pale?"

"I can try something brighter." Betsy Anne dug in one of her belt's pouches. "Candy Cane Red might work." She applied a coat of brighter red lipstick to Lisa's lips.

"Better. Let's keep moving." Alexis held up her hands, thumbs out as she framed the shot. "Here's where John tells Lisa that he's shipping out again on Christmas Day. Dave, is it possible to give his face a shadow here? Not like Humphrey Bogart in *The Maltese Falcon* but something subtle that implies he's divided or torn about leaving her."

"We'll remove the kicker when we film his close-up," Dave said, referring to a floor light.

"It might not be enough," Alexis mused.

"Noted and working to solve." Dave tried to estimate how long it would take to get the first few shots of the day, along with the trajectory of natural light coming through the windows. He'd have to work on the fly when they set up for that shot, trying different techniques. He consulted with Gregg, the director of photography.

Alexis was walking the pair of leads into the dining room where the actors playing Lisa's family were gathered around a large, festive dining room table. "How's the audio in here?" she asked. "The ceilings are so low. Are we going to be able to capture Poppa Seymore whispering to John?"

While the sound crew addressed that question, Betsy Anne moved closer to Dave. "You took off your sweater. It's not even nine o'clock."

Dave leaned closer to her. "I had to run cables around the perimeter of the room since some of the shots are going to include the main floor."

"Make sure you don't catch cold after taking everything down later." She smiled at him. She never smiled at him. Not like that. Like...she used to smile at

Marcel, all rosy-cheeked and sparkling eyes. "Promise me you'll layer up when you go out."

"Okay," he promised, feeling surreal.

*Say something else, dummy.*

"Lisa's hair looks nice," he blurted. Betsy Anne had twisted it over to the side. "But so does yours." Without thinking, he brushed a lock of it behind Betsy Anne's ear.

"Thanks." Betsy Anne got that same glazed look in her eyes that she'd had at breakfast.

---

*Fa-la-la-la-la. Hunka-la. La-la.*

Betsy Anne ran her gaze up Dave's muscular arms to those Clark Kent glasses, which amplified the power of his clear blue eyes.

*It was happening again!*

Dave turned Betsy Anne to face him, taking a gentle hold of her arms. "Are you okay?" he whispered. "Are you having a low blood sugar moment?"

*From here, he could slide his hands around my back and draw me close for a...*

"No!" she said too loudly. And then in a softer voice, since the rest of the crew turned to stare, "Sorry."

*What's happening to me today?*

Movement outside the front windows caught her eye. Quinten was inching between the snowy shrubbery and the windows, carrying what looked like a four-by-six filter and a tripod to hold it in place. Three elderly women on the sidewalk wearing knit caps, scarves, and mittens, waved at him, trying to get Quinten's attention.

The Knotty Elves.

They were the same three women who'd stopped by the shoot yesterday at the invitation of Abilene. They'd been in awe of the amount of cosmetics Betsy Anne and her assistant had at their disposal. And they'd marveled at all the attractive men running around the set outdoors, like Quinten and Dave.

*They planted the seed.*

Betsy Anne heaved a sigh of relief.

*I'm not attracted to Dave. It's just the power of suggestion.*

Dave moved closer to the windows to watch his assistant work. With the sunlight streaming in and outlining the breadth of those T-shirt-covered shoulders and how they tapered to his waist...

*Well, Merry Christmas to me and all the other folks on the crew who admired a nicely built man.*

Betsy Anne turned toward the dining room to see who else was staring at Dave, but everyone was listening to Alexis give directions.

She glanced back at Dave.

His T-shirt was a deep green and fit him snugly. With his hands on his hips, the outline of those muscular arms was a sight to behold. Not even the words on his shirt could detract from his appeal: *You can't take away my Ho-Ho-Ho.*

Yes, his black hair was in need of a trim. Yes, he wore white grandpa sneakers instead of something trendy. And yes, when he pivoted those glasses to sit up on top of his head, his hair resembled Sonic the Hedgehog's spiky hairdo. But despite that... Despite years of friendship...

The Knotty Elves weren't entirely to blame. Suggestion or not...

*Fa-la-la-la-la. Hunka-la. La-la.*

There was no other conclusion.

*I have the hots for Dave.*

# Chapter Three

W hile most of the crew broke for lunch, which was being set up in a large tent pitched in the backyard, Dave stayed in the house to adjust the lights for the next scene.

*Here comes Santa Claus...*

The catchy Christmas song played in his head while he ripped up tape, coiled yards of electrical cord, and then laid it out differently. While the tune played in his head, he coached himself on asking Betsy Anne out. He was plugging into the portable generator in the kitchen when he heard a sound.

"Hey, be careful," he called, getting to his feet, and pushing open the swinging door. "I haven't taped down the cords yet." Lark would never use him again if he caused an accident on set.

A young girl of about nine or ten whirled around, long brown hair flying. She stood in front of the Christmas tree. "I was just looking." She pointed toward the hallway, cheeks pinkening. "Someone got to the bathroom before I could."

Dave recognized her as the daughter of the caterer. "It's okay. I'm not mad. But...shouldn't you be in school?"

"I'm home schooled. At least until after the holidays. I'm Molly, Faye's pride and joy. Who are you and what do you do?"

He liked kids with inquisitive minds. "I'm Dave. It's my job to make sure the lights work and that no one stumbles on my cords."

She glanced around the room. "But you put them against the wall."

He grabbed a roll of wide tape he'd left on the table. "All it takes is one person tripping on a cord in the kitchen or in front of the Christmas tree to yank everything away from the wall."

She held up her hands. "I won't trip. I promise."

"I'll make sure you don't." Dave got down on his knees, pulling out several feet of tape before laying it down over both cord and carpet. "And I'd appreciate it if you could save me a plate—half salad, half main entrée. The food is so good here that if I'm too late, there won't be anything left."

"Will do, Mr. Dave." She saluted. "One special plate. Coming right up."

"Merry Christmas will do."

Someone exited the bathroom.

"Merry Christmas," Molly said, scampering to the facilities.

---

Betsy Anne lingered over lunch, waiting for Dave to finish his set reset. She shrugged deeper into her coat.

The portable heaters were good, but they were outdoors in the middle of winter in Maine with only a thin canvas wall as protection.

Christmas music played from a small speaker behind the buffet table. The tablecloth beneath the food display was gold with colorful wreaths on it. Silverware sat on red fuzzy Christmas stockings. The holiday was everywhere on this project. And Christmas made her think of Dave.

She'd taken a big cup of coffee, of which she'd drunk half. Her quiet time with caffeine was her form of meditation. But today... She wasn't finding her midday balance.

*I can't be attracted to Dave.*

They'd been friends for a long time. He was Dave. The guy who got excited over Christmas, who wore Christmas T-shirts, sang Christmas songs acapella, sent her small, considerate Christmas gifts, despite the fact that all she sent him was a card every year.

Betsy Anne touched her cheek. That birthmark...

She'd cried many tears over it in elementary school, keeping her head down, limiting her friendships, focusing on her studies. And then she'd earned a spot at a private middle school and her mother allowed her to wear make-up. Everything changed. Suddenly, Betsy Anne had friends. She dressed in nice clothes instead of jeans and hoodies. She became popular. All because she was hiding who she truly was—inside and out.

She was afraid of having a real relationship with someone like Dave. Afraid, because in order to go for it, she'd need to take off her layers of protection.

*I don't think I can do it.*

Even if it was Dave. And so, she was determined to fight this attraction.

*I'm just going to give him a long look-see and all that fa-la-la stuff will disappear.*

Dave entered the craft services tent. His gaze traveled a circuit around the interior until it landed on her. That wayward lock of hair tumbled onto his eyeglasses. And he smiled.

*Fa-la-la-la-la. Hunka-la. La-la.*

It was the same friendly smile she'd seen thousands of times before.

But her heart started pounding and she started to smile and, all of a sudden she was warmer than midday on the Fourth of July.

"Mr. Dave!" The young girl who helped with catering waved at him. "I saved you a plate." She produced a plate that was heaped with equal parts salad and beef tips on rice.

Dave accepted it and thanked Molly, complimenting her mother on the food.

*He's so nice.*

Marcel had been more into himself than Betsy Anne—she'd had to fight him for mirror time! And he'd never looked at her the same after he'd seen her birthmark.

"There's something different about Dave," her assistant Cecily said from a nearby seat. She got to her feet, gathering her trash. "I don't know what it is, but he seems..."

*Magnetic... Mesmerizing... Memorable...*

*Fa-la-la-la-la. Hunka-la. La-la.*

"...datable."

Betsy Anne's palms landed on the table. *He's mine,* her heart wanted to say, despite her brain protesting, *but he's Dave!*

She tensed as he walked her way. He'd put on a jacket over that T-shirt and what she imagined were his six-pack abs.

*Stop it.*

Dave sat across from Betsy Anne. He looked so sexy, she almost expected him to toss her a smooth line but instead, he said, "Either everyone cleared out fast or I'm really late for lunch."

Relieved that he was still Dave, she smiled. "You're always late for lunch."

He took a bite of his beef tips. "Oh, wow. This is so good. Can Faye cater every movie we work on from now on?"

"Now you're dreaming." Betsy Anne checked the time and then gathered her things, admitting defeat where squelching her attraction to Dave was concerned.

"Dave." Lark walked over to their table. The movie's producer always looked wired, as if she had too much on her plate but was determined to power through it all. "You're doing a great job on the lights." She looked at Betsy Anne. "And you with make-up." She rested a hand on Betsy Anne's shoulder, smiling. "You added years to Abilene's face."

"Was I not supposed to?" Betsy Anne held her breath. The actress playing Lisa's grandmother had been firm about the look she wanted. Betsy Anne didn't want to admit that Abilene had also requested she *age-up* her ex-husband Cyrus—her onscreen husband and ex in real life—even more.

"I wanted Abilene to look happy and she does. The make-up is superb. The lighting fabulous. The dailies are coming out better than I hoped." Lark bit her lip. "Uh-oh. That's a sure sign that something's about to go wrong, isn't it?"

"Only if you believe in jinxes." Dave set down his fork. "Don't stress. You'll be producing more movies because you run such a tight ship."

"I'm crossing my fingers." Lark tugged nervously at the neckline of her sweater. "We'll talk more about our future business relationships after we successfully wrap this shoot."

Someone called for Lark, and she hurried off.

"That's a nice Christmas present for us if things work out for Lark." Dave grinned at Betsy Anne. "And still...I can think of something better."

No matter how many times Betsy Anne asked, he wouldn't tell her.

# Chapter Four

"I can't believe we keep finding elves on set." Dave ate a bowl of fruit while sitting across the table from Betsy Anne at breakfast the next morning.

They'd found the green overalled elf hidden among the dining room table decorations yesterday afternoon.

"The elf is cute. But Alexis is getting upset." Betsy Anne sipped her coffee, trying not to *fa-la-la* over Dave. "I can understand it if the locals want to get excited about a movie being made about a romance that really happened here in town. But they don't understand continuity. If it's in one scene, it needs to be in all the shots for that scene."

Dave nodded. "Or it'll just be a Starbucks cup spotted in *Game of Thrones*, making a blooper reel."

"That elf should stay hidden at Posey's Diner." Given her pre-occupation with Dave and the long day ahead in close proximity to him, she hoped everything went smoothly today. A thought struck. "You don't think the caterers are behind this, do you? It's a good marketing stunt."

"Nah. The caterers are always so busy. Granted, the caterer's daughter came inside to use the facilities during lunch but there were at least a dozen locals coming on and off set all day long. When I found Molly, she was standing in front of the Christmas tree, not the table. Although, I wouldn't put it past the entire town being behind the elf effort." He finished the last of his fruit. And lifted his coffee mug, staring at Betsy Anne over the rim. "We've got that exterior scene outside this morning. Did you put your underwear on?"

"My...my what?" Betsy Anne choked on her coffee.

Dave's face flamed red, making his blue eyes stand out. "Your long johns, I meant. Boy, did that come out wrong." He tugged at his thick, black turtleneck sweater, which was trimmed with small, white snowflakes. It was toned down Christmas. Very un-Dave-like.

"Where'd you get that sweater?"

"Dockery's here in town." He glanced down. "Do you like it?"

"It's nice. Not exactly what I've come to expect from you," she allowed, smiling a little ruefully because he was spreading his wings and she was too scared to spread hers.

"You mean you expect to see me in ugly Christmas sweaters?"

"Yep." It was the truth, but she felt they knew each other well enough that he wouldn't be hurt by her observation. "But it's not a bad thing. If you want, we can wear our Knotty Elves sweaters on the same day." She refrained from rolling her eyes. Barely. This wasn't like her.

"Hey, can I ask you something?" At her nod, Dave set his coffee mug on the table, looking uncharacteristically serious. He opened his mouth and—

"There you are. Gorgeously put-together, as usual." A tall man in black slacks and a pea coat pulled a chair over to their small table and sat down. His long brown hair artfully brushed his shoulders. And when he tossed that hair, Betsy Anne finally recognized him. "I've answered your beck and call, Betsy Anne. Today, I'm yours to command."

"Marcel." She'd forgotten her ex-boyfriend/ex-business partner was working for her the next few days. She gave Dave an apologetic glance. "Marcel is here to help me with make-up for the city council scene. Lots of extras on set this afternoon."

"Which reminds me that I need to get going. I've got lighting to set up." Dave stood, gesturing across the room to Quinten to get a move on.

"Wait, Dave." Betsy Anne barely kept herself from reaching for him. "What were you going to ask me?"

"You know... I've forgotten." Dave smiled, but it wasn't a smile that made her heart pound. And he left before she could figure out why.

Marcel moved to sit at Dave's place. He began drinking Dave's coffee and eating his toast. "Same old Dave. Workaholic."

"At least, he shows up for work on time." Before their personal and professional break-up, Marcel had left Betsy Anne hanging several times.

Marcel laughed. "I'm here, aren't I?"

"Only because I arranged your transportation so that you'd arrive yesterday." She couldn't risk him being a no show.

The waitress refilled Betsy Anne's coffee. She took one look at the way Marcel was picking through the plates on the table and asked, "Can I get you a breakfast?"

"Oh. No. I'm not hungry." Marcel smiled at her, holding out Dave's coffee mug for a refill. "What are you doing tonight after we're done, Betsy Anne? There's not much action in town, is there? Do you want to drive somewhere? It's Friday night."

*Ew.* "No. Marcel, we broke up."

"So?"

"You're asking me out on a date." And he wasn't Dave.

"Well...technically. Maybe." His gaze wandered around the room the way it did when he was looking for someone more interesting to talk to. "But I thought we might go Dutch. Or maybe it'd be your treat since I'm your employee now."

Betsy Anne shook her head. "It's amazing how different you look to me now."

"*Different?*" Marcel brushed imaginary crumbs off his chest and then leaned toward the window, baring his teeth, and fluffing his hair. "I think I look great."

"On the outside," Betsy Anne murmured. "You know, surface level stuff." Unlike Dave, who she was increasingly convinced had layer upon layer of goodness and beauty in him. He listened to her. He found his work fulfilling. He had quirks and could appreciate hers.

But could he appreciate her birthmark?

Betsy Anne didn't think so. She didn't think anyone could.

———

"*You-who!*" One of the elderly women who called themselves the Knotty Elves waved at Dave from several rows back in the city council meeting room. Bangles tinkled at her wrist, a clue that she might be Odette, the one who always wore bells and tinkling trinkets. "Dave, can you let that nice director know that we *weren't* sitting here when John made his announcement concerning the carousel being in trouble?"

"That was years ago but I'm sure we were in the front row." Her friend fluffed a plush scarf up around her pointed chin and blinked at him from behind her owlish glasses. Dave thought her name was June. "That's where we always sit when we come."

"Don't filmmakers care about accuracy?" The third Knotty Elf gestured Dave closer so that he could hear her when she whispered, "*Did you ask her out?*" She smelled like candy canes, and he thought her name was Pru.

"Ladies." Dave felt his cheeks heating because he'd stumbled once more trying to ask Betsy Anne out this morning. He laid a finger over his lips. "I thought Betsy Anne was our secret." He'd met the trio while browsing the Christmas sweater racks at Dockery's. They'd somehow managed to wheedle their way in and around the set during the first few days of shooting, and they'd noticed his fascination with Betsy Anne.

Or it could have been a lucky guess. She'd been shopping the coats at Dockery's across the aisle from Dave and he'd had his eye on her.

"I haven't found the right moment to ask her." For a man who ran his own business, employing a handful of lighting technicians and interns, Dave was really bad at asking women for a date. Especially women who he considered friends...

Which, truth be told, was just about every woman he knew.

"There's no right time for love," the elderly woman with the bangles chimed.

"Or a wrong time to ask for a date," the elderly woman with the owlish glasses said.

"And you've cleaned up so well." The third Knotty Elf smoothed the sweater over his shoulders. "She's not going to turn you down."

Dave sighed, gaze drifting toward Betsy Anne, who stood between the set designer and Marcel. "That's her ex-boyfriend over there." The man was a real life underwear model. If Marcel wasn't good enough for Betsy Anne, Dave didn't stand a chance with her.

"Pfft. Not a spark between them," Odette touched her mistletoe earrings. The attached bells tinkled as if the Knotty Elf tuned her own magical sparks.

"He's fluff," added June, her chin nestled deeper into the plush nest of her scarf. "You know, he reminds me of that Warren Beatty movie where he was a philandering hair stylist. Was it *Hairspray*?"

"*Shampoo*." Pru scoffed. "He'd be perfect for the part. Dave should go ask Betsy Anne out. Now." Pru offered Dave a mint from a candy tin. "I made these myself. Peppermint for calm and courage."

Dave took a mint and a step back. "Now? In front of everyone, including her ex?" He was beginning to doubt the wisdom of taking their advice.

That troublesome lock of hair fell over his eyes. Dave shoved it out of the way.

His gaze connected with Betsy Anne. Her jaw dropped as if she was in awe of something.

He cast a glance behind him to see what had shocked her.

No one was behind him. And nothing was amiss back there either.

"She was looking at you, silly," Odette said with too much jingle of those bangles.

"He really has led a sheltered life," June noted, straightening her glasses.

"Now's the time to do the deed." Pru puffed out, her breath minty and her push against his shoulders gentle but insistent.

# Chapter Five

"Hey, Betsy Anne." Dave walked up to her after talking with the Knotty Elves. "You look nice today."

*Was I staring at him like some stalker?*

She was afraid she had been because...

*Fa-la-la-la-la. Hunka-la. La-la.*

"Dude, you saw Betsy Anne this morning." Marcel tossed his hair. "You should have complimented her then."

Betsy Anne elbowed him. "Thanks, Dave. Ignore the peanut gallery."

"Yeah. About peanuts..." Dave looked flummoxed. That lock of hair fell over his eyes.

Without thinking about it, Betsy Anne reached up and brushed it back in place with one hand. With the other hand, she drew a can of hairspray from her utility belt like a gunslinger drawing his gun. It was only when she realized Dave's eyes were as wide as saucers that she kept herself from spraying the hair in place. "Oh, sorry. Habit."

He placed his hand over the lock of hair, looking as if he was at a loss as to what to say.

"Sorry. I didn't mean to invade your personal space." *What am I doing? Emergency! Emergency! Find a diversion.* Betsy Anne nervously touched her right cheek before she caught sight of Abilene and practically ran away, calling over her shoulder, "I need to touch up Abilene's make-up. Excuse me."

"Did you just choke on asking Betsy Anne for a date?" Marcel grinned as if Dave's crash-and-burn was the funniest thing ever. "Peanuts was your transition to dinner?"

"Yes, it was a food-themed transition." And a lame one at that. Dave's shoulders slumped.

*Who am I kidding? Betsy Anne needs someone with confidence where the ladies are concerned. And experience. I'm just...trying to catch up with guys like Marcel. Decades behind at thirty-five.*

Marcel slapped him on the back. "I can help you with that."

"What are you talking about?"

"Your confidence." He slapped Dave's back once more. "Haven't you ever heard that clothes make the man?"

Dave struck the heel of his hand against his forehead. "Don't tell me I said all that out loud." All the embarrassing parts.

"You did. But at least you didn't shout." Marcel led him out of the room. "Come on. This is your lucky day. I'm going to help you." Marcel led Dave to a conference room with rollaway racks filled with outfits for actors and extras, and plastic storage bins filled with shoes. He closed the door behind them and locked it. "I like this new toned-down Christmas look you're rockin'. Ugly sweaters make you look like the guy who still lives in his mother's basement. But you need to push it one step further."

"That's not necessary." But Dave didn't unlock the door and walk away.

*What if he's right?*

"You need to class yourself up for Betsy Anne." Marcel rummaged through a shoe bin. "I always take inspiration from a good pair of shoes and build my way up." He handed Dave a pair of shiny black loafers that Dave could see his reflection in. "Those white sneakers need to go, man."

"But...they're comfortable." He slid out of them anyway. Yes, he was that desperate for something that would push him over the edge with Betsy Anne that he was taking advice from vacuous Marcel. Vacuous, suddenly kind Marcel.

The make-up artist moved to a rack filled with men's clothes. He grabbed a pair of black slacks and a black silk button-up shirt, thrusting them toward Dave. "Now, we just need a jacket. Something statement-making."

Dave stared at the silk shirt. This felt wrong. All wrong.

"This isn't me," Dave said.

"If Betsy Anne wanted you, you'd already be dating," Marcel said reasonably, scanning the racks for a jacket. "Hurry up and change."

Again, Dave did as he asked. There was a rightness to Marcel's logic, even if Dave felt he was betraying who he was inside.

"Now, when you choose a restaurant," Marcel was saying, "find something super elegant with a big price tag. She loves steak and lobster."

"She likes fish and chicken," Dave said, buttoning the silk shirt.

Marcel held up a black suit jacket briefly before shoving it back in the rack. "Bring her a bouquet of roses."

"She likes daisies."

"And talk about something other than work. Or Christmas. Or all this snow." Marcel scoffed. "Betsy Anne hates snow."

"Are you sure this isn't a list of things *you* don't like, Marcel?"

"It's absolutely what I like. But it's what she likes, too."

*He doesn't know her at all. That must be why they didn't work. And that must be why we have a chance.*

"I think all this is unnecessary," Dave said, getting to his feet just as Marcel held out a black leather motorcycle jacket.

*Oh... I always wanted to wear one of those.*

But it had been outside his comfort zone.

"I'll just try this on." And then change back to his own clothes.

"Dave!" That sounded like Alexis' voice.

Dave opened the conference room door to find the Knotty Elves clustered outside.

They gave him a quick once-over while Marcel fussed with Dave's hair.

"Oh." Odette didn't move. Not so much as a jingle emanated from her direction. "That's..."

"We were curious as to his plans for you." Pru's words sounded slightly parched. "But..."

Marcel removed Dave's glasses and placed them on top of his head. "You rock the intellectual look, buddy. Now, go get her."

"Mr. Smarty Pants, you went too far." June stepped forward and pinned a small, crocheted Santa on Dave's shirt collar. "This man isn't comfortable without some Christmas."

*So true.*

"Thank you." Dave pressed his palm over Santa. "Gotta go."

Behind him, Marcel said, "I can't believe you scorched my look with that homemade accessory. That wasn't the vibe I was going for."

"Maybe not." Pru shook meltaway mints onto her palm, her words confident. "But it was the vibe he needed."

"Dave! Where's Dave?" That was definitely Alexis.

Dave hurried to find her.

---

"Dave! Where's Dave?" Alexis called for a second time.

"Right here." Dave strode down the steps of the town council meeting room toward the dais, looking as if he was a polished talk show host prepping to start the show. His black hair was carefully styled. His glasses were well-placed on top of his head, not spiking like Sonic the Hedgehog. He wore all black—shiny loafers, black slacks, and a black leather jacket over a black silk shirt. And the smile on his face...

*Fa-la-la-la-la. Hunka-la. La-la.*

Well, let's just say that it wasn't the smile Santa sent out in his press packet.

That smile said Dave was sexy, and he knew it.

The crew heaved a collective gasp, catching on to what Betsy Anne had only recently become aware of.

*Dave is smokin' hot.*

But... He didn't seem like Dave anymore. Where was the Christmas? Betsy Anne longed for something familiar, something true.

And there it was. A small Santa pin on his lapel.

She sighed dreamily, reassured.

*Hang on. If I prefer Dave true to himself and his love of Christmas, wouldn't he prefer me showing him my true self?*

*Bare my birthmark?* Her pulse raced for all the wrong reasons. *No. Nope. No-no-no.*

History had shown her that revealing her birthmark was the quickest way to distance people, making them uncomfortable when she caught them staring, which she always did, which made her uncomfortable too.

She touched her right cheek gingerly with the back of her hand.

"Who changed up Dave's look?" someone asked, drawing Betsy Anne back to the present.

Who indeed? She glanced around.

Not Cecily. She was a few feet away, putting a knit beret over an extra's bright red hair so that it wouldn't stand out so much in the background shot. The wardrobe folks were clustered in the back of the meeting room, doling out holiday sweaters and jackets for the extras. Which meant...

*Marcel?*

She shook her head in disbelief, touching her right cheek briefly once more.

He'd never do something that nice. Nor would Dave let him. The two had always been like oil and vinegar.

Alexis was brainstorming lighting ideas with Dave, tossing out buzz-words—stops, filter nets, grid cloths, and hot lights. And then Dave leaped into action, giving orders to his crew.

Several minutes later, when he was finished adjusting the lights, Dave came up to Betsy Anne, still exuding that confidence. "Hey, I was wondering if you'd like to have lunch with me tomorrow. It's Saturday and I thought we could explore Christmas Town."

"Are you not having breakfast?" She frowned. "We could just head out after breakfast."

Some of his confidence dimmed. "I plan to sleep in. I've been up late every night with the production team reviewing the dailies. And after a morning without an alarm, I plan to work out. Esther has a small exercise room in the basement."

"Oh." Far be it for her to keep him from his exercise regimen. That would be a crime. "Lunch. Lunch would be great."

"Really?" Dave covered the Santa pin with his palm. "I didn't think you'd... Just so we're clear, I'm asking you on a date." He said this last bit more forcefully, as if bracing himself for rejection.

"And I'm accepting. I knew the context of your question right away." Betsy Anne smiled, just so he'd know they were on the same page.

His grin was positively delightful.

"Dave!" Alexis called.

After Dave moved away, Marcel came to stand next to Betsy Anne, beaming.

"Are you behind that transformation?" she asked.

"Yep. I raided the wardrobe department. He's hot when he cleans up, isn't he?"

"Yes, but I..." Her gaze drifted toward Dave. "I think he always has been."

# Chapter Six

"You look so pretty." Dave shot to his feet when Betsy Anne came down the stairs late Saturday morning for their lunch date. "Not that you don't look pretty every day." He was nervous and stumbling over himself. "But today you look...special."

"Thanks." Betsy Anne blushed, apparently just as nervous as he was. She wore a red wool dress over black tights and black boots. She touched her right cheek and then gestured toward Dave. "Another new, not-so-ugly Christmas sweater?"

"Yes, do you mind that I'm stepping out of my comfort zone?" Because he was. The classier sweaters. Asking her out. His pulse was pounding so fast, he wouldn't have passed a simple blood pressure test. "I mean, I'm not completely out of my comfort zone. Let's be honest. I am who I am—lover of Christmas and a lighting geek." He waited for Betsy Anne to toss back something similar.

And waited.

She drew a deep breath and swung her arms. "So... Where are we going for lunch?"

*Not the best of starts.* "There's a really interesting sandwich place not too far from here. Three Elves Sandwich Shoppe. Have you tried it?"

"Not yet." Why was she *not* surprised that they were going to a restaurant with a Christmas theme? "What? No Posey's Diner?"

Dave helped her into her coat. "Do you really want to spend our free time looking for an elf when that's what we're going to be doing on every scene until the end of the film?"

"Nope. The sandwich place sounds fantastic."

He put on his coat, and they headed outside into the gently falling snow, taking a moment to admire the kids lining up to see Santa on the stage set up in the town square.

"What a line." Dave waved to one of the crew, who walked by Esther's carrying a cup of coffee. "I hear Santa gives out candy canes to every kid who tells him what they want for Christmas. You have to lick the candy cane to make your wish come true." Three times, he thought the saying went.

Betsy Anne scoffed. "If that were the case, I'd have had a pony when I was five. I sat on Santa's lap in three department stores and candy canes were my favorite thing about Christmas other than presents."

Dave offered his arm. The sidewalks were slippery in the snowy, winter wonderland. "I'm sorry you didn't get your Christmas wish."

She laid her mittened hand on the crook of his arm, eyes sparkling with amusement. "Somehow, I don't think a pony would have done well on the back porch of my family's New York City brownstone. What was it that you wished for when you were a kid?"

"I wanted a movie camera." He sighed, remembering that most important of Christmases vividly as they headed toward The Tea Pot where they'd turn onto the main drag. "I was six and I told Santa that I needed a camera because our family holiday videos were so terrible. Too dark. Bad audio."

"I bet even the hair and make-up was bad." Betsy Anne laughed, which was a good sign considering that rocky start in the lobby.

Dave nodded, smiling at her the way he'd always wanted to, as if she was unique and special to him, because she was. "Do you know what I got instead?"

Betsy Anne shook her head, returning his smile with equal interest.

"The Hungry, Hungry Hippos game."

"Oh, that's sad. But funny, too." She touched her right cheek with a mittened hand. "I got the Barbie Styling Head, complete with hair and make-up accessories."

"Instead of the pony?" That was odd. He would've expected a stuffed pony or even a stuffed unicorn under the tree. "Was your mom a make-up artist?"

"No. I had this birthmark on my cheek that I wasn't comfortable with." She gestured to her right cheek and stopped talking.

"A birthmark?" Dave asked, sensing they were suddenly on dangerous ice. "Where? I've never seen it."

"Can we talk about something else?" She sounded nervous, scared even.

"Sure."

But instead, they said nothing.

They turned when they reached The Tea Pot, which had great coffee and pastries. Several members of the production crew occupied tables inside, looking laid back and relaxed. The sidewalks were crowded with shoppers. A Victorian quartet burst into song on the other side of the street.

*Deck the halls...*

"*Fa-la-la-la-la. La-la-la-la.*" Dave took Betsy Anne's hand and pulled her through the crowd, chastising himself for being a nerd and bursting into song. "I'm sorry. I know it makes you uncomfortable when I sing."

"Don't be sorry." She hurried to catch up to him. "You have a beautiful voice."

"If I recall correctly, you told me to stop singing three times on the last film we worked on together." He shouldn't pick at her like this. They'd been getting along so well.

"Oh, it wasn't because you were singing, per se. I was stressed out over all my Marcel drama. It wasn't easy to dissolve a partnership and a relationship."

"Yet, you hired him to work on this film." A bit of frustrated jealousy tried to rear its ugly head. Her relationship to Marcel was none of his business and the guy had been nice to him yesterday. Misguided, but nice.

"I hired Marcel because everyone else declined. Most people I know in the industry are taking time off for the holidays."

It was a relief to hear. Dave guided her across the street toward Dockery's. And then he stopped. Right there in the flow of traffic. Because he'd spotted something unusual. "Look at that." Dave pointed, caught by the image of snow falling against a sunny, blue sky. He took out his cell phone and snapped a photograph.

"It's beautiful." Betsy Anne squeezed his hand.

"Beauty involving light inspires me." *Her beauty inspires me.* Dave spared Betsy Anne a long look before a car honked. He hurriedly led her toward the safety of the curb, and then pointed toward Dockery's, wanting her to understand him. "There aren't any gift ideas in this window display. Just wrapped gifts. They're so beautifully wrapped and softly illuminated... It's like when you recall Christmas mornings of the past. You know, when you were young and innocent. The soft glow of happy memories." Like the scenes they'd shot of John and Lisa's past.

Like the memories Dave wanted to create with her.

———❆———

*The soft glow of happy memories.*

Betsy Anne hadn't thought of that when she'd looked at Dockery's window. She'd thought the display was promoting their gift wrapping services. But now... Now she wouldn't look at a window display without thinking of Dave and what he'd taken away from it. "Do you always go through life thinking about work?"

"It's not work. It's my passion." Dave tugged her along through the crowd, walking fast and with a purpose. "Just like hair and make-up are your passions. I'm sorry." He slowed down. "I get sensitive about things that inspire me. The simplest things are sometimes a fine work of art to me. You feel it, too, when it comes to hair and make-up. I know you do. I bet you can tell me which Christmas movies that came out this year had the best hairstyles."

"All the royal movies with their formal party updos." No question. They'd been the most creative, too.

"And your favorite hair movie of all time?" He smiled at her, letting her geek out.

"Bridgerton. The hairstyles reflect their character's personalities. The queen is larger than life, and so is her hair."

"They have good lighting on that show. But back to movie hair." Dave paused at a crosswalk, waiting for a car to pass before venturing off the curb. "I would have thought you'd have picked out Jim Carrey's *Grinch* movie. For me, Cindy Lou Who had the best hairstyle, straight up in the air like a Christmas tree."

Betsy Anne grinned. "It was marvelous and iconic. I'd like to work on a project like that or a historical movie someday. But first—"

"But first, we need to establish ourselves on the production mill of TV movies," he said in a rah-rah tone.

"Right." And this project was their chance.

Speaking of chances, this was Betsy Anne's chance to let Dave know she wasn't perfect. He'd called her pretty when she first came down from her room. But Betsy Anne knew the truth. She wasn't pretty without her make-up on. She had to tell him. It was just... She didn't want him to ever see her birthmark. She didn't think she could stand seeing a look of pity in his eyes if he knew how large and red it was.

Dave held open the door to the Three Elves Sandwich Shoppe. "You're going to like this place. Every sandwich has a Christmas name." Dave's confident demeanor faltered. "At least, I hope you can appreciate it."

"I can, because you like it." She gave him a reassuring smile, swallowing nerves. *Maybe I don't have to tell him more about the birthmark yet.* "How did you come to love Christmas so much?"

"Everyone is nice on Christmas," he said, studying the menu board as they got into the queue.

A hard rock version of *We Three Kings* played on the speakers. The attendant at the cash register had purple and green hair.

Dave smiled at Betsy Anne. "My mother worked two jobs as a nursing assistant to keep a roof over our heads. She was always tired. Often cranky, although I can't blame her. Especially when my brother and I were too loud during the few hours she had to sleep."

"Oh. I'm sorry." And here, she'd been spoiled enough to dream of a pony. She'd never worried about a roof or where her next meal was coming from.

They placed their orders and found a table by the window when their food was ready. Across the street, Frosty's Donuts was doing a brisk business. Down the street a few blocks, the Mercantile she'd heard locals rave about offered indoor shopping and food booths. She hoped they'd go there after lunch.

"Why did you get into hair and make-up?" he asked. "Was it that Barbie hair toy you got for Christmas?"

"No. I was home sick one day, confined to my bedroom and staring out on my street wishing a squirrel would jump to the sill and talk to me when a film crew rolled up. They were shooting exteriors for an episode of *Law and Order*. The two principal actors walked down the street, over and over. In between, a stylist would rush in and fix someone's hair or add another coat of lipstick. You know, just fuss over them. From where I was sitting, that short amount of time and care seemed to allow them to run through the scene over and over again. It was emotional and I was exhausted just watching them." She could only imagine how drained they'd felt. And since she felt drained from school and birthmark drama some days, she yearned to be someone who could care for others during stressful times.

Dave pushed his Clark Kent glasses higher up his nose. "Were you home alone? No one to fuss over you?"

"Yes," she said slowly, realizing she'd never really thought of it that way. "But my parents had to work, like your mom. I was a latchkey kid. Weren't you?"

He nodded, bobbing his head in time to the beat of *Grandma Got Run Over by a Reindeer*.

They dug into their sandwiches in comfortable silence. Or it might have been comfortable if Betsy Anne hadn't reconsidered why she'd gone into hair and make-up. The birthmark played more of a role than she wanted to acknowledge.

After a few minutes, Dave asked, "What's your favorite scene from a Christmas movie? Something that you just wished someone would recreate so you could work on their hair or make-up?"

"*Love, Actually*." No thought needed. "Hands down. That scene where Kiera Knightley answers the door and it's her husband's best friend holding those big cue cards. And on them, he's written how he feels about her while his boom box plays *Silent Night*. Her hair is just so gorgeously casual. Her make-up, too.

You know it took someone a lot of time to create that look. And what all that non-fussiness allows her to do is showcase her emotion as the cards progress."

Dave grinned. "Love that. And here I thought you'd choose Star Wars and Princess Leia's iconic braids."

"You did say it had to be a Christmas movie," she pointed out.

His grin widened. "I did, didn't I?"

This was good. They were getting to know each other better than ever without her going into the angst related to her birthmark. "What would you choose?"

Dave didn't spend any time thinking about his answer, either. "The bridge scene toward the end of *It's a Wonderful Life*. Jimmy Stewart's face is lit in just the right way. Not so stark that you can't catch the subtlety of emotion. Not so soft that his face flirts with shadow. It's just a perfect scene where a man wants his wish and his life back because he's just realized how wonderful his life truly was."

"That scene could have been shot in the bowels of a dark basement and it would still touch your heart. The plot, the dialogue and acting were superb."

Dave nodded slowly. "I like talking to you."

Betsy Anne felt her cheeks heat. "About film?"

"About anything," Dave admitted, staring at her.

———

"Why are you staring at me?" Betsy Anne ducked her head and dabbed at her face with a napkin. "Do I have sauce somewhere?"

"No. I was just thinking that if we were eating in Esther's that I could point out the mistletoe she has above every dining room table and..." That was bold of him to say. Dave swallowed. "Um..."

"We could test out our physical chemistry since the emotional stuff seems to be clicking." Despite his assurances that she had nothing on her face, Betsy Anne continued to pat her cheeks and chin with the napkin.

"That's very matter-of-fact." But Dave found it romantic, too.

"And it's exactly what we've both been thinking in the back of our minds since I came down those stairs." She glanced up at him. "Isn't it?"

"Before that," Dave wheezed. "I wondered about it the day we first met, back when you were someone's employee, same as me. But I valued your friendship. I still do." That needed to be said, in case Betsy Anne wanted to draw the line here before things got much better or weird.

"Marcel and I were never friends," Betsy Anne admitted, tucking her dark hair behind her ear. "That's funny, isn't it? Especially since now that we aren't dating or in business together, we seem to be forming a friendship."

"What about us?" Dave wondered aloud, suddenly worried. "Will the opposite help in some way? Being friends first?"

"I don't know," Betsy Anne whispered, although she was staring at his lips, which was encouraging.

"There's one way to solve this." And reduce the tension he was feeling. Dave got out of the booth and came around to Betsy Anne's side. Then he cradled her face in his hands and kissed her.

Gently. Tenderly. The way he'd wanted to kiss her from the moment they'd met because even though she was accomplished and skilled, there was something about her that felt vulnerable. Was it that birthmark he couldn't see?

He ended the kiss by retreating a little, leaving only a hairsbreadth between their lips.

"I hope you feel how right that was." Dave opened his eyes and brushed his thumbs over her cheeks.

"Yes," Betsy Anne whispered, eyes still closed.

All that blotting with a napkin combined with his touch had removed some of the make-up on her cheeks. He could just make out the outlines of her birthmark. It was the size of a large rose petal, as delicate and beautiful as the woman herself. He traced its shape on her right cheek.

"No!" Betsy Anne jerked back, palm flying to her right cheek. "Don't look."

"I'm sorry. But you must know... It's beautiful. Like you."

"Don't look at me like that." Betsy Anne's voice rose. "I know you're pitying me."

"I'm not." Dave knew he should back away and give her space, but he wanted to comfort her. "You have to know that your birthmark doesn't change how I feel about you."

Betsy Anne shook her head vehemently. Clearly, it mattered to her. "Let me out. I need to go back to my room."

"Why? I told you—"

"Can't you tell?" she cried. "To cover it up!"

"You don't need to."

But Betsy Anne wouldn't be consoled, so Dave did as she asked, watching her run away, hand pressed to her cheek.

And feeling as if he'd lost her forever.

# Chapter Seven

It was the Knotty Elves who found Dave an hour later, still sitting in the booth at Three Elves Sandwich Shoppe.

"Something's wrong here." Odette trotted up, bells on her green elf cap jingling.

"He has the look of heartbreak about him, doesn't he?" June perched on the bench across from him, her gaze alert behind her owlish glasses.

"It's a first date." Prudence reached into an oversized gnome print tote, took out a snowman-shaped bag and unsnapped it to reveal a stash of round full-sized candy canes. She tossed candy canes on the table as if she already knew her homemade melt-aways couldn't cure this problem. Then the concerned retiree squeezed in beside June. "How could that go wrong?"

How indeed?

Dave explained about Betsy Anne's birthmark. "She's never mentioned it before. I hadn't realized she was so sensitive about it. But now it all makes sense. Her mother wanted it covered. Betsy Anne always has her face made up so you can't see it. I need to do something. To make her feel...that I don't see this as an imperfection. It's a part of her."

The Knotty Elves considered him with silent, curious gazes.

"WWSD," Odette mused.

Dave shook his head. "What?"

"What would Santa do?" June translated.

"If a child sat on his lap and was embarrassed by a visible birthmark."
Prudence unwrapped a candy cane. The plastic crinkled in her fingers as her
eyebrows creased together.

"I already tried to tell her it wasn't a big deal." Dave slouched in his seat. "She
didn't believe me. What else can I say?"

"WWTMD." Odette adjusted her elf hat over her bun, keeping both from
slipping off her head. She beamed at Dave.

June frowned. "I'm afraid you've lost me, dear."

"What would *the movies do*." Prudence brandished her candy cane like her
personal magic wand. "I love puzzles." She took Dave's hand. "If this were one
of your films, how would they prove to Betsy Anne that her birthmark doesn't
matter?"

"You ladies are brilliant!" Dave leaped out of his seat and hugged them each
in turn. "I know exactly what to do. But I'm going to need some help."

---

Betsy Anne lay on her bed with a facial cloth drying on her face.

She'd run all the way back to Esther's after her date with Dave, fighting tears.
Now, she was treating her pores to thirty minutes of love. The facial cloth had
dried on her face until it felt almost like a second skin.

But it wouldn't lift away her birthmark.

*You can't show anyone that mark,* her mother had said. *They'll tease you.*

"Stupid birthmark." Maybe if she got a regular contract with Lark for more
movies, she could afford to have a plastic surgeon lighten it.

She'd never let a man touch her face while kissing for just that reason. But
Dave had swept her off her feet.

*And now...I have to face him on Monday.*

Outside, carolers began to sing *Silent Night.*

Betsy Anne glanced at the small, pink-flocked Christmas tree in her room,
thinking of Dave and feeling as if Rudolph had slid down the chimney and
landed on her chest.

Something rattled against her window. The wind?

The carolers lifted their voices.

Sighing, Betsy Anne got to her feet and went to the window, which was covered by sheer curtains that let in the light during the day but gave her some privacy.

A crowd had gathered on the sidewalk below her room, familiar faces of the crew, as well as the Knotty Elves. They were singing as the snow fell. And in the center of the assembled carolers stood Dave.

He wore an ugly Christmas sweater—bright green with a gingerbread man in a Santa cap. Dave waved at her and lifted a white cue card on which he'd written: *This is me apologizing.*

*Oh.* Betsy Anne clung to the curtains.

Dave dropped the card to reveal another: *I never meant for you to feel vulnerable.*

She smiled. That was so Dave. Always kind. Always considerate.

The carolers kept singing. They were good, but they could have been off-key, and Betsy Anne still would have heard the song as if it had been sung by angels. All because Dave had arranged this.

He dropped another card, revealing: *You are beautiful—inside and out.*

Betsy Anne held her breath.

Dave uncovered the next card: *We all have scars—inside and out.*

He flashed the card so those around him could read it. A few nodded and raised their hands, as if in agreement. And those few... They were people Betsy Anne knew because they worked together.

Abilene, the actress who'd had shoulder surgery and confessed that, because of her scar, she no longer wore sleeveless clothes.

Cecily, Betsy Anne's assistant, who'd survived an abusive relationship.

Quinten, the best boy, who had a scar through an eyebrow that he didn't like to talk about.

Dave, whose mother couldn't relate to his dream of working in film.

As Betsy Anne got a little choked up, Dave revealed another card: *Christmas is the time for truth, love, and forgiveness.*

Betsy Anne leaned closer to the glass, nose pressed against the sheer curtain, anxious to see what message came next.

*I know your truth. If you forgive me, we could work on the love part.*

Another card fell to the ground as her work family lifted their voices to close out the song: *Sleep in heavenly peace.*

Another card fell to the ground: *You're perfect, Betsy Anne.*

The group cheered and hugged.

Betsy Anne ran from the window.

———❦———

"Is she still standing at the window?" Abilene pet her fluffy, furry dog, the one that reminded Dave of Clifford the Big Red Dog. "I can't see her silhouette."

Dave couldn't, either. He held his breath, waiting for a sign.

The front door of Esther's slammed. "Oh, my gosh! You guys are awesome!"

They all turned toward the corner, awaiting the audience of their impromptu show—Betsy Anne. Dave fully expected to see her in the clothes she'd worn last, the make-up she valued so much put skillfully over that birthmark.

But the Betsy Anne who ran around the corner wore gray flannel pants decorated with Santas and reindeer slippers and a green sweater with a gingerbread Mrs. Santa. On her face... Dave didn't know what it was, but it was white and covered everything on her face but her eyes, nostrils, and mouth.

Betsy Anne jogged toward them. "That was so special. You're all so special."

"Um..." Abilene waved a hand in front of her face.

"Betsy Anne!" Cecily charged out to meet her boss and peeled off whatever was on her face.

"Oh." Betsy Anne's expression fell. She looked as if she was going to flee back inside.

It was Dave's turn to rush forward. "We don't care about how you look, honey." He took her into his arms and kissed her birthmark, which was clearly visible on her right cheek. "Just like you don't care how we look or what we wear or what scars or insecurities we have."

The friends he'd gathered surrounded them, chiming in.

Betsy Anne started to cry, but she didn't pull away from Dave. Or rather, she did, but it was to hug everyone who'd come to support her.

And Dave. Because that's where she ended her hugfest.

"You know I don't care what you wear or if you have bed head or that rosy birthmark is showing on your cheek," Dave told her as earnestly as possible. "You're beautiful to me because of *who* you are, not how you look." He leaned down to whisper in her ear, "But you're rocking that ugly Christmas sweater. And it matches mine."

"I love it when a plan comes together." June high fived the other Knotty Elves.

"I want you to know me, Dave." Betsy Anne started crying again. "All the parts of me that I'm not comfortable with. I also wanted to tell you what inspired me and my craft. I want to tell you so much." She paused to sniff. One of the Knotty Elves handed her a snowflake-print handkerchief.

"We'll have time for all of that, honey. We'll go at your pace," Dave promised, feeling like the luckiest man in the world with her in his arms.

After her tears had dried and Dave escorted her back inside where it was warm, he had the moment of privacy he'd been waiting for. And the right words to say. The words he'd never said to any female ever before.

"Betsy Anne, do you want to go steady?"

She answered by flinging her arms around him and kissing him.

When they were done, at least for now, Dave held her close and whispered, "Merry Christmas, love."

She laughed, kissed him, and then made the sweetest of requests. "Say that again."

The End

# Her Second-Story Santa

## Book 4: Lights, Camera, Christmas Town

### Cheryl Harper

ChelseaBeth Publishing

# Chapter One

*December 10th*

D Alexis Dorsey had always believed Christmas Town was pure magic at night. She had fallen under the town's spell on her first visit, when her stuffy, older brother Steven had been invited to town for an old friend's wedding while she was in college.

And then Steven had tumbled into love with Beth Long, and Christmas Town had become the home for Christmas Alexis and Steven both needed. During the day, the town was a cheerful celebration with music and happy shoppers.

At night, Christmas Town was enchanting.

The town square twinkled with multi-colored lights, couples strolled hand-in-hand along the cleared sidewalks and dodged snow drifts here and there. The gazebo waited to bestow happily-ever-afters on those who shared a kiss there during the Christmas season. Warm light from the shop windows lining the square and wreath-decked lamp posts added a hazy glow without illuminating much of anything directly.

As a fan of beautiful scenes in general and the holidays always, Alexis loved everything about Christmas Town after dark.

As a director charged with making a movie in such conditions? Alexis knew how much of a challenge the ambient lighting would present for her night shoots. She trailed behind the film's producer, Lark Matthews, and Dave Walsh, the unfortunate soul who was going to be lighting their first night shoot in less than twenty-four hours. She resisted the urge to chew nervously on her thumbnail.

Alexis missed the new mittens the Knotty Elves had presented to her on her first day back in town. It would be much more difficult to bite her fingernails if a knitted Mrs. Claus stared back at her each time the urge hit. That was an old, bad habit that returned in times of stress.

So far, *The Wedding Carousel* was proceeding according to the shot plan she'd meticulously laid out, and she was meeting the budget she and Lark had discussed at length.

All in all, she should be feeling secure.

So when would the crushing weight of anxiety let up? It had no place here. Or...it shouldn't.

But Alexis had a lot to prove to her critics, her friends in Christmas Town, and herself. Everything had to be right.

"We'll move the crew out here early afternoon to set up," Dave said with an enthusiastic nod of his head.

Lark was equally upbeat. "I confirmed our start time with Griffin Walker, so we'll have security on hand to direct the crowds as we work. I'm not going to lie. This is going to be a challenge on several levels—lighting, sound, actor distractions."

Why was Lark saying that as if she was cheerfully anticipating conquering each obstacle? All Alexis could see was the millions of places where disaster lurked.

"We've got permission to close down the gazebo for one night and one night only," Lark continued. "If we have any extra time, I have a list of library shots we can run through, things we can use for the title sequence or advertising...you know, scene-setting footage of the carousel and the gazebo at night." Lark balanced her laptop in one hand and tapped the keys with the other. She never went anywhere without her laptop. "The weather forecast is for snow flurries, which is great for these scenes. Let's get everything we need. Re-shoots will be difficult and expensive."

Alexis nodded. Every producer *ever* had said the same thing, so this was nothing new, but she understood what Lark meant here. They were disturbing life and business by closing off portions of the town square. Since she and Lark both had Christmas Town roots, neither of them wanted to disrupt their neighbors any more than they had to.

"Have you made a decision on the crane shots yet?" Dave asked as he pointed to the busiest corner of the green. "We could set up there and capture a crowd, busy shoppers, give a sense of space but the lighting is going to be tricky."

Alexis wanted every tool at her disposal, so her first impulse was always to say yes, but this was her first job for Lark. The precarious state of her future career choices urged caution, especially with the budget. Coming under budget would increase her chances of working on Lark's next project. "Let's finish this first night, Dave. If we meet the schedule and have anything left in the budget, we can work in a short night before we wrap this shoot."

Lark's sigh of relief confirmed Alexis was on the right track.

"Expect a crowd," Alexis added with a nod at the people who were clustered here and there, watching them closely. Bulging bags from Christmas Town's shops and steaming cups of hot chocolate cradled in their hands were proof that holiday shopping was proceeding along the square even as the movie production distracted locals and visitors alike.

Gus, Barty, and Marv had set up shop temporarily wherever the filming was around town, and they were glued to the action on the snow-blanketed green. She should enlist their help to find the practical joker who kept hiding Elmer the Elf in her shots. If she missed one in a take she needed at the end of all this, it could be a problem.

"Elmer the Elf is popping up where I least expect it." Lark shook her head. "Until we ran through the list of shots we've finished so far, I didn't realize how many takes Elmer has photobombed."

It didn't surprise Alexis that Lark's brain was moving along the same lines as hers. Directors and producers often struggled for control of a movie; their focuses were usually divided by the importance of artistic vision versus financial success. But she and Lark had gelled from their first phone call.

"Since we only expect to find Elmer contained within Posey's, he is really expanding his territory." Alexis forced her shoulders to relax. She had a history of pranks herself, all focused on loosening up her very proud older brother Steven, so she admired whoever was pulling this off. The first time Steven visited her in California, he'd immediately stripped the guest bed because he'd expected her to have short-sheeted it. She had done it so often in his New York penthouse that it made sense.

That was why she had skipped it for that particular visit, to set him up as unsuspecting for the next.

"If we're done here, I'll go check for Elmer in the diner. I've been daydreaming about their shepherd's pie all day long." Dave waved over his shoulder to where Betsy Anne Gleason waited on the sidewalk.

Reminded again how lucky she was to be working with such a solid crew, Alexis nodded. "Thanks for all your hard work, Dave."

He clasped his hands together as if he was giving heartfelt thanks and then trotted through the snow. Alexis and Lark watched him press a kiss to Betsy Anne's lips before the couple turned to walk into Posey's.

"This crew you've put together is good," Alexis said as she shoved her small notebook into her coat pocket. She still had some work to do on the call lists for the next few days, but she had the time. Ever since she'd learned the producer on her last project had been spreading the word that she was difficult, dramatic, emotional, and impossible to work with, she'd spent less time sleeping. That left more time for worrying about her career. Tonight, she could distract herself by running through the schedule for taping on the town square at night.

Lark shrugged. "I like to work with people I know."

Alexis bit her lip. The urge to ask Lark why she'd reached out to Alexis was on the tip of her tongue, but she wasn't sure she wanted to hear the answer.

Lark must have noticed her hesitation. "I haven't seen anything but professionalism from you, Alexis. What I don't know is how I got an award-nominated film director for my made-for-TV project." Lark pursed her lips as she seemingly chose her words with care. "Although sometimes... Never mind. You're demanding, but that's the director in you. Never met a good one who was easy to please."

There were mixed messages in there. Anxiety crowded her chest once more.

Alexis matched Lark's pace as they strolled back across the snowy green. They passed a full-figured snowman facing the street corner as if he was waiting for the imaginary traffic light to change. Alexis was rarely alone with Lark and had been wanting to say something to her in private. Perhaps now was her chance.

"If you're pleased with the movie we make together, please call me for other projects." She'd dreamed of accepting an Oscar one day for a sprawling historical piece that changed the future of moviemaking, but Alexis had learned practicality during her stint in Hollywood.

A good job was a good job, and Lark had given her that.

"When John and Lisa named you as someone they wanted working on their movie, the only person they mentioned by name, by the way, I thought they were joking." Lark shook her head. "Absolutely no one even loosely connected to film or TV production missed the buzz about you the year *Hitching Home* came out. You made a viral sensation. It was amazing how this little film spread, mostly by word of mouth, until everyone was speculating on what Alexis Dorsey might do someday." Lark bumped her shoulder, as if they were good friends...or could be. "No way did I think you'd even take my call."

Alexis tilted her head back to study the dark sky overhead. It was a fairly clear night, so there were faint stars visible even in the glow of the town square. The music playing from one of the storefronts was faint, but Alexis thought it was *It Came Upon a Midnight Clear*. One of her favorites and absolutely perfect for the moment.

"I guess it takes Hollywood gossip a minute to filter all the way to New York." Alexis sighed. "I'm not sure it's anything as organized as a blacklist, but I've had free time since the last producer I worked with decided he had done me enough favors along the way." She pushed her shoulders back, determined to confess her concerns all at once, like ripping off a bandage. "Apparently, his high regard was dependent on pulling in Steven Dorsey as an investor." Her wealthy older brother. "I refused to ask for a check that could prop up future Rafe Costelli productions and..." Alexis held out her hands. "As a result, Rafe claims I'm too hard to work with, and that smart producers should avoid me."

Alexis had expected concern, shock, perhaps even guarded sincerity.

Instead, Lark snorted. Then she sputtered a laugh. "Ridiculous. No one would believe that." Then she bent closer. "Don't tell me anyone is falling for that."

Lark's reaction made it easier for Alexis to breathe. "Your phone call was a no-brainer to answer because it was the only one coming in. I'm used to some people expecting any Dorsey to be privileged and lucky instead of talented. Nepotism is alive and well in Hollywood, right? I thought I had proven myself to some of my peers already." She gripped Lark's hands. "But I'm happy to be doing this project. I love Christmas Town. It has been too long since I met Steven and Beth here for Christmas."

"I bet your brother makes a splash every time he rolls into town."

"In his limousine? Yep." Alexis grinned. "One year, I managed to book him into a moving truck at the airport instead of a luxury sedan. I have pictures of his arrival here. Now, he refuses to let me make any travel arrangements for him anymore."

Lark tipped her head back and laughed loudly.

More of the tension that had been crushing Alexis floated away. Anyone who could laugh like that was her kind of person. Playing pranks on Steven had gotten harder because her older brother was smart, but every now and then, she was inspired.

"I met your brother once in New York. He's very..." Lark narrowed her eyes as she considered her description.

"Proud? Annoying? Reserved? Rich?" Alexis offered, although she knew her brother was so much more. People tended to consider him an uptight robot. Marrying Beth had changed that a bit. "I've heard some people say the same things about me."

"Fancy. I was going to say fancy." Lark frowned. "But that's not the right word, either. Since I've been back in town, I've heard folks sing his praises because he's so generous, but they also make sure to mention his high *standards*."

Her emphasis on the last word was amusing, mainly because Alexis had heard some version of that sentiment her whole life but never so politely.

"Yes, I expect to hear him complain loudly about the fact that I took the big bedroom in Beth's house with the best view of the square." Alexis tilted her chin up. "I'm the younger sister. It's my job to humble him."

Lark grinned. "I'm glad John and Lisa asked for you, that I took a shot, and that you answered that call."

"If I can keep an eagle eye out for Elmer and his shenanigans, I expect this entire shoot to go smoothly." Reassuring Lark that she was in control after she'd confessed the downturn in her career was critical. "Then we can discuss our next project together."

Lark started to speak but then looked as if she changed her mind. Alexis realized she was half a second from considering her thumbnail again when Lark sighed loudly. "We're so lucky to have you."

"But..." Alexis removed the notebook and pen from her pocket. Jotting down notes would make it easier to accept the criticism calmly.

"Not a *but*...more like an *and*." Lark wrinkled her nose. "You're so perfect for this project. John and Lisa's wedding was what brought you and your brother to Christmas Town in the first place, right?"

"Yes." When Steven had been called to Christmas Town to be one of John's groomsmen, Alexis had been adrift, thanks to her jet-setting absent parents and the first in a long line of boyfriends who were only after her money. So, Steven had invited her along. Christmas Town and Beth had charmed them both.

Lark touched her arm. "Your experience shines through, Alexis. Every shot furthers the story. The framing is solid, but the piece I'm missing is the joy. Your joy."

Alexis shoved her pen and notebook back in her pocket because it wouldn't take notes to remember those words. She might not forget them for the rest of her life. She loved making movies. How could that not show in her work?

"I tracked down a copy of *Hitching Home* after I read this raving review in one of the movie blogs I followed when I was starting out." Lark waved her arms wildly. "The reviewer kept using the word 'bubble' and all this imagery to describe how this girl who is trying to make it home to Pennsylvania before her baby comes is hopeful, bright, and fun. I couldn't understand how it could be done. Make the subject matter and the hardships on the road encouraging *and* fun? No way, but you did it. No real experience. No studios behind you. No producers breathing down your neck." Lark pointed to herself. "Complete freedom and the joy of doing what you loved. It showed."

Alexis was proud of *Hitching Home*. It was special. A once-in-a-lifetime adventure.

The entire experience had been tarnished a bit by the realization that her invitation to work with the students who had hashed out a script came along with the expectation that she or her brother could bankroll the project, too. She'd ended up getting caught in the excitement of the project and financing it on a shoestring budget. But that had been a lesson in thoroughly investigating people and their motivations.

Since she'd fallen for the same thing, only on a larger scale with Rafe and a personal scale with a string of boyfriends, Alexis knew she hadn't learned that lesson well enough. But that was then. This was now.

"Joy." Alexis bit her bottom lip. "You're not getting that in my dailies." *A week's worth of work and only now was she mentioning it?*

"Not yet," Lark said slowly, "but you have a rogue elf popping up in shots, Knotty Elves lurking nearby, extras prepared to steal the show at any moment, and a sweet story to tell here. I know you know this. You've got to love the story enough to lean into it, sometimes at the expense of being technically correct or spot on with the script."

*Take chances*, Alexis thought she meant. But taking chances in film involved risking one's reputation. Bad reviews. A silent cell phone instead of a constant ring and stream of job offers.

Lark waited for Alexis to meet her stare before continuing. "I want to do movies like no one else is doing, Alexis. I believe you can make that happen."

"If I find the joy." In herself. In the story.

"Which you will." Lark turned, walking away from Alexis backward. "I have some numbers to crunch and emails to send before I can sleep. But you need rest. Another day of work tomorrow. Good night!"

Alexis nodded and returned to the sidewalk that circled the town square. Most of the shops were closing soon for the evening, but the atmosphere was still cheerful, accented by multicolored lights and the happy chatter of late night shoppers. It didn't match her mood. She shoved her hands in her pockets as she walked slowly home.

Home. She was staying in Beth and Steven's holiday home. Alexis had hung Beth's wreaths in the windows and put out the family of merry foxes wearing bright red scarves that glowed on the small porch. Someday, she wanted a home like this one. In a town like this one. The opposite of the mansions and penthouses she'd grown up in. But even though she loved her brother and sister-in-law, she was staying in their home. Not hers.

*I'm beginning to feel like the Grinch.*

How did she find joy on a low budget TV film under a very tight schedule?

A noise had her looking up as Alexis neared home. A noise from above.

There were no reindeer on the roof next door. But Santa Claus was there, red suit, red cap and all. Old Saint Nick was shimmying up the front porch railing on the house next door to Beth's. Alexis doubted he was there to deliver early Christmas presents.

But he did give her an unexpected burst of joy.

# Chapter Two

F lynn Sullivan wondered if the universe was encouraging him to spend more time in the gym.

He struggled to pull himself up onto the narrow roof covering the small porch of his grandmother's house outside his childhood window. When she'd taken him in as a teenager, that was how he snuck in and out. Years later, he was out of climbing practice. Not even the removal of the Santa Claus mittens the Knotty Elves had presented him with was helping.

His only comfort was that he had no audience.

The same could not be said for earlier at Holly Haven Animal Rescue, where the renowned actress Abilene had proclaimed Flynn's Santa performance uninspired. And Prudence Parker had informed Flynn that if he intended to be a convincing Kris Kringle, everything about him had to be magical, including his breath. The spry Knotty Elf had slipped a small tin of her homemade meltaway mints into his pocket with instructions to call her for a refill. Then Pru had nudged her elbow into his ribs and assured him minty magic made kisses sweeter too before whisking off to join her two cohorts entertaining the kittens up for adoption.

Since Flynn had been subduing an overexcited chihuahua at the time, he'd taken Abilene's and Pru's comments personally. Maybe he wasn't typically jolly, but he'd still wanted to assist with the shelter's fundraising and be nothing but a magical Kris Kringle.

After all, he needed as many volunteer opportunities as he could get to repair his bad boy reputation, the one he'd made as a teenager, along with his partner in trouble Kaleb Matthews. For so long, he'd been on the Naughty list, but he hoped to be promoted to Nice again.

At least, Abilene had fussed over him, fluffing his beard, and patting his "bowl full of jelly" stomach pillow. He'd popped several meltaway mints into his mouth and soaked in Abilene's whispered words of encouragement. "Santa would laugh off any mishaps. He's a hard worker, but he's still a little mischievous boy at heart."

That was Santa. And Flynn. He'd taken a counseling job at Christmas Town High School this year, but as for a town welcoming committee... It would take a while to make the town see the good in him the way his grandmother had, when his parents gave up on him.

He swung his leg up over the snowy ledge and rolled in the snow toward relative safety.

"The more things change," he heard a feminine voice say from below, "the more things stay the same. The Santa costume? That's an interesting choice, but you used to be better at breaking and entering, Flynn."

Flynn popped his head back over the edge of the roof to find Alexis Dorsey grinning up at him from the front yard. She was wearing a puffy purple jacket, an obnoxiously green knit hat with tassels dangling from the crown, and sensible boots.

The way his heart stopped and then resumed beating double-time had nothing to do with the strain of pulling himself up to the second story.

"It's the suit." Moving into a sitting position, he held out his arms to show her the velvety red of his Santa suit. "Slippery. Increases the degree of difficulty, Lex."

"Santa is supposed to use the chimney, Flynn. I expected you to commit to the role." She sobered, changing the subject. "Should I call the fire department? Or do you need an ambulance? You aren't going to fall, are you?"

Flynn inched back from the edge before waving his hand confidently. "Of course not. Have I ever wanted to meet the police?"

She shrugged, grinning.

Their friendship had formed the first time Alexis had visited Christmas Town while they were both in college. They'd bonded over a love of visual arts—cameras. Their friendship was kept alive by vacation visits, occasional phone calls, frequent texts, and the power of the perfect meme. Although they lived far apart and didn't see each other daily, she was important to him.

"I thought you were adulting now?" She hunched her shoulders as a gust of wind struck, swirling snow around her ankles. "Why are you breaking into your own house?"

Didn't feel at all good to be an adult still living with his grandmother. "My grandmother borrowed my truck earlier to spend a weekend shopping with friends in Portland. My house key and hers are most likely sitting in her purse." And Flynn never secured his bedroom window. Old habits died hard. "How's the movie coming along?"

"Okay." Lex shrugged her shoulders. The world might believe that one word and gesture, but Flynn had known her for long enough to recognize something was bothering her.

"Get out the eggnog, the spiked kind. I'll be over in a minute." He opened the window and fell inside to the sound of her chuckles. "It's the suit!"

If Alexis answered, he didn't hear her.

Changed, feeling more like himself, Flynn grabbed his camera, the one his grandmother had given him to distract him from finding trouble when he was a teen. He shoved it into a jacket pocket, and almost barreled out the kitchen door without grabbing two of Gram's incredible sticky buns. He couldn't show up next door without them. It was something of a tradition.

Buns in hand, Flynn hurried out the door, across the backyard, and through a gate that stuffy Steven had reluctantly installed when he couldn't discourage Alexis from a friendship with one of the local bad boys. Fact was, they didn't go out at night and create mayhem or even kiss. They spent more time together talking about new techniques or something someone else had captured on film that inspired them. And life. They talked about life. Lex had helped him realize his passion was in helping kids in trouble, the way he'd been, even if he also loved taking photos. He reassured Alexis whenever she doubted herself. Was she doubting herself now?

Flynn pounded up the back porch stairs to the kitchen door.

"I was expecting you to come down the chimney." She pushed the door wider to let him in, which gave him a full view of her, from her black stockinged feet to her black skinny jeans to her black cable knit sweater to her short black hair and equally dark eyes. All that black. Others might look at her and assume she worked in advertising on Madison Avenue. Flynn saw a woman who wanted to look put-together every day but didn't want to deal with wardrobe decisions. He saw a woman who cared more about her current project than taking care of herself. He saw a kind, talented, insecure woman who would have made his heart pound with love and longing even if she wasn't beautiful.

Her eyes lit up when she spotted the container he held. "Are those Grams' sticky buns?"

"To bring anyone else's buns into that house would be a fighting offense." Grams had a lot of pride in her signature treat.

Alexis wrapped her hand around Flynn's to tow him over to the kitchen island. That was the thing about their relationship. Alexis saw no physical boundaries and Flynn couldn't have been happier. "Sit. We haven't had a chance to catch up all week. How's your job? Your grandmother? Your campaign to change your bad boy reputation?"

"Don't take the spotlight off you." Flynn slid onto the stool and immediately took a sip of eggnog from a reindeer mug. The sweetness had a nice alcohol finish that promised to warm inside, although not as much as being with Alexis did. "Something's bothering you. Tell me everything. The bad boy doctor is in."

Alexis put a plate with the sticky buns in the microwave and punched a button.

"I know you hear me, Lex. Talk." Flynn waited patiently while she stared at the numbers counting down. Then he noticed the mittens on the island countertop. The Knotty Elves had made Alexis a pair, too. And for some reason, she'd gotten the matching Mrs. Claus to his Santa ones.

The microwave dinged. Flynn kept quiet, sipping his eggnog.

"There's not much to tell. The movie is on schedule and under budget." She shrugged slightly before offering him a plate and a fork. "Overall, Lark seems pleased." She settled next to him. Her mug had a cat on the front, all cozied up under a Christmas tree.

Flynn braced an elbow on the counter. "And?"

"I didn't sign up for a therapy session, Flynn." She shook her fork at him. "You can take your counselor hat off."

"Fair." Flynn nodded. "Let's reboot. I'm here as a friend and I can tell that something isn't quite right in your world." He sighed forlornly, pouting. "Now, this is friendly intervention, not official counseling. Collect your thoughts. I'm here when you're ready."

Alexis grimaced. Fidgeted. Ate a few bites of sticky bun. "In all honesty...my career isn't...going well." She slumped on the counter. "Why is it so hard to admit that?" She dragged herself back into an upright, sitting position. "And I'm mad about it. I've been blaming others. That stupid producer who only hired me for my family's money." Alexis frowned, lowering her voice. "But tonight Lark told me that my shots were good, but she couldn't see any joy in them." There was a raw note in her voice, the way there was upon discovering long-hidden truths. "I hate that she's right. When I did *Hitching Home*, I did things my own way in part because I didn't know any better."

"What's the difference between then and now? Apart from us not having more regular conversations where we geek out over the latest tech and creative camerawork?" Flynn didn't move, didn't want to distract her from this emotional place of truth.

She shook her head. "I didn't have anything to lose. I was young. I had money to explore a passion project. It wasn't a job, or a career on the line. That makes it easier to be fearless."

Flynn scoffed. "The pains of adulting."

"It doesn't come with a manual, does it?" Finishing her sticky bun, Lex crumpled up her Christmas green-and-gold plaid paper napkin and tossed it at his head. "But you know what I mean."

"I do. This isn't the plan you made for your life." Flynn braced his foot on the bottom rung of her stool to scoot it toward him. Being close to her made it easier for him to admit some of his own fears. "I've been volunteering for anything I hear about. Reading to seniors at Over the River, playing Santa for pet photos, helping with the school choir you're using in the film. All because I have to play some game to erase the past instead of forging ahead, helping kids keep their lives on track. We are a product of our past, our families, even the places we grew up in. Maybe it's time you got used to the fact that life isn't fair when you're born with a silver spoon any more than it is when you're born without one."

"Choir?" Alexis covered her mouth with one hand, gasping dramatically. "Have you been a singer all this time?"

Leave it to Alexis to try and distract from the emotional message he'd been trying to send.

Flynn propped his elbow on the counter and rested his chin on his hand. "The choir director asked for help *supervising*, not singing. I couldn't say no. Besides, it allowed me to take some good shots that I'm going to offer for the yearbook. My students will definitely want to remember that a movie came to town this year. You deserve to feel hurt, by the way, and if you want to fight for your opportunities and the life you want, you should do that. I would." That was part of why he was here. Now.

She sipped her eggnog. "From what you told me, you used to want to fight if someone looked at you the wrong way." Alexis tapped his knee. "I lost count of all the people who warned Steven that I should definitely not be spending time with you."

"Yeah. We call that growth." Flynn paused, considering his next words, his next action. "We both have to push through the difficult stuff to achieve the lives we dream of." He wrapped his hand around hers, knowing that he was telling her one of his own, deeply buried truths without saying a word. "And it isn't wrong to reach for each other to help each other get there. I have you to thank for where I am now."

Her mouth dropped open, and Flynn wondered if he'd blown it, if he was misreading things between them or just overlaying his vision of Lex and him onto this scene.

# Chapter Three

A lexis wasn't sure if Flynn meant to pull her closer as he spoke, but she couldn't find any clever way to point out that he was close enough to kiss. Tilting forward a few inches would put her lips on his—not an unattractive option.

He'd always been devil-may-care handsome. Dark hair, dark eyes, tempting smile. She'd always registered that on some level. But that wasn't who they were to each other. They were friends, creative muses, a lifeline when things threatened to scrape rock bottom. Nothing more.

Or they'd never explored more before. Should they now?

Alexis shook her head to clear the strange impulse away. "What do you mean you have me to thank? You don't owe me a thing. If anything, I should write you a check for listening to my worries." When he didn't return her smile, she poked his chest.

His very close, very firm chest.

"It was a joke." Alexis took a chance and rested her hands on his knees where they framed her legs. "My friend, Flynn... You made something incredible of your life. You should be so proud of yourself. I had nothing to do with it."

Flynn covered her hands with his, rubbing the sensitive skin of her wrists with his thumbs.

*Oh, my.* Alexis did her best to contain her eyebrows. They wanted to race up her forehead.

"Do you remember that first walk I dared you to come on?" Flynn asked softly. "We met at midnight and walked through town."

Alexis nodded. "Yeah. That was the first time I really understood that Christmas Town is nothing like other places. It was only the two of us. The snow hushed any other noises, and you could almost hear snowflakes landing. Without all the flashing lights and the music and chatter, there was nothing but peace. I needed that peace."

He nodded. "Very few people have ever mentioned peace and me together, but with you, I felt it. All the pain of abandonment inside me settled a bit, and I could understand that I wouldn't always feel short-fused. My grandmother had been trying for years to tell me I didn't need to go through life with so much anger, but that night, I got a peek at what life might hold someday if I let it go."

The twist in the center of her chest surprised Alexis. It complimented the sting of tears burning her nose. There was something important going on here. Now wasn't the time to point out he'd mentioned the famous song lyrics from *Frozen*. "I did that? For you?"

Flynn blinked. "You aren't going to cry, are you?"

Alexis laughed at his panicked tone. "You should be used to that. The kids who come to you for help cry, I'm sure."

He tipped the napkin holder in the center of the island over and shook out another bright plaid napkin. "They aren't you."

Alexis accepted the napkin he shoved in her direction. "Okay. The danger has passed. Your loving concern is duly noted."

When he settled back on his stool, Flynn ran his hands through his hair as if the near brush with her tears had shaken him.

Alexis realized they were doing this strange thing where they stared into each other's eyes and smiled. Her hands were back in his. She would have happily sat there all night.

Flynn passed his thumbs over her skin in a light touch. "What can I do to help you find the joy in making this film?"

Joy. She'd forgotten all about that.

Alexis inhaled slowly, freeing herself from the hypnotic power of his attention, freeing herself from his touch, and his personal space by getting to her feet. "We could try a walk?" The uncertainty in her voice wasn't normal. "I want to try to see this film through your eyes. That is, unless you have to do something important tomorrow morning, like work, and need your beauty sleep."

"I can always spare you my time." Flynn tugged a camera from his pocket. He had a way of seeing things through the lens that inspired her. "Good thing I brought this."

Alexis led him to the front door and shrugged into her coat. She tugged the hat the Knotty Elves had given her down over his ears and pulled on Beth's pretty faux fur headwrap. Her sister-in-law's taste was good. Alexis immediately felt more confident. That was a boost she needed.

"Grab your mittens. It's cold out there tonight." Flynn held the pair she'd left in the kitchen.

Alexis tugged them on and joined him at the door.

"We need to be quiet." Flynn's dark eyes sparkled with that mischief she so loved. "Wouldn't want anyone to see us and snitch to Steven."

"You aren't scared of my brother. You never were."

Flynn scoffed, taking her hand as they went down the front walk. "I do a good job of pretending. He's a master at intimidation."

"Don't I know it. He wanted me to have a curfew in college, remember? Sneaking out with you to talk about anything and everything was freeing." Alexis tightened her hand on Flynn's. He'd shown her a different perspective. How there was beauty in a snow drift, as much beauty as there was in a crystal vase. He'd challenged her to think outside of the rules someone else had created. That truth had been her goal with every shot in *Hitching Home*. "If you were so scared of rich and powerful Steven Dorsey, why'd you risk spending time with me?" Often, people pursued friendships or romance with Alexis to gain favors from Steven.

"From the moment I saw you filming, I felt connected with you, as if you would understand how viewing the world through a lens gave you both distance and a window into something's soul." Flynn pulled his camera up and snapped a quick shot of the deserted green. "For the first time in my life, I'd met someone who understood how the lens makes things so much clearer. I would have taken any chance to spend time with you. Besides, you enjoyed sneaking out at night as much as I did."

"It's not exactly sneaking when you're twenty and in college." Although her brother had thought so. Alexis slipped on a patch of ice mid-step and caught herself on Flynn's arm.

"Whoa. Don't forget how easy it is to fall around here." Flynn waited for her to nod and then pointed. "I have an idea for a shot of the gazebo."

He clasped her hand and led the way while Alexis tried to remind herself of other walks and other nights and other times she and Flynn had chased inspiration like this. They were friends. They were bound by this shared love of creative ideas and how light falls and the kind of story they could tell within the frame of a lens.

Flynn had never kissed her, and if Alexis was being honest, she'd never imagined wanting him to. That wasn't their story. She needed to shift her point of view. He was her friend, maybe her best friend. Changing their focus by adding a kiss could be a big mistake.

# Chapter Four

The next night, Flynn scuffed his feet and blew warm air into his Santa Claus mittens as he watched Alexis work.

Being behind the scenes of a movie production was interesting, but to be here with a purpose—supporting Alexis and the choir—was heaven. Or it would have been if the temperature hadn't been below freezing.

The high school choir had nailed five takes singing *Deck the Halls*. The first take had ended with the crowd gathered outside the taped-off areas applauding so loudly that Alexis had to yell, "Cut!" more than once to be heard. They'd finished singing long ago, cleared out for the next scenes to be filmed.

Alexis and Lark had done a decent job of balancing the enthusiasm of the town with the business of getting the night shots they needed, but Flynn had been watching the set of Alexis' jaw and shoulders all night long. Her tension was growing as the hours stretched later, but he wasn't sure what to do about it. Right now, Alexis and Lark were staring down at a monitor, reviewing film. Even from this distance he could see her shoulders sink. Lark patted her on the back.

That seemed like a bad sign. They were filming the two actors inside the gazebo. This had to be an important scene. That gazebo had played a big part in countless Christmas Town love stories.

"Sullivan! Flynn Sullivan!" someone yelled as the crew re-set the marks for the actors and changed camera positions.

Flynn turned to find Alexis' brother, Steven, standing next to Gus, Barty, and Marv. Immediately the muscles across his shoulders tightened. That man could pluck the string of Flynn's last nerve just by showing up.

Flynn ambled over to join them. "Steven, I didn't know you were in town. I didn't see the limo block the street in front of Beth's house."

The Three Wise Men chortled.

The longsuffering sigh that Steven released was familiar. "Walk with me." Steven motioned toward an empty stretch of sidewalk away from filming. He nodded at Gus, Barty, and Marv. "Gentlemen, good to visit with you again."

"You, too, your excellency," Barty said. "Merry Christmas."

Gus tipped his knit cap and Marv solemnly bowed.

Steven shook his head as he walked away.

Flynn applauded the Three Wise Men before following Steven.

When they were alone, Steven crossed his arms and stared intently at Flynn. "How long are you going to let her struggle like this?"

"Excuse me?" Steven ordering Flynn to speak was strange enough, but his demanding question was even more unexpected. Steven Dorsey had once made it very clear that he'd prefer Flynn on another planet far, far away from his sister. "Who? What do you mean?"

"Don't play games, Sullivan. Why haven't you worked your magic with my sister yet? She's obviously struggling and when she struggles, it's you she calls. Not me." Steven didn't look happy about that. "This film is important to her. And I...I need you to do this for me. For her." The mogul shook himself, as if he hated having this conversation. "Alexis is smart. She's strong. I don't want her to be cynical and I certainly don't want my sister to be afraid to trust herself. You helped the first time she realized being a Dorsey meant that it would be difficult sometimes. Go. Do that again."

Flynn rubbed his forehead, reluctantly sharing, "We talked last night. She needs some time to... I'm not convinced she wants interference. Yours or mine." Not in a heavy-handed way.

Steven glowered. And then he walked away.

"That's a wrap for tonight, everyone," Alexis called. "Thank you for your hard work." She turned to have a word with Lark.

The crowd dispersed, shivering and talking about getting warm. The experienced movie crew immediately sprang into action to clear cables and equipment. By morning, the town square would be open for normal December shopping and tourism.

Flynn hurried over to the catering table, grabbing two cups of hot chocolate being handed out by Faye and her assistant. And then he walked toward Alexis.

"We're getting there. Don't worry about it, okay?" Lark patted Alexis on the shoulder before moving away to talk with someone else on the crew.

"Ugh." Alexis accepted a cup of hot chocolate, a worried cast to her pretty eyes. "One step forward..."

She needed a distraction.

"Just FYI. Your brother ordered me to come over and fix you." Flynn sipped his hot chocolate as if this was no big deal. "This confidence thing you're having... He seems to think I have the solution."

Alexis huffed out a breath. "Nice. You and I both know that I'm the only one who can find the answer to my problem." She shook her head, trying her best to smile.

"You're right. But I did find it interesting that your brother..." He gripped Alexis' coat sleeve to make sure she was following his train of thought. "Your brother ordered me, the bad influence from next door, to help you. It's almost like he..." Flynn stared up at the dark, cloudy sky as he followed that idea to the conclusion. "Approves of our friendship?" That was mind-blowing.

Her laughter floated on the crisp air between them. "See? Even a stuffed shirt like my brother can change his opinion of you."

"And all of this happened *before* I completed my plan to win over the town."

"There's a plan *after* your plan to win over the town?" She elbowed him lightly. "Spill."

"I'm really thinking it's time..." Flynn closed his eyes. "To settle down or settle in? What's the way to say that? I want my own place. I want a wife. And I want to build the family I can almost picture in my head." He tapped his temple with a Santa Claus mitten. "That's wild, isn't it? I just said it aloud for the first time."

They stood in the warm glow of the gazebo with activity all around them, but it felt as if they were alone.

Because Alexis was looking at him differently. "More adulting. I'm impressed." There was no tease in her tone.

Deflated that her answer wasn't more...*something*, Flynn tipped his head back, staring at the occasional star peeking through the clouds. "I shared. That was difficult, so tell me what went wrong tonight. Not that I'm trying to fix you. There's nothing broken about you." Despite what her brother said, she was perfect, inside and out.

Alexis' shoulders slumped. "I took your advice and tried a different camera angle for the gazebo scene. Lark said it was good, moving to where she wants. But she didn't get the *quote-unquote* joy." She held up her mittened, Mrs. Claus hands to make air quotes.

"You'll get there." Flynn flashed his Santa mittens to her.

"We match," she said slowly. "Did the Knotty Elves do that on purpose?'

Flynn dipped his head to catch her attention. "I don't have to answer that question." But he suspected they had.

"Huh." Alexis put her mittens next to him. "Cute."

She was more than cute. She was beautiful and more than anything, Flynn wanted to sweep her into his arms and tell her so. But she had filmmaking on her mind, and he had to find a way to divert that brilliant brain of hers so that she'd be able to reconnect with her feelings. And then maybe...just maybe...she'd realize she had feelings for him, too.

He grinned at her, struck by inspiration. "Remember that first night we snuck out? We were so awkward with each other. Strangers who both had these cameras that we loved and all these ideas about how to capture a story, the story of the town square." Flynn bent down to sit in the snow. Cold immediately seeped into his jeans. Hoo-boy, he hoped this idea paid off. "I suggested a real moose walking across in the early morning, or anything in your frame that wasn't normally there." He looked up at her. "Are you going to sit with me or what?"

"Aren't we too smart to get cold and wet so late at night?" Alexis rolled her eyes as she sat next to him. "Your point was to capture the one little detail, the one incongruity that an object or change in direction might capture. Tell me how freezing our butts and talking about moose tracks is going to bring joy in my filmmaking."

"You're getting lost in the mire of details, Lex." Flynn set his hot chocolate in the snow, far away from his feet and then stretched out to make a snow angel. "Do you remember why we were talking about story that night? It was because when I saw you filming that day, you were capturing your brother's reaction to a prank you pulled. And you, Alexis Dorsey, used to be the most inventive prankster I knew." Flynn flapped his arms, continuing to make the wings on his snow angel. "What does that make you think of?"

He listened to the shush of snow as Alexis flopped back into the drift and made her wings.

The production crew had mostly finished on the square. Because of the cold, almost everyone else had scurried on their way. Silence made it easy to hear her breaths. Love made it easy to handle the cold on his backside.

"I haven't pulled a prank in I don't know how long." Alexis heaved a puff of air that took her concerns, bundled them like a fluffy cloud, and made them dissipate. "You think that's why I'm not being more creative on this film."

"I didn't say that."

"I love the way the world looks from this angle," she said softly. "The lights are softer, and everything is in sharp focus. So clear." She turned to face him. "This feels pretty magical to me, joyful almost."

Flynn rolled closer so that he could see the emotion in her eyes. "Sharp focus."

Alexis licked her lips before wrinkling her nose. "I almost kissed you last night. If you aren't careful, I'll do it tonight."

The shot of energy that sizzled through Flynn made it seem possible to leap up into the air and fly high above the town, like Santa in his sleigh powered by magic. Instead, he brushed his hand over her cheek. "What stopped you?"

Alexis blinked and he noted the moment understanding filled her eyes. "I needed a different point of view." She pulled him closer and the kiss there in the snow in the center of Christmas Town tilted his lens on its axis. The world shrank down, the night fading away, until only he and Alexis were there.

This had to be the biggest gamble of his life. The risk of losing Alexis Dorsey's friendship was enormous.

But the potential payoff, the future that unrolled in his mind frame by frame with her lips on his, was infinite.

# Chapter Five

S unlight streaming through a gap between the curtains woke Alexis the next
morning. She rolled over stared at the ceiling, thinking about The Kiss.

In her head, that meeting of lips would forever and always be The Kiss.

In her life, there would be Before The Kiss and After The Kiss.

Alexis knew Flynn had measured that event the same way. When The Kiss
had ended and she'd opened her eyes to a new world, Flynn had blinked as if he
was seeing the world for the first time, too. As if he wasn't quite sure what that
meant.

"There's a very real possibility of frostbite if we stay here much longer," he'd
said but the look in his eyes conveyed he wouldn't mind so much.

She'd laughed, grateful that he'd given them both time to process what could
be a very big change in their lives.

They'd walked home quietly, hand in hand like the couples she'd watched
strolling on the snowy green the night before. After she'd stepped inside Beth's
house, Alexis had rested against the front door, staring at the cozy, cluttered
living room but replaying the events of the evening in her mind, starting with
the normal.

*The shoot proceeding smoothly.*

*Waving to Steven and Beth when they arrived to watch her work.*

*Feeling Flynn's comfortable presence in the background.*

*Hating the pressure but loving the story she was telling.*

*Watching the takes with Lark on the monitor as the night went on.*

*Realizing that Elmer was peeking around the corner of the gazebo at her in her very first shots of the night.*

*Listening to the obnoxious voice in her head, the one that sounded a lot like that first college boyfriend who had tried to take advantage of her heart to reach the Dorsey money, as it promised she'd never manage to prove herself apart from her family's name and influence.*

*Turning to find the bad boy who'd become her best friend making snow angels next to her.*

*Realizing how much of the magic she loved about Christmas Town and the creative joy of telling her kind of stories in film.*

All of that was wrapped up with Flynn Sullivan.

Kissing him had been the only choice.

Falling in love with Flynn Sullivan was simple. She'd been doing it for years without knowing it. But snow angels in the center of Christmas Town cast a spell, revealing everything at once. Love, a feeling of home, the promise of joy.

She had time to figure things out with Flynn. But the film...

She'd gone to the kitchen. It was the safest, quietest place to pace without waking up Steven and his wife. Pacing led to sitting in front of her laptop at the island where she'd drank eggnog with Flynn earlier. She had the tiniest seed of a plan to solve the Elmer the Elf problem. That could add some story magic. And if she changed up some of her shots, that would add some joy. All it would take was a little extra time, an extra line of dialogue or two, and a bump in the budget.

She'd propped her elbow on the counter to create a spreadsheet with a list of shots, equipment, and estimate of the cost for each as she rehearsed what she'd say to Lark.

By the time she'd stretched out in bed to sleep, she'd started replaying The Kiss in her head again. The absolute certainty that it gave her settled her anxious mind and she'd drifted off to sleep.

And now? Today? Everything was clear. But first, she had to sell her idea to Lark. Thank heavens most of the day had been scheduled as time off.

After she talked with Lark, Alexis was going to sell Flynn on a different kind of proposal.

Filled with energy and excitement for the day, Alexis hurried into the shower and managed to dress herself before rushing down the stairs.

Steven was stringing garland made of large red and white pompoms along the mantel. Beth was kneeling next to several boxes of decorations spread across the floor.

"Good morning," she said as she whizzed through the kitchen to pour a cup of coffee.

"It's nearly afternoon," Steven said slowly. "Do my eyes deceive me or do you appear to be in a much better mood than the last time I saw you?"

She hurried over to squeeze him tightly before doing the same to a laughing Beth. "Kisses, Steven. They change everything!"

He frowned. "Oh?"

Alexis tilted her head down. "Don't give me that. You like Flynn. You know you do."

Beth's lips were twitching as she smiled up at Steven.

Her brother sniffed. "I know *you* like him and that's all that matters to me."

Alexis launched herself at him again and closed her eyes when her brother brought her close. "Want to invest in my new business?"

"Of course." Steven set her down and returned to fiddling with the garland.

Beth met Alexis' glance as they waited for him to say more.

When it was apparent that Steven wasn't going to demand any conditions because he was already signing up for whatever Alexis had in mind, Alexis nodded. "I need to go talk to someone before I tell you how much you're in for."

Steven was nodding when she yanked the loud green knit hat over her hair and tugged on her Mrs. Claus mittens. She slung her laptop bag to her shoulder and missed whatever Beth called as she ran out the door, one arm in one sleeve and her coat dragging behind her. Alexis paused at the end of the walkway to check for any sign of Flynn next door, but it was a school day, so he was probably already at work.

"Lark and then Flynn." Alexis hurried through town and texted Lark to find her location. She was inside the old bank building on the square, but she agreed to a quick meeting.

By the time Alexis stepped inside, she had rehearsed her pitch a couple of different ways, but when she saw Lark, all she said was "I know how to add joy to the film. I need to change some camera shots to capture the quirkiness of the town. But the joy is multiplied by our photobombing elf. The shots... The elf... A slight change to the script... It will cost money, but I'll invest in the production. In fact, we should be partners. Develop projects together." Alexis yanked her hat off and opened up her laptop.

It didn't take long to boot, which was a good thing because it didn't give Lark a chance to talk.

"*Hitching Home* was a viral success," Alexis continued. "The rules were there were no rules for that short film."

"We do have some restrictions on this film," Lark began.

"But I'm not talking avant-garde techniques," Alexis was quick to point out. "But what if we make use of the Elmer footage. He becomes an Easter egg for viewers. We can add something in the script about him going missing from Posey's. But that's not all. What if separately we made a short piece featuring Elmer? Think of the social media possibilities. In my head, it's shot through Elmer's point of view. His level. What he sees. We'll need a drone. A cute dog could be necessary." Alexis waved that thought aside. "Or not. I don't know about lighting or sound, so this could be an expensive first go, but I'll back it. I want to try it. Here's my proposed budget." She flashed Lark her computer screen.

Her boss bent closer to the screen.

"I like working for you, Lark. I'd like to discuss how we might work together in the future if you're interested. And if you're not..." Alexis shook her head. "Well, I don't know. I didn't get that far in my head. But I'm sure this is the kind of joy you wanted, the loving, surprising elements found in a small town. In *this* small town. The Wise Men. The Knotty Elves. Elmer." She suddenly ground to a halt and took a breath. "I'm all over the place. Do I need to start again? Slower this time?" And leave out the part about working together in the future?

Alexis wasn't aware that she'd been shifting back and forth like an antsy elf herself until Lark clasped her arm and held her still. "I love it. All of it. Especially the Elmer idea." She bit her lip. "And I like how you're already thinking of the future. We can make movies that no one else is making. That's what I want. But I'm going to do that from *here*." She pointed at the floor. "This space. Right here. Not New York, Hollywood or LA. Small towns. These stories." She crossed her arms over her chest. "What does that do to your partnership plan?"

"Only makes it better." She'd be here with Flynn. Alexis closed her laptop, tucking it away. "Have you ever been so relieved and happy and excited to work that you didn't know how to contain it all?"

Lark smiled slowly. "I have. I am. You're in?"

Alexis rushed Lark for a quick and heartfelt hug. "You haven't said whether I can have a drone for Elmer's mini-movie."

Lark laughed. "I understand the vision. Let me take a look at the numbers and talk to my bosses in New York. Then let's talk. But they'll probably approve it if you agree to pay for any overages."

Alexis offered Lark her hand to shake. "I have faith in you."

"Things are still very much in the conceptual stage, so I'm asking for secrecy," Lark said as she followed Alexis to the door. "And can we set up a meeting to discuss this further?"

"My lips are sealed and yes on the meeting," Alexis said as she backed out onto the sidewalk. She couldn't wait to find Flynn. She hurried toward Christmas Town High School. She spotted Flynn walking toward the music building where the choir practiced.

"Hey," Alexis said as she slid to a stop in front of him.

"Hey." Flynn wrapped his hands around her arms to keep her upright. "Where are you going in such a hurry?"

"To find you." When he frowned, Alexis realized she'd answered so quickly that the words bled together so she repeated herself slowly. "To. Find. You."

"What a coincidence." Flynn shoved his hands in his pockets. "It's my lunch break. I was coming to find you."

Alexis licked her lips, prepared to bare her soul, but he held up a hand.

"Don't apologize for the kiss," he said. "Yes, you're my best friend but what we have is too special to be afraid to try for more. The only thing I want in my life is you, your kiss, and your future tangled up in mine. Not as friends." He frowned. "I mean, yes, as friends but more than that. I don't know how that works with your career, but I want to find out." He rocked back on his heels as if he was bracing himself for her response.

"Do you think the choir will spare time for me? Because I need their help and yours concerning a prank that Steven will definitely never see coming." Alexis stepped closer. "But before we go there, can I kiss you again? I hate that we've already wasted so much time not kissing."

His chuckle sent a shiver down her spine.

"Forget your career and the questions? Just kiss?" he asked as he bent his head to press his lips to hers.

When their lips touched and the magic swirled between them again, Alexis knew everything was going to work out.

"I found the answer to that joy problem. I wouldn't have made that leap without you." Alexis wrapped her arms around his shoulders. "You helped me realize it isn't enough to check the boxes. That will never satisfy the haters or make them look past the Dorsey name to see that I have real talent." She kissed his chin. "I have to show them. You believe I have talent. So does Steven. And Lark. And now, I believe it, too."

"What about the awards? The fame?" he asked carefully.

Alexis considered that. "Maybe they'll come. Maybe they won't. But I won't have a single regret, I promise. And...there might be a way for me to live here. Permanently."

Flynn pulled her hand into his pocket as he turned them toward the music building. "I hope you don't mean with me in my grandmother's house. Or with you in Steven's."

# Chapter Six

That night, as Flynn stood behind the small group of choir kids who'd agreed to help him with this prank, he wondered if he'd fully considered all the consequences. Someone could call the cops or file a complaint.

"Too late now," he muttered as he tossed a snowball up at the bedroom window. When the light came on inside, he pointed at Amelia Carstairs. "Hit it."

Amelia and the rest of the choir sailed through the first verse of *All I Want for Christmas* before Alexis' brother shoved the upstairs window open and leaned out with a shout, "Hey!"

"Hey," Flynn called back with a wave, relieved Beth poked her head out, too. Surely she'd stop Steven from yelling angrily at high school carolers.

Beth must have said something to Steven because the choir finished their song without further interruption.

"Nice gesture, Sullivan." Steven was surprisingly not angry. "But my sister took the corner bedroom with a window on the side. You'll have to do it all over again for her."

The choir parted down the middle to reveal Alexis stepping out from behind Flynn, her phone held up to capture her brother's reaction to the latest in a long line of pranks. Alexis Dorsey was back and in fine form.

"Of course, that wasn't for Alexis," Steven said dryly. "Wouldn't be the holidays without a prank from my adoring sister. Merry Christmas, everybody." He slammed the window shut.

"Thank you. Thank you all." Lex wrapped her arms around Flynn's shoulders for a quick, sweet kiss.

Oh, yeah. He'd happily support any plot Alexis Dorsey drew up.

After the laughter faded and the choir dispersed, Flynn and Alexis were left with easy silence and peace. Snow drifted around them, binding them, connecting them.

As a kid too rowdy for his parents to handle, he'd wondered if anything would ever feel right like this again.

As a man, he understood how much sweeter his world was with Alexis Dorsey next door. Whatever came next for them was going to be magical.

"I like this," Alexis whispered on a happy sigh. "You and me. Couldn't have written a more joyous ending myself."

"Ending? To the first act, maybe." Flynn kissed her again. "The best part of our story is just getting started."

The End

# Christmas Take Two

## Book 5: Lights, Camera, Christmas Town

### Liz Flaherty

ChelseaBeth Publishing

# Chapter One

*D*ecember 13*th*

"Time to get you to Pine Tree Inn." Abby Nash clipped the leash onto Jolly's collar and lost herself in her rescue dog's warm brown eyes. Eyes that reminded her of... Well, someone else's. But she'd stopped being captivated by her ex-husband's appealing gaze years ago. She rubbed Jolly's ears. "And if Cyrus Nash still wanders through my dreams upon occasion, well, that's our secret, Jolly."

Abby was about to walk Jolly to the Pine Tree Inn, where he was staying with her assistant, Miranda, in her closet-sized motel room. While the managers at Over the River were welcoming and the residents even more so, large dogs weren't allowed to stay for reasons of safety. The remainder of her evening, she planned to run lines for tomorrow's early morning casting call.

"Abby." Odette King bustled through the sliding glass doors at the Over the River Retirement Home, where Abby was temporarily living during the filming of *The Christmas Carousel* movie.

Odette's two friends, Prudence Parker and June Baxter, trailed close behind her. The trio of knitters, known collectively as the Knotty Elves, had gone out of their way to make Abby feel welcome in the senior living community.

Odette cradled a potted poinsettia against her chest and waved her free arm. "Abby, dear, your ride is here."

Abby worked on keeping an excited Jolly in a sit position. Patience was a virtue in a good dog, but not always in a young dog. "I didn't order a ride."

Pru patted Jolly affectionately and slipped him a doggy biscuit from her pocket. Her words were unapologetic, her expression polite. "We called a ride for you."

"I believe he's here now." June motioned toward the dark SUV pulling into the carport. "And right on time."

"Punctuality is a good trait." Odette offered Jolly another treat. "Now you can get to the good part of your evening faster."

The SUV parked, the driver's side door opened, and her ex-husband stepped out. Cyrus looked as gorgeous as ever in a peacoat and a newsboy cap with his short brown hair a neat fringe beneath it. His brown gaze fixed on Abby and warmed her from the inside out.

June poked her bony elbow into Abby's side. "Cyrus' scarf looks as good on him as yours does on you, dear."

*Yes, it certainly does.*

The Knotty Elves had gifted Abby and Cyrus matching scarves. The silver, purple, and teal scarf had horrified her at first glance but touched her with its handmade softness. She'd quickly grown fond of it and gained permission to wear it in the film.

"Well, we're off to see Zoey Hansen about a special postcard project for Holly Haven Rescue," Pru announced. "We'll just leave you two to enjoy this beautiful evening."

Like that, the Knotty Elves were gone, and Abby was alone with Jolly and her ex-husband. Abby reminded herself that falling into Cyrus Nash's eyes was part of her past. "Cy, what are you doing here?"

"Evening, Abby." Cyrus tweaked Abby's scarf when he came to stand in front of her on the sidewalk. "I think the Knotty Elves were afraid you intended to walk into town."

That was exactly what she'd intended. "It's a perfect night for a walk. Jolly seemed to like the idea too."

"It is," he agreed, looking around at the starlit sky, "but it's dark, Abby, and the inn is clear across town. Now, while your new dog is definitely a 'jolly good fellow,' he's not what you'd call a level-headed protector."

As if to prove his point, Jolly jumped up, wiggling for more attention.

They laughed at her dog's antics.

"Your concern is duly noted." Abby and her ex were friends of sorts, but she was always having to assert her independence. "I've been living in Vermont for a long time, Cy. I walk everywhere."

He frowned, took Jolly's leash, and opened the passenger door so Jolly could hop in the back. Then he opened the front door for her and waited while she climbed in. Once he was settled into the driver seat, he said, "I'm almost sure they have violence and crime in Vermont, too, and you may not be on the screen that much anymore, but you're still a celebrity."

"Well, Vermont does have crime," she admitted. "But I'm never afraid there. It's where I grew up, where I always felt at home even when..."

"*Where you always felt at home.*" Cyrus raised a sardonic eyebrow, still managing to look handsome. "Even when we were married and I forced you to live in Southern California, you mean?"

Abby's nose had a habit of rising in the air when she became annoyed. A tell Cyrus knew all too well. There was a time he claimed her pique was charming. She supposed that wasn't true anymore. "You didn't *force me* to do anything, Cy. I stayed in California a long time after we weren't married anymore."

It was true that he hadn't forced anything, but he'd liked their Hollywood lifestyle better than she did. He had never seemed to mind being recognized, doing interviews, or stopping whatever he was doing to talk to fans. "*They're our bread and butter,*" he'd tell her when she objected, "*and they're mostly nice people.*"

Maybe they were, but Abby had longed for privacy. For a house with a picket fence and flower gardens she cultivated herself. For a family to share it with. She loved acting, always, but she couldn't say she liked what came with it.

Cyrus was frowning. "But are you happy in Vermont?"

That was an odd question. Surely he knew. They'd seen each other a few times a year since the divorce twenty years ago. He'd come to the grand opening of Steeping on Main, her teashop in Vermont. She'd even attended a few of his movie premieres with him.

"Yes, I'm happy." Although it had taken her a long time, and there were still holes that had never been filled, like that one corner of her garden that didn't get enough sun. "I don't miss California. I do miss the rush that comes with a great role, but not the headaches and heartaches that accompany it." She lifted her shoulders in a shrug. "I miss the income." She missed him, too, sometimes. She always had, but there was no point in saying so.

Jolly made an impatient noise in the back seat.

"Let's go, shall we?" Abby buckled her seat belt.

Across town at the Pine Tree Inn, Jolly practically bolted when he saw Miranda standing outside with Dustin Burnside. Miranda and Dustin's relationship was blossoming and for that, Abby was grateful. She'd always wanted her assistant to find her own true happiness.

"I'd say he's ready for bed," she told Miranda, "But I doubt it."

"That's okay. He can walk to the green with Dustin and me. I'll keep him from kissing a pretty girl in the gazebo." Miranda bent to give the dog a rub, her light titian curls blending prettily with Jolly's red coat.

Abby gave Miranda a hug. "See you in the morning. Have a nice walk."

"How about a drink?" Cyrus suggested when Abby turned back to him. "Eli, who owns the cottage I'm staying in, introduced me to the Snowed In Pub. Hardly anyone from the film has discovered it, and it's a quiet place."

"Sounds nice." Abby was tired—filming took more out of her than it had when she was younger, slimmer, and still a natural blonde. She couldn't have said why—Miranda did all the heavy lifting, both figuratively and literally. She even walked Jolly most afternoons, although the dog's presence was a calming influence for Abby throughout the long work days. On set, Jolly was as popular as Elmer, the elusive elf from Posey's Diner who seemed to disappear and reappear in unexpected places during filming.

"Did Elmer show up on set today?" Abby sank into the car's plush leather passenger seat. "I didn't hear about it if he did."

"He did." Cyrus headed toward downtown.

"Pru claims he's magic," said Abby. "She believes you just never know where or when he's going to show up. When I explained not everyone on the movie appreciated that kind of magic, June said those folks should learn to embrace Christmas and be grateful for it. I've learned not to argue with the Elves, but I don't think I buy the magic part."

"Why would you have trouble believing in magic?" Cyrus brought his fancy car to a stop at an intersection. "Your acting career had a lot of it." He raised a hand to touch her cheek lightly. "And us. We had magic."

Oh, they had been magical together. The darlings of the red carpet for the trio of years they were married. Although Cyrus' acting star rose higher than hers, she'd never been without work, and they'd reached the point of being recognized everywhere they went.

That had been the beginning of the end, although Abby hadn't realized it at the time. While in the process of becoming the striking young couple beaming loving smiles at each other wherever they went, they'd lost track of who they really were.

Inside the Snowed In Pub, no one seemed to recognize Abby or Cyrus, much to her relief. She slid into the corner booth, appreciating being normal and unnoticed and hummed along with a jaunty rendition of *Holly, Jolly Christmas*.

"Wine?" Cyrus hung their coats on the hooks at the end of the booth.

Abby shook her head. "This is Christmas Town, remember? I want some really decadent hot chocolate with a peppermint swizzle stick and real whipped cream on top."

He grinned, sparking some of that old magic that she'd never admit he had. "By decadent, I'm assuming you mean including a jigger of Captain Morgan?"

She grinned back. "I wouldn't turn it down."

He put the orders in at the polished bar, then sat across from her, his dark gaze steady on her. "Does working again make you want to get back into it?"

"I do work, Cy," Abby said evenly. "I run a semi-successful teashop and volunteer at the animal shelter. I don't do much on-screen other than the occasional cameo or guest shot, but I still do commercial voiceovers and narrate audiobooks. I'm enjoying making this movie. I even like working with you again." And wasn't that a surprise. "But life in the public eye is like a hamster wheel to me, and I never want to get on it again."

The bartender, a smiling woman near Abby's age, brought their drinks on a tray that included a platter of cheese and crackers. She looked familiar, but Abby couldn't place her.

Cyrus could, naturally. He never forgot anyone. And that was part of his charm, especially to his fans. "Abby, you remember Christy. She's helping in wardrobe for the production. And I think we met her mother-in-law at Over the River."

"Oh, of course," Abby said graciously. "You made me look like I'm still a size six."

Christy offered a rueful smile. "Believe me, that's my expertise. I left a size ten behind me a few years back." She turned her head slightly as if looking over her shoulder. "And I do mean literally behind me."

Cyrus and Abby laughed.

"You work at Candlelight and Lace, the bridal shop, don't you?" Abby remembered because she'd walked past the store earlier and recognized Christy helping a customer.

"Two days a week and work I take home. One night a week here at the pub. When Rob and I remarried two years ago, I thought I might stop working so we could travel more. However, his cabinet-building caught on to the point that if I stopped working, I'd have to dust while I waited for him to come home. *That* certainly wasn't going to happen."

Abby laughed again, delighted with Christy's story. "Housework? It wouldn't happen with me, either. Now gardening..." She paused. "Hang on. Did you say *re*married?"

The other woman's cheeks pinkened. "Yes. We were divorced for a few years, but we weren't all that good at it, so when I bought him off the auction block for a Valentine's Day fundraiser a few years back, I kept him."

"There's something I haven't tried," Cyrus riffed. "Would you buy me if I went up for auction, Abby?"

"She knows better than to answer that question," Christy said in feminine solidarity.

Abby stirred her drink. Would she buy Cyrus if given the chance? She didn't know.

# Chapter Two

C yrus Nash had been in love once in his life.

He'd fallen hard and fast and proposed to beautiful, blond Abilene on their second date. She'd laughed in soprano disbelief, but when he repeated the question after the cast party of the film they'd just finished, she'd said she might as well marry him, because she was unemployed and didn't have anything better to do. But her heart had been in her eyes, as his had been in the proposal.

The marriage lasted three years. They were the shortest, longest, best, and worst years of his life. They'd both been such consummate actors, as in love with their shared profession as they were with each other, that in retrospect, he wasn't sure they'd ever known each other at all.

In the end, though, they'd become so estranged that she'd come to think of him as a notorious flirt and he'd believed she really was the prima donna her reputation had dubbed her.

Looking at her across the thick pine table at the Snowed In Pub, Cyrus wondered if he'd ever really known her. She looked so different now, with her hair pearly gray, swirling around her shoulders with eyes the same color as her hair. She used to have to wear blue contacts in movies because her eyes didn't photograph well. But he could lose himself in the softness of them. Then. And now.

She had some laugh lines and crows' feet, although not many, and she didn't bother covering them up. The makeup artists on set had to work a lot harder to make her look the eighty years old their parts called for than they did him. Or so Betsy Anne, the head of the make-up department, told him. Recalling the comment made Cyrus laugh. He was far into the journey of heading over the hill.

Abby raised an eyebrow. "Do I have whipped cream on my upper lip?"

If she had, he'd have felt compelled to kiss it off, just to see if kissing her still felt same as it always had, back when they'd been able to shut out the rest of the world with the lightest of touches, the tenderest of embraces. In the years they'd been apart, they'd fallen into the habit of doing airy cheek kisses when they parted. They felt phony to him, but the brief hug that accompanied the tiny smooches made it worthwhile.

"I was thinking of makeup," he confessed. "Of how much less you've aged than I have. Have you had work done I don't know about?" He hadn't, although his agent had suggested it. He was fifty-five. He thought he probably looked it but didn't particularly mind.

"Thank you," said Abby. "I don't think much about it anymore. How I look, I mean." She smiled at him, but he thought her eyes looked sad. "It's not true, though, you know about our ages. You look wonderful, and you look young, too. The screen and stage are both kind to you, and you are kind to them."

Her words were sincere, but it was the look in her eyes that held his attention. "What made you decide what we had wasn't worth keeping? I never quite understood why you wanted out."

"I know. And I don't know how to make you understand now, either."

"Try me."

She leaned her elbows on the table and considered him. "You were moving to New York to work in theater, Cy, and my work was in California where I didn't like living. We'd been apart more than we'd been together the whole time we were married. How were we supposed to start a family when we were both more committed to our careers than each other?"

"You and I were a family. And Queenie." The mother of her second dog Duchess.

He'd gotten Queenie for her so that she'd have company while he was gone. The little dog wasn't meant to be his replacement. They'd both loved Queenie.

They'd known their lives would have to be a series of separations while they were building their careers. He didn't like it, but he hadn't understood how much she'd hated it. Maybe he didn't want to back then.

"We weren't a family." She shook her head, and tears glinted in her eyes. "I know we loved each other, but we weren't together in any way that mattered. Do you remember when I walked to Delilah's?"

He did. It had been the day after their friend Delilah's husband was buried. Abby had wanted to visit Delilah to see if she could do anything for her friend. Cyrus had been surprised when she appeared at the door with no makeup, her hair scraped back in a ponytail, and wearing jeans and a T-shirt. The jeans were baggy, and the shirt had a stain on it.

Idiot that he was, he'd said, "I don't mind at all, but you know you're going to show up in the tabloids dressed for working in the garden. Are you sure you're okay with that?"

She'd shrugged. "What difference does it make? If Delilah wants to work in her plants, I want to be prepared."

Abby and her little dog had left, and helped Delilah in her greenhouse, and by the time they'd walked back home, Abby's baggy jeans were muddy and so was Queenie. The paparazzi had taken her picture. She hadn't been smiling in the tabloid photos; rather, her look had been fierce. At least, as fierce as she was capable of, kindhearted soul that she was.

Cy had been supportive but annoyed. The studio where Abby was working hadn't been thrilled and her agent had been aghast, but Abby hadn't cared.

"I handled that badly," he admitted, fishing the soft cotton handkerchief he always carried out of his jacket pocket and giving it to her. "Maybe worse than that."

"Not badly, maybe." She wiped the dampness on her cheeks away and looked at him. "But not how I needed you to. The other side of that is you needed me to be Abilene whenever I was in public, but I was just done. Done with always being 'on,' and done with relationships that weren't real. I wanted to be just Abby, but that wasn't who you wanted or who show business wanted."

"You're half right." He got up, taking their empty cups to the bar to order re-fills from Christy. When he came back, he hesitated before continuing. "Maybe more than half. It's true that I wanted Abilene, but I wanted *just Abby*, too."

"Behind closed doors."

He wanted to say she was wrong, that even though he loved his profes-sion, he'd never chosen it over her. But he knew he had. Pretending otherwise wouldn't help the seesaw condition of their fragile friendship, and it wasn't like they were going to get back together at this time in their lives.

Or that they'd even want to.

His smile felt as though he had to build it, muscle by muscle, but he got it done. "I think the reason I didn't understand was because I didn't want to admit things about myself I didn't like."

Christy brought their second round of drinks a few minutes later, leaning close to the table to set the cups down carefully. "There's a couple in another booth being pretty curious," she said very quietly. "They want to know if you're from the movie that's being filmed here in town. I told them I wasn't sure who you were but that you'd expressed an interest in not wishing to be disturbed while you're here. Was that right, or would you rather meet them?"

Cyrus's first inclination was to meet them, because that's what he always did, but the look of resignation that crossed Abby's face stopped him. "We're really wanting privacy right now," he said. "Maybe they could catch us another time."

"Sounds good to me." Christy nodded. "If you decide you want to leave without passing both the bar and the entire row of booths, give me a sign. I'll let you out the back door."

When Christy returned to the bar, Cyrus asked Abby, "When you left Cal-ifornia and disappeared almost into the night, was it because the industry was unkind or because you disliked yourself?"

"Both. And also because of Aunt Greevy."

He frowned. He'd loved the old lady, too. "You moved back east because of her?"

"During the last years of her life, I didn't see her enough—although, if you'll remember, she was a whiz at texting. After she died, Miranda and I found every piece of printed news about you and me there'd ever been. Aunt Greevy had scrapbooks for you, for me, and for us. She had every letter I wrote her and every card you ever sent. She left me everything. All I'd done for her was call her every Sunday afternoon."

He remembered it differently. They used to fly to Vermont for the sole purpose of taking Aunt Greevy to their movies at the Star Theater in St. Johnsbury. They had fresh lobster delivered because she loved it so much. When Abby filmed in Italy, she took her aunt along because it was where Greevy and her husband had spent their honeymoon. Cyrus had even collected autographs for her from actors and directors she liked.

"I guess I wanted that picket fence I always dreamed about. Even though our life was exciting, when you weren't in it anymore, I didn't have any idea who I was." Abby shook her head. "When I went back to Vermont, I found me. Mostly. That's just a pathetic thing to admit, isn't it?"

"I'm sorry," he said, feeling guilty. "If I was insistent on having things always my way. If I didn't see things I should have."

"Oh, good grief, Cy, it wasn't *your* fault. I loved our life when we were together, and I loved acting. I *still* love acting. But the time came when we couldn't manage the together part anymore, and loving acting didn't make up for the fact that I hated virtually everything else."

They talked longer. About Duchess, her teashop, his family—he was unsurprised she knew more about his nephews than he did.

He told her his plan to head back to Broadway when the filming wrapped in Christmas Town, a part of him wishing she'd offer to visit New York to spend time with him, see if they could recapture at least some of what they'd once had. But she just listened, asking interested questions about the project he was going back to.

When they'd finished their second orders of spiked hot chocolate, he lifted a hand in Christy's direction. She came to let them out the back door. It was snowing lightly, although the flakes were big and fluffy. Cyrus slipped on a patch of ice and Abby reached for his hand to help him steady himself. They laughed a little about their diminishing grace, and he didn't let go of her hand.

And she didn't let go of his, either.

# Chapter Three

Outside her wreath-decorated front door at Over the River, Abby melted into Cyrus' embrace, cherishing the warmth and sweetness of it. Relishing being held in a way that was exciting but not purely so, loving but not quite romantically so, knowing but not in a taking-for-granted sort of way.

They took their time kissing, reacquainting and reconnecting in a way so unexpected and so...wonderful.

Muted laughter from down the hall drifted around them and Cyrus pulled away, pressing the softest kiss on her cheek. He leaned in, his whisper husky and intimate, warmed her ear. His words her heart. "Remember when we called kisses promises?"

Oh, how she did.

"I leave you with one last promise." Cyrus worked his way back to her mouth, brushed his lips against hers, and released her. "Until tomorrow."

Abby slipped inside her apartment and sighed, trying to process the sweet barrage of feelings Cyrus' touches had brought to life. She was still sighing even after she'd tugged on her soft sweats with a reeling, possibly tipsy reindeer on her shirt and knitted red slippers one of the residents of Over the River had left at her door.

Restless, she went down to the large social area outside the Carriage Room Dining Hall. She'd stayed at the retirement complex long enough to know everyone's sleeping hours varied, so she wasn't surprised to find several people reading, doing handwork, and playing chess. A fire snapped in the fireplace. Lights twinkled in the garland draped across the mantle and stockings hung from every available surface. A big tree filled a corner, with the stack of presents under it growing every day.

The Knotty Elves invited her to join them, and she curled into a comfortable chair at the large table.

"You look a little melancholy, dear," said Pru, who was knitting a long scarf in Harry Potter's Gryffindor colors. "Was your evening not what you expected?"

The kiss was better than she'd expected. Abby laughed, the sound catching in her throat. "We took Jolly to Miranda, then went to the Snowed In Pub for some hot chocolate." She smiled at Austen Rahilly, who was seated near the fireplace. "Your daughter-in-law was there. She's lovely."

The older woman smiled back. "She is, and she makes very good hot chocolate."

"Tell us about your teashop, Abby." Odette's smile was as bright as the colorful bracelets she wore, the ones that tinkled as her knitting needles clacked. "Is it like Gina's Tea Pot here in town?"

Abby liked Gina Banning's bustling shop, but it felt very different from Steeping. "Quieter," she said. "While I offer a bigger variety of tea and some coffee as well, the only food is a small selection of scones. I keep thinking I should create a breakfast and lunch menu, but I like it as it is. Then I wonder if that's enough."

"Feeling torn, are you?" June was working on a red and white knit elf hat. "Between the life you had and the one you're living now?"

"Maybe a little." Abby picked up a pair of knitting needles from the yarn basket, noticing that someone had fixed the dropped stitches in the scarf she'd left last night. "I don't act very much anymore. I'd almost forgotten about the flow of adrenaline that acting brings. I'm really enjoying it, but I'm homesick, too."

Abby knew that while she was enjoying making this movie, she'd be happy when it was over, and she could go back to the life she'd made, complete with the pretty front yard and flower gardens at Aunt Greevy's house. But she would miss seeing Cyrus every day. The time together recently felt like it had in the very early days of their relationship—talking, teasing, tempting.

"Do you miss being married?" Odette's question brought Abby out of her reverie.

Abby gave her a sharp glance. "Did I say something?"

"No, you didn't say anything." June laughed. "But we've seen that look before."

Pru snorted. "We've *worn* it before."

"I don't miss being married so much as I miss being in love," Abby said. She'd had relationships since her divorce, and she knew Cyrus had, too. Nothing that lasted. For either of them. There'd always been something between them that hinted at more. Sad that they'd screwed it up so badly. "However, I like my life and the only man I've ever truly been in love with likes his. It's a twain that will never meet."

*Again. It will never meet again. You don't get that lucky twice.*

"Personally," came a voice from a chair in front of the fire, "I'd prefer a nice dog to having a man around."

"You're allergic, Doris," Pru quipped.

"Hmph. Too bad it's to dogs instead of men," said Doris, whose crankiness was apparently no secret, judging by the eyerolls generated by her comments. "Just stick with that nice dog you got from the shelter, girlie. You'll be a lot happier."

Laughter, including Abby's, rippled through the room.

She set her unworked knitting back in the basket, then looked at the lacy white ornaments Austen was crocheting. "I can do that. My aunt Greevy taught me the basics when I was a kid and helped hone my skills later. She said I didn't crochet well, but I was good at covering up my mistakes."

Every time Abby had wanted to give up, her aunt put the hook and the project back into her hands. "Never give up on what you can fix." She'd picked up Abby's first pathetic effort and tossed it into the trash basket beside the bed. "Of course, it's important to know *when to* give up, too." Like with her marriage.

Together, she and Aunt Greevy had made enough lacy white Christmas ornaments that Abby put up a small tree just for them, adding more she found when traveling. She called it her memory tree.

She'd crocheted off and on since then, creating ornaments to add to the tree in the teashop. She'd made a teacup so often she thought she could do it with her eyes closed.

Austen laughed. "I must have learned from an Aunt Greevy of my own, because I have a lot of mistakes." She rummaged in the bag on the table in front of her, bringing out a crochet hook and some thread. "Here you go."

It felt good to hold the hook. As she worked the thread between her fingers, the tension left Abby's shoulders and neck. The work took shape in her hands, becoming a snowflake. She would need to add something shiny to it. Unless... She looked up. "Do you have—"

Before she had the question asked, Austen pushed a spool of glittery thread over to her. Abby began to work the sparkle into her snowflake. Thoughts of Cyrus's kisses and her eager return of them lingered like a sparkle of light across a fresh layer of snow. The fire crackled. Around her, conversations continued.

A while later, Abby held up the nearly finished ornament, taking in the twinkle lent by the textured thread. Such a small effort to produce such a big effect.

How long had she been missing sparkle in her quiet life? And how much effort would it take to get it back?

# Chapter Four

"They're the grandparents everyone wants and hardly anyone gets," Lisa Richardson said with warmth and pride. "This is my Poppa Seymore and my Nana Elaine Garland. I know you met them the other night, but they were in their ugly sweaters, and you might not have been able to recognize how cute they really are, Abby."

Lisa, one half of the couple that the film was about, was right. Her grandparents were a gorgeous couple, so clearly in love. Abby was proud to be playing one half of the real-life couple in the movie.

But she also felt a twinge of curiosity. How would she and Cyrus have looked at the Garlands' age if they'd stayed together?

She pushed the thought aside. "I can never play you—you're too pretty," she gushed to Elaine, not caring that she probably sounded like a rock band groupie.

"And here I was thinking you were the only one pretty enough to play her." Seymore came forward, limping a little, and gave Abby a hug.

She thought maybe sounding like a groupie had paid off—the man was a champion hugger. Abby laughed. "Well-played, Mr. Garland. I see now why your marriage has lasted."

"He has his moments." Elaine smiled at her husband, then held out a large Christmas tin toward Abby. "I wanted to give you some baked treats. There are several kinds. Fudge is my only claim to fame and the reason I've become so fluffy in my old age. I can't make anything without tasting it."

"Oh, thank you!" Abby tilted a glance at Cyrus, just a few feet away. "Am I supposed to share it?"

The Garlands spoke in unison, with Elaine saying, "Only if you want to," and Seymore saying, "Of course."

"We have to do some work now," said Cyrus, raising his hand to acknowledge a call from one of the crew. "We have a short day today, though. Would you have lunch with us?" He caught Abby's eye. "Okay?"

"I'd love it if you could." Abby grinned at the older couple. "Please choose where we can go and make it expensive—Cy's buying."

"We'd love to," said Elaine, exchanging one of those silent conversation looks with her husband to make sure he was on board.

Seymore nodded enthusiastically. "We know just the place to go, too."

Abby looked over her shoulder. "Miranda, will you find the Garlands front row seats to watch Cyrus flub his lines?"

"Certainly." Miranda stepped forward, joining in the laughter at Cyrus' expense. "Have you met Jolly? He likes to watch, too."

Cyrus rubbed the dog's head. "He laughs when I flub the lines. Is that what you're trying to say, Miranda?"

"Yep." Abby's assistant grinned.

The scene they were shooting was a favorite of Abby's. She tried to add some of Elaine's twinkle to her performance, and Cyrus as Seymore had the slightest limp to his step that hadn't been there before.

He was gifted.

She would have so loved if he'd chosen her over their careers and settled for taking jobs that would have allowed them to be together. He could have worked on a TV series—the opportunities had been there—but it wouldn't have been enough. He loved movies. He loved theater. He wouldn't have been happy in a series, although he would have been brilliant at it.

At the end of the day, would she have been happy if he wasn't?

Probably not.

When the scene was wrapped, they arranged to meet Seymore and Elaine at Twelve Nights Restaurant. They quickly changed and removed the aging make-up and wigs. And then they left the set together.

"Go help Dustin with the adventure tours while you have this free time," Abby urged Miranda. "Can you take Jolly?"

"Sure. He loves it when we're outside with Dustin." Miranda's joy at being in love might have been contagious, might have made Abby more vulnerable to the feelings toward Cy from their past.

Abby decided not to worry about it.

Lunch was wonderful. They lingered over coffee, listening to Christmas Town tales from the older couple.

"There's so much magic here." Elaine's bright blue eyes met her husband's, gazes clinging in a way that made Abby exchange looks with Cyrus.

*It's as if they're the only people in the room.*

Cy nodded, and Abby wondered for just an instant if she'd said the words aloud.

Seymore launched into another intriguing tidbit about Christmas Town. "You want to talk about Christmas Town magic? There's a red-and-white stocking that's been making its way around town for several years now. It will always have a note in it that's meant for the person who finds it." He chuckled, and Abby heard Santa's *ho-ho-ho* in his depth and cadence. "I thought that was on the south side of crazy when I first heard about it, but I've learned not to question some things."

"Like Elmer the Elf," said Cyrus. "He keeps showing up at the set, sometimes in places he shouldn't. We had to refilm a segment because first he was there and then he wasn't. It was hard because we kept laughing. We never had to reshoot because of a toy before."

Abby laughed, leaning in so that her shoulder bumped against Cyrus'. "And believe me, we've had our share of adventures on set."

Their eyes met, and for a moment it was as if *they* were the only ones in the room. The sensation was both familiar and precious.

"The Knotty Elves are great." Elaine drew Abby's attention back to earth. "They help keep the magic going as well."

"That's the real secret of love," Seymore added, his hand covering his wife's. "Keeping the magic alive."

When they left the restaurant, Abby felt as if a little magic dust had been sifted over her during the conversation. She prided herself on being a pragmatist—show business wasn't a good place to be otherwise—but there was no avoiding the hopefulness and joy that seemed to be the state of mind in this pretty town.

"I'll take you to Over the River, but let's get Jolly from Miranda and take him for a walk," suggested Cyrus. "It's always dark when we're downtown after work. And even though the holiday lights are spectacular, it would be nice to get a look at downtown in daylight."

Abby wanted to say no, because she was almost certain the streets of Christmas Town were going to be lined with heartbreak if she didn't back away from spending so much time with Cyrus, but she couldn't make herself do it. Removing herself from his company would be what Aunt Greevy had referred to as cutting off her nose to spite her face.

"That sounds like fun," she said instead.

Jolly, who obviously knew nothing of loyalty, insisted on Cyrus holding his leash when they got out of the car in front of Dockery's Department Store. The red, furry traitor heeled and sat like a perfect gentleman. When Guy Williams, the barber, stepped out of Kringle Cuts to say hello, Jolly offered his paw politely.

They were recognized as they walked, and signed a few autographs, but it wasn't enough of an interruption to make Abby want to retreat.

"Tell me more about the teashop," Cyrus requested. "Who's running it while you're gone?"

"Margie, the previous owner, manages it whenever I'm away." Abby laughed ruefully. "In truth, she's better at it than I am, but ownership had become more of a load than she could carry."

"Have you kept it the way it was when you bought it?" Cyrus had come to her grand opening, bringing such a big bouquet of flowers she'd been able to separate it for the vases on all the tables.

"I've added coffee and I've had bookshelves built in the seating area, where customers can take a book and leave a book. A few authors have been so charmed by Steeping that they've come in and done signings and author talks."

"Do you ever get bored?"

She smiled at the display of Christmas socks and gloves decorating a tree in the window of Fingers and Feet. Teddy bears in scarves and stocking caps sat under the tree. According to Elaine, this was the store where the legend of the red-and-white stocking had originated. "No, I don't get bored. I like the shop and I like being part of the community. It's fun being a performer, the work is exciting, but I don't want to live that way. *We* were fun until we weren't. At the end of the day, I'm still the person in the back row in the picture who people don't quite remember."

Cyrus scowled at her. "You were never that."

She laughed, feeling relief in it, and turned to him, laying her hands on the sleeves of his peacoat. "Oh, Cy, of course I was. I still am. I have no wish to be anyone else. Even when I was well known, it was because I was married to you, and it was *painful* for me. Not the being with you part but being a public figure." She felt tears pushing behind her eyes and had to hold them wide to keep from blinking. "Don't you see? You loved the woman who looked good on the red carpet, and I loved the man who stood in the rain in his tux and changed a tire for a woman who had a carload of kids when we were on our way to an awards show. It was incidental to me that you were a celebrity, and it was incidental to you that in my heart, I wasn't."

His face changed, frustration kindling in his warm brown eyes. He laid his palm against her cheek, the gentleness of his touch not reflecting his expression. "You were never incidental," he said. "You were never an afterthought or less in any way. We couldn't make each other happy back then—I'll own that—but I always loved you. Always."

"I know." Just as she'd always loved him. But there was no reason to go there again. Love hadn't been enough, and it still wouldn't be.

"Look," she said, hating the rusty sound of her own voice, "let's get some socks for your nephews for Christmas."

His eyebrows rose. "They're in college. I buy them gift cards at Starbucks, not socks."

"Oh, well, okay." She shrugged. "I still buy them socks. They give those young men personality."

Leaving him standing on the sidewalk, she went into Fingers and Feet. She took her time, buying socks and gloves and hats for the three boys she knew mostly through Facebook and texts with her former sister-in-law.

When she returned to the sidewalk, Cyrus was sitting on the bench in front of the store, Jolly leaning against his leg. Cyrus spoke to another man and looked at what appeared to be plans on graph paper. "Abby, this is Rob Rahilly, Christy's husband."

She shook hands with the handsome man, who told her he remembered her from the movies she'd been in and that she'd aged much better than Cyrus had.

She laughed. "You and Cy dip out of the same blarney bucket, don't you?" But there was no denying she enjoyed the compliment.

"Not a bit," he said, smiling at her. "Cyrus, I'm pretty sure I have what you need. I'll give you a call."

"What was that about?" She patted Jolly's head and watched Rob walk away.

"Just something Lark was talking about for the set," he said vaguely, taking the largest bag from her. Lark was the talented young executive producer of the film—she and director Alexis Dorsey combined were every actor's dream team. "This is all for my nephews?"

"Mostly." Abby grinned at him. "Want to grab a piece of peppermint pie from Posey's and take it to go? I met Posey at Over the River and made the mistake of asking her if she was retiring." Posey had a temper. "Now, I can make it up to her by being a customer."

Cyrus chuckled. "I'll take Jolly and all this to the car while you grab the pie."

When Posey brought out their to-go order, Abby pulled a crocheted snowflake from her coat pocket and looked around the diner—almost every inch of it was covered with Christmas decorations. "I don't know where you can put it, but I'd like you to have this, Posey. I put my initials down there in red thread—that's what the Knotty Elves said everyone does."

"Oh, I love it." Posey went to where pine garland was festooned over the breakfast counter and felt along its looping length until she located what must have been a hook. A few seconds later, the star sparkled from its place in the greenery. "There. Even when you leave, a part of you will always be in Christmas Town."

Abby had a feeling she was leaving little pieces of herself all over town. "I'll be back," she promised.

---

After enjoying the pie on a bench sheltered from the snow, they walked Jolly to the Pine Tree Inn, where Miranda and Dustin were waiting for him.

"He's a tired boy," Abby promised, bending down to give the overgrown puppy a hug. "Aren't you, love?"

"I have an idea." Cyrus smiled at the young couple, an expression that could send a surge of warmth into the coldest of hearts. "I'll text to double-check with Eli and Cass, but I'm almost sure I could keep Jolly at their guest cottage with me. That would give you two some time when you weren't chaperoned by either the entire film crew or one very furry security guard." Belatedly, he dropped his gaze to Abby. "Would that be okay with you?"

It was another one of those times, she realized, when life was going to change. She'd known it the day she'd met the handsome guy who'd been one of the other leading actors in the first movie role she'd landed after moving to California. Who'd ever have thought making a commercial for shampoo would pave the way to the most important relationship of her life?

But he'd ended their first shoot by saying, "I've gotten used to being your boyfriend and I kinda like it. Want to go to dinner on payday?"

There'd been no going back after that. Twenty-some years later, she knew if Jolly stayed with Cyrus, it would only deepen the connection they shared. But Abby sighed. Miranda had never said no to any request Abby made, and there had been many. The least Abby could do was give her uninterrupted time with the man who appeared to have stolen her assistant's heart.

"What a great idea." Abby nodded at Cyrus. "Go ahead and text them. I feel a bit on the selfish side because I didn't think of it."

Just that quickly—which Abby was learning happened a lot in Christmas Town—the arrangements were made. They drove to the Pine Tree Inn and transferred possession of Jolly's food, bowls, dried liver treats, and toys to Cy's SUV while Jolly dozed on Miranda's bed, snoring delicately.

The couples parted. Cy drove Abby and Jolly to the property where he was staying. He left the SUV there because after his power nap, Jolly was more than ready for another walk. The dog led the way toward the town square, where the snowy green was a hive of activity.

"I love the cheerful bustle here," said Abby. "Sometimes it doesn't seem quite real, but then I think of the people we've met and that the movie we're making is a true life story and realize it is. I'm surprised there aren't a million people in Christmas Town, jostling to make it into a place of Disney proportions."

"I think it's been suggested and maybe even tried, but much of its charm is its small town vibe," Cyrus said. "Combine that with its idiosyncrasies and its tendency toward horrible weather, and it can be discouraging to developers. Thank goodness. I'd hate to see it change. It didn't take long to work its magic on me—that's for sure."

She slipped her hand into his, grinning when Jolly gave a woof of approval from Cyrus's other side. "Me, too."

# Chapter Five

Cyrus wasn't much of a believer in perfection. He thought some of the best scenes he'd ever watched or taken part in had been far different at the finish of production than they'd been at the beginning.

But walking around a pretty little town with snow wafting down the way it seemed to have been doing ever since the cast had arrived bordered on flawless. Add to it holding both your still-loved ex-wife's hand and the leash of her funny, galumphing dog and there was perfection.

"How old were we," he mused, looking around as they walked—there were so many lights, so many singers, so much joy, "when we discovered that perfection comes in moments, not lifetimes? Not even years."

"Well, speaking for myself, I was probably forty-eight. That's when I moved back to Vermont. I had good moments when I grew some faith in my own decisions, and good moments" —she stopped, looking up and meeting his eyes—"after Duchess died."

"After she died?" He tilted his head, not understanding.

"You flew in from England when she passed, Cy, just like you did for Aunt Greevy's funeral. But for Duchess, you were on your first vacation in goodness knows how long with your whole family and you came back. You flew all night to be with me, and two days later, you flew back to your family." Tears slipped down her cheeks—a surprise because she wasn't a crier—and he reached to wipe them with his thumb. "Moments, Cy. Moments are perfect."

He nodded. "You're right." But there was more. There was a question he'd never asked her. "Why have you—"

They were interrupted by an autograph seeker.

And then they stopped for some hot chocolate complete with peppermint swizzle sticks, then went on, stopping to watch the middle school choir sing on a stage on the snowy town square and act out *Up on the Housetop*.

"Cy." Abby touched his arm. "Why what?"

"Oh." He gestured toward a bench along the walkway. "Let's sit for a minute and give Jolly and me a rest. We worked hard today."

Her snort made him laugh. "It was the shortest day we've had since we started filming." Abby brushed snow off the seat before sitting down. "I think they should find a way to heat these seats. And maybe keep them dry at the same time."

He sat beside her, close enough for them to share each other's warmth. Despite the snow, it wasn't that cold outside, but the proximity was...pleasant. "You should write a letter to Mayor Banning with that idea," he suggested, and laughed again at the look she gave him. "I know it was a short day, but we've walked all over town since...some places more than once. I don't often log that many steps."

"Me, either. It's been fun though." She tilted her head. "But what were you asking me? I thought we'd covered all the hard questions."

"Why you never got married again."

"Oh."

He waited a moment, his hand resting on Jolly's silky red head. "I came close once," he admitted when she didn't expand on her answer.

"I remember. You introduced us. She was nice."

Brandi Giles *was* a nice person. She was also twenty years younger than Cy was, which at the time put her in her mid-twenties. While Cyrus didn't have any problem with age differences—he had a lot of friends whose spouses were from different generations—in the long run, it didn't work for him, and it wasn't fair to her. Not that age had ended up being the real reason they'd broken up.

"She had awful taste in music, though," he said, trying for levity. That hadn't been the reason, either.

Abby nodded. "But she had everything else. She was pretty and smart and funny and—"

"And she looked like you." Which Brandi figured out before Cy did. He'd been so mad when she said it to him that he could hardly speak. But she'd been right.

He'd never married again because—

Abby interrupted his train of thought. "I never married again because whoever the man was, he wouldn't have been you." Her voice was low, musical.

If he closed his eyes, he could remember hearing it for the first time when she was auditioning for the film he had the lead role in. She'd been sitting across from him at the table on the stage, and he'd hardly even looked at her. But then she'd spoken, and he couldn't look away. He couldn't look away now, either. Not when she'd just said what he'd been thinking. He'd never come close to marriage again after Brandi. In truth, he'd never even had what he'd consider a serious relationship.

He wanted to say something. Not just any something, but the right thing. How did you do that, though? How did you just act as if the last twenty years hadn't even happened?

"It's not that we kept loving each other," she said, gazing out over the snow-covered green toward the Tea Pot. "But that we made each other unable to love anyone else. That's kind of sad, isn't it?"

———

When Jolly showed signs of getting restless and their hot chocolate was gone, Abby and Cyrus got up. They'd talked all afternoon and into the evening, and there seemed to be nothing left to say.

*What do I say after admitting I can't love anyone else?*

Abby knew what Aunt Greevy would say. She'd say an offer to try again should be made. But Aunt Greevy had been a romantic. And divorce... Divorce hadn't been popular with her generation. Mostly, they stuck things out. That made her feel something of a quitter.

Abby didn't pay attention to where they were going. She'd been to the green several times and was always charmed by it, especially the gazebo, where couples stood in line to share kisses and hopes for the future.

Suddenly, maybe by a little bit of that magic that seemed to have so many believers in this town, the gazebo was in front of her, festooned with soft lights and garland. Christmas music flowed from an unseen speaker system.

"That song," she said to Cy. "It's familiar, but I can't place it. I think I've heard so much holiday music since we came here that I've become almost deaf to it." It was true—music was as ubiquitous as lights and decorations.

Cyrus raised his head, listening. "It's *The Wexford Carol*. Remember? We sang it in church a few times when we were in the choir scenes for this movie."

Abby was sure they didn't get in the gazebo line on purpose. Jolly was rubbing noses with another dog, one she thought had been his friend at the rescue. It was a comfortable queue—everyone talked. After a few "aren't you in the movie?" inquiries, no one paid undue attention to her and Cyrus, and she was grateful for the privacy. When the music in the gazebo played *Joy to the World*, Cyrus started singing and within seconds had formed a choir from couples in line.

Before they'd realized what was happening, it was their turn. Cyrus made a donation in a discreet tin and then swept Abby into his arms beneath the gazebo mistletoe. Every move was familiar, but it wasn't real, was it?

It was a performance and nothing more. Yet his lips captured hers and refamiliarized themselves as if the discovery was the most wonderful thing ever. And the kiss was as genuine as they always had been. It *was*, in that moment, the most wonderful thing ever.

Long after their marriage had ended, they were still a couple in the eyes of many, so even now cameras flashed, and their kiss earned applause. Abby drew back, cheeks heating, waiting for Cy to swing them into the hands-clasped bow they'd executed more times than she could remember. Instead, he just drew her to his side and waved to the accidental audience. As if this was real, not a performance.

Abby was stunned into silence.

They started back with Jolly in the direction from which they'd come.

In the SUV, Cyrus looked over at Abby in the dusky glow from both the vehicle's interior lights and the ones that lit the holiday decorations around Christmas Town. "Do you want to come to the guesthouse where I'm staying for a while?"

Did she? Did she want to go down the path that choice would surely lead her on?

She thought of the long and longing kiss in the gazebo, and yearning moved through her. The gazebo promised a future, and it was reckless to believe in things like that after all this time. The next thing she knew, she'd be seeking out red-and-white striped stockings, searching for magic outside of the small town's borders.

But just this once... Maybe?

She nodded. "I'd like to see where you and Jolly are staying. And then home." To the retirement home. Abby laughed. "This place gets you all turned around, doesn't it?"

Cy grinned. "I was thinking just the opposite."

---

Jolly looked worried when Cyrus left the guest house to take Abby to Over the River.

Abby assured him he'd enjoy his sleepovers in a bigger place than Miranda's tiny room. Cyrus turned on the TV for the dog and promised he'd be back soon.

For better or worse—the thought brought a dry chuckle from Cyrus that made Abby look at him across the car's console—their relationship had changed on this long and wonderful day in Christmas Town.

"What?" said Abby. "You're too quiet."

He had to drag himself back to the dark confines of the SUV. "Just my mind going in weird places." He reached for her hand, clasping it. "Like where do we go from here?"

She hesitated, her fingers curling into his. "Our own homes, I think. The real ones. The differences between us are still there. Although the things that were right are still there, too. I'm enjoying making this movie, working with you and this cast and crew in this wonderful location. But I'm homesick, too. I imagine you're missing New York, too."

*Not so much.* He *did* miss it, but not like he'd expected he would. "Are you sure? I don't know that I can ever be happy again without you."

"Oh, Cy."

Not the answer he'd hoped for, although he wasn't certain what he'd expected. He parked by Over the River's front entrance. "Come on. I'll walk you to your door. After all, I'm still a good date."

"You're the best date," she said, at odds with her brush-off of their relationship.

They kissed in the hallway at her door, finding themselves snickering because they were acting like high school juniors who hated to say goodnight.

On the drive back to the guesthouse, Cyrus reflected that it wasn't the *goodnight* that was tough, but the *goodbye* that would come when filming wrapped just in time for everyone to make it home for Christmas.

A large carton sat on the covered porch of the Welcomes' guesthouse. A note was attached to the top.

Like I thought, I had this. It was finished except for the name on it. I hope it works. If not, let me know and we'll work up something else. —Rob

The object was hard to manhandle out of the box, but Cyrus finally managed it.

Perfect. It was perfect.

# Chapter Six

"Oh, I love that," Abby said.

The Knotty Elves were in the rec room when Abby went down to wait for Miranda to arrive the next day. A stocking, complete with red-and-white stripes and a green cuff at its top, lay on the table before them.

"Which one of you made it? Can I buy it?" Abby touched the soft stocking, thinking of wishes and dreams.

"It's not for sale." June peered at her through her thick glasses. "But we might be able to work out a trade. How many of those crocheted ornaments have you made?"

"Only a few. I just started them the day before yesterday."

"Do you think you can finish six by the time your movie's done?" June exchanged glances with her partners in crime.

Abby considered the timeline. "Sure. Angels? Snowflakes?"

"Anything you like," Odette assured her "And you don't even have to starch them. We can do that."

"It's a deal."

"Well, then, here you go." June pushed the stocking in her direction. "Do you want a name on the cuff?"

"Not a name." Abby frowned. "A message. Maybe just 'Take Two.' Would that work?"

"Oh, easy." June looked over her glasses at Abby, the glance speculative. "We all need a do-over once in a while, don't we?" She drew the stocking back. "We'll have it done by noon and bring it to the carousel today. That's where you're filming, isn't it?"

"It is. I'm excited to see it."

Miranda texted that she'd arrived. Abby said her goodbyes and moved on, still thinking about the carousel.

She'd read about the Christmas Town Carousel as part of her preparation for playing Elaine Garland. She wouldn't get to ride on it—portraying Elaine at eighty precluded it, although she thought the woman would have done it in a heartbeat.

The carousel was beautiful. She'd also seen it yesterday with Cyrus but since they had Jolly with them, they'd been unable to ride. The scenes in a mural on the wall behind it made its riders feel as if they were in a special, exciting place.

The venue had been closed for the morning to allow shooting to go forward, so even though she didn't get to ride, Abby walked around and looked at the animals. A scene was being shot with Cyrus as Seymore Garland playing Santa Claus. Abby sat on one of the benches on the carousel and watched in silence, joining the applause when the scene was completed.

"Of course, I did it in one," he said when Alexis congratulated him on getting it in one take. "How can you screw up Santa Claus?"

Flynn Sullivan, a school counselor and part-time photographer who was Alexis's best friend—and maybe more—had volunteered as Santa at Holly Haven's fundraiser, where Abby had gotten Jolly. He came over to her now, grinning. "Screwing up Santa can be done, can't it, Abilene? I almost did."

She grinned back, remembering when she'd insisted Flynn was too cranky to be Santa Claus. "*Mea culpa*, Flynn. You're a wonderful Santa with the right direction." She elbowed Cyrus when he came to stand beside her. "Almost as good as the old guy here."

The Knotty Elves appeared just before the crew broke for lunch, bringing a gift bag Pru passed to Abby with a conspiratorial wink. Posey's great-grand-daughter Molly followed, carrying totes holding dozens of still-warm cookies.

It was another short day for Abby. Cyrus claimed to have business to attend to this afternoon and evening.

She had a twinge of misgiving, not because they were going to be apart for the evening. But because being apart and not understanding each other's needs had caused their divorce in the first place. She thought of the stocking in the gift bag. It was like a promise she wasn't sure she could keep.

She took the present with her when her scene was finished, and her work was done for the day. She urged Miranda to spend the rest of the afternoon with Dustin and Jolly. And then she rode the Christmas Town Trolley with the Knotty Elves back to Over the River.

"You know," said June, as they entered the Carriage Room together, "most of us are alone by choice, and it works well for us. I spent forty years as a high school principal and I loved it, but when I retired, I was thrilled to be in the company of adults—and even then, only when I wanted to be. When my husband died, I had no inclination to marry again." She stopped, and Abby stopped, too, compelled by the intensity of the older woman's gaze behind her round glasses. "But there's nothing wrong with not wanting to be alone, Abby. It doesn't make you weak or namby-pamby."

"Yes," said Odette, from June's other side, "she did just say namby-pamby. That's how old she is."

"Hey, Abby," called Austen from across the room, "look what got delivered while you were at work."

The box on top of a round table was at least three feet square, maybe larger, and wrapped in the kind of shiny gift wrap she'd seen at For Christmas' Sake downtown.

"There's a note," said Austen. "And it took all I had to keep from steaming it open. Why would anyone seal an envelope and then have it delivered where a bunch of nosy old people live?"

"Thoughtless, indeed." Pru tsked. "If you'd like privacy to open it, dear, you're obviously in the wrong place."

Abby laughed, opened the red envelope with her thumbnail and removed the handmade, folded card. The artwork on the front was lovely. She turned it over to read the name of the artist on the back and then admired the front again.

Her audience mumbled about Abby taking too long to read the message inside. It was wonderful, holding them at bay like that.

"What a lovely card," she said, holding it up so they could see the picture of books under a Christmas tree on its front.

"They sell those at nearly every store in town," said Grace Blessing from another table. "The artist is local. Unless I'm mistaken, that particular card is blank inside. Perhaps someone wrote a note. Hint-hint."

Abby beamed at her. "Oh, do you think so?"

The audience groaned.

She took pity on them—and herself—and opened the card. The note was short and cryptic or would have been if she hadn't understood it.

"I've always known who you are," she read aloud. "No signature."

The Knotty Elves and everyone else in the room exchanged looks.

"Is it from a stalker?" asked Clancy Gallagher, the complex's administrator, who was passing around glasses of wine.

"Oh, the very best kind," Abby assured him, accepting a glass. "Should I open the package, or should I take it to my room?"

"You'll take it to your room over our dead bodies," said Austen pleasantly. "We're all old enough it wouldn't be hard to do, but you wouldn't want it on your conscience, would you, dear?"

Abby pretended to give that some thought, but catcalls made her laugh and apply her trusty thumbnail to the seams of the wrapping paper. It was far too pretty to rip off.

The box had been constructed around the gift, using packing tape. Clancy handed her a knife from a drawer in the kitchen area of the large room. "Don't let them near the knife," he warned, jerking his head at the residents. "They can't be trusted."

That earned him some ribbing.

Abby cut the tape slowly until the side of the box marked front fell loose. "Oh," she said, delight making her voice light and high. "It's a library."

The Little Free Library was painted burgundy and cream, with reading on main painted over its door in blue letters that matched the ones on the front of her teashop. A pile of books was inside, including a couple of signed mysteries by author E. W. Doherty, which was Eli Welcome's pen name. A copy of *Charming Christmas Town*, a beautiful volume of photographic essays by local photojournalist Dean Galloway, also autographed, was at the bottom of the stack.

It was perfect. Perfect.

———❦———

Abby rode the Christmas Town Trolley to the town square, bundled in her puffy white jacket and the colorful scarf the Elves had made for her. The package holding the stocking was looking a little worse for wear, but she carried it anyway. Cyrus had texted her, asking her to have dinner with him at Silver Bells Café.

She responded with, Meet me at the gazebo.

He was waiting when she stepped off the trolley, his Santa Claus suit replaced by his peacoat and newsboy cap and faded jeans. His face lit when he saw her, and she closed her eyes for a second, remembering the note.

"Thank you," she said, when he drew her in for a hug. "It's the nicest present I've ever had."

"Rob Rahilly had it already built, or I couldn't have gotten it done. You really do like it?"

"I love it." She met his eyes, holding his gaze. "I love you, Cyrus Nash, and I know who you are, too." She handed him the gift bag.

"This is nice. I spent this afternoon handing out presents to kids at the hospital in my Santa costume." He opened the gift bag, grinning at the hand-knit red and white stocking. He raised a questioning eyebrow when he read the letters knitted into the cuff. "Take Two?"

"You know the story of the stocking. There's always a note inside."

"Oh, right." He handed her the bag and reached into the stocking, coming out with what looked like a train schedule.

"If you don't feel like driving to St. Johnsbury from New York, you can take the train," she explained. "It takes longer, but it would be less exhausting, and you could sleep or read—I'll have books in the Little Library. I could pick you up at the station, and sometimes I can stay in New York with you. I'm not sure what we'd do if you go on location, but..."

She was interrupted just wonderfully by his lips on hers, where he took his sweet and lingering time convincing her he meant business.

"We'll work it out," he said, the words the same kind of promise she'd made with the stocking. It would fade, become worn, seams tested, but it was a promise, nonetheless. "Even when it's hard. I love you back, Abby Nash."

"When it's hard," she said, feeling as if her heart might burst through her chest. "We'll come back to Christmas Town and do another take in the gazebo. What do you think?"

He rolled the stocking up as small as he could and put it in his pocket along with the train schedule, then wrapped his arm around her to go to the back of the queue waiting their turn to kiss in the gazebo. "I think that's a fabulous idea."

"Hey, the movie's coolest couple. Weren't you two here last night?" Flynn Sullivan was volunteering his photography skills in the gazebo. He grinned at them when they stepped into the structure.

"We were," said Cyrus agreeably. "We're just going through again in case the first take wasn't strong enough. We don't need a picture, though." His smile was as warm as the scarf around Abby's neck. "We know who we are."

The End

# Cocoa Kisses and Marshmallow Hugs

## Book 6: Lights, Camera, Christmas Town

### Tanya Agler

ChelseaBeth Publishing

# Chapter One

*D*ecember 16*th*

Who had time for Christmas with three jobs, two leaky faucets, and a nearly zero bank account?

It was a good thing Zoey Hansen's parents were ensconced in Arizona for her dad's health. They'd be aghast at how little decorating she'd done for her first Christmas as the owner of her childhood home. Their potential disappointment only made Zoey feel their absence that much stronger.

Zoey found her lucky holiday scarf and zipped up her coat, cutting it close in terms of making a dinner meeting with a new client for her graphic design firm. This weekend she'd try to get around to the detailed list of winter prep her father left behind, such as checking on the sump pump and backup generator along with weather stripping the upstairs windows. Then there was the irritable heater that kept giving her fits, no matter what she tried after watching heater repair instructional videos on YouTube during her work breaks. If she could somehow swing the cost of a furnace repair instead of doing it herself, she could spend her spare time unpacking her mother's box of twenty-seven nutcrackers, one for every year of Zoey's life, left behind for her enjoyment. Those should be safe from her rescue kitten, Marshmallow, and vice versa.

Zoey gave Marshmallow a snuggly hug, then put her in her cat bed, and locked her front door.

It was dark. The snow was gently falling, making all of Christmas Town glow in twinkling splendor. At least, all the houses and businesses were decorated for Christmas. Not her house.

Zoey picked up her pace until she turned onto Main Street where she admired the storefront windows. A Victorian village. So adorable! A scene from the North Pole with elves loading Santa's sleigh. How festive! She passed a vendor hawking chestnuts and popcorn, the smells heavenly.

One of Santa's elves stood in front of Comfort and Joy, handing out candy canes. Zoey smiled and accepted hers before setting out for the Silver Bells Café where she'd meet her newest client, Lia Logan, the owner of the local animal rescue shelter.

The restaurant came in view. A crowd was gathered around a group of carolers singing a rousing rendition of *Joy to the World*. Everyone joined in the final refrain before clapping. She placed a dollar in the bucket, the happy song buoying her spirits.

"Zoey Hansen." June Baxter separated herself from the caroler audience, followed by Prudence Parker and Odette King. The trio of knitters was known around town as the Knotty Elves.

*What do the Knotty Elves want with me?*

Volunteers for charity? Cash donations? Attendance at some event? She was too busy, and cash strapped for any of it. Her humbug mood returned.

"Just the person we've been looking for." Pru pushed aside her silver bangs as if to see Zoey better.

"I'm flattered, but I have to decline," Zoey blurted.

"Decline what, dear?" June tittered and plucked the hood attached to her downy soft scarf over her head. "Our earmuffs? They'll keep you plenty warm."

Odette reached into her voluminous velvet bag like Mrs. Claus offering an assist to Mr. Claus and pulled out an adorable pair of earmuffs with snowmen on each ear. "Your mother is worried about you. We assured her we'd look out for you. These will keep you cozy as you head out to your various jobs."

Zoey accepted them. "Thank you. This is very kind." Especially since her attitude was more likely to earn her a lump of coal in her stocking than her wish for a Christmas surrounded by family.

She bit her lip to stem tears from the first present she'd received since her parents left. It was beyond kind.

Odette patted Zoey's shoulder. Her holiday bangles chimed. The fresh lavender sprigs pinned to her bonnet-style wool hat spiced the air with a comforting floral fragrance the same as her words encouraged. "Pass it on and do something for someone who doesn't expect it. That's how friendships blossom."

The Knotty Elves waved goodbye.

Still feeling guilty, Zoey rubbed the soft earmuffs before heading to her meeting.

Zoey entered the Silver Bells Café, relieved she'd arrived ahead of Lia. She found an empty booth by the window near where film director Alexis Dorsey sat. Zoey greeted her and asked the server for coffee.

Zoey extracted her tablet and drawings for Holly Haven, Lia's animal rescue at Two Sticks Farm. Lia had liked the logo Zoey had designed for their mutual friend Dustin's new adventure zipline company and hired her to update the rescue's graphics and website.

A few minutes later, Lia made her entrance, black jacket dusted with animal hair, smile widening when she caught sight of Zoey. "Merry Christmas! I'm so happy you agreed to help the animals." Lia gave Zoey a quick embrace, took off her scarf decorated with gingerbread men and placed it on the hook next to the booth along with her coat.

"Anything for the rescue that matched me with Marshmallow." It didn't matter that Zoey was still paying the vet bills from her kitten's mild case of anemia, which was now cured. "I have a couple of different graphics for you to review." Especially given that Zoey could work for Lia and keep her temporary job as a swing shift stocker at Dockery's and an extra on *The Christmas Carousel* film set. Today she'd ridden on the carousel multiple times during numerous takes. It was a good thing she didn't get motion sickness. She needed that job.

"Since you're charging me a pittance for your graphic design services, I insist that tonight's dinner is my treat." Lia settled into the booth and picked up the menu.

"Thank you." Zoey focused on her designs, stopping when the server conveyed the day's specials and took their orders.

Roasted turkey with dressing for Zoey and hearty lentil soup for Lia.

And then Zoey continued with her pitch. "This new logo will pop out more than your current one on mobile devices."

"Hold that thought. I see someone who expressed interest in adopting a pet. Be back in a few." Lia chuckled and then winked. "I've also always found that leaving the table is the best way to ensure our food is delivered soon."

After she left, Zoey checked her email and found an inquiry about her graphic design business. Yay! She started calculating a bid.

A loud burst of laughter at the front of the café brought Zoey out of her work daze. West Coogan kissed the movie's producer, Lark Matthews.

"Go make your dreams come true. See you later tonight." West left and Lark headed to a booth behind Zoey, the one with Alexis.

Love. Zoey sighed.

Someday when she wasn't so busy, she'd like to find someone. The problem was that few guys compared to her older brother Jonah's best friend, Sean Carmichael. She'd first met him when she was a senior in high school, and Sean had spent Christmas with her family. Sean's brown eyes were the exact color of melted chocolate, and his laugh always sent ripples down her spine. Even living here in Christmas Town, she'd never met someone who loved Christmas as much as Sean. He always threw his whole self into the season. He packed as much as he could into each holiday visit. Reading to residents on Christmas Eve at Over the River Retirement Home. Feeding the animals at Holly Haven. Helping her dad hang the exterior lights. Although her brother kept in touch with him, Zoey hadn't seen Sean in over five years. Had he lost his Christmas spirit the way she had?

"We might have to shut down," Lark's panicked voice rose above *Deck the Halls*, halting Zoey's daydream. "Are you sure Gregg won't be coming back? We were lucky to get him as our director of photography." Even with her hushed tones, Lark sounded distressed.

Zoey could hardly blame her. This production was the biggest thing to hit Christmas Town, even bigger than last year's Bake-Off. The town was benefitting with a boost to the economy, tourism, and jobs. Including Zoey's! If they shut down... That would put her behind on paying those vet bills on time.

"I know lots of people are taking the holiday off," Alexis said. "But I scoured my contacts and called—"

"Here you are." The server arrived with their food just as Lia returned.

Zoey would have to wait until tomorrow to discover what solution Alexis was sharing with Lark and if it would work. As she and Lia continued their review of creative, Zoey tried not to panic as Lark and Alexis left.

After dinner, Zoey hurried along Main Street, the delicious smell of popcorn tantalizing her but that would have to wait until her next paycheck. She waved and thanked the elf for another candy cane while taking care to avoid any icy spots on her way to her house on Angel Avenue. She had just enough time to feed Marshmallow, change for her evening job, and get one quick cuddle session in before she left for Dockery's.

She'd bought her childhood home when her parents moved somewhere that wouldn't aggravate Dad's severe asthma. Yet she feared she might have overextended herself. Things were looking grim. Especially when she rounded the corner and saw her dark, gloomy house.

Something caught her eye in the shadows of her porch. More like two large somethings along with an unfamiliar SUV in her driveway. She hadn't ordered any packages, so who had business at her door at this time of night?

———◈———

Sean stood on Zoey Hansen's darkened porch, petting his dog Cocoa, and wondering where all the Christmas decorations were.

Did he have the right house?

"Sean Carmichael?" A woman's voice cut through the dark.

An angel approached him from the shadows. An angel he recognized. "Zoey?" Relief coursed through him. "Hey, what's it been? Five years?"

"Near about." Zoey joined him on the porch. "I think my porch light burnt out."

"And your outdoor light timer isn't working either." Easy enough to fix. He kept a tight hand on Cocoa's leash so the big dog wouldn't bowl her over with affection. "It doesn't matter."

"It doesn't matter?" Zoey chuckled. "We're standing in the dark."

But the lights from the other holiday displays were enough to reveal Zoey. She'd matured into a stunning beauty with a cute pair of blue earmuffs covering her blond hair. Her eyes—were they blue?—settled on Cocoa. "And who's this handsome fellow?"

"This pretty girl is Cocoa." He gave the brown Chesapeake Bay-Labrador mix a hearty thump.

"You both must be freezing. Come on inside." Zoey passed him, smelling of candy canes. She inserted her key into the lock and paused. "Is Cocoa good around cats?"

"The rescue agency said she is." But Sean was suddenly unsure. "I've never had her around them before. This is our first Christmas together."

"It's my first Christmas with Marshmallow, too." Her gaze went to his dog and then to Sean. "Hold her just in case?"

"Of course."

She unlocked the door and snapped on a light.

Sean's jaw dropped as he held Cocoa back. "Where are all the decorations? The nutcrackers on the fireplace mantel? The Christmas village? The tree?" It was as if the Grinch had snuck in and removed all vestiges of Sean's favorite holiday.

"Where indeed?" Zoey closed the door behind him.

An orange-and-white tabby peeked out from behind the sofa and decided to come forth in an obvious ploy to ensure everyone knew this was her domain. Cocoa investigated the pretty kitten, a wispy creature who lacked in physical stature but had a big personality. She meowed, and Sean knelt beside her, allowing her to sniff his hand. He must have passed her test because she rubbed her lithe body along his leg. And then she did the same with Cocoa.

"That's Marshmallow." Zoey had removed her outer gear and disappeared into the kitchen.

"She likes us." Sean stood. "Good girl, Cocoa. Looks like the rescue agency was right." He snapped off Cocoa's leash, being careful to continue to keep an eye on the animals.

Zoey reappeared, holding a can of cat food, still looking like an angel, if a tired one. "Sorry, Sean, but you caught me at a bad time. I have to feed Marshmallow then leave for my evening position at Dockery's."

"Oh. I should have called first, but everything happened so fast. One minute I was working a job for my stepfather, and the next Alexis called asking if I could get up here pronto and step in for the cinematographer—"

"That will be such a relief for Lark and Alexis." She tucked a lock of long blond hair behind one ear, her smile brightening the room. "For all of us, really. Including me. I was worried because... Well, I'm an extra."

Sean was unexpectedly pleased that his being here made her happier. "Wow. Two jobs."

"Three actually." Her smile faded. Her gaze drifted around the living room, probably looking for the things he'd pointed out were missing.

"Listen, I'm sorry to barge in here without warning and for sticking my foot in my mouth. I was super excited to be back in town and I wanted to say hi before I found accommodations. Frankly, I was hoping to get my Hansen Christmas fix."

"Me, too," she murmured.

"You're obviously busy with work, trying to make ends meet and..." *Way to stick your foot in your mouth, Sean.* "I haven't been in constant contact with your brother Jonah since he started working on that cruise ship."

Her kitten was purring almost loud enough to cover most of the awkwardness.

Sean's phone pinged. He checked his phone and groaned. "Shoot."

She switched the cat food to her other hand as Marshmallow wove through her legs. "Everything okay?"

He kept reading the text. "Alexis hasn't had any luck finding a place for me to stay. She's going to ask her brother if I can sleep on his couch." He glanced at his dog, currently giving herself a back scratch on Zoey's carpet. "I need to text her about Cocoa. Some people are taken aback at her size, but she's a sweetheart."

"You don't have a place to sleep?" Zoey gave each pet a worried look. "Jonah's room is available." She unpeeled the aluminum top of the cat food can.

"Are you sure?" He accepted her offer, happy he'd be spending the holiday in the home he loved. "Thank you. Cocoa and I won't be any trouble."

Zoey glanced at her watch. "I have to change and go to work. Please help yourself to whatever's in the kitchen. And you know where to find the clean linens." A reference to how often he'd visited the Hansen home in the past.

He sent her a grateful smile. "I'm going to enjoy staying at the Hansen Hotel."

"Hardly a hotel." Zoey wrinkled her nose and laughed. "There's no room service, and there aren't any amenities."

But he owed her for the privilege of staying here. "I'll pay whatever you're charging."

She scoffed and shooed at him with her hand. "You're Jonah's friend, and his room is empty."

"The film production company is giving me a stipend. If it helps a Hansen, so much the better." Sean glanced around the living room with fresh eyes. Even without the holiday décor, it looked sparse. There were blank walls and empty spaces where her parents' furniture and decorations used to be.

"You can say it. I haven't replaced much after my parents moved." Zoey sighed. "I've had a few unexpected expenses and could use the extra money, but it doesn't feel right taking money from Jonah's best friend."

"I insist on giving you my hotel stipend. You won't even notice Cocoa and I are here." That brought another laugh, and he found himself wanting to hear more before he returned home. "Thanks, Zoey. Merry Christmas." He held out his hand to shake.

Zoey hesitated, and then laid her hand in his with a gentle but firm grip that had him not wanting to let her go. But he did.

She picked up Marshmallow and gave her a caring caress. "I'll see you on the movie set tomorrow. And…" She looked into his eyes. "I'm happy you're here."

"I'm happy to be here." *With you.*

———

It was almost midnight when Zoey inserted her key in the front door. With a start, she remembered her houseguest in time to stay as quiet as possible.

She'd been so close to sending Sean on his way earlier. And then Odette King's words had come back to her. *Pass it on and do something kind for someone who doesn't expect it. That's how friendships blossom.* Zoey wasn't sure her deed counted as kind now that Sean was paying her to stay in Jonah's room, but Jonah would approve.

She was sure she hadn't imagined that spark when they shook on the deal, but friendship was all they had to offer each other. According to Jonah, Sean lived in Springfield, and her life was here in Christmas Town. She closed the door behind her, somewhat floored that her crush was back in town. Back under the same roof.

She flicked on the living room light and gasped, her mouth dropping open in shock. The room sparked to life with her nutcracker collection on its familiar place on the mantel. Mom had taken most of her other decorations but somehow, Sean had found enough Christmas that it was as if Shelly Hansen would suddenly appear with a plate of warm cookies and a warmer hug.

Marshmallow mewed from a curled position on the couch, her paw resting on a length of gold, sparkly garland.

"Were you and Sean in cahoots?" Zoey whispered, brushing back a tear. A familiar creak sounded on the staircase. "Sean?"

"Busted." Sean came into view, a welcome sight in red flannel pants with Santas all over them and a dark green T-shirt. "I was hoping you wouldn't see this until after tomorrow's filming."

"Why?" She moved to the fireplace to touch the nutcracker her mother had gifted her on her thirteenth birthday. "You must have been tired from your long car trip, yet you did all of this."

Cocoa stumbled down the stairs, yawning. She ambled over to Zoey for a pat, then sat on Sean's foot and gazed up at him lovingly.

Zoey imagined she was staring at him the same way.

"Christmas is my favorite holiday." Sean rubbed Cocoa's ears. "Christmas Town has always reeled me in, hook, line, and sinker. Seemed a shame that there wasn't some of it inside."

Her heart raced. "Are you staying in town after the film shoot then?"

Sean shook his head. "My mother remarried this summer, and I'm working for my stepfather now. She needs me. *They* need me."

"Is that why you gave up your filmmaking career?" Zoey's heart went out to him when he nodded.

He picked up a snow globe on an end table. "After my dad died on Christmas, Mom stopped celebrating the holiday, the holiday my dad loved. We'd take vacations instead. But I missed Christmas. After I met Jonah in college, I jumped at the chance to spend Christmas in Christmas Town. Mom started to vacation without me. Last year, she met my stepfather. They discovered they lived ten miles from each other and haven't spent a day apart since. But...My stepfather made some bad business decisions and had to let staff go. At the same time, my career was floundering. So..."

"You came together for family." In a house where the holiday he loved, the one that reminded him of his father, wasn't celebrated. "You're a good man, Sean."

Marshmallow trotted over to Zoey, purring loudly. Zoey picked her up for a cuddle. There was something about having Sean in the house that made Zoey realize just how morose and lonely she'd been. All work and no play couldn't replace the void that had been left after her parents and brother left.

"Merry Christmas, Zoey." Sean's gaze met hers with that electricity she'd felt when their hands touched.

*Yes, a kiss under the mistletoe would be nice.*

Zoey looked away. She blamed the thought on her childhood crush, her exhaustion, and her addiction to romance movies.

Even so, Sean was turning her first Christmas away from her family into something special, something unexpected.

She just had to keep herself from falling into his sweet arms and making a fool of herself like a love-struck teenager.

# Chapter Two

Outside the barn where the interior shooting was taking place, Zoey arrived at the makeup trailer.

Betsy Anne, the lead hair and makeup artist, was currently applying cake powder to the face of a supporting actor. One benefit of the filming was getting to know Betsy Anne, whose warm yet businesslike demeanor impressed Zoey. Betsy Anne was a model she longed to emulate with her graphic design business.

Betsy Anne nodded at Zoey. "I'm running a few minutes behind, so feel free to hang out at the catering table with the other extras."

Zoey had overslept and skipped breakfast and didn't need a second invitation. Another joy of being an extra was partaking of the delicious food.

Zoey hurried to the craft services tent. The caterer, Faye Burlew, had outdone herself this morning with a fine selection of fruit, miniature omelets, and toast. English muffins and bagels shared space on a holiday tablecloth decorated with candy canes. Nearby, a beverage station offered an assortment of bottled juices and soda along with huge silver urns of coffee and hot water for tea or cocoa. Zoey made a beeline for the coffee.

The production believed in using as many conservation measures as possible, so Faye had set out mugs with the film title on them rather than Styrofoam cups. Zoey filled her mug. Steam curled into the air, the rich aroma reaching her. Faye had learned her culinary skills from the best, her grandmother Posey who owned Christmas Town's favorite diner. Zoey started for the pitcher of creamer when she saw something out of the corner of her eye.

Sean approached the table and stopped short, his arms full of two long boxes stacked on top of each other. This morning he seemed ready to take on the cold weather of Maine with holiday spirit. That wool cap with reindeer on the brim was adorably geeky and merry. His brown gaze settled on her. Recognition and pleasure made his broad face that much more handsome.

She tamped down that spark inside her. He made it quite clear last night he couldn't stay in Christmas Town. It was hard enough saying goodbye to Mom and Dad with the moving van in sight. She couldn't get attached to him, only to say goodbye too.

Still, it was obvious he needed a helping hand. He was Jonah's friend, and friendship crossed state lines.

"How can I help?" she asked, rushing to his side.

"Could you introduce me to the caterer?" Sean's impish smile almost convinced her that one little holiday romance fling wouldn't be a bad thing. She hadn't dated in forever. But she wouldn't do anything to damage their friendship. "When I accepted the cinematography position here, I emailed Gina Banning at The Tea Pot and ordered three dozen gingerbread scones."

"The ones with maple syrup icing drizzled on them?" They were her favorite. "These will put you at the top of Santa's nice list for sure."

As if Sean's thoughtfulness in decorating her house wasn't enough for that.

Zoey spotted Faye heading their way with a tray of breakfast burritos. "Here comes Faye now."

Sean introduced himself and gave her the box of scones then turned back to Zoey. "I don't think I'm paying you enough. That was the best night's sleep I've had in years."

Zoey started laughing. "Pay me extra? You brought gingerbread scones, provided me with professional Christmas decoration services, plus rent money. I'm the one who should be thanking you." She'd given notice at Dockery's last night. They'd assured her they had plenty of staff to pick up her two shifts a week.

Sean's meltable brown eyes were focused on her. "Speaking of decorations, you need a Christmas tree."

For the past few years, Mom and Dad relied on a fake tree. Zoey missed the family trips to Holly Acres Tree Farm, where Dad would always flex his muscles before cutting down the selected Fraser fir. That was another ache that three jobs hadn't been able to fill. "Okay."

"Maybe you and I could find the perfect tree together." Sean's eyes held a hint of promise.

*Or that could be my imagination again.*

"I'd like that," she said, proud of herself for not gushing and embarrassing herself.

---

Sean stood next to Alexis, trying to blend what she was saying about blocking the shot with the emotion they were trying to convey in this scene.

He was nervous about this job. He was qualified, if not extremely experienced. But his mother didn't approve of him working in film and hadn't approved of him leaving on a moment's notice. But Sean couldn't pass up this opportunity or let Alexis down. He'd met her while he was in film school. She'd used interns, him included, to make *Hitching Home*. She was creative, organized and demanding.

Alexis was the opposite of Zoey, who was gentle, soft spoken, and accommodating. He'd never really noticed her much on previous visits. She'd always been shy. There but in the background. Happy to sing Christmas carols with him but busy with her friends while he'd been busy exploring the town. She'd been hustling to keep her family's home, a home that had more meaning to her than it did to him, obviously. But he hadn't realized until he'd set out some decorations how much it felt like home to him, too.

"Sean," Alexis said. "I've rambled enough. What do you think?"

Sean proposed the best angle and depth for the sensitive scene between the child actor who played the younger version of the hero and the actress who played his mother. The scene was where they'd learned of the boy's father's death.

"Quiet on the set." Sean settled behind the camera.

"Roll film," Alexis said. "And...action."

The actors were professionals and worked through the long shots and then the close-ups, including one Sean proposed of having a camera set on the table in front of the actress to intimately capture her range of emotions. Every bit of dialogue touched Sean deeply. His father had died unexpectedly. His mother had struggled to help him heal.

"I think we've got it." Alexis left for the black tent outside the barn to review the footage.

Sean helped move the cameras to a different corner of the barn for the montage involving the carousel repair itself.

"Nice work," Dave, the lighting guru, told him. He wore a really ugly Christmas sweater with snowmen whose yarn arms dangled.

"Thanks. I love film, don't you?"

"I was talking about the scones." At Sean's startled look, Dave clapped a hand on his shoulder. "I'm kidding. You're talented. Thanks for coming."

As the morning wore on, Sean realized how much he'd missed everything about film production. The camaraderie. The determination to capture the emotion of a piece. The thrill of a perfect take. When he and Alexis conferred on the staging of a scene for maximum emotional impact, it was like coming home, much the same way as yesterday when he and Cocoa settled in at the Hansen house.

He pushed that thought aside and ate lunch with Dave and Betsy Anne, two crew members who were dating. He looked for Zoey, but the extras were gathered off-site.

After lunch, Sean and Dave conferred with Alexis, who then gathered the cast and crew. She delivered guidance about her vision for the next scene to the actors and extras. Then she turned to Sean with a thumbs up. "Ready when you are."

The afternoon scenes went well. They were repairing the mechanics of the carousel in the scene, so it wasn't exactly heart-wrenching. But there were close-ups of tools and hands to be navigated around gears and pistons.

Everyone was ready for the mandated break. The caterer, Faye, along with her young daughter, went around carrying trays of snacks and bottled drinks. A few crew members went to the catering tent to see if there were any scones left. Sean wished them luck. From what he'd seen, the scones were the hottest ticket around.

An older woman with silver bangs approached him, brandishing a scone and wide grin. "Are you the young man who had the good sense to buy Gina's gingerbread scones?"

"Yes, ma'am."

Two other women appeared, both with scones in hand. One of them gave him the distinct impression he was back in the principal's office. The other brushed crumbs off her long flowery dress.

"Next time tell Faye so she can bring eggnog," the silver-banged woman said. "It's the perfect accompaniment for these scones."

Her friends nodded in agreement. And then they exchanged introductions.

"People around here call us the Knotty Elves. We've a penchant for knitting." June tapped her round glasses into place and eyed him. Her gaze steady, clear and unflinching. "Where are you staying? We haven't seen you before."

"I'm Jonah Hansen's friend and was lucky enough that he's out of town." Sean grinned. "Zoey's letting me stay in Jonah's room. She and her new kitten Marshmallow welcomed my dog Cocoa and me. She's something else."

All three seemed to perk up at his words.

"Very good taste." Speculation lit Pru's gaze.

"And good common sense," June concurred.

"Unless you meant the kitten was something else?" The lightness in Odette's words harmonized with the soft jingle of her bell bracelet as she nudged her elbow into his side.

"No, ma'am. I meant Zoey." His gaze swept the makeshift studio, looking for her bright blond hair and sunny smile.

"Merry Christmas, Sean." Odette sing-songed, her expression vibrant like her smile. "We hope to see more of you before you go. Ladies, let's find some eggnog."

They conferred about something as they headed to the exit, presumably for a place offering eggnog.

Filming resumed shortly thereafter.

After a few takes, Sean noticed something amiss and cut the scene. "What's that?" Sean pointed at the offending object in his shot. It was red and green and... He squinted. "Is that Posey's Elmer?"

"Good eye." Alexis smiled, visibly relaxing. "Elmer strikes again. Continuity would have discovered it, and we might have had to retake the shot another day, adding to the budget and possibly a delay to the filming schedule." She waved over an assistant, who carried the misbehaving elf away.

Dave sent Sean a thumbs-up, and Sean grinned back.

Maybe he had left his parents in a bit of a lurch to come here. But it was the first bright spot he'd had in months.

And he still had a date with Zoey to choose a Christmas tree.

# Chapter Three

Cocoa was positively adorable, as was his owner.

Zoey had a feeling this trip to Holly Acres Tree Farm after a long day of filming was a bad idea as far as her heart was concerned. What was once a crush on Sean could easily turn to something more when her batteries weren't fully charged. Night had fallen and the tree lot was lit by blazing lights. Everything smelled like Christmas.

"Earth to Zoey." Sean waved his hand in front of her face. "I said, do you see any good trees?"

"Uh, nope." Those magnetic brown eyes captivated her. Sean approached Christmas with a fervor that Elmer the Elf would envy. Some might find that cloying or artificial, but Sean's inner sweetness was as real as the Fraser firs surrounding them. Family cheer had been missing this season. And Sean was filling the gap.

"What about this one?" He pointed to a tree.

She shook her head. "It's too tall. I like the star topper to be visible, so we've always picked a shorter tree."

"Stars, like people, deserve to shine," Sean said, his smile sending flutters through her.

"Oh, that's sweet." Zoey turned to Cocoa and pitched her voice high. *"He's sweet, isn't he?"*

Her tone excited Cocoa. She barked and ran in circles until Zoey and Sean were both entwined in her long leash, bringing Zoey closer to Sean. Close enough to kiss.

Zoey's heart pounded. Her lips parted.

Sean's arms came around her, steadying, for her feet anyway. "For the record, I didn't train Cocoa to do this. But it's kind of nice."

*He might kiss me after all!*

"Ah, so Cocoa's a matchmaker of her own accord?" Zoey laughed, loosening up for the first time in too long. Sean was handsome. Christmas was everywhere. And his dog... "I guess Cocoa's a fan of *101 Dalmatians*." Where two dalmatians ensured their owners fell in love. Zoey laughed again, thinking of Cocoa and Marshmallow doing the same.

Cocoa lurched forward once more. Sean stumbled into Zoey's arms, and they tumbled into a snow drift at the base of a tree.

"Sorry," Sean murmured, smelling of peppermint and winter dreams. "Are you all right?"

"Yes." Although Cocoa decided they were having too much fun without her and leaped on them, trying to lick their faces. "Girl, these aren't the kind of kisses I had in mind."

Sean had managed to wrestle Cocoa off them. He swung around, grinning. "You had kisses in mind?"

Zoey's cheeks heated. *Think fast.* "It's mistletoe season. Every girl has kissing on her mind." And to prove it was no big deal, she quickly kissed his cheek.

Had she sold it? Zoey wasn't sure. If she wasn't already sinking into a snow drift, she might have dove in one.

Sean took it all in stride, laughing and unwinding Cocoa's leash.

She pulled her gaze away to stare at an average tree a few feet away. It wasn't the tallest, the fullest, or the prettiest. It was one of those trees that just endured.

*Like me.*

"Good news." Zoey scrambled to her feet, gathering the shreds of her dignity. "I found the perfect tree."

She brushed off the snow and touched her earmuffs, the thoughtful gesture on behalf of the Knotty Elves. And then she glanced at Sean, who was walking around her choice. He was rubbing off on her. She was starting to see the joy in the season, instead of dwelling on her low bank balance. There was hope for that, after all.

"It's a nice tree," Sean said. "It's growing on me."

"Me, too." Zoey could envision its full potential for filling her living space with beauty and warmth. "It brings nostalgia and heart. We can decorate it with giant white snowflake ornaments, golden bells, and bright colorful balls. There'll be lots of glowing lights. The big bright ones. And my grandma's star. So that anyone who has ever lived in my home or visited knows they can always find their way back."

The instantaneous pull toward this tree reminded her of the way she'd bonded with Marshmallow the second she held the kitten. It was the same way she was starting to feel about the man who stood beside her.

"It's the one," he whispered, his gaze fixed on hers.

---

The snow had stopped.

Downtown Christmas Town looked like a New England holiday, snow-capped postcard with red bows gracing the black lampposts and poinsettias as far as the eye could see. Sean loved this town. The aroma of the roasted chestnuts coming from the street vendor at the corner of the green. The giant tree sparkling with colored lights, its branches extending toward the famous gazebo in the square. The residents waving and greeting him like an old friend.

If he could live anywhere, he'd live here. Zoey was a bonus beyond compare. Earlier at the tree farm, he sensed a change between them. They'd flirted. For a second, he'd even considered kissing her. He hadn't been thinking about selling bicycles or staring at his bedroom ceiling in Massachusetts, unable to sleep because he missed being creative and capturing characters and stories on film.

But now, outside of The Tea Pot with a Christmas tree on the roof of his SUV, Sean did think about those things. The good and the not so great. It had always been his mother and him against the world. Mom needed Sean in her life, too much for him to leave her and his stepfather behind. She'd made the call to bring him home from New York. She'd expressed concern about him leaving for Christmas Town, her worried gaze had drifted to his stepfather.

"I'll stay out here on the bench with Cocoa, the dog," Zoey offered, smiling. "While you get cocoa, the drink."

"Got it." Sean realized he'd been standing on the sidewalk, thinking not moving. "Thanks."

After a quick pat on Cocoa's head, Sean headed toward the entrance of The Tea Pot, the small shop only open for another hour. He dipped his head at three older gentlemen walking toward the coffee and pastry shop.

"Good evening." He stopped and opened the door for them to enter. "Merry Christmas!"

The old man in a faded red hunting cap and flannel jacket lingered behind as the others proceeded toward the counter. "You look familiar." The older man's voice came out in a rasp, the cloud of vapor hanging in the air for a second before evaporating. "Have we met before?"

"I'm here with the film crew, and I'm a friend of Jonah Hansen. I'm staying with his sister, Zoey," Sean offered more information than he would have in New York.

"Now I recognize you." A gnarled hand landed on Sean's shoulder. "You used to volunteer to read at Over the River on Christmas Eve. We don't get too many volunteers your age over there."

Sean didn't like tooting his own horn. But he remembered the gentleman now, from years past and his presence on the set today by the Knotty Elves. "Barty, isn't it?"

"Yep, and I'm here with my best friends, Gus and Marv." Barty extended his hand, and Sean gave him a hearty handshake. "There's nothing like friendship to bind people together."

"Yes, sir. Jonah and I go way back. Some of my best Christmas memories involve being here."

"The town is open all year for full-time memory-making. Something to keep in mind." Barty tipped his faded red cap and joined his friends inside The Tea Pot. "Merry Christmas, Sean."

"Merry Christmas, sir." Sean smiled as the older gentleman left him. And then, Sean paused.

He could see himself here, becoming a part of the fabric of the town and its traditions. He could even imagine a life with Zoey here. But there'd be an ache in his heart from two losses—his mother wouldn't be near and after this film ended, neither would the opportunities to pursue his passion. He was stuck at a crossroads, unsure which path to take.

A family, their arms filled with wrapped packages, slipped past Sean as he held the door open before he realized he was letting the cold air inside.

"Sean?" Zoey called from the bench. "Are you okay?"

He gave her a wave and a nod before heading inside.

When Sean attempted to pay for his and Zoey's drinks, the attendant shook her head. "You're Sean, right?" She prepared two cups of hot cocoa, heavy on the whipped cream and chocolate shavings, and presented them to him. "The Three Wise Men said to take good care of you. Their treat. Merry Christmas."

"Merry Christmas." He looked for the elderly men, but they'd gone. He made his way outside.

"Sean! Over here." Zoey came from the direction of the town square, with Cocoa walking jauntily beside her. Her cheeks were bright and rosy. "I saw an old friend from high school and his fiancée. Her name is Lane and she asked me to contact her tomorrow about updating her architect firm's logo and website. Isn't that wonderful?"

"And I ran into Barty and two other men who paid for these." He exchanged the cups of cocoa for his dog's leash. "It's our lucky night."

"That was so sweet of them. People like Lane and the Three Wise Men are the reason I didn't move to Arizona with my parents. Well, and Christmas. I do love Christmas. I hope Jonah reconsiders and doesn't sign another contract with the cruise ship next year." Zoey sighed. For a minute, it looked as though her eyes were about to tear up. "Christmas Town is one-of-a-kind. If you hadn't come to stay at the Hansen Hotel and insisted on looking for a tree, I'd be working tonight, and I'd never have talked to Lane. You've reminded me to enjoy the season. Thank you."

Her smile was as glorious as the lights surrounding them.

And it seemed to light which branch of the crossroads he should take.

# Chapter Four

Inside the barn, which was serving as the staging area for today's exterior scene, Zoey yawned on account of the early call.

Alexis began delivering instructions to the larger than usual group of extras. It seemed like every resident of Christmas Town was appearing in the recreation of the town's Thanksgiving parade, either on the sidelines or as a participant.

Today was a particularly important scene where heroine Lisa's longing for John forced her to confront her true feelings. Although Lisa discovered she couldn't rewrite the past, she could write her own future.

Zoey shifted, suddenly uncomfortable at how closely that could apply to her own life.

"When our heroine Lisa locates the missing lord-a-leaping," said Alexis, consulting the clipboard her assistant handed her, "the maids-a-milking and dancers all walk in a straight line behind Lisa while those on the sidelines move to your spot on the parade route. Stay right here until we call you to assemble in your groups. Any questions?"

There were none.

Zoey glanced at her maids-a-milking costume. The long, ice-blue dress with accompanying white apron was rather loose-fitting, and she hoped she didn't trip over the hem. Zoey held a wooden bucket, which had candy inside for her to toss to children during the parade.

The Knotty Elves approached her.

"Good morning, Zoey. We heard you and Sean had a wonderful evening." Prudence thanked the props master for a chair and slipped what looked to be a colorful candy tin into his hands. They had to be on the sidelines for filming, but Zoey had a feeling they would always be in the thick of everything that was happening.

"Good morning." Zoey decided to stay in keeping with her costume and curtsy.

"Well, you're just the person we were looking for." June unraveled a plush scarf, revealing her thin neck. A cartoon cardinal tangled in Christmas lights was on her eggshell-colored sweater. The words: *'Tis the season for Preening* were embroidered in swirly cursive below the bird. June added, "We made fruitcakes yesterday at Over the River, and we have one more."

"Thanks, but I've never acquired a taste for fruitcake." Zoey held out her bucket. "Not only that, I have no place to put it."

"Sorry, dear. June should have asked straightaway for your parents' new address." Odette removed her wool bucket hat and patted the fresh lavender sprigs she'd twined around her bun. Her bracelets jingled, a counterpoint to the excited chatter all around them. "Your father loves our fruitcake. We wanted to send him one."

"That's so sweet." Zoey felt a pinch of longing in her chest for a family Christmas. "I wish I could deliver it in person."

"The first holiday without loved ones is always the hardest." Odette laid her hand on Zoey's arm, her long fingernails painted with individual candy canes. "I've known your mom for years, and she'd want me to give you a pep talk. You're a strong woman, Zoey Hansen. I'm glad you decided Christmas Town is where you belong. She'd also want me to give you this."

Odette pulled her into an unexpected hug.

*This.* This was another reason Zoey hadn't left Christmas Town. Everyone supported each other. A little schmaltzy perhaps, but Zoey craved moments like these. Snow, schmaltz, and support. That had made the decision to stay almost a no-brainer.

"Excuse me." Sean's layer of stubble made him that much more attractive, but she noticed dark circles around his eyes. Had he not slept well?

"Is everything okay?" she asked.

Sean looked as if he had something important to say. She waited patiently. He held a dark folder to his chest. "Marshmallow, Cocoa, and I missed you at breakfast this morning." His voice was husky, and his eyes were full of longing.

She smiled, thinking she'd missed seeing them too. "The extras had to report earlier than usual today."

Odette looked at Sean, then Zoey. She smiled and dug into her voluminous knitting bag. "Sean, you'll need these when you're not working that camera." She handed him a pair of earmuffs.

"These are like Zoey's," Sean said, examining them. "Thank you."

"They're a matched set," Odette crooned, sashaying toward her chair.

Sean cleared his throat. "I...uh...I need to get back to work." He walked away then glanced over his shoulder, a long, lingering gaze that caused the good kind of goose bumps.

Zoey stood there, stunned. So much so that she missed her stage call.

—— ❁ ——

Sean settled behind the camera for the ninth take of the day. There was a reason crowd scenes were so difficult to film, and they'd encountered too many of them. Missed cues. The clouds covering the sunlight at the wrong moment. A firetruck's siren piercing the air in the middle of a take.

In the distance, he saw extras returning to their marks, including the group of maids-a-milking, all holding their wooden milk buckets. His gaze sought out Zoey, who looked especially lovely today with her halo of blonde hair and pink, rosy cheeks. It had taken everything in him to head upstairs last night when he'd wanted to kiss her goodnight.

"Action!" Alexis called.

This time, everything went off without a hitch.

While production reset the cast, Sean handled a briefing with the drone operator. He seemed to know what he was doing and what Sean and Alexis wanted.

Sean checked the schedule for the rest of the day. He needed to call home, but it wasn't going to be a quick conversation. He hummed along to the faint chorus of *Holly, Jolly Christmas.*

Faye and her daughter rolled around a cart with a choice of holiday snack mix in green cellophane wrap tied with reindeer ribbons or Christmas cookies in red bags. Sean chose a bell sugar cookie with peppermint frosting. By the time Betsy Anne refreshed Macy Winter's makeup and spritzed on some extra hairspray, Alexis had returned. Everyone assumed their places. Sean and the continuity supervisor checked that no wrappers or water bottles were in sight.

"Action," Alexis called.

"Wait. Sorry." The drone operator trotted over to the drone. "Elmer wanted to fly without a ticket."

Sure enough, the elf sat on top of the drone, which was only a little larger than a Roomba vacuum.

"Holy smokes, that was a close call," Alexis said, completely sincere. "Whoever the elf prankster is, they should at least have given Elmer a seat belt."

Zoey was right. Everyone was important and caring in Christmas Town. Even of miniature elves.

# Chapter Five

After a successful afternoon presentation at Tanner and Dunn Architect Firm culminating in a new retainer, Zoey walked into Posey's Diner.

Since Sean came back to town, everything was going right for her. She'd even been asked to meet with Alexis. Maybe she'd get a speaking role in the film. The atmosphere in Posey's was festive and lively, elevating her mood.

Zoey spotted Alexis, Lark and Faye waiting for her at a back booth. She hadn't been expecting the others. Suddenly, her steps faltered. "Am I... Did I do something wrong?"

"No," Lark said. "Have a seat."

Zoey removed her coat and sat while Lark placed a sheet of paper on the table with scribbles and a sketch.

Before Zoey could look at it, Posey came over, pencil in hand. "Merry Christmas! Always love seeing my granddaughter taking a break." She winked at Faye. "Molly's having a blast in the kitchen decorating sugar cookies for tomorrow." Posey raised her pencil. "Will this be separate checks?"

Lark shook her head. "It's business, so only one tab, and it comes to me."

Zoey looked beyond Posey and found Elmer tucked away on an upper tree branch on a shelf across the room. "I'm glad Elmer's no worse for wear considering yesterday's adventure."

"That imposter..." Posey laughed, shaking her head. "My Elmer hasn't left this dining room, much less this building in decades. Consider your free piece of peppermint pie part of your meal."

242

"Thanks." Zoey grinned, feeling the need to converse because she was nervous. "No need to hide him again. But what's this rumor I hear about you—"

Across from her, Faye made a quick, cutting motion across her throat.

"—retiring?"

Posey made a growling sound deep in her throat. "All I did was sell my house and move to Over the River." Posey snapped her order pad closed, even her beehive vibrated on her head. "No need to order. I know what you ladies need for dinner. And I retract pie for you, Zoey."

"I'm sorry," Zoey called after her, repeating to Faye, "I'm sorry. I'll pay for everyone's meal if Posey serves us liver and onions."

That garnered a laugh.

And then Lark got right down to business. She slid the scribbles toward Zoey. "We'd like your opinion about this."

Zoey started to sweat. This felt like an unexpected algebra test. "Pixie Pop Productions. That's a great name, but you have some issues with the main graphic. This pixie can't look like Tinkerbell. Her image is trademarked." When they didn't say, *"Well, duh,"* she continued. "I'm not sure if you want a literal interpretation of a pixie or something else, something playful could be named Pixie, like a kitten or something." She thought of sweet Marshmallow and smiled. "Whatever you want your audience to think about when they see the logo should influence the colors, fonts, and design styles you use."

Lark, Alexis, and Faye exchanged glances. And smiles.

"Did I... Did I pass?" Zoey asked.

"Yes." Lark reclaimed the drawing and put it in her tote. "I'm starting a production company. Me, Alexis, and Faye."

Posey delivered four mugs of hot cocoa to the table, mumbling, "Retirement," before marching away.

"We'd like to offer you a position as our graphic designer," Lark said as if they hadn't been interrupted. "We need a brand package—the works for our company. We'll also need film design—logos, titles and credits, promo materials for each film. You get the idea. You could still take on other freelance projects, but this would be a full-time job with benefits."

"You had me at *we'd like to offer you.*" Zoey was practically hyperventilating. Of course, she was going to say something stupid.

But they laughed as if Zoey was already one of them.

She glanced out the front window and saw Sean walking past with Cocoa.

Over the past few days, she hadn't just reclaimed her holiday spirit. She'd also reconnected with the part of herself that made things happen. She no longer sat back and kept her feelings to herself. She spoke up. She laughed. She was more than just the part-time help or an extra on set.

She was... She was... Growing into her own and...

Sean disappeared from sight.

She was falling in love with Sean.

Zoey scooted out of the booth and stood. "Ladies, I accept your offer, contingent on a formal contract with everything spelled out." Yes, that was businesslike. "But I have to tell someone something, and it can't wait."

She donned her coat and her earmuffs, a smaller version than the pair Sean wore, and she hurried out the door.

Odette was right. Zoey was a strong, independent woman who could make it on her own. But sharing her life with someone, especially someone who encouraged her to connect with the world around her, didn't take anything away from that. It only made everything sweeter, right down to those Marshmallow hugs that had turned her world around earlier this year.

———

Sean patted the backpack with his early Christmas present for Zoey.

"What do you think, Cocoa?" he asked his dog, who was sniffing the snow covering the bushes near the gazebo. The line wasn't too long tonight, somewhat surprising, as even he knew the town legend that couples who kissed there in the month of December would find their happily-ever-afters.

"Sean!" Zoey exited Posey's Diner.

The Knotty Elves held the door open for her, exchanging enthusiastic greetings and laughter.

In no time, Zoey reached him, cheeks rosy, slightly out of breath. "Merry Christmas... Um, hi, Cocoa."

His dog wasted no time shimmying up to her for some affection.

"Merry Christmas." Sean reached into his backpack and pulled out a wrapped present. "I got this for you. I know it's early. But I saw it and thought of you."

"An early Christmas present? I love it!" Her blue eyes sparkled.

And he knew. Sean knew he wanted to spend the rest of his life with this woman in this town. The difficult conversation he'd had earlier with his mother had been the right path to take.

Sean's pulse raced, and he stopped fighting the wave of emotion. He gave into it. He was falling in love with Zoey Hansen.

But first, he had to explain his gift. "My dad loved Christmas," Sean said in a soft voice. "Dad said it was because Christmas was the time of year when people let their guard down and shined a light on the world, a light powered by love for their fellow man. And my gift... Go ahead and open it."

Zoey unwrapped the small box, revealing a small, red Christmas light bulb. Her smile softened, all happiness and mush. "It's a light."

He took the bulb out of the box and flipped a small switch, making the bulb glow red. "When I showed up at your house the other day, there wasn't a single light on."

"And now, you're giving me light, literally and figuratively. But..." Tears flowed down Zoey's cheeks, spilling from her big blue eyes. "Did something go wrong with the film? Are you leaving?"

"No." Sean inhaled a deep breath and slowly exhaled. "I talked with my mom today. She and my stepfather accepted my resignation. She told me she raised me so I could live my life on my terms, not hers. I put in my time to help my stepfather's business get back on its feet, but she knew I wasn't happy."

"That must have been so hard for you." Zoey laid a hand on his arm. "I know how hard it is to choose between your family and the place you're meant to be."

He nodded. "I'm not supposed to tell anyone yet until the end of the film. But I...I'm meant to be here. In Christmas Town. With you, I hope."

Zoey's face clouded with a mixture of hope and confusion. "I hope, too, but... What will you do when the film is over?"

Sean leaned close to whisper in her ear. "I'm going to work for Lark, working with Alexis." He drew back.

"You, too?" Those blue eyes glowed brighter than any of the Christmas Town lights. "They just asked me to come on board as the in-house graphic artist."

"Shh." Sean put a finger to her lips.

They both laughed, moving closer.

"You were the first person I wanted to tell," Zoey whispered.

"I wanted to tell you this morning when you were dressed like a pretty milk maid." He gave into impulse and sifted his fingers through her silky blond hair. "I..."

"I think I'm falling in love with you," Zoey said, leaning into his touch. "You and Cocoa."

Sean nodded. "We're a package deal."

"Don't forget Marshmallow." She took the light bulb he'd given her and held it close to her palm.

"Do you know what this means?" Sean shifted his gaze toward the gazebo.

"I'm game." Zoey threw herself into his arms. "But first, a dress rehearsal."

Sean lowered his lips to hers, the taste of peppermint, sugar and everything sweet about Christmas flooding him with happiness.

Cocoa barked and bumped into their legs, probably intent upon tangling them up again.

"Girl, you already worked your matchmaking magic," Zoey told her.

"Want to wait in the gazebo line?" He tilted his head toward the crowd.

Zoey stared into his eyes. "You know, we have the entire season for that. I'd rather spend tonight with you and Marshmallow and Cocoa, creating special memories in front of our tree." Zoey laid her head on his shoulder. "Marshmallow hugs and Cocoa kisses. So many possibilities."

"Let's go home." Sean wrapped his arm around Zoey. "We'll make this the best Christmas ever."

She grinned. "Until next year."

The End

# Red, White & Blue Christmas

## Book 7: Lights, Camera, Christmas Town

### LeAnne Bristow

ChelseaBeth Publishing

# Chapter One

*D*ecember 19*th*

      Christmas lights and decorations lined the driveway through the Pine Tree Inn and RV Resort.

Griffin Walker walked past the motel part of the inn and on to the RV section. Most of the RVs and camp trailers were lit up, too, or at the very least, had Christmas decorations in front of their yard. There were three exceptions. The two large motorhomes that served as his temporary home and his boss', and the fifth-wheel camper parked next to his slot.

Griffin would have assumed the trailer was empty except for the fact that he sometimes saw a light coming from the windows when he got home from working as the head of security for the film production company making a movie in Christmas Town. He'd been curious about the occupant. Whoever he or she was. There was a ramp that led up to the door of the RV, implying that whoever lived there wasn't as agile as a cat.

He reached his RV just as the door to the fifth-wheel opened. Griffin suppressed a grin. Curiosity satisfied. His neighbor had emerged from seclusion. And then Griffin's smile faded.

An elderly man wearing burgundy slacks, a blue-checked wool shirt and a thin coat was trying to wrangle a walker through the narrow trailer door. The walker wasn't folded. It was fully extended.

Griffin hurried up the snowy ramp to the man's door. "Can I help you?"

The man's bushy eyebrows bunched together. "I can manage."

Griffin smiled gently. "I know you can, but why not take advantage of help when it's offered?"

"Hmph. That's what my granddaughter says, too. I just want to go to the store and get some milk." The man had just managed to get the walker out the door and onto the ramp when a phone inside began to ring. He left the walker where it was and levered himself back inside to answer, slamming the door in Griffin's face.

Muffled voices were all Griffin heard. It was cold. And snowing. Yet, Griffin couldn't in good conscience leave without making sure the man was safe, staying or going.

"You," the old man called to Griffin a few minutes later. "Get that contraption back in my house."

"Is the door open?" Griffin folded the walker in half. The door wasn't locked. He entered the trailer, shutting the door behind him. Pictures decorated the walls and lace doilies were draped over the cushions of the sofa. It looked like a home. "No Christmas decorations?"

"Humbug." The man's gruff voice was painted with sarcasm. He pointed to the only empty spot inside the cramped trailer. "It goes right there."

Griffin wasn't put off by the man's grumpiness. As a physical fitness trainer for people with disabilities, he worked with a lot of elderly people. He knew from experience that for many of them, their attitude was a defensive mechanism. "Weren't you leaving?"

"I was going to get some groceries, but my granddaughter is on her way over with them."

Griffin's shoulders relaxed a little. He was glad to know that the man wasn't completely alone. He introduced himself and held out his hand.

"Murray Anderson." The man shook Griffin's hand, eying the dark blue baseball cap with the United States Navy emblem Griffin was wearing. "You a squid?"

"I was, yes, sir." Griffin laughed. "I've been out of the Navy for four years, now."

The older man nodded. "How long were you in?"

"Eight years," he answered.

"Why'd you leave?" Murray looked like the iciness of their first encounter was melting.

But Griffin wasn't fooled. He was being tested, allowed to stay, and possibly help as long as he passed. "My dad was having some health issues, so I wanted to be available if he needed anything." Griffin glanced out the window. He didn't want to outlast his welcome. "I'm staying next door if you need anything."

"Hmph." The man's eyes narrowed. He nodded toward the door. "My granddaughter will be here soon."

Obviously, the man wanted him to leave. Griffin scanned the cramped trailer and spotted a pen lying on the table. He picked it up and wrote his number on the back of a piece of junk mail. "Call me if you need anything."

"I won't but thank you." That last was begrudgingly given.

Griffin made his exit, pulling the door closed behind him. He trudged through the snow to the RV that was his temporary home. The motorhome was large and roomy, especially compared to the older model fifth-wheel Murray lived in.

Christmas Town was a nice place, but it wasn't equipped to accommodate the large number of people involved in shooting a movie. Actors, directors, producers, assistants, managers, camera operators, sound, lighting, art, costumes, hair, make-up, caterer...the list went on and on. And they all needed a place to stay.

Griffin was lucky. Some of the crew members had to stay in neighboring towns and commute every day. Lark Matthews, the producer, wanted to make sure that Griffin was close to the set, so she'd managed to talk the owner of the RV into letting him use it during filming. Being the head of security for a film had some perks, at least.

He changed into a pair of flannel pajama bottoms and sat down in the U-shaped dinette area with his laptop. The screen lit up and he opened a website for real estate in the Los Angeles area. He'd been looking at homes for months but hadn't found what he was looking for. The truth was, he didn't really know what he wanted.

Growing up in a military family, then serving in the military himself, he'd never had what he'd call a permanent home. He moved to LA when his father had some health issues. But now that he was better, his parents had sold their home, invested in a catamaran and were sailing the world. It wasn't that they didn't love him. They were taking advantage of life while they still could.

Griffin didn't give much thought about where he was stationed...*living*. LA seemed just as good a place as another. At least, that's what he thought until he visited Christmas Town.

For the last two weeks, he'd observed the small town on his early morning jogs. He'd never been in a place that seemed so welcoming and friendly. Sure, the town oozed with Christmas spirit. With a name like Christmas Town, that was a given, but it was more than that. He suspected the town was like that all year long.

Realization struck him. That's what he'd been missing. What he wanted was a place that felt like home. As a certified physical fitness trainer, he often trained actors and actresses while on location for the production company, but what he really wanted to do was open a fitness facility for people who weren't comfortable going to a traditional gym. Disabled veterans. Adults and kids with special needs. Elderly people.

Until he could build up enough clientele to be a full-time fitness instructor, he was stuck working for the movie industry...and stuck in LA. Could he find a place like Christmas Town on the outskirts of Los Angeles? He expanded his search area, but most of the homes were well out of his price range.

A loud knock at the door rattled the windows. It must be Lark. Or Alexis. Besides the producer and the director of the film, no one else ever contacted him outside of business hours.

Before he could get to the door, a loud voice called, "Christmas Town Sheriff. Open the door."

# Chapter Two

D ale Anderson could hear someone moving inside the motorhome. Her hand instinctively touched the weapon at her side. At least once a week, her grandfather called to report squatters at the Pine Tree Inn and RV Resort. For once, it looked like he was correct.

The door opened slightly, and a face appeared. Confusion clouded his hazel eyes, but not fear or guilt. Dale relaxed a little.

"Can you step outside, please?" She backed off the porch to allow the man some space.

"Is there a problem, officer?" He opened the door and stepped out of the motorhome onto the snowy ground with only a pair of socks on his feet.

At least Dale didn't need to worry about him trying to run away. "What's your name, sir?"

"Griffin Walker."

Dale kept one hand on the radio clipped to her belt while she did a quick inventory of his identifying characteristics. *Six foot. Square jaw. Crisp cut, short brown hair. Cowlick on the right. Steady gaze. Determined? No. Resigned. Nose might have been broken. Muscular. No stranger to the gym.* "Mr. Walker, this is private property. Do you have permission from the owner to be here?"

"Of course."

She arched one eyebrow. "Do you mind if I contact the owner to verify that?"

He rubbed his hands together against the cold. He only wore a T-shirt over those broad shoulders.

*Posture: military.*

He drew a breath. "Honestly, I don't know the owner. My boss made all the arrangements. I can give you her number and she can put you in touch with the owner."

Dale didn't need the owner's number. She had it. Dean Galloway.

"Who's your boss?" She pulled a notepad out of her pocket.

"Lark Matthews, the movie producer," he said, not the least bit impatient or disrespectful.

Relief rushed through her. She hadn't wanted to arrest a man in his stocking feet. The filming of a movie in Christmas Town was all anyone could talk about. Every room in town had been rented out. It didn't surprise her that Dean Galloway had offered the use of his motorhome.

"You're with the film company?"

"Yes." He crossed his arms over his chest, causing his biceps to bulge under the long-sleeved T-shirt he was wearing. It wasn't a look-at-me move.

But she was looking.

Strictly as an on-duty officer. Or not.

Dale glanced at Griffin again. He was tall. Built. And had the kind of rugged good looks that made women swoon. "You're an actor then?"

He gave her an amused look. "No. I'm the head of security."

Now Dale understood his amusement. "It wouldn't look good for the head of security to get arrested for trespassing."

"It would not," he said without a trace of amusement. "Would you like Lark's number?"

She shook her head. "That's okay. I know how to get in touch with her if I need to. Sorry to bother you. Have a good night." She turned away, noting her grandfather peeping out his trailer window.

"Wait. Don't you need my ID? For the report?"

Dale pressed her lips together. He was familiar with procedure, too. That meant he was more than hired muscle. He was smart. "Technically speaking, this is all off the record."

His gaze swept over her uniform. Over her. And not dispassionately, which was odd. In uniform, she was usually asexual, annoying to folks more than anything. "Meaning, you just got off duty. What brought you out here?"

The door of the fifth-wheel trailer opened. "Are you arresting him, Dale?" Her grandfather's voice was high-pitched, strained, like her patience with him lately.

"No, Grandpa," she called. "He's got permission to be here."

Griffin chuckled. "I guess that answers my question."

"Sorry." She shrugged, outwardly calm, she hoped. For some reason, she didn't want Griffin to have a bad opinion of her. "Ever since his hip surgery, all he does is sit around and watch detective shows. He's a retired cop. And you were probably the first real excitement he's seen in a while."

"That's okay." Griffin smiled. "Better safe than sorry."

The smile he gave her shot straight to Dale's heart. Most men would have been irritated, if not downright angry, about being accused of trespassing. It was odd talking to him out here in the cold and shadows. Odd because she didn't want their conversation to end.

A strangled cry, followed by a thud, could be heard next door.

"Grandpa!" Dale rushed over to her grandpa's yard.

Her grandfather was sprawled in the snow on the ramp, his walker nowhere in sight.

"Don't move him," Griffin cautioned, and Dale stilled, because he was right. Her emotions—her fear—were getting the best of her. Then Griffin asked, "Murray, did you hit your head?"

"I'm fine." Her grandfather propped himself up on his elbows on the snowy ramp, frowning. "Well, don't just stand there, squid. Help me up."

Griffin knelt down next to her grandfather, carefully checking him for injuries.

"You're not fine, Grandpa." Dale choked back a sob and struggled to keep from hyperventilating. Her pulse thundered in her ears and her breath came in short gasps.

Griffin assisted her grandfather to his feet and escorted him into the trailer.

Dale stood. Hands fisted. She wore a badge. Officers in uniform didn't cry. A moment later, Griffin touched her shoulder. "He's okay. Are you?"

"No." She let out a shaky breath. "I'm sorry. Throw bad guys with guns in front of me and I never blink. My grandpa falls down and I turn into a whimpering mess."

He cocked his head. "Christmas Town has a lot of shoot-outs?"

She gave a nervous laugh. "No. But I saw my share of them in New York."

He rubbed the top of his arms with his hands. She'd forgotten he was out here in his jammies.

"You were on the force in New York City?"

"Queens. For six years." She looked at the open door to the trailer. "Can you help me get him to my patrol car?"

"I'm not going to the hospital, Dale Marie Anderson," her grandfather bellowed from inside. "So, if that's what you're thinking, you can just forget it."

Dale hurried into the trailer with Griffin right behind her. "I want to have you checked out, just to make sure."

"I don't think that's necessary." Griffin walked over to where her grandfather was sitting on his favorite chair. "Murray, you'll tell her if something starts to hurt, right?"

"Nothing hurts," her grandfather barked, adding in a quieter voice, "Just my pride, squid."

Griffin turned to Dale. "If it'll put your mind at ease, I can call Stefan Adamidis. He's the EMT on set. Maybe he can come check him out."

Dale draped a fleece blanket across her grandfather's lap. "No need. I have Sophie's number."

"Sophie?" Griffin gave her a puzzled look.

"Sophie Banning. She's a trauma nurse at the hospital and her husband is the surgeon that replaced Grandpa's hip."

He shook his head. "I guess it's true what they say about small towns. Everyone knows everyone."

She laughed. "For better or worse, yes."

Griffin gave a brief nod. "Since you have everything under control, I'm going to head back to my RV before I end up in the ER with frost-bit toes."

Dale's gaze dropped to his sock feet, now wet from melted snow. "Oh. I'm so sorry! Thank you for all your help."

"No problem. Good night, Murray." He turned his gaze and smile to Dale. "Good night, Dale. Merry Christmas."

Heat flushed her neck. "Merry Christmas."

She stared at the door for a long time after he left.

# Chapter Three

The next morning, Griffin waited in line to grab a scone and a cup of coffee inside The Tea Pot. His early morning jogs always ended here. He could wait until he got to the film set to eat, since Faye Burlew, the set's caterer, always had plenty of great food, but he enjoyed visiting The Tea Pot every morning. From its mismatched wooden tables and chairs to the antique snowshoes on the wall, the place hummed with the feel of an old-fashioned Christmas.

In truth, he enjoyed everything about the small town. And if he happened to run into one of Christmas Town's law officers, that wouldn't bother him, either. He'd thought about Dale all night. Her green eyes. Her careful smile that deepened into dimples.

"Good morning. Your usual?" Gina, the owner of The Tea Pot, greeted him.

"Yes, ma'am." He heard a trio of harmonizing to the last lines of *Let it Snow* behind him and turned to see three older women congratulating each other on their perfect pitches. He tipped his baseball cap toward the caroling ladies' table. "Good morning, ladies."

He'd met the Knotty Elves the first time he'd come into the shop, but he couldn't remember which one was which.

"We hear you had some excitement last night." One of the ladies squeezed honey into her tea with precision and eyed him over the rims of her round glasses.

"Huh?"

"Murray Anderson," another one of the ladies answered. The bells on her bracelets jingled in time to the clack of her knitting needles. "Lucky for Dale that you were there when he fell."

"Poor Dale." The third Knotty Elf paused her teal knitting needles long enough to reach up and fluff her silver hair. "She's tried so hard to encourage him to get out of the trailer since his surgery, but he's a stubborn man."

"Pru is right." The second Knotty Elf angled her knitting needles at him and eyed him thoughtfully. "Maybe you can get him out and about. You're strong enough. And Murray used to come to game night at Over the River."

"That's a wonderful idea, Odette." The first lady pointed chin dipped decisively in approval. "Murray's been cooped up so long, he's forgotten why he moved to Christmas Town in the first place."

Griffin remembered her name now. June. Her accomplices, Prudence and Odette, watched him too. Their holiday spirit was on bold display from their colorful sweaters to their themed accessories. Yet not even the sparkle in Pru's snowflake print scarf dimmed the clever glint in her gaze. He shifted on his feet. "Why do you think he'd listen to me?"

Pru raised her eyebrows beneath her bangs. "He did try to have you arrested. If nothing else, you can use that to make him feel too guilty to say no."

His mouth dropped open. "How did you know that?"

The women all returned to their knitting, ignoring his question. Griffin looked at Gina.

Gina put the lid on his coffee and handed it to him. "Don't ask me. But if you hang out in Christmas Town very long, you'll learn two things. One, we watch out for each other. And two, not much happens around here that the Knotty Elves don't know about. Their spy network rivals the CIA."

"I can see that," Griffin said as he received his change.

He thought about Murray sitting in that tiny trailer. On his way to the exit, he stopped by the Knotty Elves' table. "I'll see if I can talk Murray into taking me on a tour of Christmas Town."

"Lovely idea." Odette grinned. "It wouldn't hurt Dale to accompany you, too. She needs... Well, we'll let you figure that out."

The thought of spending more time with Dale was definitely appealing. He nodded at them. "Merry Christmas, ladies."

He stepped out of The Tea Pot and continued down the sidewalk, tucking his scone in his pocket. His breath came out in white puffs and the cold air burned his lungs, but he found it invigorating. His early morning jogs seemed so much nicer in the snow than on the sidewalks of LA.

Just as he reached the end of the building someone came around the corner and smacked into him, knocking his coffee cup out of kilter.

"Oh." The wide, green eyes of Dale Anderson met his gaze with horror. "I'm so sorry."

"Didn't get me. All is good."

"Are you sure?" She pulled off her gloves, then one of his, and took his bare hand, examining it.

Shots of electricity traveled up his arm where she touched him. Her eyes were almost as green as the Christmas tree in the square across the street and filled with concern. This was... She was... As unexpected as she'd been last night.

"Let me buy you another cup of coffee." She'd obviously been out for a morning run as well. Her long dark hair was pulled into a messy bun and was poking up out of the center of the gingerbread-decorated beanie she wore. She returned his glove.

"Don't worry about it. There's plenty of coffee on set." He moved away from the street corner where anyone in The Tea Pot could see them to stand closer to the edge of the vacant bank building. Without the physical exertion of jogging, the cold was beginning to seep through his fleece-lined jacket, and the building provided a bit of windbreak as well as privacy from the inquisitive Knotty Elves.

She followed his example and sought shelter near the building, too. "If coffee is on set, why do you buy it in town?"

He touched the white paper bag in his pocket. "The scones. They're amazing."

Dale laughed, revealing her dimples. "Can't argue with you there."

She turned as if she was going to continue on her way, but Griffin wasn't ready to see her leave yet. "I've been jogging here every morning for almost two weeks. How come I haven't run into you before?"

The wind teased a slim lock of hair across her face. "I've been on the night shift for the last two weeks. I get four days off before switching to the day shift." She tucked the stray strand back into her beanie. "Where are you filming today?"

"Gingerbread Lane." He had looked at the location yesterday. The quaint street, lined with gingerbread and Victorian-style homes was beautiful. "Then at the barn."

"Gingerbread Lane, I get," Dale said. "The houses on that street are beautiful. What are you filming at the barn?"

"They're using the inside as a set for the bridal shower scene." He liked talking to her, liked noting her composure and economy of movement, at odds with those sparkling eyes and dimples. "It allows them to move walls and shoot different angles rather than shooting at the Garland house."

"Nice." She lingered, which wasn't like her. Not talking, which wasn't like her either. "Hey, my grandpa is a huge fan of Abilene and Cyrus Nash. I was hoping to coax him out of the house by taking him to watch some scenes being filmed. And... Would it be all right if I brought him by Gingerbread Lane?" Her nose wrinkled once more. "I know I shouldn't ask."

"Ask away." *By all means, ask me on a date.* "As for your grandpa watching filming, I'll do better than that," he said, eager to please. "If I get permission, bring him to the barn after lunch. You can watch some filming and I can introduce him to Abilene and Cyrus."

"Really?" Her face broke out in a huge smile, showing off deep dimples and sparkling green eyes. "I don't want to get you into any trouble."

"It's not any trouble."

Dale grinned. "You don't know what this will mean to him."

Griffin pulled his cell phone from his pocket. "What's your number? As soon as I get the film schedule for the day, and clear it with Lark, I'll text you what time to be there."

She gave him her number and waited for him to enter it into his phone before she said goodbye and resumed her jog down Jack Frost Avenue.

He watched until she was gone, wondering at his fascination, wondering if she found him fascinating, too.

# Chapter Four

D ale knocked on her grandfather's door. She waited for a few moments before letting herself in with the key. Grandpa was sitting in his recliner, watching television. Loud. It was about all he ever did anymore. Watch TV and make noise.

"Good afternoon, Grandpa." She gave him her brightest smile, the one that brought interest to Griffin's sad eyes.

"Hmph." Her grandfather flipped through channels on the screen. Silence. The roar of an excited football crowd. Silence. The pleasant voiceover urging them to place their order now before the deal expired. Silence. A gun shoot-out.

Dale took the tv remote from him and turned it off. "Shower and get dressed please." Oh, that was her cop voice. Oops.

Grandpa pounded his hands on his chair arms. "What in tarnation for? The doctor? I told you I was fine."

"Well." She tried to act casual. "If you want to meet Abilene and Cyrus Nash in your pajamas, I'm sure they won't mind."

The look on her grandfather's face almost made her laugh. His mouth dropped open, and he stood up as tall as he could. "What are you talking about?"

"Your next-door neighbor, the one you accused of trespassing, is the head of security for the movie Abilene and Cyrus Nash are filming." Dale crossed her arms over her chest and shrugged. "He's offered to let us come watch them film. And if you're very good, you can even meet some of the stars."

"Including Abilene?" His creaky voice held a certain amount of awe.

She nodded. "Including Abilene. But you have to hurry. We're supposed to be there by two." She'd been excited to receive Griffin's text earlier. It had been succinct and to the point. No emojis. He probably didn't know how rare and appreciated that was.

Grandpa hobbled to the tiny bathroom with a bit more vigor than usual. As soon as he disappeared, she started picking up the trailer. It shouldn't be so hard to keep such a small area clean, but it was a mess. Used paper plates were on the table from previous meals. Dirty clothes were scattered across the sofa.

There weren't even any Christmas decorations out. Where was the table-top Christmas tree he'd insisted on buying last year? She glanced at the walls. The stockings her grandmother had crocheted were missing from the spot he always hung them. They were probably in boxes in the exterior storage locker. She sighed. Her grandfather had lost his Christmas spirit when he'd lost his original hip.

She threw away the trash and put the dirty silverware and cups in the sink. She started a load of laundry in his miniscule, stackable unit. By the time she was finished washing the dishes and scrubbing the counters, Grandpa emerged from the bathroom.

He frowned, wrinkled storm clouds on the horizon. "You don't need to clean up after me."

"I don't mind." Guilt pressed on her chest. She'd promised her mom she would help Grandpa as much as she could. "I'm sorry I haven't been around much."

Grandpa reached into his closet and pulled out a bright red and green knit scarf. It looked like something the Knotty Elves would make. "It's okay, pumpkin. I know it's hard when you're on night shift. I spent my fair share of time on the same shift myself."

Her spirits rose a little when she saw him wrapping his favorite Christmas scarf around his neck. "That's no excuse. Admit it, you've barely left the house in weeks."

"We're leaving the house now, ain't we?"

She noted the stubborn tilt of his jaw and knew the conversation was over...for now.

# Chapter Five

G riffin walked through the building one more time. Unlike some places where he'd worked, the biggest problem on this set hadn't been rabid fans or protesters, but the continued appearance of an annoying little elf. No one seemed to know how the doll got there—anywhere it pleased, apparently—but the small creature kept randomly appearing in scenes. And although Griffin took it personally, the crew had accepted Elmer as more of a mascot.

"Griff," his walkie-talkie screeched. "You copy?"

"Yes." Eric was his second in command and rarely called him unless it was important.

"You've got visitors," Eric announced.

Griffin smiled. Dale and Murray had arrived. All day he had looked forward to seeing Dale again. "I'll be right there."

The set was busy. Betsy Anne was touching up make-up in one area of the building while Dave was fiddling with lighting and Sean was busy checking the cameras. Filming would be starting soon, so Dale's timing was perfect.

Griffin's heart did a stutter step when he saw her. With her hair down, the deep chestnut locks hung in soft waves past her shoulders. Her face was almost bare of makeup, but she didn't need any. He liked that he could see the soft spray of freckles across her nose. "Hi."

"Hi." Relief flashed in her eyes. "Are we too late?"

"No, you're right on time." Griffin reached his hand out to her grandfather. "Hello, Murray. Nice to see you again."

"Squid." The old man's grip was firm, and he seemed to be standing a little straighter than before.

Griffin glanced around. "Where's your walker?"

"I left it at home," Murray said with conviction. "You don't dawdle in the presence of royalty."

Dale pressed her lips together and shook her head. "It's in the trunk of the car in case he needs it."

Griffin motioned for them to follow him to the set, walking slowly to accommodate Murray's pace.

Dale leaned close to Griffin to whisper. "He didn't want to meet Abilene looking like an old man."

"Ah." Made sense, Griffin supposed. As long as he didn't fall and break another hip.

Electrical cords of all shapes and sizes stretched across the building. Griffin led them through a maze of cords and make-shift walls.

"Make-up and hair are in this area over here." He pointed out different parts of the set as they passed. "Set dressing is over here."

Lark approached them with a clipboard tucked under her arm, eyebrows raised, a silent question asked.

Griffin nodded. "Lark, this is Dale Anderson and her grandfather, Murray."

"Hello." Lark smiled at them, a dynamo on pause, full of welcome and grace. She looked Dale over. "Welcome to the set. Have you lived in Christmas Town long?"

"Just a couple of years." Dale cocked her head, burnished hair spilling over one shoulder. "How did you know I didn't grow up here? People usually assume everyone that lives here grew up here."

Lark laughed. "I *did* grow up here and I would've remembered going to school with a girl named Dale. It's an unusual name."

"I'm afraid my father was a huge fan of Roy Rogers and Dale Evans." Dale smirked. "I don't ride or sing, so don't ask."

"You used to sing," Murray said loyally, although he was looking around. "You used to sing as a kid. Had talent."

Dale rolled her pretty eyes.

"Lark isn't exactly a common name, either." Lark picked up the conversational ball as if she didn't have a gazillion things to do all at once. "Our names just make us more memorable. What brought you to Christmas Town?"

Griffin was just as interested in the answer. He hung back to listen as Murray walked on ahead, one deliberate step after another.

Dale nodded toward her grandfather. "My grandparents used to vacation here when they were young, and it was their dream to retire here."

"That's so sweet." Lark looked behind Dale and then over to where Murray was headed. "Where's your grandmother?"

Dale's face fell. "She died five years ago."

"Oh." Lark hesitated, and then hugged Dale briefly. "I'm sorry. Family losses are hard."

"Thank you." Dale glanced toward her grandfather. "I think being in Christmas Town has really helped."

"Of course." Lark smiled encouragingly. "This place is magic, you know."

Griffin stepped closer to Dale. "We should catch up with Murray."

"Oh, Griffin." Lark stopped him before he got too far. "Alexis and I need to talk to you about something whenever you have some free time."

"Sure. Today?"

"Any time before we wrap up filming." Lark touched the earpiece of her headset. "If you'll excuse me. Nice to meet you, Dale," she called over her shoulder.

Griffin and Dale hurried over to where Murray was watching Dave run around the set, checking the lighting from every angle.

"Wow." Dale stared at the set. "It looks like the inside of a house."

"Where's Abilene?" Murray whispered, which was odd considering he belted most words out.

Griffin pointed across the set. "She's in a cubby over there, collecting herself for the scene. I'll introduce you after they're done."

Both Lark and Alexis Dorsey, the director, were easy to work with. They were surprised when he'd asked for permission to bring visitors to the set, since he'd never asked for anything like that before. Once he explained the situation, they were willing. Finding out that Dale was a local police officer seemed to sway their decision, too. He didn't want to push his luck by interrupting their preparations for the scene.

He unfolded a couple of chairs for Dale and Murray to sit on. "Stay right here. I'll be back in a few minutes." He glanced at Dale, muting his walkie-talkie. "Cell phone on silent."

# Chapter Six

D ale watched Griffin hurry away. It had been a long time since she'd been attracted to a man. She hadn't dated at all since moving to Christmas Town. She'd been too busy with work and her grandpa to even think about it. She pressed her lips together as she watched Griffin stop and talk to people.

She was so busy watching Griffin; she didn't even notice all the activity around her until Grandpa squeezed her arm.

"Can you believe how realistic the house looks?" His excitement was bubbling over in his voice. "Well, except for the green windows."

"It's called a green screen," a man Dale's age standing nearby told him. He took a step closer. "During production, wherever you see a green screen, it will be replaced with an outside scene."

Grandpa looked intrigued. "What kind of scene?"

"Most likely a snowy street, since the house is supposed to be on Gingerbread Lane." The man spared Dale a friendly smile. "I'm Sean Carmichael, the director of photography. Are you enjoying your visit to the set?"

Dale nodded. "Very much. I had no idea how much detail goes into making movies."

"You're friends with Griffin, right?" Sean asked. "We receive visitor notifications, and it lists who requested passes."

Before she could answer, people started entering from different directions. Sean turned toward a camera. Several actresses moved into position, including Abilene.

Dale tapped her grandfather's arm. "There's Abilene," she whispered.

He frowned. "She looks a lot older than I remember." He didn't whisper. Grumpy Grandpa never whispered.

"I'll take that as a compliment," a young woman said. She opened a folding chair that was leaning against the wall and settled next to them. "I'm Betsy Anne, the makeup artist."

Dale had heard that Abilene was playing Elaine Garland, but she hadn't overlaid the age of Elaine over the beautiful Abilene. "So, it's your job to make Abilene look older?"

"Exactly." Betsy Anne nodded. "How do you know Griffin?"

"He's staying in the RV next door to me," Grandpa answered. "He's a squid." Betsy Anne and Dale exchanged amused smiles.

"Quiet on the set!" Sean shouted.

Dale reached over and squeezed her grandfather's hand. This was so exciting! The lights where they were sitting dimmed and the lights on the set came on. Dale was mesmerized as the actresses stilled.

If it wasn't for the few times that lines got messed up and they had to start again, Dale would've forgotten that it wasn't real. In between takes, Betsy Anne touched up make-up and someone else adjusted lights. Sean fiddled with a camera. The entire process amazed her.

"Mind if I sit here?" A gentleman nodded at the vacant chair next to them.

Dale looked up and her mouth dropped open. It was him. Cyrus Nash. Her heart raced. She'd loved him in the classic *Christmas Moon*.

Her grandfather nodded enthusiastically. "Sit, Mr. Nash." He leaned over to Dale and whispered, "That's Cyrus Nash."

Her grandfather hadn't been this excited in ages. As the two men talked quietly, she glanced around for Griffin. She hadn't seen him since filming started. Once, she thought she saw him at the far end of the building, but he disappeared so fast she wasn't sure.

A little girl walked by and waved at Cyrus.

"Hello, Molly." Cyrus greeted her. "Did you help your mom make the donuts this morning?"

"Yes," she said solemnly. "Did you like the cream-filled ones? I made the custard myself."

Cyrus smiled. "You did a very good job. Those were my favorite."

After Molly walked away, Cyrus said, "That's Faye Burlew's daughter. I heard rumors that Faye is moving back to Christmas Town and will be working with her grandmother at Posey's doing the books, payroll, and inventory."

"It's about time Posey got someone to help her." Grandpa nodded, sounding as if he'd just eaten at Posey's yesterday. "She's been doing it by herself for far too long."

"I heard she's retiring," Dale said.

Cyrus waggled his finger at her. "She'll deny it and deny you peppermint pie if you ask her."

"Thanks for the warning." Dale was rather fond of that pie.

The adjustments between takes were completed and things got quiet as they prepared to film again.

Griffin appeared out of nowhere and stood behind Dale's chair.

He bent to whisper in Dale's ear, "Are you having a good time?"

"Yes," she whispered back. "Thanks so much."

Dale settled back to watch the scene when she noticed something she hadn't seen before. "Griffin." She tapped his arm. "Why is Elmer hiding behind the wreath?"

"What?" His head jerked to look at the set. "Good grief," he muttered. "I have to tell Alexis." He hurried over to the director.

"Cut!" Alexis yelled. "The elf is back."

Laughter erupted from the crew as Griffin removed the toy from its hiding place.

Griffin walked back to Dale, a frown on his handsome face.

"I take it Elmer wasn't supposed to make a cameo appearance?" Dale chuckled.

"No," he sighed. "He keeps randomly showing up in shots. Every time he does, scenes have to be redone and they may even have to use a different camera angle than they wanted to. I'm head of security, but I can't figure out how he keeps showing up."

"Simple." Dale grinned. "It's Christmas Town magic."

He snorted. "Well, I wish he'd stop. He's making me look bad."

Dale reached over and covered Elmer's tiny ears. "Don't listen to him." She talked to the elf in the same tone of voice one would use to talk to a small child.

Griffin laughed. "You're funny." He handed the elf to someone efficient-looking, who whisked away with him. "Want to go to Posey's later to see if the little troublemaker makes it back safely?"

"Our Elmer is a stunt double." Cyrus winked. "For the action shots, you know."

They chuckled.

"About later..." Griffin let his invitation dangle between them.

"Sounds good. I haven't had a piece of Posey's peppermint pie this Christmas season. That should be against the law." Dale looked at her grandfather. "What do you say, Grandpa? Want to go to Posey's after we're done?"

Her grandpa puffed out his chest. "No. I already have plans."

She cocked her head. "Since when?"

Cyrus leaned over from his chair on the other side of Grandpa. "I invited him to have dinner with Abilene and me. And after, we're going to game night at Over the River."

"Oh." Dale glanced at Griffin, smile growing. "Looks like it's just you and me."

"It's a date." He smiled right back. "I'll meet you back here as soon as everything is done. Or if you don't want to wait, I can meet you at Posey's."

"I don't mind waiting," she said. Her heart lodged in her throat as she watched him walk away. *A date. Wow. I have a date.*

Grandpa leaned close to her. "He's just in town for the movie. When it's done, he'll be gone. All these people will be gone."

"I know that, Grandpa." Dale bit the inside of her cheek because, even though he was right, the thought of a date with Griffin made her smile.

# Chapter Seven

A bilene made her appearance shortly after the last scene wrapped up. Cyrus greeted her with a kiss and introduced her to Dale and Murray. Griffin had always admired the fact that Abilene and Cyrus were so down to earth, but now he could've kissed them. The joy on Murray's face was evident and getting to have time alone with Dale was a bonus for Griffin.

By the time things were put away, it was almost six o'clock. Murray had already left with Cyrus and Abilene, so Dale was sitting alone, waiting for him.

"Go ahead, boss." Eric gestured to where Dale was sitting, engrossed in her phone. "We're almost done anyway. Enjoy your evening."

Griffin scanned the area. Everything was put away and the actors had already gone. The only ones still left were some of the camera crew and the cleanup crew.

He nodded. "Thanks. I owe you one." He grabbed his jacket and hurried toward his date.

Dale glanced up from her screen and saw him approaching. She stood and shoved her phone in her back pocket, then put on her jacket. "Done?"

"Eric is going to finish. I'm sorry you had to wait."

"It's okay. I really enjoyed myself." They started walking towards the door, shoulder to shoulder. "Will you be done filming soon?"

"Christmas Eve." He held the door open for her and they stepped outside.

Dale frowned. At least Griffin thought she did. Did the thought of him leaving in a few days bother her? It bothered him. He was really getting attached to the small town. Why couldn't he have met Dale when he first arrived?

They drove downtown, talking about the weather and the lights.

"It must be hard to be away from your family so close to Christmas," Dale said carefully after she'd parked and they'd got out, digging for information without asking. A true cop.

He shrugged, fighting a smile. "That's one of the reasons I took this assignment. My parents are sailing around the world right now, so I have nothing else to do."

"You're going to be alone on Christmas?" She covered her chest with one hand, looking truly distraught. "I'm sorry."

"It's okay." He was used to spending holidays away from home or alone, but he liked that she felt bad for him. "I'll be here. The production crew is sort of like family."

The concern on Dale's face was quickly masked by a bright smile. She buttoned her jacket, and they started walking toward Posey's.

Griffin nodded at the town square. "I can't believe you get to experience this all the time."

Christmas lights twinkled across the square. The main Christmas tree was decorated with red garland, giant ornaments, and light. The twinkling lights in the gazebo made it look like fairies were dancing in it. He didn't think he'd ever get tired of looking at it.

Dale followed the direction of his gaze and sighed. "When Grandpa first told me he was leaving New York for a tiny town in Maine, I thought he'd lost his mind. One visit in December, and I was hooked, too."

Griffin took her hand in his and guided her to the edge of the sidewalk to allow a group of carolers to go by. Their beautiful voices filled the square. He glanced at the gazebo again. A line of people waited for their turn to get under the fabled rafters.

He didn't let go of her hand once the carolers were gone. It was soft and warm in his. He half expected Dale to pull away, but she didn't.

"I've heard a lot about that gazebo." He smiled in that direction. "Is it really as magical as they say?"

"Of course, it is," Dale gushed. "Legend says that a kiss in the gazebo during the Christmas holidays means a wedding in the next year. Bonus points if you kiss there on Christmas."

"Really? You know people this has happened to?" Griffin teased.

"You wouldn't believe how many." Dale started naming couples that kissed in the gazebo and were now married. Before long, they were standing outside of Posey's Diner.

A blast of warm air hit them when he opened the door. Christmas music played from the speakers and the chatter of customers was joyful.

"Officer Anderson!" A woman with a bright red bee-hive hairdo hurried over to meet them. Her name tag identified her as the diner's namesake: Posey. "I hear Elmer was accused of making mischief again. I'm here to say he's innocent. I'm his alibi. I've known where he's been all day long."

Griffin laughed.

"Two for dinner," Dale said. Then she looked abashed. "Sorry. The man usually says that."

"I'm an equal opportunity dater," he assured her.

Posey handed them menus and pointed to the back where they took the last empty booth.

Griffin scanned the menu while he waited. "What's good here?"

"Everything." She rested her forearms on the table. "Personally, my favorite is the shepherd's pie."

"Sounds good." He laid the menu on the table. "I'll have that. And if I don't have a piece of that peppermint pie Lark and Faye keep talking about, I'll never hear the end of it."

"Are you ready to order?"

Griffin looked up at the waitress and did a double-take. "Faye. What are you doing here?"

The caterer for the production company gave him a big smile. "I'm helping out my grandmother. There are a lot of activities going on this time of year, so I've been covering shifts for some of the servers so they can enjoy the season."

"That's nice." Dale leaned back in her seat. "We'll have two shepherd's pies and two pieces of peppermint pie. Oh, and two hot chocolates."

A few moments later, hot chocolate was delivered to the table. Griffin stared at the mugs. The whipped cream was as tall as the cups and sprinkled with chocolate shavings. His mouth watered. "I could get used to this. Might need to run extra tomorrow."

Dale took a sip of her hot chocolate. When she set the cup back on the table, whipped cream clung to the end of her nose. Griffin was stuck with an urge to kiss it off.

Her eyes crossed as she spotted it and she laughed. "Whoops." She picked up a napkin and wiped it off.

"What made you move to Christmas Town?" he asked, still thinking about kissing her. "You said your grandparents wanted to retire here. Did you move with him?"

"Actually, he relocated first. I arrived to talk him into coming home." She rolled her eyes. "He told me to spend a week here and I would know why he loved the place so much."

Griffin smiled. "And you decided to stay, too."

"Yes." She nodded. "They had an opening in the sheriff's department, so I took that as a sign."

"You gave up the excitement of New York City to come here." His respect for her grew even more.

"It was worth it. I love Christmas Town." She glowed. Burnished hair, sparkling eyes. And those dimples. Yep, she loved this town. "What about you? What do you do when you're not keeping elves off movie sets?"

"When I'm not working for a production company, I'm a fitness trainer." That sounded so...superficial.

"So, you're the reason all the movie stars look so good," Dale teased.

"I have trained a few actors." Griffin cupped the hot chocolate, wishing it was her hands he was holding instead. "But I specialize in helping disabled and elderly people find ways to be active. That's what I want to do full time."

"Noble. I'm impressed." There was warm authenticity to her praise. "If you can get my grandfather to work out, I'll be super impressed."

"Challenge accepted." As soon as he said it, he frowned. He only had a few more days until the film wrapped up. How had he become so attached to a place in such a short time?

Faye appeared at the table, with a spring of holly tucked in her hair, and two steaming bowls of shepherd's pie. "I'll bring your desserts when you're about done with your food."

"I can't wait," Griffin promised, but he doubted he'd have room.

Dale scooped up a spoonful of food and took a tentative bite. "Too hot." She waved her hand in front of her mouth with one hand and reached for her glass of water with the other.

"Patience." Griffin dipped his spoon into the crust and opened it, allowing the heat to escape.

Dale shrugged. "One of my many flaws. When I see something I like, I go for it."

Griffin hoped she liked him.

# Chapter Eight

D ale took her time finishing dinner. Partly because she wanted to give her grandfather time with his idols, but mostly because she enjoyed talking to Griffin. He didn't seem to be in too big of a rush either.

She pushed her almost empty plate to the side. "Do you travel a lot for your job?"

"Not really." He smoothed his brown hair away from his face. "Most of the films I work on are at their main headquarters. Studio lots. Getting to film on location is a treat."

"And where is home?" Dale hoped it was in New York or some place on the east coast.

"Los Angeles."

"Oh." Of course, he would not only be leaving soon, but would be on the other side of the country. She forced herself to smile as if she wasn't disappointed. "How do your fitness clients feel about you being away for this long?"

"I think they handle it better than I do." Griffin took one last bite of food. "Because most of them are older, or dependent on family, they usually take time off for the holidays. And when I say time, I mean weeks. And weeks. And weeks."

"I get the idea." She cocked her head to the side. "And you miss them?"

"Yes." He patted his stomach. "But right now, I'm missing my gym. I haven't had a good work out since I arrived."

"Christmas Town does have a gym, you know." She belonged.

Griffin pointed his fork at her. "Only open to guests during regular business hours."

Dale nodded. Deck the Barbells was located in the downtown district. It was open to everyone during the day but from eight at night until six a.m. entrance required an electric key card only given to full members. She rarely made it during normal hours, so she was glad her membership offered her twenty-four-hour access.

She waved Faye over. "Can you put our peppermint pie in to-go boxes?"

Griffin cast her a confused look. "Are we leaving?"

"I'm going to pick up my grandfather and take him home. Then you and I are going to work out at Deck the Barbells. You can have dessert after I kick your butt in the gym."

He grinned. "Challenge accepted."

Faye returned with the check and handed it to Griffin.

"I'll pay for my own," Dale said, reaching for the slip of paper. "I requested our table for two."

Griffin waved her hand away. "No way. My treat. I invited you."

"Thank you," Dale said graciously as they exited Posey's. "I'll take you to your RV to drop off the pie and you can grab some workout clothes."

A few minutes later, they pulled into the entrance of the Pine Tree Inn.

"Do you want me to pick you up when I bring Grandpa home, or do you want to meet me at the gym?"

Griffin's brow furrowed. "If you don't mind, I'll ride with you to pick up Murray. I'd like to say hello to Cyrus and Abilene."

Warmth radiated through her, secretly pleased to spend more time with Griffin. When he got out of the car to go into his RV and change, she leaned her head back on the headrest and closed her eyes. What was she doing? She liked Griffin more than she should, and he'd be leaving soon.

The opening of the car door startled her. "That was fast." She kept her eyes averted from him in his workout gear.

Griffin fastened his seatbelt. "Do you need to go change, too?"

"No." She didn't look at him when she backed up. Or when she faced forward to drive. "I have clothes in my locker at the gym. Have you seen much of Christmas Town, outside of the square, I mean?"

"Not much. I run. I work. I walk. There are enough Christmas lights on these houses to put Clark Griswold to shame."

She laughed at his *National Lampoon Christmas Vacation* movie reference. She didn't always catch on to movie references. "That's Reindeer Meadow." Dale pointed out the area past the fence to the sign announcing the second annual Bake-Off which had wrapped up a few days ago. "They have a show of it online. I've never seen so many desserts in one place."

"Sounds amazing. Did they have gingerbread houses?"

"Houses? *Puh-lease.*" She snorted. "This is Christmas Town. There was a separate competition just for that. Gingerbread mansions. Gingerbread castles. Gingerbread buildings of every shape and size."

"Sorry I missed it. Gingerbread is my favorite."

"Mine, too." Dale's cheeks heated. Why did it make her happy that they shared the same taste in desserts?

She parked her car in front of Over the River, and he followed her inside to the common room. He stopped, staring at the chaos with wide eyes.

Dale tried to see it through his eyes.

The first thing he saw were several women scattered about with yarn. The click of their knitting needles didn't even slow down as they glanced at them. Music blared through the open double doors on one side of the room and on the opposite side, two sets of double doors marked the entrance into the Carriage Room, the retirement home's restaurant and common room.

June Baxter brushed her hands over her sweater adorned with a pair of lovebirds perched underneath mistletoe and approached them. Her grey eyes gleamed, and she gave Dale a quick hug. "Instead of hugging you, I ought to be putting you in time out, young lady. What are you doing letting a card shark into our midst?" June didn't wait for a reply and turned her attention to Griffin. "How are you enjoying Christmas Town at night?"

"I'll let you in on a secret." Griffin leaned closer to June. "I'm breaking into the local gym tonight."

"Don't start rumors," Dale warned him. "He's kidding. Where's my grandfather?"

"Playing games." Odette King, another Knotty Elf, tugged off a pair of vibrant purple gardening gloves and stepped away from a round table filled with potted poinsettia plants. "I'm glad to see you, Griffin."

A few seconds later, the third Knotty Elf, Prudence Parker bustled through the swinging door leading to the kitchen, smelling of peppermint and vanilla. "Griffin! We made something for you." She picked up a knit beanie from a side table and handed it to him.

"Thank you." Griffin slipped the gingerbread beanie on his head and grinned at Dale. "This one almost matches yours."

"Does it?" There was a definite twinkle in Odette's gaze. "Isn't that a coincidence."

Dale wasn't about to make too much of identical beanies. "Excuse me, ladies." She headed toward the common room, not waiting to see if Griffin was following.

She stopped and scanned the room. Tables were scattered throughout the space. Each had a different game and groups of people were either watching or playing. Several tables were playing card games like Rummy, other tables had dominoes, checkers, or chess. Finally, she spotted her grandfather sitting at a table with Cyrus, Abilene, and several others.

As she approached, the table roared with laughter. "What did I miss?" Dale asked.

Abilene waved at her, her face red. "We're playing Cards Against Humanity."

"Oh." Now Dale understood the laughter. The game had a tendency to get a little rowdy.

"Griffin!" Cyrus waved across the room and poked the man he was sitting next to. "That's the one I was telling you about. I bet he could help you."

Griffin cocked his head as he approached. "Help with what?"

The older man reached out his hand. "I'm Stan Fromer. My doctor told me I need to lose some weight. Cyrus says you can tailor a workout program for me."

Griffin cast a sideways glance at Cyrus and nodded his thanks. "I'd be glad to sit down and help you come up with a plan that will work for you."

Dale leaned against the wall, waiting for her grandfather to finish his game.

Griffin walked over to wait with her. "When was the last time your grandfather hung out with people like this?"

She shook her head. "When we first moved here, he spent a lot of time at the Christmas Town Workshop with Barty, Marv and Gus. They're the male equivalent of the Knotty Elves. We call them the Three Wise Men, but since his hip surgery, all he does is sit in his chair in that tiny trailer."

"Maybe this will remind him how much he's missing out on."

"I hope you're right." She waited for the round to be over before leaning close to Grandpa's ear. "Are you ready to go?"

Grandpa shot her an irritated look. "What's your hurry?"

"Well..."

Grandpa's gaze darted from her to Griffin and back. "If you've got plans, go ahead. I'll get a ride home."

Clancy Gallagher, Over the River's administrator, was watching the game and overheard. "I'll be glad to take Murray home when he's ready."

"See?" Grandpa snorted. "Comes a certain age and relatives think you need a keeper."

Dale's heart leaped in her chest. She wasn't sure if it was from happiness that her grandfather seemed more like his old self than he had in months, or at the thought of spending time alone with Griffin.

# Chapter Nine

G riffin had only been downtown a couple of times. He had walked through the district on his way to North Pole Grocery and did some shopping at the mom-and-pop stores housed in the buildings along Joyful Street. He'd bought his mother a handmade ornament from Boxes and Boughs, and a new tie for his father at Fir Tree Fashion.

He hadn't been down here at night, though. The lights and decorations were every bit as beautiful as those on the square and he was surprised more people hadn't ventured down the street from the square to look at the window displays. The shops were closed for the evening, so the street wasn't busy, and Dale parked her car right in front of the gym. He waited while she unlocked the door by using her key card.

"I'm going to change." She pointed toward the women's locker room. "I'm sure you're familiar with the machines, so go ahead and get started."

Griffin nodded and headed for one of the treadmills. His body hummed with excitement. In LA, he worked out at the gym at least three times a week and his body missed it. He'd probably push himself too hard and be sore tomorrow, but he didn't care. He stretched his muscles a little and warmed up on the treadmill. By the time Dale returned, he'd finished warming up and was on a rowing machine.

An hour later, his muscles ached, and they were both out of breath. He had beat her at hanging crunches, but she managed to do more pull-ups than him. Only because she had less weight to lift, he'd jokingly told her. He'd always been competitive, but he didn't mind losing to her.

There was a stack of towels by the door, and she tossed him one as they made their way back to the lobby.

"What's on the upper floors?" Griffin wiped the sweat from his face with the towel.

"Personal training rooms. I think there's a physical therapy room, too." She had her towel wrapped around her neck, her hands fisted in the ends. "There's another fitness studio in town. I teach a few karate classes there when my schedule allows. Never during the holidays."

His eyes widened. "You teach karate?"

"Karate, jiu-jitsu and wrestling." She gave him a pointed look. "Care to spar a few rounds?"

"No way." Griffin laughed. "You'd have me pinned in three minutes." Wrestling was one sport he'd never participated in. Although he never had a wrestling partner as attractive as Dale. "I had no idea that Christmas Town offered so many things."

"For a small town, we have a lot to offer." She snapped him with her towel. "Do not take that the wrong way."

"Never crossed my mind." He looked over one of the bulletin boards on the wall. He skimmed the list of classes. "Do they offer classes for disabled people? Older people?"

"Over the River has a bus that brings residents into town for shopping and appointments. I'm sure they could take the bus here if they wanted to. Also, Pete Ford, he's the physical therapist at Over the River, sets up classes for the residents. They do yoga, chair exercises, and things like that. Is that what you mean?"

He shook his head and scanned the list of classes again. "Do they have classes that specialize in that age group? What about disabled adults and kids?"

"Not that I know of. Chase Bailey would probably be the one to talk to about that." She took his towel from him and went to drop them in the laundry bin in front of the locker rooms. "I'm going to change. Be right back."

He was still staring at the class list when she returned. "Who's Chase Bailey?"

"He's a realtor and runs a home for adults on the autism spectrum." She cocked her head. "Are you interested in starting a program in Christmas Town?"

"I...I wish..." Griffin sighed. "I'm only in town another week at the most."

"Does the film company have another job lined up for you?"

"Not yet."

She gave him a long look. "So, what's your hurry to leave?"

# Chapter Ten

The next morning, Dale parked at her grandfather's trailer at eight, just as the sun had decided the world should be fully light. She doubted he was up and moving yet, but she always came to eat lunch with him on her days off.

Today, she thought she'd surprise him by taking him to breakfast. It had absolutely nothing to do with her grandfather's handsome neighbor, whom she might also invite along.

She knocked on the door, but there was no answer.

"Grandpa!" She pounded on the door harder, concern creeping in.

When there was still no response, she pulled her key out and unlocked the door. He wasn't there. Her heart raced. Where was he? She took her cell phone out of her purse and called Griffin. "Hi, Griff. Have you seen my grandfather? He's not home and I'm really worried." Had he come home last night?

"Look down the street," Griffin said.

She tumbled out of the trailer, scrambling through the snow to the end of her grandfather's RV space. At the end of the trail leading past the RV park, she saw her grandfather and Griffin walking slowly toward her.

She walked to meet them, trying to stay calm when she'd just been on full alert. "What are you doing?"

Her grandfather waved off her concern, smiling. "I was showing Griffin Mistletoe Park."

"Did you know fairies live there?" Griffin asked her. He was smiling, too.

Dale might have liked their smiles if she'd arrived ten minutes later and not been blindsided by her tottering grandfather walking on the snow and ice! She reached for her cop detachment. "Fairies? I've heard rumors a gang of them moved in. I can't say for sure." She did a visual scan of her grandfather. Her heart was pounding too fast, and everything felt wrong, like a bike chain right before it slipped. She did a visual check of her grandfather to make sure he was okay.

"What are you doing here so early?" Grandpa had snow boots on, so at least there was that to be happy about. "It's your day off."

Yes, yes it was. "I thought I'd take you to breakfast, and you could tell me all about your evening with Cyrus and Abilene."

"Sounds good," Grandpa said. "Want to join us, squid?"

"Sure." Griffin smiled.

Was this good? It's what she'd wanted, wasn't it? Life was coming hard and fast at Dale this morning. She hadn't had a second cup of coffee yet and she wanted to get off this emotional rollercoaster.

"I heard Lynn's Pudding and Pie Shop has a great breakfast special," Griffin was saying.

The way Griffin looked at her made her heart race all over again. *He's leaving in a week.* She focused on that smile. It was hard not to. That smile was worth something. *Heartbreak?*

Dale swallowed. "You don't have to work this morning?"

"I took the morning off," he said. And that was that.

When they got to her grandfather's trailer, Grandpa went inside, leaving Dale and Griffin alone. "I can't believe you got him out of the house so early. I'm sorry if I freaked out."

"I should have told you. He likes telling stories and once he got started..." Griffin pulled his new gingerbread beanie down a little more on his head.

"I think he forgot how much he likes it, too." She bit her lip. "If you hadn't invited us to the movie set, he'd still be sitting in that chair watching TV. Thank you." She reached out and squeezed his gloved hand. "Why did you take the morning off? Are you sore from the gym?"

His brown eyes searched hers. "I was thinking about something you said to me."

"About what?" The intensity of his gaze sent shivers dancing down her spine.

"I emailed Chase Bailey last night and he replied back right away to set up a meeting later."

Her heart raced. "What did he want?" *What do you want from Chase?*

"Chase thinks True North and Over the River would be interested in having me develop a fitness program for their residents. Something more than restorative physical therapy or gentle weight-lifting while sitting in a chair. Not that there's anything wrong with that, but some people want more. Some people need more."

"Sounds like a full-time job." Dale tried to keep her voice light, but inside she was shaking, afraid to put to words what this might mean.

"I can't quit my day job yet," he said staring at her levelly. "But I am going to take unpaid time off until I can determine if there's enough of a demand to keep me here."

"So, you're going to stay for a while?" Dale smiled. And she couldn't seem to stop.

"Yeah," Griffin said. "I hope you don't mind."

"Not at all. You'll be helping a lot of people in Christmas Town."

Grandpa opened the door and started down the ramp. "What's this about you helping people, squid?"

Griffin stood close enough to Grandpa to catch him if he slipped. "I'm going to stay in Christmas Town and develop some fitness programs for Over the River and True North. Might work into something full time and permanent."

"Call Jack." Grandpa continued toward the car.

"Dr. Banning?" The physician who'd done his knee replacement surgery? Dale looked her grandfather over. "Are you hurting? Do we need to go to the ER?"

"Calm down," Grandpa barked. "I meant squid should call Jack."

"Why?" Griffin walked next to him along the path.

"He's not only a surgeon at Christmas Town Memorial Hospital, he's also a veteran." Grandpa scoffed. "I'm sure he could get you in touch with people who might want you to work with disabled veterans in the area."

"That's a great idea, Grandpa!" Dale opened the car door for him, and Griffin stood close to make sure he didn't fall before he got into the backseat.

Once they were all seated, Griffin reached over from the passenger seat and took her hand.

On the way to Lynn's, Grandpa told them all about his evening with Cyrus and Abilene. He was amazed that they were charming, intelligent people, just like everyone else. Of course, he knew they were. Dale laughed. Grandpa didn't seem to catch that he was contradicting himself.

"I'm really surprised the restaurant at Over the River was so good." Grandpa switched gears. "Do you know The Carriage House is completely run by the residents? If Posey does retire, how long do you think it'll be before she's cooking there?"

"I'm not going to ask her." Dale smiled.

Griffin was smiling, too.

Grandpa was still talking when she parked in front of Lynn's Pudding and Pie Shop. As they walked inside, Griffin's phone rang. He motioned for them to go on inside while he answered the call.

Lynn's was much smaller than Posey's with only five tables, but it was just as festive.

Julianna Fisher brought over two menus for them. "Merry Christmas."

"Could we get one more menu?" Dale asked, removing her beanie and fluffing her hair. "We've got one more coming."

As if on cue, the bells on the door chimed and Griffin walked in with a big smile.

Julianna glanced at Griffin's beanie. "I recognize the Knotty Elves handiwork on both of you. How do they know who gets what?" She winked at Dale before going to get another menu.

Griffin watched Julianna walk away. "What did she say about the Knotty Elves?"

"It's not important." Dale would ponder the matching beanies later. She hadn't seen other couples with them, but she had seen matching scarves worn by Cyrus and Abilene. "What time are you meeting Chase?"

"Ten." He still stood next to the table. "Can I talk to you alone for a minute?" Dale nodded and followed him outside.

"That was Lark on the phone," Griffin said in a serious voice, the tone of voice that doctors delivered bad news with. "Lark, Faye, and Alexis are opening their own production company, right here in Christmas Town and they asked me if I would be interested in working for them setting security at their home base and coordinating it for when they film on location. Dean is willing to let me keep renting his RV until I find a place of my own."

"What?" Her breath escaped in a rush. "Does that mean you're really going to stay?"

"It does." He took one of her hands in his, his thumb traced her knuckles. "And I'm just warning you that I want to get to know you a lot better, so if you don't feel the same way... If I'm misreading things... Please tell me now."

Her heart skipped a beat. As much as she liked him, she didn't want to be responsible for Griffin altering his entire life just because there was something yet-to-be-discovered between them. She lifted her chin. "If I said no, would you still stay? I don't want to take the blame if—"

"I fell in love with Christmas Town first." Griffin pushed a strand of her hair away from her face. Gently, so gently. "So yes. I would be staying, even if I wasn't already half in love with you."

Her heart pounded. "So, you'd stay no matter what?"

"Yes." He lifted her chin and kissed her.

He tasted of chocolate and peppermint, and she'd never found the combination more appealing. She wrapped her arms around his neck and kissed him back.

"Knew there was something I liked about you from the start, squid." Her grandfather's admission interrupted the kiss. He stood in the doorway to Lynn's. "The gazebo magic is in that direction."

Griffin grinned at Dale. "Who needs a gazebo, Murray? I have my own magic right here."

The End

# Catering Christmas

## Book 8: Lights, Camera, Christmas Town

Cari Lynn Webb

ChelseaBeth Publishing

# Chapter One

*December 22ⁿᵈ*

Three more days and Faye Burlew could fall face-first into her bed and sleep for sixteen hours straight.

But right now, there was absolutely no time for face-plants or sleeping.

The craft services tent for *The Wedding Carousel* had to be restocked. The film production's cast and crew needed to be fed hot meals over the next two days. As the catering manager on set, that was Faye's responsibility. Not to mention overseeing the Christmas Eve wrap party. And those were only her paid work tasks.

Bookkeeping, payroll and inventory waited at her grandmother's restaurant—Posey's Diner. There was more Christmas shopping to finish. Her best friend and boss Lark had invited her to join her new production company as an assistant producer. Always it seemed there was more to do. But if it meant giving her daughter a perfect Christmas in Christmas Town then Faye would get it all done.

A quick glance at the clock confirmed the evening was quickly passing her by. So, for now, it was all systems—and ovens—on go.

Faye tightened the sash on her elf apron and smiled at her nine-year-old daughter. "Molly, turn up the tunes. It's time to get cooking."

"You gotta wear the hat too, Mom." Molly handed Faye a slouchy elf hat with Fa-La-La Faye embroidered on the white velvet trim.

Faye adjusted the knit hat on her head, added an exaggerated flick of the giant white pom over her shoulder and shimmied around the large kitchen island. "Give me something upbeat, Molls."

"You got it." Molly hit the volume on the portable speaker. *Jingle Bell Rock* filled the kitchen. Molly secured her Molly McJolly elf hat on her forehead and twirled in her fuzzy penguin slippers. "It's our own Christmas dance party, Mom."

Faye belted out every word to the Christmas song and got busy mixing donut hole batter. She had dozens to bake and prepare tonight. Donut holes were the start of tomorrow's breakfast prep that would ensure she was ready for the sunrise cast call. Three songs later, the doorbell chimed, interrupting the last verse of *Holly, Jolly Christmas*.

"Pizza is here." Swiping the cash from the counter where Faye left it, Molly dashed into the living room. "I'm starving. I'll get it."

Faye slid the first tray of donut holes into the oven and set the timer.

"Mom?" Molly called out. That was quickly followed by, "Mom. It's *not* the pizza guy."

Smiling at her daughter's disgruntled announcement, Faye joined Molly in the entryway. "Who is. . ."

Her gaze collided with a pair of startlingly familiar eyes. Ones she knew to be steely gray in the daylight but were muted under the dim porch lamp. Her words dissolved as her breath puffed out. *Kaleb Matthews. It couldn't be.*

"Merry Christmas, Faye." The smallest grin stirred across Lark's brother's lips.

It had been on track to be a very merry Christmas. Yet Kaleb's unexpected arrival was certainly a wrinkle in her *Fa-la-la*. Faye reached up, catching her elf hat as it slid sideways. "Kaleb."

Amusement flickered across his face. His gaze traveled from her head to her toes and back.

Faye's mind raced. Her heart kept pace. "What are you doing here?" She sounded breathless. For no good reason. He was her best friend's older brother. *Estranged older brother.* Only Faye took him in as if he was her secret Christmas wish come true. *Get it together, Faye.* She stammered, "You're supposed to be on an oil rig in the gulf."

Surprise lifted his eyebrows. One corner of his mouth edged further into his cheek. "Faye Burlew, have you been keeping tabs on me?"

*Yes. No. Would you mind so very much?* Faye opened and closed her mouth without saying a word.

"I got some unexpected time off." Kaleb tapped the snow from his boots onto the porch. "I didn't have plans, so I came home for the holidays."

"Right. Home." Faye paused, then blinked. "This is your house. We're in your house." She sprung into motion. Gave a quick introduction to her daughter and pulled Molly aside to let Kaleb in.

Kaleb came to a standstill in the entryway.

Too late, Faye realized she should have warned him.

His gaze tracked around the open living space, his expression reserved.

Faye bit her bottom lip. She was fully aware even Mrs. Claus would suggest a holiday décor edit with the intent of toning things down. Christmas literally covered every wall and window of the family room before spilling like an out-of-control holiday parade into the kitchen and sunroom beyond. At Molly's request, Faye had unpacked every dust-coated Christmas bin in the attic and scoured the local stores for even more decorations.

If only those tabs she'd been keeping on Kaleb had included his holiday preferences. Or even details of his last trip home. Were the antique Santas on the mantle and oversized silver bells trimming the stairway comforting memories? Or was it all just one painful reminder of the parents he'd lost? Same as it was for his sister.

Faye willed him to say something. Anything. *Take it down. Put it all away. Get out.* Well, anything except the last. Molly was enjoying staying in this house.

The silence stretched. He never flinched.

Faye cleared her throat. "The house was on the accommodation list we received for the cast and crew."

He nodded and reached out, running his fingertip lightly over the wing of a glass angel figurine. Angels had been his mother's favorite—and were Faye's too. A collection of new and old angels filled the entryway table. A frame in the center read: *Open your heart. Hear an angel's blessing. For Christmas and always.*

She knew his eye color, but not the man who'd spent ten years grieving alone. Still, she was drawn to him. Wanted to wrap her arms around his waist and hold him close. Comfort him as if . . . Faye stuffed her hands into the fur-lined red mittens sewn on her apron. "Lark urged us to stay here and also encouraged us to decorate."

"Mom went all-out since it's our first Christmas in a real house. We live in a teeny, tiny, itsy-bitsy apartment." Molly skipped into the family room. The fluffy white pom on her elf hat swung against her back. "Kaleb, Mom says your mom liked Christmas more than Mrs. Claus. And she always gave out frosted cookies with extra-warm hugs."

"My mom always did give the best hugs." Kaleb glanced at Faye. More than grief swirled through his steady gaze. A small rasp scratched through his words. "It looks like I remember and so much more."

Funny, she could say the same about him. She saw hints of the boy she'd known, yet looking at the man, she saw so much more. "I always felt more at home here with Lark and your family than my own," Faye admitted. His gaze softened, even his shoulders seemed to relax. Faye lifted one shoulder. "I wanted Molly to feel that here, too."

Just once. Then perhaps her daughter would find her place in Christmas Town and feel like she truly belonged somewhere. And it would be the start of the perfect childhood Faye always imagined giving Molly. The childhood Faye had always wished for growing up, but never had.

Kaleb stepped further inside. "Where's my sister?"

"Aunty Lark is most likely with West." Molly wiggled behind the Christmas tree. Within seconds, the colorful lights sparkled all over the tall tree. "They're *always* together."

Kaleb arched an eyebrow at Faye. "Seems I have a lot of catching up to do."

"And decorating. We have loads more decorations to put up." Molly peeked around a tree branch and grinned. "We only holiday-ed my room that used to be

Aunty Lark's, but we can do your room too, Kaleb." Molly paused and frowned. "Except Mom is in your room. It's closest to mine."

Amusement curved across Kaleb's face. He eyed Faye. "Now, there is a twist I didn't see coming," he teased.

Faye's cheeks warmed. There was a reaction she hadn't seen coming either. She blurted, "I can move rooms."

"No. Stay where you are." He stepped closer to her, bent down, and picked up the bag he'd set near the door. Straightening, he leaned in, and whispered, "If I had known Faye Burlew was in my bed, I just might have come home sooner."

Just like that the charming bad-boy Faye had once barely resisted was back. Her cheeks flamed. Her heart pounded. Words failed her.

As for Kaleb, he whistled his way upstairs. When the doorbell chimed again, he called out, "Hey, Molly McJolly, if you save me a piece of pizza, ice cream from The Sweet Shop is on me."

"I'll save you two pieces, Kaleb," Molly shouted and raced to the front door.

Faye decided to save her refusal for later. There wasn't time for trips to the ice cream parlor or down memory lane. Same as there wasn't room in her life for dates, dating, and daydreaming about a certain ruggedly handsome oil worker.

Besides, she'd long ago given up all things heart-related after one high school class valedictorian and all-star athlete had left Faye pregnant and alone days after their graduation. Lesson learned. Love was clearly not to be trusted.

As for her best friend's big brother, well, he could be very bad for her heart. Especially one that seemed all too ready to forget that lesson learned all those years ago.

# Chapter Two

T he timer in the kitchen chimed.

Faye thanked the pizza delivery boy, headed to the ovens and the task at hand: donut holes. One pan out, the next pan in. Faye switched on the mixer to beat more batter. She made a third bowl of salad. Meanwhile, her mind circled back to Kaleb. As if that was where her heart wanted to be.

But Kaleb wasn't supposed to be home. He was supposed to be on some offshore oil rig. Where he'd been working since he'd accepted his high school diploma, hopped on his motorcycle and hightailed it out of town.

Faye had only seen him one other time since then. When he'd returned for his parents' funeral.

But then Faye and Lark had hightailed it out of Christmas Town without a goodbye or an explanation soon after that fateful memorial service, Faye's positive pregnancy test, and their high school graduation. Leaving Kaleb to deal with the fallout of losing his parents alone. Faye had heard from her grandmother that Kaleb had closed up the house with help from friends, taken his own leave and headed back offshore. While Lark and Faye had headed for their new lives in New York City.

As for Lark and her brother, their relationship was non-existent. Faye had never pressed her best friend for details. Faye had been too busy adjusting to her single mom status and silently taken her best friend's side as she always had. Always would. As for Lark, she had never discussed her brother. But she had ignored his calls and texts over the years. Until finally, Kaleb had seemed to stop trying.

Faye should call Lark. Tell her best friend that her big brother was home.

But Lark had a movie to finish and a production company to launch. Lark had just found her happy again with West. How would her friend take this news? Worse, what if Kaleb hadn't come home for a reconciliation?

There was only one thing to do. She would figure out Kaleb's intentions, then proceed with caution.

Surely, she could handle Kaleb. She hadn't fallen for his charming daredevil ways back in high school. No, instead she'd chosen the perfect, parent-approved boy and look where that had gotten her. Still, she was older and wiser now. Knew better than to get distracted by the good-looking, head-turner Kaleb had turned out to be.

Faye heard Kaleb's deep voice in the family room, talking to Molly.

Her pulse picked up. Not exactly the indifference she was going for. She concentrated on glazing donut holes, not whether the timbre in Kaleb's voice had gotten deeper. She dipped a donut hole in the melted butter, rolled it in the apple cider glaze and set it on a wire rack.

Kaleb walked in, swiped the donut hole from the rack and popped it in his mouth before she could stop him. He grinned around the mouthful and reached for another.

"No more." Faye pushed his hand away. "There's a salad and pizza for you."

"But I want these," Kaleb countered.

*And I want...*

Faye focused on her donut holes, not Kaleb's still damp hair and his appealing half-grin.

"You gotta eat your vegetables first, Kaleb." Molly circled the island as if determining the best corner for a snatch and run. "That's Mom's rule."

"Does your mom have a lot of rules?" Kaleb asked, amusement in his words.

Faye was coming up with even more by the minute. For example: *Don't get lost in a pair of intriguing gray eyes. Don't get distracted by a charmer. Don't trust in the power of a man's kiss.*

"Mom has rules." Molly nodded. Her gaze fixed on the bowl of cinnamon sugar donut holes. "You gotta follow her rules, too. Otherwise, she'll tell Santa. Then it's a no-present, no-party Christmas."

"We definitely can't have that." Kaleb picked up a fork and his salad bowl, took a large bite and proceeded to finish his vegetables in record time.

Molly giggled.

Kaleb had his salad bowl in the sink and the donut hole bowl lifted over his head and out of Faye's reach even faster.

Molly's laughter spilled around the kitchen. She clutched her stomach, doubled over, and cheered Kaleb on.

Kaleb fended Faye off with his free hand and grinned. "I finished all my vegetables. I followed the rules."

Faye crossed her arms over her chest and stared him down, using her best *don't-mess-with-me-I'm-a-mom* look. "You can't eat the entire bowl of donut holes."

"I'm not." He lowered the bowl slightly, took one out and handed it to Molly. "I plan to share them with Molly."

Her daughter wiggled her hips in silent celebration.

"Molly has had more than enough sweets for one night," Faye countered.

Molly stuck the entire donut hole in her mouth, preventing Faye from taking it back, and edged noticeably closer to Kaleb.

Faye studied the pair. Matching mischievous grins. Gazes gleaming brighter than the lights chasing each other around the Christmas tree. *Trouble.* A double dose. This pair she would have to keep her eye on. Why couldn't Kaleb have shown up after the movie was done filming?

"This is the only time of the year when we can eat too much sugar and get away with it." Kaleb slipped another donut hole to Molly before offering one to Faye. "Come on, Faye. Live a little."

Faye's gaze connected with Kaleb's. She completely forgot her most recent new rules. His eyes were impossibly appealing. His grin far too captivating. His words entirely too tempting, the same way they'd been all those years ago when they were teenagers. *Come on, Faye. One date. It's all I'm asking. What are you afraid of?* The same thing she feared now. Losing her heart to the wrong guy again. Kaleb was the wrong guy, wasn't he?

The oven timer chimed.

Faye turned, secured her heart, and stuffed her hands into a pair of oven mitts. "I've got work to do. Try not to get cinnamon sugar all over the couch, please."

Behind her, a bowl plunked on the granite counter.

Faye turned back and struggled not to smile. Both Kaleb and Molly were seated at the kitchen island, elbows braced on the granite, chins anchored on their raised hands. Faye smoothed the laughter from her words. "What are you two doing exactly?"

"Well, you ruined it with all that talk about work," Kaleb grumbled.

Molly pursed her lips. "It's no fun if you can't get sugar all over."

Faye set the pan down and tried to look sympathetic. "What's the plan now?"

"We help you." Kaleb plucked a still hot donut hole from the pan. "We can dip and glaze for you, so it goes faster."

"And sample." Molly held her hand out, palm up to Kaleb.

"Right." Kaleb smiled and gave Molly a plain donut hole. "Consider us your quality control."

Faye wasn't sure *what* she wanted to consider Kaleb. But it wasn't *her* anything. "You really want to help?"

"I do," he assured her. "What? Are you afraid I'll mess something up?"

*No. I'm afraid I might like having you around a little too much.* Faye pushed her shoulders back. Reminded herself she was more than fine on her own. Nothing would change that. Not even her handsome helper.

"Well, let's get started. We've got more batter to make." She handed Kaleb a stainless-steel bowl and set of measuring cups. "The only rule in baking is measure everything."

And the only real rule in love: *don't ever fall.*

# Chapter Three

There were moments in life that could only be described as surreal.

Watching the sunrise alone on a platform in the middle of the gulf.

Getting a midnight phone call from the Christmas Town sheriff and wondering how you were supposed to keep going without your parents.

And right now. Standing in the kitchen he'd grown up in. With the woman he'd had a crush on. Yeah, surreal.

Only now Faye was a woman and proving exactly why she was so unforgettable. She was prettier now with her expressive hazel eyes and long blonde hair streaked with gold. Her laugh still enchanted him. Her smile still captivated him. And she was still as off limits now as she had been back then.

Kaleb wasn't home to start something he couldn't finish. He was home to finally tie up loose ends. Sell his family's house and leave like he always did. Since his parents' funeral, he'd been chasing the money, one promotion at a time and building his career. Always looking forward. Never looking back.

Yet when he looked at Faye, humming and scrubbing a mixing bowl to the beat of the Christmas song playing in the background, he thought of beginnings, not ends. Staying, not leaving.

But he'd never been one for wishful thinking, no matter how tempting.

After Molly had been put to bed without that promised trip to the ice cream parlor, Faye rinsed the last of the soap bubbles from the bowl and handed it to Kaleb to dry. "We're finished. There's nothing left to prep for tomorrow morning."

"It feels like we prepped enough for the entire weekend." He would've happily done more if it meant more time with Faye. Kaleb stacked the bowl under the counter, tucked away his foolish thoughts, and hung the towel on the oven handle.

"Trust me. It won't last through lunch tomorrow." She dried her hands and considered him. A soft smile teased her lips. "Now, it's time for our reward."

A chance to extend the evening with her was reward enough. "You're going to let me eat the almond blueberry French toast casserole."

She laughed and shook her head. "I've got something even better."

There wasn't much he could think of that was better than the sound of her happiness. It filled him. Made him feel lighter. He would've claimed it was impossible to breathe easy in his family's home. But right now, with Faye, he was doing just that.

"I found your mother's recipe for her homemade peppermint hot chocolate." She tapped the side of a coffee carafe on the counter. "There was a holiday recipe book packed with the decorations."

"Please tell me that is *the* hot chocolate we were forbidden to drink as kids?"

"Yes." Her gaze twinkled. She opened a cabinet and took out a pair of insulated tumblers. Amusement swirled through her words. "And the very same hot cocoa I caught you sipping on the back porch after the winter dance."

That had been the same winter dance he'd ask her to go to. But Faye had turned him down and chosen Troy Denhouse instead. Kaleb had skipped the dance and spent the evening at Reindeer Meadow with friends. He'd returned minutes before his sister and Faye were dropped off, wanting to see how beautiful Faye looked. Yeah, he was a glutton for punishment.

In the here and now, Kaleb grinned. "You don't know what I was drinking."

"I know you wouldn't let me have any." She filled the tumblers. "Not even a tiny sip. And you said it was hot chocolate."

He couldn't share his drink with her because then she would've been too close. Close enough to kiss. Like she was now. And that would've been bad. Like it would be now. He stepped closer to Faye anyway. "It was for your own good."

"I'll be the judge of what's good for me." She dolloped whipped cream onto the hot chocolate and pressed the green tumbler into his hand. "Now try it and tell me if it's as good as you remember."

His gaze traveled over her face. "I can already tell you that it's better."

A blush bloomed in her cheeks. She quickly finished fixing her hot cocoa and tapped her tumbler against his. "To your parents and the Elf Patrol."

Kaleb finally glanced at the holly green tumbler he held. The words: *Assistant Elf Patrol* were engraved in white bold letters on the outside. "This was my dad's special mug."

"And this was your mother's." Faye held up her red tumbler engraved with: *Head Elf Patrol*. "These were the only mugs in your entire house we were forbidden to use."

"I can't believe these are here." Kaleb traced the lettering. Memories from his childhood came floating back. His mom's endless cheer. His dad's off-key singing. His parents holding hands, their love tying them together like a giant satin bow. "I thought most everything had been sold at the estate sale or donated when I..." He tightened his grip on the tumbler. Grateful it was still here.

"Is that where everything I remember went?" Faye walked into the family room.

Kaleb followed and sat on the couch beside her. "I came back a little over a year after the funeral." He'd left Lark a message to meet him. His sister had never responded. "I had a lot of help from West and his family. Your grandma and her friends, plus Prudence, June, and Odette. They helped me decide what to keep and store in the attic, what to sell and what to donate."

"They're the reason you still have all your parents' holiday decor." She motioned toward the array of Christmas decorations he remembered from his childhood.

The Santas lobbying for room among the holly berry and pine branch garland stretching across the fireplace mantle. The dozen handsewn ornaments his mother had patiently crafted. The angel tree topper. He inhaled, tested that tightness in his chest for grief's jagged edge. Nothing there, but a faint sense of contentment.

"Your grandma and her friends told me it was too soon to decide how I felt about the Christmas stuff." He sipped the hot cocoa and settled back into the couch. "They said one day I might find comfort in it." Joy, when he was ready, they had promised. He hadn't believed them.

She shifted and looked at him. "How do you feel?"

"Better than I thought I would." He tapped his tumbler lightly against hers. "This is helping." *You are helping.*

"Well, it seems you've been remodeling and refurnishing the house. It looks terrific, by the way." She sipped her cocoa. "So, you must come back often."

"Not a lot," he admitted. The renovations had been necessary for the sale. The furnishings he'd added for his own use on those infrequent visits and for renters. "I've never been back at Christmas. Until now." His first holiday back was going to be his last. Now he felt it. The slightest catch in his chest.

Faye's gasp was whisper soft. "Are you sure this is okay?" She reached over and touched his arm. "Are you sure this isn't too much?"

If he had to face the past, he couldn't think of anyone else he wanted beside him. He nodded and took the long route to those memories from long ago. "So, Molly is really sweet."

"She's pretty great." Faye's shoulder bumped against his. Her voice melted like the whipped cream in the hot chocolate. "Molly has been my whole world for the past nine years."

Kaleb scratched his cheek and ran a quick calculation. He'd known Faye had a child, but not exactly when.

She lifted her mug in a mock toast. "Yeah, it looks like you were right, after all."

"How's that?" He kept his words even, his expression neutral, despite the bad feeling seeping through him.

"You warned me about Troy Denhouse." She met his gaze. Her expression reserved. "You warned me Troy would use me and discard me like he did all those other girls."

*Go on then, Faye. Date Troy. But don't come running to me when he casts you aside. And he will. That's what he really excels at.* Faye had lifted her chin and never backed down. *When would we date, Kaleb? You spend more time in the principal's office than class. If you're not at after-school detention, you're grounded.* She hadn't been wrong. Kaleb had broken one too many rules growing up. More than once. But he drew the line at hearts, especially Faye's.

Faye hadn't stopped there that day. *Troy's at the top of our class. Even my parents approve of him.* Kaleb had nodded. *Looks like you made your choice, Faye.* She'd walked away and slowed, only to toss over her shoulder: *I won't regret it, either. You'll see.*

Kaleb hadn't *seen* because he'd graduated and left town. He hadn't returned that Christmas of Lark and Faye's senior year. Didn't know if Faye dated Troy consistently or off and on. One year later, he lost his parents and all he saw were his own regrets. Not coming home more often. Leaving too soon. Not appreciating the time he'd had with his parents when he'd had it.

Now he had this time with Faye.

He took Faye's hand in his. Her fingers were chilled. He set his mug on the coffee table and gathered her closer. "I'm really sorry, Faye. That's the last thing I ever wanted to be right about."

"It's fine." She settled against him as if she'd always snuggled close to him. Her head rested on his chest. Her words were quiet. "Or it would be fine I suppose if it wasn't only my heart."

"So, Troy isn't in Molly's life?" Kaleb tamped down the anger on their behalf.

Faye shook her head. "He had plans after we graduated. None of which included me or a baby."

Kaleb had known Troy hadn't been the best boyfriend material. Still, he'd expected Troy would've shown up for his own kid at the very least. Kaleb wanted to believe he would've been there. But he, too, had been a selfish teenager, bent on breaking rules and living on his own terms. Faye had stepped up for her daughter. All on her own. A teenager herself. His admiration for her grew. "Where is Troy now?"

One of Faye's shoulders lifted in a half-hearted shrug. "I stopped trying to keep in contact a few years after Lark and I settled in New York. His continued silence was answer enough."

He knew the feeling. The silence from his sister had been more than deafening. "Well, you've done a terrific job raising Molly."

"I had help," she said. "Lark has been with us every step of the way."

"I'm glad you had each other," he said and meant it. "I wish I had known. I would've helped, too."

"You already had too much to deal with." She lifted her head and looked at him.

"I would've made time for you." He reached up and touched her cheek. "I would've definitely done that."

"You're serious?" Her gaze searched his. "What exactly would you have done?"

"I would've started with a few words for Troy." He held her gaze. His words serious. "If you knew where Troy was now, I'd be more than happy to have a long overdue conversation with him."

She curved her fingers around his, linking their hands together. "You're a good guy, Kaleb Matthews."

"You don't need to sound so surprised," he teased. He stroked his thumb across Faye's palm, felt her relax against him. Felt himself do the same.

"I can't promise Lark is going to react well to you being here," she whispered, sounding tense.

"I didn't think my sister would," he admitted.

"You *are* here to see Lark, aren't you?" Faye pushed against him so she could look in her eyes. "This house is... Lark hasn't come here since we arrived. You can remind her of the good memories you relived by being here tonight. She needs that. She needs her family. She needs *you*."

*I'm here to sell this house.* That was nothing Faye would want to hear. A definite moment buster for sure. "You just told me my sister might not want me here. But you think I should talk to her?"

"You should do what feels right." Faye settled back in the couch, not leaning on him.

Suddenly, Kaleb was second-guessing what felt right. Knew only that everything felt right with Faye here, with him.

Faye sighed. "Can I ask what happened between you two?"

Now it was Kaleb's turn to shrug. But it was far from indifference he was feeling. "I wasn't here to protect my parents or her. I abandoned them. I'm sure Lark hates me. At the very least, I should have taken her with me. Instead, I let her live alone in this house. She was only eighteen."

"You were nineteen and grieving." Faye sat up, framed his face in her hands, her words and expression earnest. "And honestly, I don't know if Lark would have been grateful that you stayed. Not then."

"But she would have now," he said in a voice raked with regret. "That time... It all feels so hollow. Their deaths. Lark being alone."

"Then let me tell you," she urged and held his gaze. "The hollowness can be filled. If you reach out to Lark. If you bridge that divide. She's ready... Well, she's crazy busy and super stressed, but she won't turn away from you. Not this time."

Kaleb inhaled. Felt those cold spaces inside him ease. The ones no amount of distance or time or even sun on a hot oil rig could ever seem to thaw.

There was one thing he didn't want to let go. One person. He tightened his arms around her.

And vowed tomorrow he'd let go of all his wishful thinking and Faye Burlew.

# Chapter Four

*H*ey *Lark. About Kaleb.* Faye inhaled and silently rehearsed how to break the news to her best friend. *Your brother is home. He's back. With me.*

Well, Kaleb wasn't with Faye. Hadn't been with Faye since last night. When they'd sat on the couch, holding hands, and talking into the early hours of the morning. She hadn't wanted it to end.

*So not the point. Stay on task.*

Faye concentrated on setting up the taco table in craft services. Lunch was ten minutes away. From the grumblings Faye had heard when she'd replenished the snack table after the sunrise breakfast, the retakes had not been going well. When she'd returned from prepping the taco bar fillings at her grandmother's diner, her catering assistant warned Faye tension on set was high.

Faye added serving spoons to the salsa section. Checked the warmer lamps under the shredded chicken and ground beef chafing dishes. Restocked the utensils. Kept debating whether to tell Lark about her brother's return. The news wouldn't improve Lark's mood. But Faye should give Lark a heads-up. There wasn't any real harm in waiting until after filming wrapped for the day, was there?

Same as there wasn't any real harm in spending time with Kaleb. Getting to know him. After all, they were friends of sorts. *I want more.* She batted that thought away. When the door swung open, she sighed in relief.

Cold air drafted inside. The adorable couple, wearing coordinating Christmas sweaters and looking more in love than they had yesterday, hardly seemed to notice. Dave, the lighting specialist rubbed Betsy Anne's hands between his own. The makeup artist shifted into Dave's side as if drawn there. Same as Faye had fitted herself against Kaleb last night. Faye's cheeks warmed.

*Get to work.* Faye stepped behind the taco table. More cast and crew arrived. A line formed. People were served. Came back for seconds. And dessert. The lunch hour was almost over when Lark finally arrived.

Faye handed Lark the plate of loaded nachos she'd prepared for her and readied that early warning.

The door swung open. A chorus of *We Wish You a Merry Christmas* rattled through the oversized tent, interrupting Faye. A familiar trio of spirited retirees bustled inside with Faye's daughter.

Molly spotted Miranda and Dustin and bee-lined for the couple. No doubt to inquire if Dustin had welcomed any new rescues at the shelter. Molly was convinced adopting a dog would help her transition from homeschooling to the Christmas Town Elementary school after the holiday break.

The Knotty Elves finished their warbly chorus about glad tidings and figgy pudding. They reveled in the cheerful round of applause before making their way to the serving table. The Knotty Elves were frequent guests. Lark had given up barring them from set one day into filming after they'd snuck in, wearing their own hand-made VIP passes. Even Griffin, head of security, indulged them.

Prudence Parker wrapped an arm around Lark. "We've just had the most wonderful time with Molly and Kaleb."

Lark went statue still.

*I should have told her.* Faye swallowed. The guilt made her throat sandpaper dry.

"Lark, your brother is so entertaining." June Baxter flitted to Lark's other side.

"Not to mention quite handsome," Odette King chimed. She pinned Faye as if sighting her for a private snowball attack or more likely one of Cupid's arrows. Faye hadn't failed to notice how couples were wearing matching knitted items from the Knotty Elves.

Faye wanted to shout that she hadn't noticed how handsome Kaleb was. But that would be a lie. Faye looked at Lark, trying not to squirm.

Odette's shrewd gaze gleamed as if she'd recently become a Cupid-in-training and as such knew Faye's thoughts before Faye did. "Kaleb told us he spent the night with Faye." Odette paused and added in a stage whisper, *"At the house."*

Lark fixed her attention on Faye, eyebrows raised.

"Don't look at me. I didn't plan it." Faye also hadn't planned for the evening to feel so right with Kaleb. *Perfect, really. Like everything I've been missing. Needing.* Faye snapped her fingers and disrupted her thoughts. "Kaleb showed up out of the blue. We thought he was the pizza delivery boy."

Lark's words were precise and measured. "Why didn't you tell me?"

*That I like him? I only just admitted that to myself.* Faye touched her forehead, her cheek and then reminded herself that the question was about Kaleb's presence, not Faye's feelings for him. She took a breath and...blinked. "Look. Lark." She paused, staring across the tent.

"You were saying," Lark urged in a chilly voice.

"No. Really. *Look.*" Faye pointed at the table across the tent. The one where the cast and crew set props. The same table where Faye had instructed the florist from Glad Tidings Floral Shop to leave the bridal bouquet for the wedding scene being shot early tomorrow morning.

"Is that Elmer tangled up in Lisa's bouquet?" June used one finger to nudge her glasses up her nose. Approval filled her words. She was a supporter of this copycat Elmer's shenanigans.

"Looks like Elmer is getting ready for the wedding scene finale." Odette beamed as bright as her yellow Christmas light bulb earrings.

"Which reminds me." Pru turned to Lark. "We prefer to be prepared. Where will we be seated for the wedding scene tomorrow?"

"Will it be on the bride's side or the groom's?" June's thin eyebrows arched in sharp curves over her too-round glasses.

"I suppose we could go either way," Pru mused.

Odette nodded. "We do have a history with both sides—the Garlands and the Richardsons."

Lark rubbed the back of neck. "We framed the scene for only a few extras at the ceremony."

Pru pursed her lips. "That's hardly authentic."

"Are you filming the wedding at the carousel?" Odette's disappointment was obvious. "Or is that unnecessary too?"

Lark cast a wide-eyed, *please-run-interference* glance at Faye.

Coming to her aid, Faye stepped around the table and joined Lark. "Of course, the wedding will be filmed at the carousel, just as it was in real life." The trio relaxed, but their smiles remained doubtful. "Maybe if we talk to Alexis, she'll know how to make room for a few more."

"I wouldn't be surprised if Lark edited out Elmer, too," June accused.

"What do you know about Elmer on set?" Lark asked a bit sharply, even though she'd admitted to Faye last week that she'd given up finding the culprit behind Elmer's unexpected appearances.

"We know Elmer is part of the very fabric of this town." Pru tipped her head toward the prop table. A group was gathered there, snapping pictures of Elmer, and laughing.

"We know Elmer brings joy wherever he is," Odette chimed in.

"Sometimes it's the smallest things that mean the most," Pru offered casually. "When they're asked about the movie your crew might not remember costume details or on set frustrations. But they will recall how they feel right now. The joy and camaraderie."

"Isn't that what matters most?" June peered at them. "How we make each other feel?"

Kaleb made Faye *feel*. Things she hadn't in a long time. Things she'd believed she wouldn't feel again. But could she trust those feelings?

"Well, I'd like to try my hand at a selfie with Elmer before he's snatched away again." Odette smiled and waggled her eyebrows. "Shall we, ladies?"

The trio cheerfully drifted toward the prop table to join the revelry.

Lark set her untouched plate of nachos on the table. "So, Kaleb is really here."

"Sorry I didn't tell you sooner. I wanted to break it to you gently and in person." Faye stepped over to the beverage table. She picked up Lark's travel mug, which was imprinted with the words *Producer of Joy and Happiness*. She filled it to the brim, put the lid on, and handed it to Lark. "Isn't it past time you two talked?"

"I shut him out," Lark said, her words lacking her usual confidence. "Maybe he doesn't want to talk to me."

"You know that's not true." Faye reached for her mug, which was imprinted with the words: *I'm a big cup of Christmas cheer.*

"What did Kaleb tell you?" Lark sipped her coffee. Her expression resigned.

"That he felt guilty for leaving you alone after the accident." *And that he would've been there for me when I was pregnant and scared.* Instead, Faye had chosen dreamy-eyed Troy Denhouse, who had a gift for saying all the right things. The boy her parents, who never agreed on anything, even custody of their only daughter, had liked. Look where that had gotten her. If only she'd chosen a ruggedly handsome, straight talker instead. *It isn't too late.*

Faye shut down that thought and concentrated on her best friend. "Talk to Kaleb. He's your family, Lark."

"I need time to think." Lark slid a candy cane cozy on her travel mug. "I need to finish this movie. Clear my head."

Faye touched her friend's arm. "It's going to be fine."

"Tell me Kaleb isn't coming here." Lark lowered her voice. "I can't talk to him *here.* I'm working. Corporate needs to hear that my sets are always professional."

"You won't have to see him here," Faye assured her. "If Kaleb comes, Molly and I will keep him occupied. Concentrate on those last retakes. I've got Kaleb covered." At least for now.

Lark sighed. "I don't know what I would do without you."

"Right back at you." Relief settled on Faye's shoulders where there'd been tension before.

Lark sipped her coffee. "Sorry about putting you in the middle."

Faye wasn't. She cared about both Lark and Kaleb and wanted the siblings to work things out. She wanted other things too. "Go finish your best film yet." Rah-rah!

"I need to run through some script changes with Abilene and Cyrus. See you later?" At Faye's nod, Lark called out to the middle-aged couple and walked away.

Faye skipped her gaze around the crowded tent. Heard the laughter and merriment that good food and full stomachs tended to bring. She noticed something else. So many happy couples.

Alexis, the director, held hands with Flynn Sullivan and chatted with graphic designer, Zoey Hansen and Sean Carmichael, the director of photography. The lively foursome sounded as if they were discussing a double date, not work. Love was, as they say, in the air and on the set, despite Lark's claims about personal not blending with professional.

Faye exhaled. It wasn't her fault she was thinking about Kaleb and crossing those friendship boundaries. It was Christmas Town's fault. Here, love was celebrated with the same exuberance as Christmas. Case in point, the line for the famed gazebo in the square where starry-eyed couples kissed to seal their future together often outpaced the line for Santa.

Of course, Faye would get swept up, too. Even Lark glowed these days, now that she'd reunited with West Coogan, her first and only love. All Faye had to do was get through the weekend of shooting. The film would wrap. Christmas would arrive. All would settle again.

It would be Faye and Molly, helping Faye's grandmother at the diner and building their new lives in Christmas Town. There was nothing more Faye needed.

After all, she'd fallen under the spell of Christmas Town's love lore once before and ended up heartbroken with a newborn. Now was *not* the time to make the same mistake. Besides, Faye suspected her heart had nothing left to give.

# Chapter Five

T he last double decker cheeseburger and slice of peppermint pie had been
served at Posey's Diner over an hour ago. The closed sign flashed in the
window. The industrial dishwashers hummed in the commercial kitchen.

Posey, Faye's grandmother and diner namesake, sat in a booth with the
Knotty Elves. The women shimmied their shoulders to the upbeat tempo of
*Run, Run Rudolph*. Kaleb twirled Molly around the cleaned tables, closing out
the pair's Christmas dance-a-long.

Kaleb couldn't remember the last time he'd danced. Or had so much fun
doing it.

Molly spun to a stop and grinned. "Can we play another song?"

"Only if it's *Silent Night*." Faye stepped from behind the counter where she'd
been closing out the cash register. She slipped the purple apron over her head.

"Mom, you can't jingle bell hop to *Silent Night*." Molly scooted closer to the
jukebox. "It's too slow."

"That's the point." Faye rubbed her forehead, then pointed out the window.
"The van is here to take grandma and her friends to Over the River."

At Molly's frown, Posey stood and consoled her great-granddaughter. "Tomorrow is another day for dancing. Rest up."

"As for us, it's definitely time for a slow down, too," Faye added, as if wanting
to head off any negotiating between Posey and Molly.

Faye looked run down. Faye and Molly had been gone hours before Kaleb had
woken up. He'd met with Chase Bailey, his real estate agent. The rest of the day
had been spent with his former rule-breaker compatriot, Flynn Sullivan. The

pair had helped ready the square for the annual Christmas Pageant, building booths and helping set up the stage under the direction of Gus, Barty, and Marv, the town's Three Wise Men. Flynn and Kaleb had run into even more friends from high school, which hadn't been awkward or painful, but rather enjoyable and comfortable.

He'd avoided the set after Molly answered her mom's phone and informed him that Aunty Lark wasn't having a good day on account of nothing going according to her plan. Seeing as he wasn't in Lark's plans, he took the easy way out and kept his distance. He finally met up with Faye and Molly at the diner.

Kaleb caught Faye's attention. "I could use a bit of a wind down myself."

Faye's gaze brightened.

"You two look like Kaleb's parents when they'd been sipping that Elf Patrol cocoa and shared those private smiles with each other." Pru arched an eyebrow. There were murmurs of agreement from Pru's cohorts.

Faye caught her laughter behind her hands.

"Guilty. We had some last night." Kaleb shrugged and grinned. "I'm not apologizing. That cocoa is really good."

"Don't we know it." Pru slid out of the booth. Kaleb helped the older woman with her snowflake print faux fur lined trench coat. She peered at him over her shoulder and asked, "What do you think we wind down with at home these days?"

"It's certainly not prune juice." Odette's yellow Christmas light bulb earrings sparkled. She eased her arms into a green-and-white plaid wool coat Kaleb held for her.

"Although we've been forced to limit our whipped cream usage these days. Doctor's orders and all." June wrapped a fluffy candy-cane red striped scarf around her thin neck and tugged on her matching gloves. "The recipe is still the same as the one Kaleb's mother shared with us ages ago."

Odette flipped her silver tinsel trimmed hood over her head and eyed him. "We discovered some things are best when not meddled with."

Kaleb kept his expression neutral. Love was not in his new year forecast.

"We can also assure you that most things are better when shared." Pru eyed him for a beat before bustling toward the door beside Odette.

Kaleb couldn't deny her words. He'd shared an evening with Faye and was better for it. He checked to make sure Posey, Faye, and Molly were bundled up then held the door for the Mrs. Claus stand-ins.

June paused in the doorway and patted his cheek. "You've become a fine man, Kaleb Matthews. Your parents would be proud."

That was high praise coming from the former school principal. He wanted to hug her. But she was already taking the hand of the waiting bus driver and climbing inside the passenger van.

Still, he got that hug. From Posey. Warm and affectionate. She touched his cheek. "June is right." Posey looked at her granddaughter. "This here is a fine young man, Faye. What did I always tell you?"

Faye tipped her head. "Gram always told me if I only get one bite of pie, make sure it's the best bite ever."

Molly giggled. Faye's lips quivered as if she fought to contain her laughter.

"Sassy elf." Posey's mouth pursed. "That's what Pru should've stitched on your elf hat, Faye Burlew."

"But those were your words." Faye hugged her grandmother and whispered in her ear.

"It's good to know you listened." Posey beamed. "I stand by my advice. Every word of it, too."

Faye helped her grandmother into the van. One horn honk, several waves, and the van disappeared around the corner.

Before Kaleb could inquire about Posey's advice, Molly asked, "Can I have Elf Patrol juice when we get home?"

Kaleb met Faye's stare over Molly's head. At the same time, they said, "You're not old enough."

Molly's eyebrows slammed together.

"But you can have a ride back to your car." Kaleb dropped to one knee. "Hop on."

Molly climbed onto his back and laughed as he stood and pretended to drop her. Argument successfully averted, Faye offered him a grateful smile.

It wasn't long before they were back at Kaleb's house. Molly in a pair of pink unicorn pajamas proclaiming she should sparkle all year. Faye in fleece pants and a fuzzy sweatshirt.

"Kaleb, can I have one more piggyback ride upstairs?" Molly asked, collapsing on the floor and pretending to be exhausted. "My legs are so tired."

Kaleb laughed and shifted to let the little girl climb on. One stop at the island for Faye to kiss Molly goodnight and he headed upstairs. He returned to find Faye on the same stool she'd been on. Her head in her hands. Her eyes half closed. He never hesitated. Just plucked Faye up into his arms and walked into the family room.

"Kaleb." Faye wrapped her arms around his neck. "What are you doing?"

"You're so exhausted, you're about to fall off the stool." He settled on the couch with Faye on his lap.

"I should go to bed." She yawned but didn't move. "It's another early morning call tomorrow."

He covered them with a blanket. "All work. No sleep."

"Next week, I'll sleep in." She smoothed his T-shirt and pressed her cheek against his chest. "Maybe even play a little."

He chuckled. "What's that look like?"

"I have no idea." Amusement curved through her words. "I haven't done it in a while."

"That's a shame," he said. "I hear it's supposed to be fun."

"So, you don't play either."

"Like you, I work a lot." He'd buried himself in work since his parents' accident. Lost and found himself offshore on those oil rigs. Now he was finding he wanted more out of life.

She peered at him. "Maybe we should work on changing that for ourselves."

Change. He wanted to do that for her. He brushed his hand over her hair. "What do you have in mind?"

"Molly wants to ice skate at Reindeer Meadow," she said sleepily. "Sled at Merryman Slope and ski at Blue Spruce."

"All good choices." He chuckled. "What about you? What does Faye's fun day look like?"

"This," she said simply before adding, "For me, it looks like this. My feet up. Someone else cooking. Sipping your mom's hot cocoa. A movie marathon. It's much less busy. Probably sounds boring."

"It sounds perfect." But only with her. He tightened his arms around her, held onto her and the moment.

Her quiet words filtered through the silence. "Do you remember back in high school, when I turned you down for the winter dance?"

"Yeah." He wasn't sure where this was headed. But he knew she'd deserved better than him.

"It wasn't you," she whispered.

He held his breath.

"I know now I was just trying to win my parent's approval." She paused, sighing. "Really, I was trying to get their attention for once. When I dated Troy, I had it. He was the son they wanted. They were so convinced he would be good for me. That he would help me achieve all my dreams." She went silent again, adding in a small voice, "I can't believe he strung me along for a year."

Neither could Kaleb. "What happened when your parents found out you were pregnant?"

"They told me I ruined my life," she said, her voice quiet. "Like they always knew I would."

Kaleb brushed a tear off her cheek. "I'm sorry, Faye."

"It's why I spent so much time here before and after my parents' divorce," she confessed. "Your parents always seemed to want me. I miss that. I miss them."

"I do, too." He gathered her closer.

"Molly wasn't a mistake." Faye tilted her head up and met his gaze. Tears shimmered in her eyes. "The only mistake I made was being too scared to follow my heart back then. I should have..."

"Shh." There'd always been something about Faye. Something that made Kaleb want to follow her. He skimmed his fingers over her cheek, catching another tear. "What about now?"

"Still scared." She leaned toward him. Her words gentle yet charged. "But I'm listening to my heart."

He knew the feeling. He exhaled and closed the distance between them. Before his lips brushed hers, he said, "We can be scared together."

Her eyes flared slightly. Their lips met. For a kiss that didn't hesitate. Or hold back. One that spoke of promises. Hopes and wishes. Futures.

He was breathless when he pulled away. Speechless while searching for something to say. "Fun fact. I'm a pretty good cook."

Her smile was slow and enchanting. "Now that is good information."

They talked until only cinders pulsed in the fireplace. Faye fell asleep. Kaleb held Faye for a while longer before carrying her upstairs. He settled her in his bed, slipped out and peeked in on Molly. He picked up Jingles from the floor and tucked the stuffed penguin back under the covers.

Molly blinked at him. "Do we gotta get up already?"

Kaleb shook his head. "You still have time to dream about sugarplum wishes and reindeer rides."

Molly's giggle seeped through her yawn. "And candy cane cottages."

"Filled with gumdrops," he added.

Molly shifted, flung her arms around his neck, and pressed a soft kiss on his cheek. "Thanks for making my mom happy, Kaleb. I know you can make Aunty Lark happy, too."

Unable to find his voice, Kaleb squeezed the little girl before tucking her back in.

In his parents' bedroom, sleep eluded him. Two kisses. Same night. Both upended his world. Both imprinted on his heart. Nothing he'd ever expected when he'd caught that flight home. Nothing he'd ever dared imagine. Molly thought Kaleb made her mom happy. The truth was Molly and her mom showed Kaleb what happiness could be.

But he was leaving. Not to mention selling the house. A future with Faye wasn't possible. Faye and Molly deserved someone who would be around for the long haul. That had never been his plan. Even if he wanted to change plans, Faye may not want him or the life he offered.

It was best for everyone if he stuck to his plan.

Now he just needed to convince his heart to follow his lead.

# Chapter Six

K aleb should've kept his heart closed.

That truth nugget became clear seconds into answering his phone the following morning when a fragile voice cracked across the speaker, seeking Kaleb's help.

"Kaleb?" Molly whispered. "Help."

He was instantly awake. Instantly concerned. Instantly determined. More than ready to slay whatever he had to. Not that he was any kind of knight in shining armor. But for the little girl who'd captured a piece of him, he wanted to be.

Kaleb arrived at his sister's trailer and de facto film production office outside the barn in record time. The door slammed open before he reached the stairs. Molly launched herself into his arms. Her tears and her words spilled free like a burst frozen pipe. He carried her inside, grabbed a paper towel roll from the counter and settled her on the couch.

"Okay." Tearing off a paper towel, Kaleb dabbed at Molly's cheeks. "First, we're going to take three deep breaths."

Molly nodded. Her bottom lip trembled. Together they inhaled. Exhaled. Her tears slowed to a trickle.

Kaleb's heart steadied. Yet his knees wobbled, forcing him to sit beside Molly. "Okay. There's nothing we can't fix together." *Please let that be true.*

"I lost Elmer." Molly slumped against him. "Everyone is gonna hate me."

"No one is going to hate you." Kaleb couldn't claim the same about himself. He had things to confess to Faye and his sister today. That was for later. Right now, only Molly mattered. "Tell me about Elmer."

"Elmer. The elf." Molly hiccupped.

*That elf.* Kaleb's family had spent many nights at the diner searching for Elmer. All for that peppermint pie slice. "Doesn't Elmer stay at the diner?"

"Not that Elmer. I'm talking about the original Elmer that Grams showed me a long time ago. She kept him in a box in her office at the diner." Molly wiped her hand under her nose. "Grams said when she retires, she's going to take Elmer with her. They have to go together because Great Grandpa gave him to her."

Kaleb shouldn't be surprised there were two Elmers causing mischief in Christmas Town. But he was.

"Well, I've been hiding Grams' original Elmer on set so he could be in the movie, too." Molly sniffled. "But no one knows it's me."

Kaleb winced. He could only imagine the scene retakes the misplaced elf had caused. "Did Aunty Lark and the others get mad when they saw Elmer on set?"

"Maybe at first," Molly admitted, small face scrunching. "But it's Elmer. Everyone loves him. Now they all laugh when they see him. Like yesterday when he was trapped inside the wedding bouquet during lunch." Molly drew a shaky breath. "They won't laugh no more," she wailed, burying her face in his coat. "Because I lost the original Elmer. Everyone is gonna be sad, especially Grams when she goes to the retirement home without her Elmer. It's all my fault. And Mom is gonna be *really* mad."

"Not if we find him." Maybe Faye wouldn't be mad later with Kaleb if he found the right words now for Molly. If only he knew what those were. He stood and tried to sound confident. "Elmer couldn't have gone far. Where is he supposed to be?"

"Inside my elf hat." Molly smashed the paper towel into a ball. "Every morning, I get to sleep in Aunty Lark's bed 'cause it's so early when we get here."

"Show me." Kaleb followed Molly into the bedroom.

Molly picked up a white crocheted bag with a snowflake pattern and round wooden handles. "This is my special bag where I put my elf hat Ms. Pru made me."

That the Knotty Elves were somehow involved seemed somehow fitting.

"Ms. Odette made it." Molly adjusted the familiar red hat on her head. "Ms. June sewed my elf name on 'cause she's the most steady with a needle. They made Mom's too 'cause we're an elf team."

He'd seen Faye's elf hat the night he'd arrived. He'd even wondered what his elf name might be if he had a hat. But he wasn't part of their team. "Who puts Elmer in your bag?"

"He's just there when I get up in the mornings." Molly peered into the empty bag. "I looked all over. Even in the wedding bouquet. He's gone."

"Just missing," Kaleb corrected. "We will find him."

"You'll help me?" Hope widened her red-rimmed eyes.

"That's why I'm here." No sooner were those words out then Molly hugged him.

*I could get used to this.* But it wasn't fair to Molly or Faye. He was leaving. He squeezed Molly. Silently vowed he would fix this for the little girl, then batten down his heart and move on to his life overseas.

An hour later, the elf hunt was a bust. Elmer was nowhere to be found in the RV, the craft services tent, or inside the barn. The cast and crew were off-site. Molly had asked Faye's catering assistant at the snack table if there'd been any Elmer sightings at the carousel building that morning. The assistant frowned and reported not a single one.

Back in his sister's trailer, Molly was on the verge of tears again. Kaleb's phone vibrated. He checked the caller ID and sent his real estate agent to voicemail. He knew he'd most likely be letting people down soon enough, but he was determined one of them wouldn't be Molly. He just needed to locate one missing elf. That was proving to be as hard as figuring out how to tell Faye his truths. He rubbed his chest and told himself it was all going to work out.

Molly hopped up from the couch and announced, "Santa."

It was Christmas Eve. Kaleb supposed it was only fitting that the jolly man in red was on Molly's mind. "What about Santa?"

"Santa will bring Elmer home," Molly rushed on. Her words gained speed. "But we must talk to him right now."

"You want to go see Santa?" Kaleb needed to call Chase back, find out what his real estate agent wanted. See his sister. Make sure she was okay. Talk to Faye. Face all those hard conversations he'd been avoiding while he chased down an elf. Unfortunately, a visit with Mr. Kringle wasn't on his list.

"Please," Molly pleaded. "This is important."

"But your mom..." He would start with Faye and finally come clean.

"She's prepping lunch at the diner. I told Ms. Pru that you were coming to spend the day with me, so they didn't need to watch me." Molly wiped the back of her hand under her nose. "Mom can't take me. The Knotty Elves are at the carousel. Please, Kaleb."

When had Kaleb developed such a soft spot for big brown eyes and little kids? He crossed his arms over his chest. His little sister had used the same tactics on him growing up—the same plea in her voice. The same hope in her round eyes. He'd always given in, too.

Molly sniffed and looked even more downtrodden. "Santa is my last chance to make it right."

Kaleb knew a thing or two about wanting to make things right. He wanted to see Molly smile, not cry. "I can't just take you from the set."

"We can go and come right back," Molly suggested. "Mom won't even know we left."

Kaleb scrubbed his hands over his face. "I don't know, Molly."

"I'll be with you." Molly grabbed his hand. "You'll protect me, right?"

Kaleb glanced at her. "Always."

"I'll be super-fast, Kaleb. I won't even tell Santa about my own list. Just Elmer. Then I'll lick the candy cane three times and Elmer will appear." Molly bobbed in her snow boots and squeezed his hand between both of hers. "It's magic."

Kaleb had stopped believing in magic when his parents died. But he'd been lost the moment he answered the phone this morning. He couldn't turn Molly down. Heck, he'd been lost the moment he returned and found the adorable mother-daughter duo in his house. He leaned into his most serious tone. "Santa. He's our only stop. There and back."

"Don't worry, Kaleb." Molly tugged him toward the door. "Mom and I will go see Santa this afternoon like we always do on Christmas Eve, and I'll give him my wishes then."

Kaleb went as cold as if he dove headfirst into frozen Moose Lake. "What do you mean like you always do?"

"Pictures with Santa is our Christmas Eve tradition." Molly yanked on his arm to get him moving across the parking lot. "Since I was a baby. 'Cause Mom says no matter where we were, even if it was in the desert, we could always find Santa together."

*No. Nope.* Kaleb wasn't going to ruin a family tradition, too. He wasn't a grinch. He pulled his cell phone from his pocket and sent a quick text.

No, he wasn't a grinch. But he feared he was much worse.

He feared he was a heartbreaker.

# Chapter Seven

*M*eet me at the square.

      That was all the text from Kaleb said. Faye could've simply texted back *no*. Or: *can't*. Or: *I'm busy*. Instead, Faye dropped everything and was now rushing to the square to see him.

She slowed her steps, if only to prove one kiss—however magical—would not have her tripping over her own heart.

Faye skirted down the middle of Main Street. It was already blocked off for the Annual Christmas Eve Pageant that had delayed opening until the afternoon to allow Lark to finish filming her last exterior shots that morning. Lunchtime was fast approaching. The square was already bustling. Final touches of garland and colorful lights were being added to the booths that lined the square for locals to sell their handmade crafts and homemade treats. The sound system was being tested on the stage where the children's choir would perform. The scent of fresh pine thickened the air. A deeper breath drew in hints of vanilla, cinnamon, and orange as she passed the mulled wine and cider booth. She waved to familiar faces and promised to stop by later for samples.

All the while she searched for Kaleb's dark hair. She found him easy enough. He was taller than most and standing near the front of a long line. Her pulse picked up. Molly was next to Kaleb, waving and calling out, "Mom. Over here."

Faye joined the pair, took in her daughter's flushed cheeks and red-rimmed eyes, and felt that first pinch of worry. "What's going on?"

"I need to see Santa. It's super important," Molly blurted. "But Kaleb said it was super important we tell you. 'Cause it's what we do."

Faye's gaze skipped from Kaleb, his face reserved, to the front of the line that ended at Santa's village. They weren't too far from Santa's lap. Less than a handful of families were ahead of them. If she'd lingered at the diner, she would've missed Santa with Molly. Unease sifted through her, slight and nothing she could hang onto, much like the light snow falling around them.

"I'm gonna show Kaleb our special Santa photo album when we get home," Molly continued as if all was as it should be. "He says he can't wait to see it, even the one where I'm crying, and my face is redder than Santa's suit."

Kaleb leaned closer to Faye and whispered, "We've got a bit of a situation."

They certainly did. Their Santa tradition was expanding to include one more. And Faye wasn't stopping it. She simply moved forward in the line. "I'm going to need more than that."

"I promised I wouldn't say anything." Kaleb tipped his head toward Molly, who was selecting a candy cane from the straw basket one of Santa's elves held.

*And I promised I wouldn't fall for you.* Faye cleared the catch from her whisper. "But I'm Mom. That trumps everything."

"I know." Kaleb adjusted her scarf around her chin. "But Molly called me. She was crying and wanted my help."

And he rushed over to her daughter. Faye's heart tumbled. Not a complete fall. Nothing she couldn't catch. "Is everything good now?"

He shook his head. "That's why we're here. Apparently, Santa is our fix-it guy."

She was starting to think maybe Kaleb was her fix-it guy. Fixing loneliness. Fixing that feeling of not having anyone but Lark to lean on.

"Next in line," an elf called.

Startled, Faye pulled her gaze away from Kaleb and watched Molly race to Santa.

One second, Molly was whispering in his ear and the next she was tugging Faye and Kaleb back to Santa's chair. Molly put Faye behind Santa's left shoulder, Kaleb on his right before she climbed onto Santa's lap and declared, "This is going to be the best picture yet."

No sooner was an enthusiastic elf handing Faye the printed photographs than Molly was sprinting across the square to greet Miranda, who was walking Abby's dog, Jolly. Faye and Kaleb followed Molly's path toward the green.

"One conversation with Mr. Claus and all is right in the world again." Kaleb shook his head. His words bemused. "Now that's true magic."

Faye was feeling a bit of that magic herself. She reached for Kaleb's hand the same time as he turned to her and said, "Faye, we need to talk."

Those four simple words were never the problem. It was always how they were said. Faye caught her heart and tucked her arm against her side.

Someone shouted Kaleb's name. Faye turned and recognized Chase Bailey hurrying toward them, despite the snow-slick sidewalk.

The realtor's greeting was kind, but brief, his words even more hasty. "Kaleb, glad I caught you. I've been trying to reach you all morning. With it being Christmas Eve and I wanted to make sure you got my message."

Kaleb patted his pocket. "Sorry, haven't checked my phone in a while."

"I've got good news." Chase brushed the falling snow from his sweater. "I've got clients coming into town this weekend. They are serious buyers and want to see your house the day after Christmas."

*Buyers.* Faye waited. Waited for Kaleb to correct Chase. Tell the busy realtor he had the wrong house. That house was Christmas Central. That house had been her shelter. And now, it was Molly's.

*Faye, we need to talk.* That unease collected around her like a snow drift.

Kaleb nodded and shook Chase's hand. "That should work."

*No.* Faye started to shake her head, made herself stop.

"I'll text you the details. Any problems, let me know." With that, Chase was off as swiftly as he'd arrived.

Faye had a problem. A heart-sized one. Still, she stood her ground and gaped at Kaleb. "You're selling your house." *Tell me it isn't true.*

Kaleb caught her hand and tugged her toward an empty bench away from Santa and his Christmas cheer. "I wanted to tell you."

"Why didn't you?" The moment he'd walked into the door. Before she'd completely fallen for him and would forgive him anything. When Molly fell for him, too. *Molly*. Faye glanced at the picture she held. At Molly's bright smile, aimed not at Santa, but Kaleb. Faye's stomach dropped out. Her daughter had already fallen, and Faye had failed to protect her. A chill skimmed over her as if she stood inside a snow drift. "Never mind. It doesn't matter."

"Faye, I'm sorry." Kaleb motioned to the bench. They were close enough to sit.

She faced him instead. "At least tell me why. Why sell now?"

"I got a promotion overseas." Kaleb stuffed his hands in his jacket pockets and tucked his elbows against his sides. "I'm not sure when I'll be back."

Faye sucked in another deep breath, wanting the icy air to lock her buckling knees. "I see."

"No." He stepped toward her. She stepped back. He reached out but just as quickly dropped his arm. "No, Faye, you don't see. I've been thinking about this for a while. It was all arranged before."

"Before what?" She searched his face, still foolishly hoping for some Christmas magic.

"Before I came back," he said steadily. "Before I knew you would be here."

"Well, I'm here now." *With you.* Faye clenched her teeth together to keep them from chattering. A chill consumed her from her fingertips to her toes. "But that isn't enough, is it? You're just like Lark. You always run away. From the house. From each other. And now, from me."

"Faye, listen to me." He ran his fingers through his hair and tugged on the strands, dislodging the snowflakes. "The house... I wasn't comfortable in the house until you brought it back to life. And Lark... She doesn't need me. And you... My career is offshore. I'd be here part-time at best. You and Molly deserve more than that. You know it, too."

Faye knew that he wasn't willing to fight. Not for her. Not for them. Not for what they might have. She knew she was tired, down to her bones. Always the one hanging in there to give everyone what they needed. To give and give until she had nothing left. Faye inhaled the cold air and willed her heart to freeze. To numb. To ease this tremendous pain. "It looks like you have it all worked out for both of us. Thank you for saving me the time of expressing my opinion."

"Faye." His breath came out in a stiff puff. "I really am sorry." It was the right thing to say.

But it didn't change the fact that he'd handled everything all wrong. The house... Her... Lark... "At least tell your sister before she sees the sold sign in the yard. Or worse, hears it from someone else."

He nodded, gaze drifted over her face. "Merry Christmas, Faye."

She lifted her chin to smooth out the quiver, to strengthen her will to carry on as if he hadn't broken some part of her inside. "Merry Christmas, Kaleb."

Faye walked away then. Forced one snow boot in front of the other. Forced herself not to look back.

Molly saw her and rushed over. "Where's Kaleb?" Molly leaned around Faye. Confusion in her tone. "He's gone."

"He had to leave." He was always going to leave. Faye wrapped her arm around Molly's shoulders and held her tight. "Come on. We need to get to the set."

"Mom." Molly paused and studied Faye. "Are you okay? Your voice sounds funny like mine does when I'm trying not to cry."

"I'm fine." Or she would be. Her throat closed. She pulled Molly in for another hug.

Molly wrapped her arms tighter around Faye's waist. "This is a really bad Christmas, Mom."

Faye squeezed her eyes shut. That was the last thing she wanted for Molly. To ruin her first Christmas in Christmas Town. "Don't say that, Molls."

"It's true." Molly leaned away and rubbed her cheek. "I went to Santa because I lost Elmer. I thought he'd turn up here. Now. But he didn't. And now you lost Kaleb. Worst. Christmas. Ever."

Faye kissed her daughter's forehead and grabbed her hand. "We've got each other, Molls. That's what matters." That would be enough. More than enough. "Wait. What did you say about Elmer?"

# Chapter Eight

F aye and Molly slipped into Christmas Town's Carousel House through the side door and walked to the temporary snack table Faye had set up earlier.

How had things fallen apart so quickly? Molly was the Elmer mischief maker and Faye hadn't known. And then she'd lost the antique Elmer that Gramps had given to Grams in the early days of the diner. That was going to hurt. And she'd told Molly that she had to come clean with Grams and Lark. And everyone.

But surprisingly, that wasn't what made Faye's heart truly ache. It was Kaleb. He'd ridden into town forty-eight hours earlier and put everything in her life off-kilter.

"Cut," Alexis yelled cut. "Dave, the angle of that overhead spotlight is reflecting off the carousel mirrors above the unicorn like the glare on a windshield."

"On it," Dave called back.

"Where have you two been?" Lark picked up a bag of holiday-colored Jordan almonds from the table, stress snacking, for sure. "You almost missed your favorite part. You love when we shoot the wedding scenes."

*Not today. Maybe not ever again.* That was her heart talking. Faye worked her words into casual. "We went to see Santa."

"With Kaleb," Molly added.

Lark paused before popping an almond into her mouth.

Grandma Posey eased through the side door. "Have I missed it?"

"I've missed something." Accusation thickened Lark's words. "Faye took Kaleb to see Santa, too."

"That was all Molly's doing," Faye countered.

"It's good to know someone has opened her heart to Kaleb." Grandma Posey wrapped an arm around Molly and tucked her protectively into her side. Grandma Posey eyed Faye and Lark, her expression set. "As for you two sweet, misguided dears, you'd do well to follow Molly's lead. It's past time to open your hearts back up to Kaleb, too."

*Open her heart? To Kaleb?* He didn't want that. Faye exchanged a look with Lark. Her best friend looked equally flustered.

"Oh, look at that. The bride is here." Grandma Posey gave her beehive a tweak. "I'm not too late after all."

The bride wore an embroidered, fitted white gown, understated yet elegant. She had a pill box hat veil, and simple pearl stud earrings. Faye would've chosen a plush faux fur wrap, a princess gown with lace long sleeves and an even longer train if she was dreaming of her own winter white wedding and marrying her own prince charming. But that dream had passed her by, and princess weddings were best left for the movies. A dull ache built in her chest.

"It doesn't matter now." Molly pressed her cheek against Posey's side. "Christmas is already ruined, Grams."

Lark glanced from Molly to Faye. "It can't be that bad."

"I'm sure if we put our heads together, we can fix anything," Grandma Posey fiddled with the cheese sticks and slipped one in her pocket.

"That's what Kaleb said, too." Molly's bottom lip jutted out. "But Santa's magic is busted, Grams. Elmer's gone. Kaleb left. And Mom wants to cry."

Lark's eyebrows snapped high on her forehead.

"I'm fine." Faye's words lacked conviction.

Molly flung her arm out, suddenly teary. "That's what she always says when she's about to cry. And since I lost—"

"Shh." Grams drew Molly away. "Tell me what's wrong."

While Molly shed tears and whispered her secret about Elmer to Grams, Lark set her hands on her hips. Her gaze narrowed on Faye. "You know, Molly's not wrong."

"About Christmas being ruined?" Faye chewed on her bottom lip.

"No." Lark reached over and brushed a tear from Faye's cheek.

"Places," Alexis shouted.

Lark gave Faye a *we-are-so-going-to-talk-later* look before joining Alexis behind the camera.

Faye sniffed, trying to collect herself.

Odette King waved from her chair on the bride's side and motioned Grandma Posey and Molly over.

"Come on, Molly." Grandma Posey handed a bag of Jordan almonds to Molly. "I know just who we need to talk to."

Quickly Posey and Odette exchanged places. Molly settled among the Knotty Elves.

Odette shuffled toward the snack table. Her mistletoe earrings glimmered. She shimmied behind the table beside Faye. "Had to get up. It's my new hips. They like to move more often these days."

Faye blinked some more. Sniffed some more. Tried to smile as if nothing was wrong when in fact everything was.

Odette eased closer, whispering, "We know who stole Elmer and have everything under control. Molly will be fine."

"Thank you," Faye whispered on a shuddering breath.

"Places," Alexis called. "If we can get this scene finished, we can get to the wrap party and Christmas pageant early."

Cheers filled the Carousel House. Joy buzzed around from the extras filling in as wedding guests to the animated cast and crew. Faye seemed to be the only one ready to raise her hand and yell: *I object*. She held her peace and kept her sour mood to herself.

"Quiet on set," Alexis shouted followed by, "Action."

The instrumental version of The Wedding March filled the Carousel House. Macy Winter, playing the role of Lisa Garland, clutched her white-and-deep-red rose bouquet and walked down the aisle past the real Lisa Garland and John Richardson. She skirted the carousel and ended near the mural. Her groom, played by Fox Baylor, waited beneath the wedding arch wrapped in fresh garland, holly berries, and shimmering silver ribbons.

Faye got completely lost in the scene. From the love shining in the acting groom's gaze. To the bride and groom's heartfelt and emotional reciting of their handwritten vows. To their first kiss as the newly proclaimed Mr. and Mrs. Richardson.

"Cut," Alexis called, and the Carousel House erupted in applause.

Odette dabbed her eyes. "I do adore weddings, even if it is the second time, I've seen this particular one."

"Looks like you might get another chance to watch this one again." Faye pointed to Alexis and Lark huddled behind the camera, viewing the replay. "It would be nice to get a retake or two in life."

Odette touched Faye's arm. "But my dear, it's never too late to get things right."

"What if you don't know what's right?" Faye countered before she could stop herself.

"That's simple." Odette plucked a white chocolate-covered pretzel stick from a festive jar and pointed it at Faye. "Trust your heart. It'll lead you where you need to be."

Faye rubbed her chest. "I don't think I can do that." Kaleb wasn't going to be here in Christmas Town. She couldn't follow him. And besides, he didn't want her to.

Odette peeled the plastic wrapper off the pretzel. Her gaze wise, her expression sympathetic. "That's just because you're convinced love hurts too much."

Faye nodded and blinked back those tears.

"But my dear, you're hurting now, are you not?" Odette took a decisive bite of the pretzel and chewed. Then the shrewd retiree waved the pretzel stick at Faye like a broken wand. "If it's love you're wanting to avoid, you're too late. It's already found you."

*Love.* No, surely Odette was wrong. Faye could not be in love. Her heart raced. Her stomach clenched. If it was love, she'd feel way better than this. Elated. Over the moon. Not panicked. Not queasy. Faye's hands fluttered in front of her, and she fumbled her words. "I can't just. . . I don't just. . ." *Trust love.*

Odette polished off her pretzel, seemingly content to wait Faye out. Her smile was slow to spread and full of satisfaction.

Faye braced her hand on the table as if she needed an anchor. "I'm not the rush-into-things kind of person." She certainly wasn't a fall-head-over-snow-boots-in-love-instantly kind of person.

"You liked Kaleb in high school, Faye, if your grandma is to be believed, that is. One can only deny these kinds of feelings so long." Odette's words were sincere yet wry. "Love didn't creep up on you. This is much more like a slow, long slide."

A slow slide into love. Years in the making. That panic eased. Love like that could be trusted. Faye whispered, "Yes, but what now?"

"Simple." Odette beamed like Mrs. Claus instructing her elves. "You straighten things out with the man you love. You figure it out together, the same way you and Lark brought this movie to life. As a team. One step at a time."

*One step at a time.* Faye smiled. Yes, that felt right. Exactly right. She could do that. She *would* do that. She handed Odette another pretzel. "Do you happen to have your needle and thread with you?"

"Never leave home without them." Odette's gaze sparkled. "Do you have a request?"

Faye watched Macy and John move to their places under the arch and hold hands for their retake. Those two actors had worked together, like a team, to bring John and Lisa's love to life.

She grinned at the clever Knotty Elf and said, "I do."

# Chapter Nine

K aleb heard a car pull up in the driveway.

He waited in the kitchen and willed himself to stop hurting. He'd been aching since he'd walked away from Faye earlier. And now, he had to face his sister before he left town and the past behind.

The back door opened. Kaleb waited, not certain he could hurt more than he already did. Still, this conversation was long overdue.

Finally, Lark appeared and frowned at his duffle bag in the mudroom. "You're leaving already? You never even said hello."

"I thought we could do that now," Kaleb said grimly.

"What? Say hello or goodbye?" She unzipped her coat but didn't take it off, as if she wasn't certain whether she was staying or going.

He had known what he'd wanted to do when he'd stepped off the plane two days ago. Say goodbye to the past, sell the house and cut all ties to Christmas Town. Now, he didn't know much of anything. Other than he hurt so very much. "We haven't talked in years, Lark. Would it matter which word I chose?"

"This time..." Lark sat on the closest kitchen stool. Her expression unguarded, her gaze welling with sadness. "Yeah. It would have mattered."

His sister was here. She'd answered his text and met him halfway. He needed to do the same.

He sat beside her and reached for her hand. This he could get right. "I'm sorry I didn't stay after Mom and Dad died. I wasn't exactly an angel when I was a teenager, and I didn't know how to be a man when it happened. You told me you were fine."

"Several times. At the top of my lungs," Lark said. "From behind the locked door of my room. But I wasn't fine."

"You shut me out and I...I did the same to you." Kaleb stared at the kitchen, not seeing the remodeled countertops and cabinets, but seeing the dark oak and yellow Formica, seeing his parents drink their Elf Patrol hot chocolate and dance. They knew how to live. How to love. "It wasn't until later that I tried calling and texting."

"I never blamed you for leaving here." Lark squeezed his fingers until he looked at her. "Heck, I left here. But time...and hard-won perspective from talking to others about our parents has given me closure. And if you don't have it yet...you can talk to me. Anytime."

"I'd like that." He nodded.

"It feels good to be in this house." Lark stood and wandered into the family room and the over-abundance of Christmas. Surprise surrounded her words. "Never thought I'd say that."

Kaleb followed her. He'd felt good in their childhood home, too. And with Faye, it had felt like home. "Mom would've liked what Faye and Molly did."

"Yes, she would." Lark smiled. "You should come to the wrap party this afternoon. The entire cast, crew, and I imagine most of the town will be popping in."

"I appreciate the offer, but it's best if I pass." Thinking about Faye hurt, seeing her might be his undoing.

"Look, we both know I talked to Faye about you," Lark said, capturing his gaze. "After we finished filming today, she told me what happened."

He assumed as much. They'd always been close. "Well, if you've spoken to Faye, then you know not even a conversation with Santa Claus could solve things between us."

She tsked. "But another conversation with Faye might. If I'd only talked to you sooner, we wouldn't have lost so much time together," Lark urged gently. "Don't lose this time with Faye. You two have something special."

He'd been starting to feel that. To believe it, too. He tapped a sugarplum fairy ornament on the tree and sent her twirling.

"You walked away before," Lark said softly. "Where did that get you?"

"Alone," he said flatly.

"What if you stayed this time?" Lark moved next to him, fiddling with a glittery turtle dove. "What if you fought for Faye. Fought for love."

*Love.* Kaleb frowned. Was that what this was? The kind of love worth risking everything for? He crossed his arms over his chest. "I don't know what that looks like."

"It looks like giving Faye your whole heart." Lark picked up their mother's favorite snow globe with the horse-drawn sleigh inside, shook it, and set the snow swirling. "I don't mean just telling Faye you love her. You need to show Faye you love her, whether you're here or on an oil rig out in the ocean."

That meant he had to open his heart and trust she wouldn't reject him. He stared at the snow globe in Lark's hand. *Your father proposed to me during a star-lit sleigh ride. Imagine that. It was enchanting.* Mom would always cradle the snow globe and add: *But the real magic, Kaleb, is in the love we share.*

Kaleb loved Faye. He feared regret more than the risk. He knew if he didn't fight for Faye, he'd regret it. The way he regretted leaving Lark all those years ago.

"I need to go get my Christmas best on for the party." Lark wrapped her arm around his waist and squeezed. "But this hug was long overdue."

They stood there, holding on to each other, Lark seemingly just as reluctant to let go as he was. And a feeling settled deep in Kaleb's bones, a feeling that things were finally healed between them.

Kaleb heaved a sigh and let her go. "Thanks."

Lark nodded briskly. "Whatever you decide about Faye, promise you'll say good-bye before you leave."

"I promise." He watched his sister walk away. And for the first time in too long, Kaleb was more interested in sticking around, than leaving. In building relationships rather than letting them slip away.

He pulled out his cell phone and opened his contact list.

Prudence Parker answered on the first ring.

"Pru, I could use some Christmas magic. The kind my parents would approve of," Kaleb said humbly. "And I've been told you and your friends are just the ones to help me create it."

# Chapter Ten

"N ow, that's the official craft services wrap." Faye handed the last of the empty serving dishes to a diner busboy and wiped her hands on a dish towel.

Her grandmother wiped down the long counter. Both red eyebrows arched high on her forehead. "You never stopped and ate, Faye."

"There wasn't time." Faye waved to Alexis and Flynn outside the diner window, then to Miranda and Dustin. The two couples had stayed to help clean-up until Faye ordered them to leave and enjoy their evening. The rest of the cast and crew were at the snowy green for the annual Christmas pageant. The booths were open. The chestnuts roasting. The children's choir was warming up for their performance.

"Grams." Molly rushed inside, a chocolate-dipped candy cane clutched in one hand and her gloves in the other. "Ms. Pru saved us seats in the front row. She told me to come and get you."

"Well, that's the best invitation I've had all day." Grandma Posey plucked off her apron and set it under the counter. "Are you okay to lock up here, Faye?"

"Of course." Faye knew her grandmother needed to slow down. "I'll finish up and join you guys soon." Kaleb hadn't answered her phone call or text saying she wanted to talk. She needed to ask Lark where he was, how he was, and if Lark could help her open the lines of communication.

"It's good to have you here, my dear, and not just for the diner help." Grandma Posey patted Faye's cheek. "My heart is full this Christmas with my family around me."

"There's no place else I'd rather be." She hoped she could convince Kaleb of the same. She hugged her. "Merry Christmas, Grams."

"Don't be too long." Grandma Posey took Molly's hand. At the door, she called out, "I almost forgot. If you wouldn't mind taking that bin of extra lights upstairs tonight, we won't trip over it when we open after Christmas."

Faye added that to her clean up list and got to work. It wasn't long before the staff had the kitchen cleaned and Faye had the main diner ready for reopening the day after Christmas. After Christmas wishes were made to the staff and hugs given all around, Faye sent them off to the festivities. She locked up the diner and carried the plastic bin with lights to the staircase hidden in the back. The upstairs loft that had been used for storage as long as Faye could remember. She climbed the stairs.

When she got to the top, she used her hip to prop open the door, and then backed into the space and twisted to set the bin on the floor. The soft glow in the room caught her gaze. She straightened slowly and gaped.

The space had been organized and cleared in the middle, boxes lined the walls. Tiny fairy lights and potted poinsettia plants lined a path. More white lights and silver garland hung from the tall twin front windows. A vintage high-backed two-seater sofa had been positioned to face the windows. Pillar candles flared from the pine branch and mistletoe centerpiece on the coffee table.

And standing in the warm glow was Kaleb, wearing dress pants, a button-down shirt, and a soft smile.

Faye ran her hands over her hair, then over the diner apron she still wore. "What is all this?"

"This is for you, Faye Burlew." Kaleb motioned toward the sofa. "It's your chance to put your feet up and let someone else take care of everything."

Faye stepped closer. Noted the thermos and familiar red elf travel mugs from his house on the table. There was also a plush, holiday blanket. She glanced out the window, saw a clear view of the crowded town square below.

"I have it on good authority that you never stopped to eat." Kaleb extended his hand to her. "I've been ordered to remedy that, but first, we need to put your feet up and allow you a quiet moment for yourself."

"Then you're only here to see that I sit down and eat?" Faye set her hand in his, teasing a little because finally everything inside her was settling. *This.* This was the feeling...*the person* she'd been missing in her life.

Kaleb led her to the sofa. Waited for her to sit, prop her feet up, and covered her legs with the plush blanket. "I thought we'd start there."

"And then what?" Faye watched him settle beside her.

He picked up the thermos, filled the Elf Patrol mugs with his mother's special cocoa then left them untouched and turned to face her. . "And then I wanted to talk about us."

"Us." Faye liked the sound of that. She inched closer to him.

"I was told I needed to stand, not walk away when things get difficult." Kaleb shifted and took her hand in his. His gaze met hers, steady and unguarded. "So that's what I'm doing. Standing and fighting for you, Faye. For us. For Molly. And for love."

"Love." She linked their hands together, sighing.

"It's always been you, Faye." Kaleb trailed his fingers across her cheek. "And it's always been love."

"Aren't you scared?" She searched his face.

"For the first time, no." He held her gaze. His words honest. Straightforward. "I know what's in my heart. It's you. It's Molly. It's us. We're all that matters."

"Kaleb." She moved into his space. Into his arms. Where she wanted to be.

"I love you, Faye." He framed her face in his hands. His touch gentle. "I know I don't offer a traditional life. I'll be away as much as I'm here."

But he would be hers. Same as she would be his.

"When I'm here, you'll have all of me," he said earnestly. "When I'm not here, you'll have my heart."

"That's all I want, Kaleb Matthews." Faye leaned forward, pressed her lips against his but then pulled away to add, "Because I love you, too. And I trust you with my heart."

Kaleb gathered her even closer.

"I'm sorry for what I said before," she said in a soft voice. "That was my fear talking."

"And now?" He drew her closer.

"It's my heart talking." He made her breathless. *Love* made her breathless. "I want to build a family with you, Kaleb. I want a life with you. But you have to know that it might not be easy."

"Then we'll face it all together." There was conviction in his voice and tenderness in his eyes. "We won't turn our backs on each other. Or family."

"Together," she whispered. "Always."

"And forever." He kissed her.

On that red couch. In a dusty old attic. Where it was just him. Just her.

And just perfect.

# Epilogue

*December 25ᵗʰ—Christmas Day*

D Christmas morning was quickly becoming Christmas afternoon and Faye was glad she'd enjoyed a quiet moment with Kaleb in the attic the night before.

It seemed she'd been on the go ever since. Not that she minded. Not in the least. Between a late-night dinner, kisses under the mistletoe and the holiday festivities, Faye couldn't recall a better Christmas.

"Lark and West are here." Kaleb glanced out the kitchen window and grinned. "Now we have more hands for food prep."

Faye tugged on the end of his elf hat. The one she'd given him when they'd gotten home. The one the Knotty Elves had embroidered with: *Kaleb Kringle*. Making him an official member of their elf family. "Don't think this gets you out of helping me."

"I'm right where I want to be. I told Chase Bailey I'm not selling." He leaned in, reached around Faye, and picked up the colander on the counter. A teasing glint in his gaze. "Now if you'll excuse me, I've fresh fruit to wash."

"And I'm in your way," she said playfully.

"I'd like to keep you right here." His gaze warmed. "But I'm afraid nothing would get done. And you've invited half the town over for lunch."

Faye laughed and slipped around him. "It's not that many people." Not this year, anyway.

The back door opened. West bustled into the kitchen, carrying a stack of presents and smiling broadly. "Where do you want these?"

"I'll show him." Kaleb took another stack of presents from Lark and headed with West into the family room.

Faye barely had time to hug her best friend and wish her a Merry Christmas when Molly interrupted, an urgency to her words.

"Aunty Lark, we gotta talk now. Before the company gets here." Molly rubbed her forehead, knocking her *Molly McJolly* elf hat askew. "Alone, 'cause I gotta say sorry for all the trouble."

"You're not trouble." Lark hugged Molly and arched an eyebrow at Faye before adding, "Especially not on Christmas morning. Besides, we come bearing presents."

"No presents yet," Molly pouted. "Mom's rule. I gotta make it right first."

"Well, this sounds serious." Lark slipped off her coat and dropped it on a kitchen stool. "Where shall we go for this conversation?"

"Your old room," Molly suggested. "It's where I'm sleeping and you gotta see how it looks."

"I can't wait." Lark followed a defeated looking Molly toward the stairs.

Twenty minutes later, Molly skipped into the kitchen, all smiles and good cheer, and hugged Faye tight. "Aunty Lark says I don't gotta tell anyone else about Elmer."

"That's nice, honey." Faye smiled, knowing that Molly had already told Grams and the Knotty Elves. Not that those four couldn't keep a secret. But did they want to?

Lark walked into the kitchen, snatched a mini spinach-and-cheese quiche from the tray, and grinned. "Molly and I agreed Elmer's movie antics should be part of Christmas Town legend. The story can be the latest addition to our beloved Christmas Town lore."

"I just wish we knew what happened to the original Elmer." Releasing Molly, who ran into the family room, Faye took her chicken, broccoli and tortellini casserole from the oven and set it on the counter. "Grams took it well, but it was—"

"Shut up in a box in a drawer for decades." Lark nodded, more than ready to point out the irony in the situation. When Faye shot her a questioning look, she added in a conciliatory tone, "And yet, that Elmer was sentimental and magic."

"Elmer is magic." Kaleb walked around the island, a gleam in his gaze and kissed Faye. "Just like this town. How else could he have just up and walked away?"

There was magic in Kaleb's kisses. The doorbell rang before Faye could turn and pull Kaleb in for more than a peck on the cheek. Later. There would be time for that later. Now was about gathering those she cared about together to celebrate family and friendships—the things that mattered most.

Dave and Betsy Anne strolled inside, called out cheerful Christmas greetings and handed out welcome hugs.

Betsy Anne set an oversized gift bag on a kitchen stool and grinned at Faye. "We couldn't arrive empty-handed, so we picked out special Christmas sweaters for each of you."

The doorbell rang again.

"We expect you to be wearing them tomorrow night for the After Christmas game night at Posey's that the guys fully intend to win." Dave high-fived Kaleb, then West.

Faye exchanged a smile with Kaleb. She was game. He nodded. He was game, too.

The doorbell rang a third time.

Sean entered, holding Zoey's hand. "Yep, we fellas have the advantage for Christmas Town trivia."

"As if!" Zoey laughed. "Half of you guys didn't grow up here."

"We've got West, Flynn and Kaleb," Griffin Walker declared as he entered the kitchen, which was getting very crowded. "Not to mention Murray Anderson."

"I cannot believe my grandfather chose your team." Dale Anderson sounded disappointed, but the sparkle in the gaze she aimed at Griffin gave her away.

"Don't worry, ladies." Lark passed out plates for the buffet. "We have our own ringers."

The doorbell rang a fourth time.

"The Knotty Elves and Three Wise Men aren't allowed as trivia teammates." West spooned a heaping serving of apple, cranberry and bacon chopped salad onto his plate. "Those are the rules."

"But no one disqualified Grams." Molly squeezed between Kaleb and Faye, her smile triumphant.

A cheer erupted from the women. A groan from the men.

"Sorry, we're late." Miranda Paxton came in, followed by Dustin Burnside. "We got caught up at Holly Haven giving the residents a little extra Christmas attention this morning."

Dustin unzipped his coat. "What did we miss?"

"Come in and grab a plate." Faye motioned to the food covering the entire kitchen island. "We'll fill you in while we eat."

Looking around, Faye's heart was bursting with love and holiday joy.

Lark came to stand beside her, putting an arm around her shoulder. "I need to thank you."

"For cooking for Christmas?" Faye scoffed. "It's what I do."

"What we do," Kaleb said from over by the sink.

"No. You were right to push for this movie to be filmed in Christmas Town." Lark gave her a squeeze. "It was what I needed."

"What we both needed," Faye amended. "Merry Christmas, Lark."

"Merry Christmas, Faye."

The pair watched their co-workers, friends, family, and guests dive into the buffet.

The good-natured ribbing, lively conversations and belly-deep laughter spread well past the lunch hour. In fact, the merriment might have continued into the evening if the assembled hadn't needed to make their way to the gazebo for John and Lisa Richardson's vow renewal ceremony. With promises to save seats and reconvene in the town square, the upbeat group departed.

Faye, Kaleb, Lark, and West set the kitchen back to rights before preparing to follow.

Faye opened the front door to carry out the trash and nearly tripped over the shiny gift-wrapped box sitting on the welcome mat. She tossed the garbage, and then carried the shoebox-sized present inside. "Molls, looks like this one is for you."

Molly skipped over to Faye. Excitement rushed her words. "Another present? What is it?"

"How would I know? It's not from me." Faye laughed. "Santa left it on the front porch. You'll have to open it to find out."

Molly slipped the card from the envelope, opened it, and read aloud, "Dear Molly, thank you for bringing Elmer's holiday cheer to the movie set and beyond this Christmas. Even though Elmer has headed home for the holidays, it seems your work in town isn't quite done. After all, there's always more magic to spread."

Faye slipped her hand into Kaleb's and gave him a questioning look. He shrugged to let her know he wasn't responsible. The same curious confusion Faye felt washed over Lark and West's faces, too.

Molly tossed the card on the counter and tore the glittery gold wrapping paper. She lifted the lid off the box and gasped. "It's a girl elf. Just like Elmer."

Everyone moved in and gaped at the elf Molly carefully removed from the box. Molly ran in place, she was so excited. "She's so cute."

"And well outfitted." Lark picked a tiny white top and skirt embroidered with hearts from inside the box. "Is this Valentine's Day?"

Faye ran her finger over a purple-and-black elf-sized outfit. "This looks like a witch's costume. There's even a witch's hat."

"If I'm not mistaken that's a bunny costume." West pointed at the white dress with miniature bunny ears on a small headband in the box.

"There's another note." Kaleb picked up a folded gift card.

Molly fussed with the elf's Christmas red-and-green outfit, clearly enraptured. "What does it say?"

"Hello, Molly and family. I'm Ellie the Elf. And I'm thrilled to be here with you." Kaleb smiled and kept reading aloud, "I'm here to be a reminder to carry the joy of the Christmas season with you all year long. I have outfits for every holiday. But I can't spread my special year-round magic without a little help."

He paused and glanced at Molly then continued, "Molly, I'm hoping you'll be my secret personal magic ambassador."

Molly's eyes widened.

Happiness rushed through Faye, leaving behind a contentment she'd never truly known. Her daughter would be woven into the very fabric of Christmas Town for years to come. Faye along with her. They were home. Where they belonged.

Faye cleared her throat. "What do you think, Molls?"

"Oh, yes. I'm the best secret keeper." Molly hugged Ellie against her chest. Delight surrounded her words. "We can hide Ellie at Gram's diner all year round while Elmer waits for his turn at Christmas. It's our own tradition with our very own elf."

Kaleb's arm dropped around Faye's waist, anchoring her to him.

She smiled and said, "The first of many new traditions."

"Come on, Molls." Laughing, Lark took West's hand and headed toward the back door. "We'll go warm up the car and talk about how we're going to introduce Ellie to Christmas Town."

"Everyone is going to be so excited." Molly stashed Ellie carefully in the box and chased after Lark and West.

Faye sighed, content. She reached up and adjusted the elf hat on Kaleb's head. "I like this look you have going."

"I like you." He pulled her closer.

"That's nice." Faye linked her hands behind his neck. "Ellie the Elf has me thinking about traditions."

Affection and amusement flashed in his gaze. "Is that so?"

"Yeah. There's this one tradition at the gazebo in the town square." Faye tangled her fingers in his hair. "I was thinking we could give it a try later. What do you think?"

One corner of his mouth lifted. "I think we've a civic duty to uphold town traditions."

A horn honked outside.

"I think that's our cue." Faye tugged him toward the door. "Fair warning. We might want to be last in line at the gazebo tonight because I won't be rushed when I'm there."

"I have no intention of rushing one single moment of our lives." Kaleb swept her into his arms on the back steps. "I intend to cherish every minute with you, Faye Burlew."

Faye kissed Kaleb right there. In the falling snow. With the horn honking. And her family looking on. Because the true magic was in their love. And love was always worth stopping for.

---

"Ladies, I know I've said this before." Odette finished tying the red bow on the last of several dozen winter wrist corsages the trio had been crafting for Lisa and John Richardson's Christmas vow renewal ceremony. Satisfaction filled her words. "But I do believe this is the year that we've truly outdone ourselves."

"Or perhaps we've simply exceeded our own outdone-ness." Pru spritzed the silk red and white rose and holly corsages with Odette's special rose oil blend and smiled.

"Some might say we've exhausted ourselves." June added the last corsage to the straw basket on the couch beside Posey. "But I feel rather invigorated."

"It's the coffee." Odette stood, pushed her chair into Posey's table and stretched. "Too much caffeine in that extra-tall Irish coffee you were sipping earlier in the Carriage Room with Cyrus and Murray Anderson."

"I had two peppermint mochas." Pru chuckled and joined Posey on the couch. "Never could turn down anything with peppermint."

"Perhaps I should've had Irish coffee rather than that decidedly un-spiked eggnog. I could use a spot of June's vigor." Posey had her feet propped on the coffee table and a look of Christmas contentment on her face. "Aren't you going to sit, June? Even for a spell."

"There's no time." June fluttered around the Christmas tree. "We're not quite finished."

"I can't imagine what else you three need to do." Posey waved her arm in front of her. "You decorated my place better than I ever could and haven't stopped since. What with the Bake-Off, the movie, and the town's usual holiday events, I don't believe you missed anything."

June rubbed her elbow. "We had a number of nudges on our list to see to."

"We certainly did." Pru touched her own elbow. "Wouldn't change any of it though."

"Me either." Odette tidied up the table and walked into the family room. "Now we've one last present."

"We like to think we saved the best for last." June rummaged under the tree and picked up a handmade glass box. She handed it to Posey. "Welcome home, Elmer."

Posey pressed her hand over her mouth. "That's my original Elmer."

"Well, Elmer's acting debut is officially over now." Pru chuckled and bumped her shoulder against Posey's. "We knew it wouldn't feel quite like home without Elmer here watching over you."

"This is a lovely Christmas present." Posey looked like she might cry. "I'm old enough to know that nothing lasts forever. But when Molly told me what had happened, my heart broke a little. She'll be so relieved when I tell her."

"We need to talk about that." Odette checked her appearance in the hall mirror. "But right now, we've got to meet Abby and Cyrus in the lobby. We're all riding together to Lisa and John's vow renewal ceremony."

"We need to get there early to secure the best seats." Pru stood and held out her hand to help Posey up. "I do believe most of the town will be there."

"Along with a large part of the cast and crew who decided to spend Christmas here in town." Pleasure filled June's face. "Seems they discovered the appeal of our little town after all."

"That's no surprise." Odette followed her friends out into the hallway. "Love, family, and magic. Everything you need is right here in Christmas Town. All you need to do is open your heart."

The End

# More About Christmas Town

Happy holidays and thank you for reading!

We've been writing sweet holiday romances in Christmas Town for years!

To view the entire series (over 60 books and novellas in value box sets), you can check out our 2 series pages on Amazon:

*Heartwarming Christmas Town (sweet novella series page)

*The Christmas Carousel (1 short + 12 full-length sweet romances)